B

LaVyrle Spencer
novels, with over
title, *Family Blessings*, went straight into the bestseller lists, following in the tradition of such favourites as *Morning Glory* and *Bygones*, further confirming her place as one of the most successful and best loved writers of romantic fiction. She lives in Stillwater, Minnesota, with her husband, Dan.

By the same author

BYGONES
SPRING FANCY
MORNING GLORY
THE HELLION
VOWS
THE GAMBLE
A HEART SPEAKS
YEARS
SEPARATE BEDS
TWICE LOVED
HUMMINGBIRD
THE ENDEARMENT
THE FULFILMENT
FORGIVING
NOVEMBER OF THE HEART
FAMILY BLESSINGS

LAVYRLE SPENCER

Bitter Sweet

HarperCollins*Publishers*

HarperCollins*Publishers*
77–85 Fulham Palace Road,
Hammersmith, London W6 8JB

Special edition 1995

First published in Great Britain by
HarperCollins*Publishers* 1994

Previously published in paperback by Grafton 1992

First published in Great Britain by
Grafton Books 1991

ISBN 0 286 15131 6

Set in Bembo

Printed and bound in Great Britain by
HarperCollinsManufacturing Glasgow

My thanks to the following people
for their help during the research of this book:

Christine and Sverre Falck-Pedersen
of Thorp House Inn, Fish Creek, Wisconsin

Captain Paul of Captain Paul's Charter Fishing Fleet,
Gills Rock, Wisconsin

Fellow writer, Pamela Smith of Seattle, Washington

L.S.

This book is dedicated to my school friends
who have remained friends for life . . .

Dodie Fread Nelson
Carol Judd Cameron
Carol Robinson Shequin
Judean Peterson Longbella
Nancy Thorn Rebischke
and
Nancy Norgren

With love and fond memories
of all the good times,

Berle

And in my thoughts often during the writing of this book were school friends with whom I've lost touch long ago, but who linger in memory. Lona Hess . . . Timothy Bergein . . . Gaylord Olson . . . Sharon Naslund . . . Sue Staley . . . Ann Stangland . . . Janie Johnson . . . Keith Peters

Where did you go?

Chapter 1

The room held a small refrigerator stocked with apple juice and soft drinks, a two-burner hot plate, a phonograph, a circle of worn, comfortable chairs and a smeared green chalkboard that said, GRIEF GROUP 2:00–3:00.

Maggie Stearn entered with five minutes to spare, hung up her raincoat and helped herself to a tea bag and hot water. Bobbing the bag in the Styrofoam cup, she ambled across the room.

At the window she looked down. On the ship canal below, the water, pocked by the first of the August monsoons, seemed brooding and oily. The buildings of Seattle registered only in memory while Puget Sound hid behind a rainy curtain of grey. A rust-streaked tanker lumbered along the murky canal, ocean-bound, its rails and navigational aerials obscured by the downpour. On its weatherstained deck merchant marines stood motionless – blurred yellow blobs wrapped head to hip in oilskin slickers.

Rain. So much rain, and the entire winter of it ahead.

She sighed, thinking of facing it alone, and turned from the window just as two other members of the group arrived.

'Hi, Maggie,' they said in unison from the door: Diane, thirty-six, whose husband had died when a blood vessel burst in his brain while they were clamming on Whidbey Island with their three kids; and Nelda, sixty-two, whose husband fell from a roof he was shingling and never got up again.

Without Diane and Nelda, Maggie wasn't sure how she'd have survived this last year.

'Hi,' she returned, smiling.

Crossing the room, Diane asked, 'How did the date go?'

Maggie grimaced. 'Don't ask.'

'That bad, huh?'

'How do you get over feeling married when you're not anymore?' It was a question all of them were striving to answer.

'I know what you mean,' Nelda put in. 'I finally went to bingo with George – you remember, I told you about him, the man from my church? All night long I felt like I was cheating on Lou. Playing *bingo*, mind you!'

While they commiserated, a man joined them, thin and balding, in his late fifties, wearing unfashionable pleated pants and a decrepit sweater that hung on his bony frame.

'Hi, Cliff.' They widened their circle to let him in.

Cliff nodded. He was the newest member of the group. His wife had died when she ran a red light during her first time out driving after carotid surgery that had left her with no peripheral vision.

'How was your week?' Maggie asked him.

'Oh . . .' The word came out with a sigh and a shrug, but he offered no more.

Maggie rubbed his back. 'Some weeks are better than others. It takes time.' She'd had her own back rubbed more than once in this room and knew the healing power of a human touch.

'What about you?' Nelda turned the focus on Maggie. 'Your daughter leaves for college this week, right?'

'Yup,' Maggie replied with false brightness. 'Two more days.'

'I've been through that with three of my own. You call if it gets rough, will you? We'll go out and see some male strippers or something.'

Maggie laughed. Nelda would no more go see a stripper than she would become one herself. 'I wouldn't even know what to do with a stripped male anymore.' All of them laughed. It was easier to laugh about the dearth of sex in their lives than it was to do something about it.

Dr Feldstein walked in, a clipboard in one hand and a mug of steaming coffee in the other, talking with Claire, who'd lost her sixteen-year-old daughter in a motorcycle accident. Amid an exchange of greetings Dr Feldstein shut the door and headed for his favourite chair, setting his coffee on a nearby table.

'Looks like everyone's here. Let's get started.'

They all took seats, conversation trailing off, a group of healing people who cared about one another. Maggie sat on the brown sofa between Cliff and Nelda, Diane on the floor on a fat blue cushion and Claire in a chair to Dr Feldstein's right.

It was Maggie who noted the absence. Glancing around she asked, 'Shouldn't we wait for Tammi?' Tammi was their youngest, only twenty, unmarried, pregnant, abandoned by the father of the baby and struggling to overcome the recent loss of both of her parents. Tammi was everybody's darling, a surrogate daughter to everyone in the group.

Dr Feldstein set his clipboard on the floor and replied, 'Tammi won't be with us today.'

Every eye fixed on him but nobody asked.

With his elbows resting on the wooden arms of his chair, Dr Feldstein linked his hands over his stomach.

'Tammi took an overdose of sleeping pills two days ago and she's still in intensive care. We're going to be dealing with that today.'

The shock hit them full force, stunning them into silence. Maggie felt it explode like a small bomb in her stomach and spread to her extremities. She stared at the doctor with his long, intelligent face, slightly hooked nose and full, cranberry-coloured lips within a thick black beard. His eyes touched every member of the group – shrewd black eyes with flat violet planes beneath – watching their reaction.

Maggie finally broke the silence to ask what they were all wondering. 'Will she live?'

'We don't know that yet. She's developed Tylenol poisoning so it's touch and go.'

From outside came the faint bellow of a foghorn on the ship canal below. Inside, the group sat motionless, their tears beginning to build.

Claire leapt to her feet and stormed to the window, thumping the ledge with both fists. 'Goddamn it! Why did she do it!'

'Why didn't she call one of us?' Maggie asked. 'We would have helped her.'

They'd struggled with it before – the helplessness, the anger in the face of that helplessness. Every person in the circle felt the same, for a setback suffered by one of them was a setback suffered by all. They had invested time and tears in each other, had trusted each other with their innermost hurts and fears. To think they could work this hard and have it backfire was tantamount to being betrayed.

Cliff sat motionless, blinking hard.

Diane sniffed and lowered her forehead to her updrawn knees.

Dr Feldstein reached behind his chair and snagged a box of Kleenex from the top of the phonograph, stretched to place it on the table in the middle of the circle.

'All right, let's start with the basics,' he said in a no-nonsense tone. 'If she chose not to call any of us, there was no way we could have helped her.'

'But she *is* us,' Margaret reasoned, spreading her hands. 'I mean, we're all striving for the same things here, aren't we? And we thought we were making headway.'

'And if she could do it, none of you are safe, right?' Dr Feldstein demanded before answering his own question. 'Wrong! That's the first thing I want to fix in your minds. Tammi made a choice. Each of you makes choices every day. It's all right for you to be angry that she's done this, but it's not all right to see yourself in her place.'

They talked about it, a long discussion filled with passion and compassion, that grew more animated as it lengthened. They worked past their anger until it became pity, and past the pity until it became renewed ardour to do all they could to make their own lives better. When they'd worked through their feelings, Dr Feldstein announced, 'We're going to do an exercise today, something I believe each of you is ready for. If you're not, you only have to pass – no questions asked. But for those of you who want to turn around that feeling of helplessness you've experienced because of Tammi's suicide attempt, I believe it will help.'

He rose and placed a hard wooden chair in the centre of the room. 'We're going to say good-bye today to someone or something that has hindered our getting better. Someone who's left us through death, or maybe voluntarily, or something we haven't been able to face. It could be someplace we haven't been able to go or an old grudge we've carried around for too long. Whatever it is, we're going to put it in that chair and say good-bye to it aloud. And when we've said good-bye, we're going to let that person or that thing know what we're going to do now to make ourselves happier. Do you all understand?' When nobody replied, Dr Feldstein said, 'I'll be first.'

He stood before the vacant chair, opened his jaws wide and ran both palms down his beard. He drew a deep breath, looked at the floor, then at the chair.

'I'm going to say good-bye once and for all to my cigarettes. I gave you up over two years ago but I still reach towards my breast pocket for you, so I've put you in that chair and to you I say, so long, Dorals. I'm going to make myself happier in the future by giving up my resentment at quitting smoking. From now on, every time I reach for my pocket, instead of silently cursing because I find it empty,

I'm going to silently thank myself for the gift I've given me.' He waved at the chair. 'Good-bye, Dorals.'

He moved back to his own place and sat.

The tears were gone from the faces around him. In their place was candid introspection.

'Claire?' Dr Feldstein said softly.

Claire sat a full minute without moving. No one spoke a word. Finally she rose and faced the chair.

When no words came, Dr Feldstein asked, 'Who's in the chair, Claire?'

'My daughter, Jessica,' she managed.

'And what would you like to say to Jessica?'

Claire wiped her hands on her thighs and swallowed. Everyone waited. At length she began. 'I miss you a lot, Jess, but after this I'm not going to let it control my life anymore. I've got a lot of years left, and I need to make me happy before your dad and your sister can be happy, too. And the thing I'm going to do to start is to go home and take your clothes out of your closet and give them to the Goodwill. So this is good-bye, Jess.' She headed for her chair, then turned back. 'Oh, and I'm also going to forgive you for not wearing your helmet that day because I know now that's been getting in the way of my getting well, too.' She raised a hand. 'Bye, Jess.'

Maggie felt her eyes sting and watched through a blur as Claire sat down and Diane took her place.

'The person in the chair is my husband, Tim.' Diane wiped her eyes hard with a tissue. She opened her mouth, closed it and dropped her head into one hand. 'This is so hard,' she whispered.

'Would you rather wait?' Dr Feldstein asked.

Again she swabbed her eyes with stubborn determination. 'No. I want to do it.' She fixed her gaze on the chair, hardened her chin and began. 'I've been really pissed off at you, Tim, for dying. I mean, you and I went together since high school, and I'd planned on another fifty years, you know?' The Kleenex hit her eyes once more. 'Well, I just want you to know I'm not pissed off anymore, because you probably planned on fifty, too, so what right have I got, huh? And what I'm going to do . . .' She opened one palm wide and scratched at it with the opposite thumbnail, then looked up. '. . . what I'm going to do to make myself better is to take the kids and go up to our cabin on Whidbey this weekend. They've been begging to go and I keep saying no, but now I will, because until I'm better, how can they be happy? So, bye, Tim. Hang loose, huh, guy?'

She hurried to her place and sat down.

Everyone around the circle dried their eyes.

'Cliff?' Dr Feldstein invited.

'I want to pass,' Cliff whispered, looking at his lap.

'Fine. Nelda?'

Nelda said, 'I said my good-byes to Carl a long time ago. I'll pass.'

'Maggie?'

Maggie rose slowly and approached the chair. Upon it sat Phillip, with the ten extra pounds he could never seem to lose after reaching age thirty, with his green eyes that bordered on brown and his sandy hair in need of cutting (as it had been when he'd got on that plane) and his favourite Seahawks sweatshirt that she hadn't washed yet but occasionally took from the hook in the closet and smelled. She felt terrified of giving up her grief, terrified that when it left there'd be nothing in its stead and she'd be an apathetic shell incapable of feeling in any way at all. She rested an open hand on the top oak rung of the chair and drew an unsteady breath. 'Well, Phillip,' she began, 'it's been a whole year, so it's time. I'm like Diane, I guess, a little pissed off because you went on that plane for such a stupid reason – a gambling junket, when your gambling was the only thing I ever resented. No, that's not true. I've also resented the fact that you died just when Katy was about to graduate from high school and we could start travelling more and enjoying our freedom. But I promise I'll get over that and start travelling without you. Soon. Also, I'm going to stop thinking of the insurance money as blood money so I can enjoy it a little more, and I'm going to try again with Mother because I think I'm going to need her now that Katy will be gone.' She stepped back and fanned an open hand. 'So, good-bye, Phillip. I loved you.'

After Maggie was finished they sat a long time in silence. Finally Dr Feldstein asked, 'How do you feel?' It took some time before they answered.

'Tired,' Diane said.

'Better,' Claire admitted.

'Relieved,' Maggie said.

Dr Feldstein gave them a moment to acclimatize to these feelings before leaning forward and speaking in his rich, resonant voice. 'They're bygones now, all those old feelings that you've been carrying around long enough, that have been keeping you from getting better. Remember that. I think, without them, you're going to be happier, more receptive to healthy thoughts.'

He sat back.

'In spite of all that, it's not going to be an easy week. You're going to worry about Tammi, and that worry is going to translate into depression, so I'm going to give you another prescription for when that happens. This is what I want you to do. Look up old friends, the older the better, friends you've lost touch with – call them, write to them, try to get together with them.'

'You mean high school friends?' Maggie inquired.

'Sure. Talk about old times, laugh about the ridiculous things you did when you were too young to have more sense. Those days represent a time in life when most of us were at our most carefree. All we had to do, basically, was go to school, pull fairly respectable grades, handle a part-time job maybe, and have a lot of fun. By going back into the past we can often pull our present into perspective. Try it and see how you feel.' He glanced at his watch. 'Then we'll talk about it at our next session. Okay?'

The room became filled with the soft shuffle of movement signalling the end of the hour. People stretched and hitched themselves to the edges of their chairs and tucked away their sodden Kleenexes. 'We've covered a lot of ground today,' Dr Feldstein said, rising. 'I think we did very well.'

Maggie walked to the elevator with Nelda. She felt closer to her than to any of the others, for their situations were most similar. Nelda could be a bit twittery and vacant at times, but she had a heart of gold and an unfailing sense of humour.

'Have you kept in touch with friends from that long ago?' Nelda asked.

'No, it's been a while. Have you?'

'Lord, girl, I'm sixty-two years old. I'm not even sure I can find some of mine anymore.'

'Do you intend to try?'

'I might. I'll see.' In the lobby they paused to adjust their rain gear and Nelda reached up for a parting hug. 'Now you remember what I said. When your daughter leaves, you just give me a call.'

'I will. I promise.'

Outside, the rain drummed heavily, lifting miniature explosions in the puddles on the street. Maggie snapped open her umbrella and headed for her car. By the time she reached it her feet were wet, her raincoat streaming, and she was chilled clear through. She started the engine and sat a minute, her hands folded between her knees, watching her breath condense on the windows before the defroster could clear it.

It had been a particularly draining session. So much to think about: Tammi, her good-bye to Phillip, how she was going to carry out the promises she'd made, Katy's leaving – she hadn't even had a chance to bring it up, but it loomed above all other concerns, threatening to undo each bit of progress she'd made in the past year.

The weather didn't help any. Lord, she got so tired of the rain.

But Katy was still home and they had two more suppers together. Maybe tonight she'd make Katy's favourite, spaghetti and meatballs, and afterward they could build a fire in the fireplace and make plans for Thanksgiving when Katy would come home on break.

Maggie turned on the windshield wipers and headed home, out across Montlake Bridge that hummed beneath the tyres like a dentist's drill, then north towards Redmond. As the car began climbing into the foothills, the sharp, resinous scent of pines was drawn inside by the ventilation system. She passed the entrance to Bear Creek Country Club, where she and Phillip had been members for years, where, since his death, more than one of their married male friends had made advances towards her. The country club had lost its appeal in more than one way since Phillip's death.

On Lucken Lane she pulled into a driveway before a ranch-style house constructed of weathered cedar and burned orange brick, situated on the side of a wooded hill, a middle-class house with neatly tended marigolds lining the front walk and potted geraniums standing sentinel on either side of the front steps. A touch of the activator lifted the garage door and Maggie saw with disappointment that Katy's car was gone.

In the kitchen, the silence was broken only by the sound of rain dropping through the downspout outside the window and the garage door rumbling to a stop. On the table beside a half-eaten English muffin and a hot-pink hair clamp lay a note scrawled on a pad shaped like a blue foot.

Gone shopping with Smitty and to pick up a few more empty boxes. Don't fix supper for me. Love, K.

Stifling her disappointment, Maggie removed her coat

and hung it in the front closet. She wandered down the hall and stopped in the doorway of Katy's room. Clothing lay everywhere, stacked, boxed, thrown across half-filled suitcases. Two giant black plastic bags, plump with discards, lay between the bifold closet doors. A pile of jeans and another of brightly coloured sweatshirts waited at the foot of the bed to be laundered. Only the top half of the dresser mirror showed; the lower portion was hidden behind a stack of *Seventeen* magazines and a laundry basket filled with neatly folded towels and new bed linens, still in their plastic wrappers, waiting to make the move to Chicago. Strewn across the floor, separated only by narrow paths, lay seventeen years' worth of memories: a pile of portfolios fat with old school papers, their top sides covered with graffiti; a softball cap and a mitt for a twelve-year-old hand; two corsages, one dried and yellowed, the other with tea roses still pink; a dusty poster of Bruce Springsteen; a shoebox full of graduation cards and unused thank-you notes; another of perfume bottles; a bill-cap full of tangled earrings and cheap plastic rope beads; a pile of stuffed animals; a French horn case; a mauve basket holding recent correspondence from Northwestern University.

Northwestern, her and Phillip's alma mater, halfway across America. Why hadn't Katy chosen the U here instead? To get away from a mother who hadn't been the most cheerful company during the past year?

Feeling tears build in her throat, Maggie turned away, determined to make it through the remainder of the day without breaking down. In her own bedroom she avoided glancing at the queen-sized bed and the memories it evoked. Marching straight to the mirrored closet, she slid open a door, pulled out Phillip's Seahawks sweatshirt and returned to Katy's room where she buried it in one of the bags of discards.

Back in her own room she pulled on an oversized set of red-and-white Pepsi sweats, then marched into the adjacent bathroom where she found a miniature pot of makeup and began dabbing some on the purple shadows beneath her eyes.

Midway through the task, tears began to build and her hands dropped. Who was she kidding? She looked like a forty-year-old scarecrow. Since Phillip's death she'd dropped from a size 12 to a size 8, lost a full bra size, and her auburn hair had lost its lustre because she never ate right anymore. She didn't give a damn about cooking, or going back to work, or cleaning the house, or dressing decently. She did it because she knew she had to and because she didn't want to end up like Tammi.

She stared at the mirror.

I miss him and I want so damned badly to cry.

After fifteen seconds of self-pity she slammed the makeup into a drawer, switched off the light and spun from the room.

In the kitchen she wet a dishcloth and wiped up Katy's muffin crumbs. But on her way to the garbage disposal she made the mistake of taking a bite of the cold muffin. The taste of cinnamon and raisin spread with peanut butter – a favourite of both Katy and her father – keyed a reaction too powerful to fight any longer. Once more the dreaded tears came – hot, burning.

She threw the muffin into the sink with such force it ricocheted off the opposite side and landed beside the flour canister. She gripped the edge of the counter and doubled forward at the waist.

Damn you, Phillip, why did you go on that plane? You should be here now. We should be going through this together!

But Phillip was gone. And Katy soon would be. And what then? A lifetime of suppers alone?

Two days later Maggie stood in the driveway beside Katy's car, watching her daughter stuff one last tote bag behind the seat. The predawn air was chill, and mist formed a nimbus around the garage lights. Katy's car was new, expensive, a convertible with every conceivable option, paid for with a minute fraction of the insurance money from Phillip's death: a consolation prize from the airline for Katy's having to go fatherless for the remainder of her life.

'There, that's it.' Katy straightened and dropped the seat back into place. She turned to Maggie – a pretty young woman with her father's brown eyes, Maggie's cleft chin, and a cosmic hairdo appropriate for the cover of a science fiction novel, a look to which her mother had never grown accustomed. Viewing it now, at the hour of parting, Maggie recalled with a pang of nostalgia when it had been downy and she'd combed it in a top curl.

Katy broke the sad silence. 'Thanks for the peanut-butter muffins, Mom. They'll taste good around Spokane or so.'

'I put some apples in there, too, and a couple cans of cherry Coke for each of you. Now are you sure you've got enough money?'

'I've got everything, Mom.'

'Remember what I said about speeding on the interstates.'

'I'll use the cruise control, don't worry.'

'And if you get sleepy –'

'Let Smitty drive. I know, Mom.'

'I'm so glad she's going with you, that you'll be together.'

'So am I.'

'Well . . .'

The reality of parting crowded in; they had grown so close in the last year, since Phillip's death.

'I'd better go,' Katy said quietly. 'I told Smitty I'd be at her house at five-thirty sharp.'

'Yes, you'd better.'

Their eyes met, misty with good-bye, and sorrow created an awesome gulf between them.

'Oh, Mom . . .' Katy dived into her mother's arms, clinging hard, her blue jeans lost in the folds of Maggie's long quilted robe. 'I'm going to miss you.'

'I'll miss you, too, honey.' Pressed breast to breast, with the scent of marigolds hanging musty-strong in the air and droplets of moisture plopping off the house roof onto the flower beds below, they exchanged a heartrending good-bye.

'Thanks for letting me go, and for everything you bought.'

A mere movement of Maggie's head answered; her throat was too constricted to emit a sound.

'I hate leaving you here alone.'

'I know.' Maggie held her daughter fast, feeling the tears – her own? Katy's? – run in warm trickles down her neck, and Katy clinging hard and rocking her from side to side.

'I love you, Mom.'

'I love you, too.'

'And I'll be home for Thanksgiving.'

'I'll count on that. Be careful, and call really often.'

'I will, I promise.'

They walked to the car, hip to hip, chins down, idling. 'You know, it's hard to believe you're the same little girl who threw such a fit when I left her the first day of kindergarten.' Maggie rubbed Katy's arm.

Katy gave the obligatory laugh as she slid into the driver's seat.

'I'm going to be one hell of a child psychologist though, 'cause I understand days like that.' She looked up at her mother. 'And days like this.'

Their eyes exchanged a final good-bye.

Katy started the engine, Maggie slammed the door and leaned on it with both hands. The headlights came on, throwing a cone of gold into the dense haze of the wooded yard. Through the open window, Maggie kissed her daughter's lips.

'Keep mellow,' Katy said.

Maggie gave their familiar all-level sign.

'Bye,' Katy mouthed.

'Bye.' Maggie tried to say, but only her lips moved.

The car engine purred a dolorous note as the vehicle backed down the driveway, turned, stopped, changed gears. Then it was gone, the tyres hissing softly on the wet pavement, leaving a last memory of a young girl's hand waving out the open window.

Left behind in the quiet, Maggie gripped her arms, tilted her head back to its limits and searched for a hint of dawn. The tips of the pines remained invisible against the ebony sky. Droplets still fell into the marigold bed. She experienced a slight lightheadedness, a queer out-of-body sensation, as if she were Maggie Stearn, but standing apart, watching for her own reaction. To fall apart would mean certain disaster. Instead, she walked around the house, soaking her slippers in the wet grass and collecting scratchy pine needles in the hem of her robe. Heedless of them she moved past trapezoids of incandescence slanting into the yard from the windows of the bathroom, where Katy had taken her last shower, and from the kitchen, where she'd eaten her last breakfast.

I will get through this day. Just this one. And the next will be easier. And the next easier yet.

At the rear of the house she straightened a clump of petunias that had been flattened by the rain; brushed two fallen pinecones off the redwood deck; replaced three pieces of firewood that had tumbled from the tier against the rear garage wall.

The aluminium extension ladder lay on the north side of the garage. *You must put that away. It's been there since you cleaned the pine needles out of the gutters last spring. What would Phillip say?* But she walked on, leaving the ladder where it was.

In the garage her car was parked, a new luxurious Lincoln Town Car, purchased with Phillip's death money. She passed it, heading up the walk between the marigold borders. On the front step she sat, huddled, wrapped in her own arms, the moisture from the wet concrete seeping through her robe.

Afraid. Lonely. Despairing.

Thinking about Tammi and how loneliness like this had driven her over the edge. Afraid she wouldn't recognize it if she ever got that bad.

She made it through that first day by going to Woodinville High School and puttering around the home ec rooms. The building felt deserted, only the office staff working, the other faculty members not due back for another week and a half. Alone in the neat, spacious rooms, she oiled the sewing machines, scoured some sinks that had been used for summer school, unearthed dittoes and ran off copies of several first-day handouts, and decorated a bulletin board: TRUE BLUE – DENIM CLOTHING CONSTRUCTION FOR FALL.

She didn't give a damn about denim or its construction. The prospect of another year of teaching the same thing she'd been teaching for fifteen years seemed as pointless as cooking for one.

In the afternoon the house waited, permanently empty, filled with wrenching memories of the place astir with the daily activities of three. She called the hospital to check on Tammi and learned that her condition was still critical.

For supper she fried two slices of French toast and sat down to eat them at the kitchen counter, accompanied by the evening news on a ten-inch TV. In the middle of her meal the phone rang and she leapt to answer it, expecting to hear Katy's voice saying she was all right and in a motel somewhere near Butte, Montana. Instead Maggie heard a recorded voice, a trained baritone with canned conviviality following a mechanical pause. '. . . hello! . . . I have an important message for you from . . .'

She slammed down the receiver and stared at it in revulsion, as if its message had been obscene. She spun away angrily, feeling somehow threatened by the fact that the instrument whose ring had often been a source of irritation in the past could now raise her pulse with anticipation.

The remaining half-slice of French toast swam before her eyes. Without bothering to throw it away she wandered into the study and sat in Phillip's large green leather chair, gripping the arms, pressing her head against its padded back, as he had often sat.

If she'd had Phillip's Seahawks sweatshirt, she'd have put it on, but it was gone, so instead she dialled Nelda. The phone rang thirteen times without an answer. Next she tried Diane, but it rang and rang and Maggie finally realized Diane had probably gone up to Whidbey Island with her kids. At Claire's she got an answer, but Claire's daughter said her mother had gone to a meeting and wouldn't be back until late.

She hung up and sat staring at the phone with a thumbnail between her teeth.

Cliff? She threw her head back in the chair. Poor Cliff couldn't resolve his own loss much less help anyone else resolve theirs.

She thought about her mother, but the thought brought a shudder.

Only when all her other possibilities were exhausted did Maggie remember Dr Feldstein's prescription.

Call old friends, the older the better, friends you've lost touch with . . .

But who?

The answer came as if preordained: Brookie.

The name brought a flash of memory so vivid it seemed as if it had happened only yesterday. She and Glenda Holbrook – both altos – were standing side by side in the front row of the Gibraltar High School Choir, mercilessly aggravating the choir director, Mr Pruitt, by softly humming an unauthorized note on the final chord of the song, making of an unadulterated C-major, an impertinent, jazzy C-seventh.

Ain't-a that good news, lord, ain't-a that good newwwwws?

Sometimes Pruitt would let their creativity pass, but more often he'd frown and wag a finger to restore purity to the chord. Once time he'd stopped the entire choir and ordered, 'Holbrook and Pearson, go stand out in the hall and sing your dissonant notes to your hearts' content. When you're ready to sing the music the way it's written, you can come back in.'

Glenda Holbrook and Maggie Pearson had been first-graders together. They had been stood in the corner for whispering on the second day of school. In the third grade they'd received scoldings from the school principal for breaking off Timothy Ostmeier's front tooth when a rock was thrown in the middle of an acorn fight, though neither girl would divulge who'd thrown it. In the fifth grade they'd been caught by Miss Hartman during noon recess with pointed Dixie Cups inside their blouses. Miss Hartman, a flat-chested, sour-faced spinster with one crossed eye, opened the door of the girls' lavatory at the very moment Glenda had said, 'If we had titties like this we could probably be movie stars!' In the sixth grade the girls along with Lisa Eidelbach had won praises for singing in three-part harmony, 'Three White Doves Went Seaward Flying', for a monthly meeting of the PTA. In junior high they had attended Bible Study Class together and had pencilled into their Bible Study books clever, irreverent answers to the questions. In the margins of their health books they'd drawn stupendous male body parts, years before they knew what those parts really looked like.

In senior high they'd been cheerleaders, nursing aching muscles after the first practice of the season, making blue-and-gold pom-poms, riding on pep buses and attending postgame dances in the school gym. They had double-dated, worn each other's clothes, shared a thousand teenage confidences, and slept at each other's houses with such regularity that each began keeping a spare toothbrush in the other family's medicine cabinet.

Brookie and Maggie – friends forever, they'd thought back then.

But Maggie had gone to Northwestern University in Chicago, married an aeronautical engineer and moved to Seattle, while Glenda attended beauty school in Green Bay, married a Door County, Wisconsin, cherry grower, moved out to his farm, bore six – or was it seven? – of his children and had never cut hair in a beauty shop again.

How long had it been since they'd lost touch? For a while after their ten-year class reunion they'd corresponded regularly. Then time had grown longer between letters, which had dwindled to annual Christmas cards until eventually those, too, had stopped. Maggie had missed their twenty-year reunion, and on her infrequent visits to her parents she and Brookie had always managed to miss bumping into each other.

Call Brookie? And say what? What could they possibly have in common anymore?

Out of mere curiosity, Maggie leaned forward in Phillip's green chair and selected H on the metal telephone index. The top popped open revealing Phillip's neat handwriting, done in mechanical lead pencil.

Sure enough, it was still there, under her maiden name: Holbrook, Glenda (Mrs Eugene Kerschner), R.R. 1, Fish Creek, WI 54212.

On impulse, Maggie picked up the phone and dialled.

Someone answered after the third ring. 'Hullo?' A male voice, young and booming.

'Is Glenda there?'

'Ma!' the voice shouted. 'It's for you!' The phone clunked as if dropped on a wooden surface, and after a brief pause someone picked it up.

'Hello?'

'Glenda Kerschner?'

'Yo!'

Maggie was already smiling. 'Brookie, is that you?'

'Who's . . .' Even across the wire Maggie sensed Brookie's surprise. 'Maggie, is that you?'

'It's me.'

'Where are you? Are you in Door? Can you come over?'

'I wish I could but I'm in Seattle.'

'Oh, shit. Just a minute.' To someone at the other end she shouted, 'Todd, unplug that damn thing and take it in the other room so I can hear. Sorry, Maggie. Todd is making popcorn here with a bunch of his friends, and you know how loud a pack of boys can be. Gol, how *are* you?'

'I'm okay.'

'Are you really, Mag? We heard about your husband dying in that plane crash. The *Advocate* ran an article. I meant to send you a sympathy card, I even bought one, but somehow the time got away from me and I never got it in the mail. It was cherry season, and you know how crazy things get around here at picking time. Maggie, I'm so sorry about it. I've thought of you a thousand times.'

'Thanks, Brookie.'

'So how are you doing?'

'Oh. Some days are better than others.'

'Bad day today?' Brookie asked.

'Sort of . . . yeah. I've had worse, but . . .' Suddenly Maggie caved in. 'Oh shit, Brookie.' She propped an elbow on the desk and covered her eyes. 'It's awful. Katy just left for Northwestern in Chicago and a woman in my grief group tried to commit suicide last week and I'm sitting here in this empty house wondering what the hell happened to my charmed life.'

'Aw, Maggie . . .'

Sniffing against her knuckles, Maggie said, 'My psychiatrist said it sometimes helps to talk to old friends . . . laugh about old times. So here I am, crying on your shoulder just like when we were sophomores with boy troubles.'

'Oh, Maggie, I should be shot for not getting to you first.

When you've got as many kids as I do you sometimes forget there's a world beyond the kitchen and the laundry room. I'm sorry I didn't call or get in touch with you. I've got no excuse at all. Maggie, are you still there?' Brookie sounded alarmed.

'Yes,' Maggie managed.

'Aw, Maggie . . . jeez, I wish I were closer.'

'So do I. Some days I'd g-give anything to be able to sit down with you and just b-bawl my guts out.'

'Aw, Maggie . . . gol, don't cry.'

'I'm sorry. It seems like that's all I've done for the last year. It's so damned hard.'

'I know, honey, I know. I wish I were there . . . but you go on and tell me everything. I've got all the time in the world.'

Maggie dried her eyes with the heels of her hands and drew in a steadying breath.

'Well, we had to do this exercise in our grief group this week where we set a person in a chair and said good-bye to him. I put Phillip in the chair and said my good-byes, and I guess it really worked because it's finally hitting me that he's gone and he's not coming back.' It was so easy to talk to Brookie. The years of separation might never have happened. Maggie told her everything – how happy she'd been with Phillip, how she'd tried to convince him not to go on the gambling junket, how he'd finally talked her into capitulating by promising they'd plan a trip to Florida together for Easter vacation, the shock of hearing that the plane had gone down with fifty-six people aboard, the agony of sending dental records and waiting for the names of the dead to be confirmed, the bizarre sense of phantasm attending a memorial service without a body while television cameras panned her and Katy's faces.

And of what happened afterward.

'It's really strange what happens when you're widowed. Your best friends treat you as if you have leprosy. You're the one who creates an odd number of table settings, you know? The fifth at bridge. The one without a seat belt. Phillip and I belonged to a country club but even there things have changed. Our friends – well, I thought they were our friends until he died and I got propositioned by two of them while their wives teed off less than twenty feet away. After that I gave up golf. Last spring I finally let one of the faculty members talk me into going out on a blind date.'

'How was it?'

'Disastrous.'

'You mean like Frankie Peterson?'

'Frankie Peterson?'

'Yeah, you remember Frankie Peterson, don't you? A finger in every hole?'

Maggie burst out laughing. She laughed to the point of weakness until she was lying back in the chair with the phone caught on her shoulder.

'Good lord, I'd forgotten about Frankie Peterson.'

'How could any girl from Gibraltar High forget Frank the Crank? He stretched out more elastic than the Green Bay Packers!'

They laughed some more, and when it ended, Brookie said seriously, 'So tell me about this guy they lined you up with. Tried to put the shaft in you, did he?'

'Exactly. At one o'clock in the morning. On my doorstep, for pete's sake. It was horrible. You get out of practice at fighting them off, you know? It was embarrassing, and belittling and . . . and . . . well, honest to God, Brookie, it made me so angry!'

'So what'd you do, punch him out, or what?'

'I slammed the door in his face and came in the house and made meatballs.'

'M-meatballs?' Brookie was laughing so hard she could scarcely get the word out.

For the first time Maggie found the humour in the

situation that had seemed so insulting at the time. She laughed with Brookie, great shaking laughs that robbed her of breath and left her nursing a sore stomach while she curled low on her spine and grinned at the ceiling.

'God, it's good to talk to you, Brookie. I haven't laughed like this in months.'

'Well, at least I'm good for something besides spawning.'

Still more laughter before the line grew quiet and Maggie turned serious again. 'It's a real change.' Slumping comfortably, she rocked on the leather chair, toying with the phone cord. 'You're so hard up – not just for sex, but for affection. Then you go out on a date and when he tries to kiss you you stiffen up and make a fool of yourself. I did it again last week.'

'Another blind date?'

'Well, not quite blind. A man who works at my supermarket who lost his wife several years ago, too. I've known him as a passing acquaintance for years, and I could kind of sense that he liked me. Anyway, my grief group kept after me to ask him to do something, so I finally did. You don't want to think *that* doesn't feel awkward! The last time I dated it was the men who did the asking. Now it's everybody. So I asked, and he tried to kiss me, and I just . . . I just froze.'

'Hey, don't rush it, Mag. They say it takes a while, and that's only two dates.'

'Yeah . . . well . . .' Maggie sighed, braced her temple with a finger and admitted, 'A person gets horny, you know. It clouds the judgement.'

'Well, listen, you horny old broad, now that you've admitted it and I haven't died of shock, do you feel better?'

'Infinitely.'

'Well, that's a relief.'

'Dr Feldstein was right. He said talking with people from the past was healthy, that it takes us back to a time when we didn't have much to worry about. So I called, and you didn't let me down.'

'I'm so glad you did. Have you called any of the others? Fish? Lisa? Tani? I know they'd love to hear from you.'

'It's been so many years since I talked to any of them.'

'But we were the Senior Scourges, all five of us. I *know* they'd want to help if they thought they could. I'll give you their phone numbers.'

'You mean you have them? All of them?'

'I've been in charge of the class reunion invitations twice already. They pick on me because I still live around here and I've got more than half a dozen kids of my own to help me address envelopes. Fish lives in Brussels, Wisconsin; Lisa lives in Atlanta; and Tani's in Green Bay. Here, hang on a minute and I'll give you their numbers.'

While Brookie searched, Maggie pictured their faces: Lisa, their homecoming queen, who resembled Grace Kelly; Carolyn Fisher, a.k.a. Fish, with a turned-up nose which she'd always hated, and across which she'd written in everyone's yearbook; Tani, a freckled redhead.

'Maggie, you there?'

'I'm here.'

'You got a pencil?'

'Go ahead.'

She reeled off the girls' phone numbers, then added, 'I've got a couple more here. How about Dave Christianson's?'

'Dave Christianson?'

'Well, hell, who says you can't call the guys? We were all friends, weren't we? He married a girl from Green Bay and runs some kind of ball bearing factory, I think.'

Maggie took down Dave's number, then those of Kenny Hedlund (married to an underclassman named Cynthia Troy and living in Bowling Green, Kentucky), Barry Breckholdt (from upstate New York, married with two children), and Mark Mobridge (Mark, Brookie said, was a homosexual, lived in Minneapolis, and had married a man named Greg).

'Are you making this up?' Maggie demanded, wide-eyed.

'No, I'm not making it up! I sent them a wedding card. What the hell – live and let live. I had a lot of laughs with Mark on band trips.'

'You weren't kidding when you said you kept track of them all.'

'Here, I've got one more for you, Eric Severson.'

Maggie sat up straighter in her chair. The laughter left her face. 'Eric?'

'Yeah, KL5–3500, same area code as mine.'

After several minutes Maggie declared, 'I can't call Eric Severson.'

'Why not?'

'Well . . . because.' Because long ago, when they were seniors in high school, Maggie Pearson and Eric Severson had been lovers. Groping, green, first-time lovers, terrified of getting caught, or pregnant, lucky on both counts.

'He lives right here in Fish Creek. Runs a charter boat out of Gills Rock, just like his old man did.'

'Brookie, I said I can't call Eric.'

'Why not? Because you used to go all the way with him?'

Maggie's jaw dropped. 'Brook*ieee*!'

Brookie laughed. 'We didn't tell each other *quite* everything back then, did we? And don't forget, I was on his dad's boat the day after the prom, too. What else could you two have been doing down in that cabin all that time? But what does it matter now? Eric's still around, and he's just as nice as he ever was, and I know he'd love to hear from you.'

'But he's married, isn't he?'

'Yup. He's got a beautiful wife. A real stunner, and as far as I know they're very happy.'

'Well, there.' Amen.

'Maggie, for cripe's sake, *grow up*. We're adults now.'

Maggie heard the most surprising words leave her mouth. 'But what would I say to him?'

'How about, hi, Eric, how they hangin'?' Maggie could almost see Brookie flip a hand in the air. 'How the hell should I know what you'd say to him! I just gave you his number along with all the rest. I didn't think it would be such a big deal.'

'It's not.'

'Then don't make it one.'

'I . . .' On the verge of arguing further, Maggie thought better of it. 'Listen . . . thanks, Brookie. Thanks so much, and that comes straight from the heart. You were exactly what the doctor ordered tonight.'

'Blow it out your ear, Pearson. You don't thank a friend for something like this. You gonna be okay now? You won't flush yourself down the john or anything, will you?'

'I feel a hundred per cent better.'

'You sure?'

'I'm sure.'

'Okay, then, I gotta go. I got kids to get to bed. Call me anytime, okay?'

'I will, and you do the same.'

'I will. See y', Mag.'

'See y', Brookie.'

After hanging up, Maggie slouched in the chair, smiling lazily for a long time. A montage of pleasant memories reeled through her mind, of herself and the girls in high school – Fish, Tani, Lisa and Brookie. Especially Brookie – not particularly bright but liked by everyone because she had a terrific sense of humour and treated everyone equitably, never indulging in criticizing or backbiting. How wonderful to know she hadn't changed, that she was still there in Door County, a ready link with the past, the keeper of contacts.

Maggie rolled her chair closer to the desk and glanced at the telephone numbers highlighted in the beam of the banker's lamp. Fish's, Lisa's, Tani's, Dave Christianson's, Kenny Hedlund's.

Eric Severson's.

No, I couldn't.

She sat back, rocked, thought a little longer. Finally, she rose and searched the bookshelves, selecting a thin, padded volume of cream leather stamped with imitation gold that had long since tarnished.

Gibraltar, 1965.

She opened the cover and saw her own squarish handwriting, with the parenthetical instruction (*Save for Brookie*), and Brookie's abysmal chicken-scratching.

Dear Maggie,

Well, we made it, huh? God, I didn't think we ever would. I thought Morrie-baby would catch us drinking beer and expel us before we ever graduated. Boy, we sure drank a few, huh? I'll never forget all the fun we had cheering and dancing and driving thru all those cornfields in Fish's panel truck with the Senior Scourges. Remember the time we stopped it and took a leak in the middle of Main Street? God, what if we'd got caught!! Don't forget the choir trip and that green slime we put in Pruitt's thermos bottle, and all the times we drove him nuts adding notes to songs, and the time we put that poster of the nude in the boys' locker room with you-know-who's name on it! (My mother still hasn't found out about all the trouble we got into over that!) Prom was the greatest with Arnie and Eric, and the day after out in Garrett's Bay in Eric's boat. (Sigh!) I sure hope everything works out for you and Eric, and I know it will because you're such a neat couple. Even though you'll be at Northwestern and I'll be in Green Bay at Beauty School, we'll still get together weekends and pork out with Fish and Lisa and Tani so let's all keep in touch . . . fer sure, fer sure! Take it easy on the guys in Chi-town, and good luck in whatever you do. You're the one with all the brains and talent, so I know you'll be a success, no matter what. You've been the best friend ever, Mag, so whatever you do, don't change. And don't forget me. Promise!

Love, Brookie

Reaching the end of Brookie's monologue, Maggie found herself smiling wistfully. She didn't remember putting green slime in Mr Pruitt's thermos or whose name they'd written on the poster of the nude. And who was Morrie-baby? So many lost memories.

She checked out Brookie's class picture, Tani's, Lisa's, Fish's, her own (wrinkling her nose in chagrin) – all of them so girlish and unsophisticated. But the one whose picture she'd really opened the book to see was Eric Severson.

And there he was. Extraordinarily good-looking at seventeen – tall, blond and Nordic. Though the yearbook was done in black and white, Maggie imagined colour where there was none – the startling blue of his eyes, true as a field of Door County chicory in August; the sun-bleached blond of his hair, streaked like dry cornhusks; the perennial teak of his skin baked in by summers of helping his father on the fishing boat.

Eric Severson, my first lover.

She found his handwriting on the flyleaf at the end of the book.

Dear Maggie,

I never would have guessed at the beginning of this year how hard it'd be to write this to you. What a great year we had together. I remember that first night I asked if I could take you home, and when you said yes, I thought, Maggie Pearson with me, Wow!! And now look at us, graduating with a jillion memories. I'll never forget that first dance when you told me not to chew gum in your ear, and the first time I kissed you on the snowmobile trail down below Old Bluff Road, and all the times when coach Gilbert would be talking to us guys during the time-outs and I'd sneak a look at you on the other side of the gym while you were cheering. I liked you for a long time before I got up enough nerve to ask you out, and now I only wish I'd asked you about three years sooner. I'm going to miss you to beat hell this fall when I'm at Stout State, but we've got a date for Thanksgiving in The Door, and for Christmas, too. I'll never forget the day after the prom on the *Mary Deare*, and the night in old man Eastley's orchard. Don't forget Felicity and Aaron, and we've got a date in the spring of '69 to talk about you know what. Keep wearing pink (but only when you got a date at home with me). I never saw a woman who looked so great in pink. I'll never forget you, Maggie M'girl.

Lots of love, Eric

Felicity and Aaron – the names they had picked for their future children. Heavens, she'd forgotten. And the date in the spring when they had agreed to talk about getting married. And how he'd always favoured her in pink. And his own special endearment, Maggie M'girl.

Remembering him, she was gripped by nostalgia. Looking back on those giddy days through the perspective of maturity she thought, Brookie is right. He's happily married to a very beautiful wife, and we're all grown-ups now. How could a call from a girl twenty-three years in his past threaten either his marriage or my well-being? It'll be a friendly hello, that's all.

Following Dr Feldstein's orders, Maggie picked up the phone and dialled.

Chapter 2

The phone jarred Eric Severson out of a sound sleep. Beside him, Nancy mumbled and rolled over as he reached for the nightstand and answered in the dark.

'Hul –' He cleared his throat. 'Hullo?'

'Hello, is this Eric Severson?'

'Who's this?' he asked ungraciously, peering at the red numbers on the digital clock.

'It's Margaret Stearn . . . ah, Pearson.'

'Who?'

Nancy thumped a hip into the mattress and gave the covers an irritated jerk. 'Who in the world is calling at this hour of the night?'

'It's Maggie, Eric,' the woman on the phone said. 'Maggie Pearson?'

'Mag –' He struggled to think who Maggie Pearson was.

'Oh, I woke you, didn't I? I'm really sorry. How thoughtless of me. But I'm in Seattle and it's only nine o'clock here. Listen, Eric, I'll call some other time during the day when –'

'No, it's all right. Who . . . Maggie? You mean Maggie Pearson from Gibraltar High? Class of '65?' He recognized her laughter and settled onto his back, wider awake. 'Well, I'll be damned.'

Nancy rolled over and asked, 'Who is it?'

Shielding the mouthpiece, he answered. 'A girl I went to school with, Maggie Pearson.'

'Oh, great,' Nancy grumbled and rolled away again.

'There's someone with you?'

Into the phone Eric said, 'Yes, my wife.'

'I really am sorry, Eric. It was an impetuous call, anyway.

Please apologize to your wife for my waking her and go back to sleep, both of you.'

'Wait a minute!' he ordered, sitting up, dropping his feet over the edge of the bed. 'Maggie?'

'Yes?'

'I'll change phones. Hang on a minute.' He rose in the dark, flipped the covers over, leaned on them with both hands and kissed Nancy's cheek. 'Hang this up when I get downstairs, will you, honey? Sorry to disturb you.'

'What does she want?'

'I don't know,' he said, leaving the room. 'I'll tell you in the morning.'

The only other phones were downstairs. He moved familiarly along the dark hall and down the steps, across the living-room carpet and onto the cool, vinyl floor of the kitchen where he switched on the fluorescent light above the sink. In its sudden glare he squinted and reached for the phone on the counter.

'Hello?'

'Yes,' Maggie replied.

'There, we can talk now. I'm downstairs. Well, Maggie, what a surprise to hear from you.'

'I really am sorry, Eric. It was stupid of me not to consider the time difference. You see, I just finished talking to Brookie – she's the one who gave me your number and suggested I call you. We had such a great talk, by the time I hung up I never gave a second thought to the time.'

'Stop apologizing.'

'But what will your wife think?'

'She's probably already gone back to sleep.' Eric heard the click as Nancy hung up the bedside phone. Dressed only in Jockey shorts, he settled gingerly on a kitchen chair, taking the phone with him. 'She travels a lot, so she's used to sleeping in hotels and on planes, wherever she needs to. When she's here in her own bed, sleeping's no problem for her, believe me.'

'Brookie told me you were married, and to a very beautiful wife.'

'Yes, she is, thanks. Her name is Nancy.'

'She's not from Door County?'

'No, she's from Estherville, Iowa. I met her my last year in college. How about you? You're living in Seattle and –?' His inflection left an open blank.

'And I was married for eighteen years. He died a year ago.'

'I'm sorry, Maggie . . . I read a mention of it in the *Advocate.*' After a pause, he inquired, 'How about kids?'

'One. A daughter, Katy, seventeen. You?'

'No, unfortunately, none.'

His reply left a gap. Groping for something to fill in, she put in, 'Brookie says you're running your dad's charter boat.'

'Yup. Out of Gills Rock with my brother Mike. You remember Mike, don't you? He was two years ahead of us?'

'Of course I remember Mike. We used his car to go to prom.'

'That's right, I'd forgotten. We've got two boats now, and Ma mans the radio for us and does all the shore work and the bookings and sells the licences.'

'Your mother – I smile when I think of her. How is she?'

'Unstoppable. Looks the same as ever – like a cross between Burgess Meredith and a Persian lamb coat.'

Maggie laughed. The sound, coming across the wire, seemed to roll time backwards. 'Ma never changes. She's still full of sass,' Eric added, settling more comfortably in the chair.

'Your mother was such a spunky lady. I liked her so much. And your dad . . . he's gone now, I think my mother wrote.'

'Yes, six years ago.'

'You were always so close to him. I'm sure you must miss him.'

'We all do.' It was true. Even after six years, Eric still felt the loss. The values he had learned had been taught to him by the old man. He'd come by his occupation wrapped in the old man's arms, with his powerful hands covering Eric's own on the rod and reel, and his voice in Eric's ear, ordering, 'Never jerk back on the line, son! Keep 'er steady!' More than half of Eric's charter customers were old-time repeaters who'd been fishing on the *Mary Deare* since the early days of Severson Charters. Eric's voice held gruff affection as he added, 'Ah, well . . . he had a hell of a good life, drove the boat till the end and died right here at home, holding Ma's hand with all four of us kids around the bed.'

'That's right – I forgot about your other brother and sister – where are they?'

'Ruth lives in Duluth and Larry's in Milwaukee. I see your folks around every now and then, your dad mostly when I go into the store. He always wants a report on how the fish are biting.'

'I'm sure he envies you, fishing for a living.'

Eric chuckled. 'I was in there about a month ago or so and I told him to drive up sometime and I'd take him out.'

'I suppose he never came.'

'No, he didn't.'

'Mother apparently wouldn't give him permission,' Maggie remarked sardonically.

Maggie's mother had been a harridan for as long as Eric had known her. He remembered his fear of Vera Pearson when he'd dated Maggie and how the area women, in general, disliked her.

'I take it she hasn't changed.'

'Not much. At least she hadn't the last time I was home, which was . . . oh, three years ago, I guess. She's still got a ring in Daddy's nose, and she'd like to see one in mine. Consequently, I don't come home very often.'

'You didn't make the last class reunion.'

'No . . . Phillip and I lived out here in Seattle then and

. . . well, it's a long way. We just somehow never made it. We travel a lot, though . . . or . . . well, we did, I mean.'

Her slip caused a moment's awkwardness. 'Sorry', she inserted. 'I try not to do that, but sometimes it slips out.'

'No, that's . . . that's okay, Maggie.' He paused, then admitted, 'You know, I'm trying to picture you. Funny isn't it, how hard it is to picture a person older than we remember them?' In his mind she was still seventeen, thin and auburn-haired, with brown eyes, a delicate face and an attractively cleft chin. Vivacious. And laughing. He'd always been able to make her laugh so easily.

'I'm older. Definitely older.'

'Aren't we all?'

Eric picked up a teakwood pear from a wooden bowl in the centre of the table and rubbed it with his thumb. He'd never understood why Nancy put wooden fruit on the table when the genuine article grew all over Door County.

'You miss your husband a lot?'

'Yes, I do. We had a model marriage.'

He tried to think of some reply but none came. 'I'm afraid I'm not much good at this, Maggie, I'm sorry. When my dad died it was the same way. I didn't know what the hell to say to my mother.'

'It's all right, Eric. It makes a lot of people uncomfortable, even me sometimes.'

'Maggie, can I ask you something?'

'Of course.'

He paused uncertainly. 'No, I guess I'd better not.'

'No, go ahead. What?'

'I'm curious, that's all. It's . . . well . . .' Perhaps it was an impertinent question, but he couldn't stop himself from asking. 'Why did you call?'

His question startled her, too; he could tell by the seconds of silence that followed.

'I don't know. Just to say hi.'

After twenty-three years, just to say hi? It seemed odd, yet there appeared no other logical reason.

She rushed on. 'Well . . . it's late, and I'm sure you have to be up early tomorrow. Saturday in The Door . . . I remember it well. Always a lot of tourists around then, and they probably all want to go fishing for salmon, right? Listen, forgive me for waking you, and please apologize to your wife. I know I woke her, too.'

'No problem, Maggie. Hey, I'm really glad you called. I mean that.'

'So am I.'

'Well . . .' Eric waited, uneasy for no good reason he could name, finally coming up with a closing remark. 'Next time you come home, give us a call. I'd like you to meet Nancy.'

'I'll do that. And greet your mom and Mike for me.'

'I will.'

'Well, good-bye, Eric.'

'Good-bye.'

The line clicked immediately but he sat for long moments, perplexed, gazing at the phone.

What the hell?

He hung up, returned the phone to the cabinet and stood staring at it. *Eleven o'clock at night after twenty-three years Maggie calls. Why?* He slipped his hands inside the elastic waistband of his shorts and scratched his belly, wondering. He opened the refrigerator and stood a while with the chill air fanning his bare legs, registering little but the repetitive thought: *Why?*

Just to say hi, she'd said, but that sounded fishy.

He took out a container of orange juice, uncapped it and swilled half of it straight from the bottle. Backhanding his mouth, he continued standing in the wedge of light from the open door, baffled. He'd probably never know the real reason. Loneliness, maybe. Nothing more.

He put the juice away, snapped out the kitchen light and returned to his bedroom.

Nancy was sitting up cross-legged with the light on,

dressed in a peach satin teddy and tap pants, her shapely limbs gleaming in the lamplight.

'Well, that took a while,' she remarked dryly.

'Surprised the hell out of me.'

'Maggie Pearson?'

'Yup.'

'The one you took to the prom?'

'Yup.'

'What did she want?'

He dropped onto the bed, braced his hands beside her hips and kissed her left breast above an inviting edge of peach-coloured lace. 'My body, what else?'

'Eric!' Grabbing a fistful of his hair, she lifted his head. 'What did she want?'

He shrugged noncommittally. 'Damned if I know. She said she talked to Brookie and Brookie gave her my phone number and told her to call me. I still haven't figured it out.'

'Brookie?'

'Glenda Kerschner. Her maiden name was Holbrook.'

'Oh. The cherry picker's wife.'

'Yeah. She and Maggie were best friends in high school. We were all friends, a whole gang of us who ran around together.'

'That still doesn't answer my question. What is your old girlfriend doing calling you in the middle of the night?'

With his inner wrists brushing her jutting knees he smiled smugly into her face. 'Jealous?'

'Curious.'

'Well, I don't know.' He kissed Nancy's mouth. 'Her husband died.' He kissed her throat. 'She's lonely, that's all I can figure out.' He kissed her breast. 'She said to tell you she's sorry she woke you up.' He bit her nipple, silk and all.

'Where does she live?'

'Seattle.' The word was muffled against Nancy's lingerie.

'Oh . . . in that case . . .' Nancy uncrossed her legs, slid onto her back and pulled him down on top of her, linking her arms and ankles behind him. They kissed, long and lazily, rocking against each other. When he lifted his head she looked into his eyes and said, 'I miss you when I'm gone, Eric.'

'Then stop going.'

'And do what?'

'Keep the books for me, open a boutique and sell all your fancy cosmetics to the tourists here in Fish Creek . . .' He paused before adding, '. . . be a hausfrau and raise a pack of brats.' *Or even one brat would do*. But he knew better than to push the subject.

'Hey,' she scolded, 'we're starting something interesting here. Let's not spoil it with that old epistle.'

She drew his head down, invited his tongue inside her mouth and became the aggressor, stripping him of his briefs, rolling him onto his back, and slithering from her own skimpy lingerie. She was adept, very adept, and infallibly desirable. She saw to her desirability the way some wives see to their daily housework, expending much time and energy upon it, allotting it a fixed time in her schedule.

Lord, she was a beautiful creature. While she reversed their roles and seduced him, he admired her at close range, her skin with the exquisite texture of an eggshell, incredibly unaged for a woman of thirty-eight, cared for twice a day with the expensive French cosmetics she sold; her nails, professionally groomed and artificially lengthened, painted a gleaming raspberry; her hair, which was presently a deep mahogany colour, shining with highlights added by some costly beautician in some far-off city where she'd been this past week. Orlane paid their sales reps a hair and nail allowance and gave them unlimited gratis merchandise with the understanding that they present themselves as walking testimonials for their products. The company got its money's worth with Nancy Macaffee. She was the most beautiful woman he knew.

She ran one long nail across his lips and inside them. He

bit it lightly, then, still lying beneath her, reached up to stroke her hair.

'I like the new colour,' he murmured, threading his fingers back along her skull, combing her hair towards the ceiling, then letting it fall. She had hair as coarse as a mare's tail, thick and healthy. Daytime, she wore it drawn back to the nape in a classic, smooth, tucked tail, held by a sixty-dollar gold barrette. Tonight it bunched around her high cheekbones, making her look like Cleopatra in an up-draught.

She sat on his abdomen, svelte, nude, shaking her head until the hair slapped the corners of her eyes, flexing her fingers in the hair on his chest like a dozing cat.

'Maurice did it . . . in Chicago.'

'Maurice, hm?'

She gave her head a final shake and let an insinuating smile tease her lips as she studied him with hooded eyes.

'Mm-hmm . . .'

On her hips his hands flexed repeatedly. 'You know, you're incredible.'

'Why?' She scratched a dim white line from his throat down to his pelvic arch and watched it return to its natural colour.

'You wake up in the middle of the night looking as if you just got up from Maurice's chair.'

Her eyebrows were brushed upward, her eyelashes thick and black around deep brown eyes. Long ago, when she'd been in training to learn her trade, she'd told him a fact she'd learned: that most people are born with a single row of lashes, but some are blessed with a double. Nancy had a double and then some. She had incredible eyes. Lips, too.

'Come here,' he ordered gruffly, catching her by the armpits and tipping her down. 'We've got five days to make up for.' He flipped her over neatly and slipped a hand between her legs, touched her inside, found her wet and swollen with desire equalling his own. He felt her cool hand surround him at last and shuddered with her first stroke. They knew each other's sexual temperaments intrinsically, knew what the other needed, wanted, liked best.

But at the moment when he reached to place himself inside her, she pressed him away, whispering, 'Wait, sweetheart, I'll be right back.'

He stayed where he was, pinning her down. 'Why don't you forget it tonight?'

'I can't. It's too risky.'

'So what?' He continued enticing her, stroking her shallowly, strewing kisses across her face. 'Take a chance,' he murmured against her lips. 'Would it be the end of the world if you got pregnant?'

She chuckled, bit the end of his chin and repeated, 'I'll be right back,' then escaped and padded across the carpet to the bathroom down the hall.

He sighed, flopped to his back and closed his eyes. *When?* But he knew the answer. Never. She pampered her body not only for the benefit of Orlane cosmetics, not only for him, but for herself. She was afraid of jeopardizing that perfection. He had taken a chance, introducing the subject tonight. Most times when he mentioned having a baby, she grew indignant and found something in the room to occupy her attention. Afterward, for the remainder of their weekend together, the atmosphere would be strained. So he'd learned not to badger her about it. But the years were on a downhill run. In October he'd be forty-one; another two years or so and he'd be too old to want to start a family. A kid deserved an old man with a little zip and zest, one he could scrimmage and wrestle with, reel in the big ones with.

Eric recalled his earliest memory, of riding above his father's head, seated on the old man's wide, cupped palm while the gulls wheeled overhead. 'See them birds, son? Follow them and they'll tell you where there's fish.' In sharp contrast came the memory of himself and his brothers and sister standing around the bed when his father died, all with tears streaming down their faces as one by one they kissed the old man's lifeless cheek, then their ma's, before leaving her alone with him.

More than anything in the world, he wanted a family.

The mattress shifted and Eric opened his eyes.

Nancy knelt above him. 'Hi, I'm back.'

They made love, quite expertly if the books were any criteria. They were inventive and agile. They sampled three different positions. They verbalized their wishes. Eric experienced one orgasm; Nancy, two. But when it was over and the room dark, he lay studying the shadowed ceiling, cradling his head on his arms and pondering how empty the act could be when not used for its intended purpose.

Nancy rolled close, threw an arm and a leg over him and tried to finesse him into cuddling. She commandeered his arm and drew it around her waist.

But he had no desire to hold her as they drifted off to sleep.

In the morning Nancy rose at 5:30 and Eric at quarter to six, the moment the shower was free. He thought she must be the last woman in America who still used a vanity table. The house, prairie-styled, circa 1919, had never pleased Nancy. She had moved into it under duress, complaining that the kitchen was unsatisfactory, the plug-ins inadequate and the bathroom a joke. Thus the vanity table in the bedroom.

It sat against a narrow stretch of wall between two windows, accompanied by a large round makeup mirror circled by lights.

While Eric showered and dressed, Nancy went through her morning beauty rite: pots and tubes and bottles and wands; jellies and lotions, sprays and creams; hair blowers and curlers and teasers and lifters. Though he'd never been able to understand how it could take her an hour and fifteen minutes, he'd watched her often enough to know it did. The cosmetic ritual was as deeply ingrained in Nancy's life as dicting; she did both as a matter of rote, finding it unthinkable to appear even at her own breakfast table without looking as flawless as she would if she were flying into New York to meet the Orlane hierarchy.

While Nancy sat at the makeup mirror, Eric moved about the bedroom, listening to the weather on the radio, dressing in white jeans, white Reeboks and a sky-blue knit pullover with the company logo, a ship's wheel, and his name stitched on the breast pocket.

Tying his sneakers, he asked, 'Want anything from the bakery?'

She was drawing fine auburn eyelashes onto her lower lids. 'You eat too much of that stuff. You should have some wholegrain instead.'

'My only vice. Be right back.'

She watched him leave the room, proud of his continued leanness, his eye-catching good looks. He had been displeased last night, she knew, and it worried her. She wanted their relationship – just the two of them – to be enough for him, as it was for her. She'd never been able to understand why he thought he needed more.

In the kitchen he put coffee on to perk before stepping outside and pausing on the front stoop, studying the town and the water below. Main Street, a mere block away, contoured the shoreline of Fish Creek Harbor, which lay this morning beneath a patchy pink-tinged mist, obscuring the view of Peninsula State Park, due north across the water. At the town docks sailboats sat motionlessly, their masts piercing the fog, visible above the treetops and the roofs of the businesses along Main. He knew that street and the establishments on it as well as he knew the waters of the bay, from the stately old White Gull Inn on the west end to the sassy new Top of the Hill Shops at the east. He knew the people down there, too, hometown folks who waved when they saw his pickup go by and knew what time the mail came into the post office each day (between 11:00 and 12:00) and how many churches the town had, and who belonged to which congregation.

These first few minutes outside were some of the best of his day, casting a weather eye at the water and the eastern sky above the woods which crowded the town, listening to a mourning dove mimic itself from a highwire nearby, inhaling the scent of the giant cedars behind the house and the aroma of fresh bread, lifting from the bakery at the bottom of the hill.

Why did Maggie Pearson call me after twenty-three years?

Out of nowhere the thought intruded. Startled by it, Eric set his feet in motion and jogged down the hill, hollering hello to Pete Nelson through the back screen door of the bakery as he passed it and headed around the building. It was a pretty little place, set back from the street with a grassy front lawn, surrounded by a white-railed porch and beds of bright flowers that gave it a homey look. Inside, he nodded to two early tourists buying bismarcks, exchanged good mornings with the pretty, young Hawkins girl behind the counter and asked after her mother, who'd had a gallbladder operation, then exchanged pleasantries with Pete, who stuck his head out of the back room, and with Sam Ellerby, who was out collecting his usual tray of assorted rolls and breads to serve at the Summertime Restaurant on Spruce Street, two blocks away.

To Eric, this ritual trip to the bakery had become as enjoyable as Pete Nelson's pastries. He returned up the hill in blithe spirits, carrying a white waxed bag, bounded into the house and poured two cups of coffee just as Nancy entered the kitchen.

'Good morning,' she said, for the first time that day. (To Nancy it was never a good morning until her makeup ritual was complete.)

'Good morning.'

She wore a bone-coloured linen skirt and a boxy shirt with dropped shoulders, immense sleeves, and an upturned collar, covered all over with tiny green and purple cats. Who but Nancy would wear purple and green cats and look chic? Even her belt – a twisted hank of purple sisal with a buckle the size of a hubcap – would have looked stupid on anyone else. But his wife had panache, and indubitable style, and access to the discount rooms in the most elegant department stores across America. Any room Nancy Macaffee entered became eclipsed by her presence.

Watching her cross the kitchen in purple shoes, her hair confined in a neat, low tail, her eyes shaded and mascaraed, her lips painted one colour and outlined with another, Eric sipped his coffee and grinned.

'Thanks.' She accepted the cup he handed her and took a careful sip. 'Mmm . . . you look like you're in a good mood.'

'I am.'

'What brought the smile?'

He leaned against the cupboard, eating a fat, glazed doughnut, occasionally sipping. 'Just trying to imagine you as a polyester mama – say, two hundred pounds, wearing double-knit slacks and hair rollers every morning.'

'Don't hold your breath.' She raised one eyebrow and gave him a smirk. 'See anybody at the bakery?'

'Two tourists, Sam Ellerby, the Hawkins girl, and Pete stuck his head out of the kitchen.'

'Any news?'

'Nuh-uh.' He licked his fingers and downed the last of his coffee. 'What are you going to do today?'

'Weekly sales reports, what else? This job would be ideal if it weren't for all the paperwork.'

And the travel, he thought. After a full five days on the road, she spent her sixth, and often half of her seventh, doing paperwork – she was one damned hard worker, he'd give her that. But she loved the glamour associated with such stores as Bonwit Teller, Neiman-Marcus and Rocco Altobelli – all her accounts. And if travelling came along with the job, she accepted its drawbacks in exchange for that glamour.

She'd had the Orlane job when they moved back to Door County, and he'd thought she'd give it up, stay home and have a family. But instead, she'd put in longer hours both at home and on the road in order to keep the job.

'How about you?' she inquired, slipping on a pair of glasses, studying the weekly newspaper.

'We're full today, so is Mike. Taking three charter groups out.' He rinsed his cup, put it into the dishwasher and donned a white skipper's cap with a shiny black bill.

'So you won't be home till seven?'

'Probably not.'

She looked up through her oversized horn-rimmed glasses. 'Try to make it earlier.'

'I can't promise.'

'Just try, okay?'

He nodded.

'Well, I'd better get to work,' Nancy said, snapping the paper closed.

'Me, too.'

Coffee and juice in hand, she touched her cheek to his. 'See you tonight.'

She headed for her small downstairs office while he left the house and crossed a short stretch of sidewalk to a clapboard garage. He raised the door by hand, glanced at Nancy's ultra-respectable steel grey Acura and clambered into a rusty Ford pickup that twelve years ago had been white, had possessed a left rear fender and had not required wire to hold its tailpipe up. The vehicle was an embarrassment to Nancy, but Eric had grown fond of The Old Whore, as he affectionately called it. The engine was still reliable; the company name and phone number were still legible on the doors; and the driver's seat –after all these years – was shaped precisely like his backside.

Turning the key, he mumbled, 'All right, you old whore, come on.'

It took a little encouraging, but after less than a minute on the starter, the old 300 straight-six rumbled to life.

He gunned her, smiled, shifted into reverse and backed from the garage.

The ride from Fish Creek to Gills Rock covered nineteen of the prettiest miles in all of creation, Eric believed, with Green Bay intermittently visible off to his left; farms, orchards and forests to his right. From the flower-flanked Main Street of Fish Creek itself the road climbed, curved and dipped between thick walls of forest, past private cottages and resorts, heading northeast but swinging to the shore again and again: at the picturesque little village of Ephraim with its two white church steeples reflected in glassy Eagle Harbor; at Sister Bay where Al Johnson's famous goats were already grazing on the grassy roof of his restaurant; at Ellison Bay with its panoramic view from the hill behind the Grand View Hotel; and finally at Gills Rock beyond which the waters of Lake Michigan met those of Green Bay and created the hazardous currents from which the area extracted its name: Death's Door.

Eric had often wondered why a town and a rock had been named for a long-forgotten settler named Elias Gill when Seversons had been there earlier and longer, and were still here, for that matter. Why, hell, the name Gill had long ago disappeared from the area tax rolls and telephone book. But the heritage of the Seversons lived on. Eric's grandfather Severson had built the farm on the bluff above the bay, and his father had built the house tucked beneath the cedars beside Hedgehog Harbor as well as the charter boat business which he and Mike had expanded to provide a good living for two families – three if you counted Ma.

Some might not call Gills Rock a town at all. It was little more than a smattering of weatherbeaten buildings stretched like a gap-toothed smile around the southeast side of the harbour. A restaurant, a gift shop, several wooden docks, a boat landing and Ma's house were the primary obstacles keeping the trees from growing clear to the water's edge. Scattered among these were smaller buildings and the usual paraphernalia peculiar to a fishing community – boat trailers, winches, gasoline pumps and the cradles in which the big boats were dry-docked over the winter.

Turning into the driveway, the truck pitched steeply downhill and bumped over the stony earth. Maples and cedars grew haphazardly between patches of gravel and among the collection of huts near the docks. The roof of the fish-cleaning shack already sported a line of gulls whose droppings had permanently streaked the green shingles with white. Smoke from the fish-smoking shack hung in the air, pungent and blue. Permeating it all was the ever-present odour of decaying wood and fish. Pulling up beneath his favourite sugar maple, Eric noted that Mike's sons, Jerry Joe and Nicholas, were already aboard the *Mary Deare* and *The Dove*, vacuuming the decks, icing up the fish coolers and putting in a supply of refreshments. Like himself and Mike, the boys had grown up around the water and had been going out on the boats since their hands were big enough to grip a rail. At eighteen and sixteen Jerry Joe and Nicholas made responsible, knowledgeable mates on the two boats.

Slamming the truck door, he waved to the boys and headed for the house.

He'd grown up in the place and was unbothered by its doubling as the charter fishing office. The front door might be closed at times, but it was never locked; already at 6:55 it was shoved as far back as the buckled wood floor would allow and propped open by a six-pack of Coca-Cola. The walls of the office, panelled with knotty pine, were covered with lures, spoons, insect repellent, a two-way radio, fishing licence forms, Door County maps, landing nets, two mounted chinook salmon and dozens of photos of tourists with their prize catches. On one rack hung yellow slickers for sale, on another a rainbow of sweatshirts lauding

SEVERSON'S CHARTER FISHING, GILLS ROCK. Piled on the floor were more six-packs of canned soft drinks while on a card table in the corner a twenty-five-cup coffeepot was already steaming with free brew for the customers.

Circling the counter with its vintage brass cash register, Eric headed for the back, through a narrow door into a room that had once been a side porch but now housed a supply of Styrofoam coolers and the ice machine.

On the far side of the porch another door led into the kitchen.

'Mornin', Ma,' he said, walking in.

'Mornin' yourself.'

He reached into the cupboard for a thick, white cup and poured himself coffee from a chipped enamel pot on a chipped enamel gas range – the same one that had been there since he was a boy. Its grates were thick with charred boilover, and the paint on the wall behind it wore a yellow halo, but Ma was unapologetically undomestic – with one exception: she baked bread twice each week, refusing to put store-bought bread in her mouth, claiming, 'That stuff'll kill you!'

She was mixing bread dough this morning, on an old gateleg table covered with blue oilcloth. To the best of Eric's memory that oilcloth was the only thing that had been replaced in the room since 1959 when the antique wooden icebox had gone and Ma had bought the Gibson refrigerator, which now was a yellowed relic, but still running.

Ma never threw anything away with a day's use left in it.

She was dressed in her usual getup, blue jeans and a tight aqua-blue T-shirt that made her resemble a stack of three inner tubes. Anna Severson loved T-shirts with slogans. Today's bore the words I DO IT WITH YOUNGER MEN, and a picture of an old woman and a young man fishing. Her tight, nickel-coloured curls held the fresh shape of home-permanent rods, and her nose – what there was of it – held up a pair of glasses that were nearly as old as the Gibson and their lenses nearly as yellowed.

Turning with the cup in his hand, Eric watched her move to a cupboard to unearth bread pans.

'How're you today?' he inquired.

'Huh?'

'That ornery, huh?'

'You come in here just to drink my coffee and give me grief?'

'That what you call this?' He looked into the cup. 'It'd make a truck driver wince.'

'Then drink that coloured water in the office.'

'You know I hate those buffalo board cups.'

'Then drink your coffee at home. Or don't that wife of yours know how to make it? She get home last night?'

'Yup. About ten-fifteen.'

'Ha.'

'Ma, don't start with me.'

'That's some kind of life, you living there and her living all over the US of A.' She smeared lard in a bread pan and clunked it down on the oilcloth. 'Your dad would of come and dragged me home by the hair if I'd've tried something like that.'

'You haven't got enough hair. What'd you do to it, by the way?' He pretended a serious assessment of her ugly, tight curls.

'Went over to Barbara's last night and had her kink me up.' Barbara was Mike's wife. They lived in the woods not fifty feet up the shoreline.

'Looks like it hurts.'

She slapped him with a bread pan, then plopped a loaf into it. 'I ain't got time for hair fussing and you know it. You had your breakfast?'

'Yup.'

'What? Glazed doughnuts?'

'Ma, you're meddling again.'

She stuck the loaf in the oven. 'What else are mothers for? God didn't make no commandment named "thou shalt not meddle," so I meddle. That's what mothers are for.'

'I thought they were for selling fish licences and booking charters.'

'If you want that leftover sausage, eat it.' She nodded towards an iron skillet on top of the stove and began wiping the flour off the oilcloth with the edge of her hand.

He lifted a cover and found two nearly cold Polish sausages – one for him, one for Mike as usual – picked one up with his fingers and leaned against the stove, eating it, pondering. 'Ma, you remember Maggie Pearson?'

'Of course I remember Maggie Pearson. My hair ain't kinked up that tight. What brought her up?'

'She called me last night.'

For the first time since he'd entered the room his mother stopped moving. She turned from the sink and looked back over her shoulder.

'She called you? For what?'

'Just to say hello.'

'She lives out west someplace, doesn't she?'

'Seattle.'

'She called you from *Seattle* just to say hello?'

Eric shrugged.

'She's widowed, ain't she?'

'Yes.'

'Ah, that's it then.'

'What's it then?'

'She always was sweet on you. Sniffin' around, that's what she's doing. Widows get to sniffin' when they need a man.'

'Oh, Ma, for cryin' out loud, Nancy was right beside me when she called.'

'When who called?' Mike interrupted, arriving in the middle of the exchange. He had thirty pounds and two years on his brother, plus a full brown beard.

'His old flame,' Anna Severson answered.

'She's not my old flame!'

'Who?' Mike repeated, going straight to the cupboard for a coffee cup and filling it at the stove.

'That Pearson girl, the one he used to trade spit with on that back porch right there when he thought the rest of us had gone to bed.'

'Oh, Judas,' Eric groaned.

'*Maggie Pearson?*' Mike's eyebrows shot up.

'Vera and Leroy Pearson's daughter – you remember her,' Anna clarified.

Testing the steaming coffee with his lips, Mike grinned at his brother. 'Hoo-ey! You and old Maggie used to nearly set that old daybed on fire back in high school.'

'If I'd've known I was going to take all this flak I wouldn't have told you two.'

'So what did she want?' Mike found the leftover sausage and helped himself.

'I don't know. She and Glenda Holbrook kept in touch, and she just . . .' Eric shrugged. 'Called, that's all. Said hi, how y' doing, are you married, you got kids, that sort of thing.'

'Sniffin',' Anna put in again from the sink, her back to the boys.

'Ma!'

'Yeah, I heard you. Just to say hi.'

'She said hi to both of you, too, but I don't know why the hell I bother.'

'Mmm . . . something's missing here,' Mike speculated.

'Well, when you figure out what it is, I'm sure you'll let me know,' Eric told his brother sarcastically.

Out in the office the radio crackled and Jerry Joe's voice came on.

'*Mary Deare* to base, you up there, Grandma?'

Eric, closest to the office, went out to answer. 'This is Eric. Go ahead, Jerry Joe.'

'Mornin', Cap'n. Our seven o'clock parties are here. Just sent 'em up to the office. Nick and me could use some help down here.'

'Be right there.'

Eric glanced through the open office door and saw a group of men crossing the blacktop from the dock, heading in to register, pay and buy licences – Ma's department. Beyond the fish-cleaning tables he saw Tim Rooney, their handyman, directing a boat that was being backed into the water on their ramp, while another pickup and boat had just pulled into the parking lot.

Switching off the mike, Eric called, 'Ma? Mike? Customers coming from all directions. I'm heading for the boat.'

At precisely 7:30 A.M. the *Mary Deare*'s engines chortled to life with Eric at the wheel. Jerry Joe released the mooring lines and leapt aboard as Eric pulled the cord for the air horn and it split the silence in a long, deafening blast. From the cockpit of *The Dove*, Mike answered with a matching blast, as he, too, revved his engines.

Beneath Eric's hands the wide wooden wheel shuddered as he threw the engine from reverse into forward and headed at a crawl out of Hedgehog Harbor.

This was the time of day Eric liked best, early morning, with the sun coming up behind him and fingers of steam rising from the water, parting and curling as the boat nudged through; and overhead, a battalion of herring gulls acting as escort, screaking loudly with their white heads cocked in the sun; and to the west Door Bluff rising sharp and green against a violet horizon.

He pointed the bow northward, leaving behind the damp-wood-and-fish smells of the harbour for the bracing freshness of the open water. Switching on the depth sounder, he plucked the radio mike off the ceiling.

'This is the *Mary Deare* on ten. Who's out there this morning?'

A moment later a voice came back. 'This is the *Mermaid* off Table Bluff.'

'Hi, Rog, any luck this morning?'

'Nothing yet but we're marking 'em at fifty-five feet.'

'Anyone else out?'

'*Mariner* was heading towards Washington Island, but she's under fog, so they pulled line and went east.'

'Maybe I'll head around Door Bluff then.'

'Might as well. No action out here.'

'What depth you running?'

'My deep line is shallow – oh, forty-five or so.'

'We'll try a little deeper, then. Thanks, Rog.'

'Good luck, Eric.'

Among Door County guides it was customary to share information liberally in an effort to help each fishing party fill out, for successful trips brought fishermen back.

Eric made one more call. '*Mary Deare* to base.'

Ma's voice came on, scratchy and gruff. 'Go ahead, Eric.'

'Heading out around Door Bluff.'

'I hear you.'

'See you at eleven. Have that bread baked, okay?'

She clicked on in the middle of a chuckle. 'Aye-aye, brat. Base out.'

Smiling over his shoulder as he hung up the mike, Eric heralded Jerry Joe. 'Take over here while I set the lines.'

For the next thirty minutes he was busy baiting rods and reels with shiny lures, attaching them to the downriggers on the stern, counting the times each line crossed the reel as it payed out, setting the depth accordingly. He assigned lines, checked the multicoloured radar screen for sign of baitfish or salmon and kept a constant eye on the tips of the reels in their scabbards along the side and rear rails. All the while he bantered with his customers, getting to know the first-timers, rehashing past catches with the repeaters, joshing and charming them all into coming back again.

He was good at his job, good with people, good with the

lines. When the first fish was hooked his enthusiasm added as much to the excitement as the bowed rod. He plucked it from its holder, bellowing out instructions, putting it in the hands of a thin, bald man from Wisconsin, then hurriedly buckling around the man's waist a heavy leather belt to hold the butt of the rod, shouting the directives his father had issued years before: 'Don't jerk back! Stay close to the rail!' and to Jerry Joe, 'Throttle down, circle right! We got him!' He scolded and encouraged with equal likeability, as excited as if this were the first catch he'd ever overseen, manning the landing net himself and hauling the catch over the rail.

He'd been fishing these waters all his life so it was no surprise that they filled out: six salmon for six fishermen.

Returning to port at eleven, he weighed the fish, hung them on a hook board reading SEVERSON'S CHARTERS, GILLS ROCK, lined the proud fishermen up behind their catch, took the customary series of Polaroid photographs, gave one to each customer, cleaned the fish, sold four Styrofoam coolers and four bags of ice and went up to Ma's for dinner.

By seven o'clock that night he'd repeated the same routine three times. He'd baited lines a total of forty-two times, had met eight new customers and eleven old ones, helped them land fifteen chinook salmon and three brown trout, had cleaned all eighteen fish and had still managed to think of Maggie Pearson more times than he cared to admit. Odd, what a call like hers began. Old memories, nostalgia, questions like, *what if?*

Climbing the incline to Ma's house for the last time, he thought of Maggie again. He checked his watch. Seven-fifteen and Nancy would have supper waiting, but his mind was made up. He was going to make one phone call before heading home.

Mike and the boys had gone home, and Ma was closing up the front office as he went through.

'Big day,' Ma said, unplugging the coffeepot.

'Yeah.'

In the kitchen the Door County phone book hung on a dirty string from the wall phone beside the refrigerator. Looking up the number, he knew Ma would be coming in right behind him, but he had nothing to hide. He dialled. The phone rang in his ear and he propped an elbow against the top of the refrigerator. Sure enough, Ma came in with the percolator and started emptying coffee grounds into the sink while he listened to the fourth ring.

'Hello?' a child answered.

'Is Glenda there?'

'Just a minute.' The phone clunked loudly in his ear. The child returned and said, 'She wants to know who this is.'

'Eric Severson.'

'Okay, just a minute.' He heard the child shout, 'Eric Severson!' while Ma moved about the room and listened.

Moments later Glenda came on. 'Eric, hello! Speaking of the devil.'

'Hi, Brookie.'

'Did she call you?'

'Maggie? Yeah. Surprised the hell out of me.'

'Me, too. I'm sure worried about her.'

'Worried?'

'Well, yeah, I mean, gosh . . . aren't you?'

He did a mental double take. 'Should I be?'

'Well, couldn't you tell how depressed she was?'

'No, I mean, she didn't say a word. We just – you know – caught up, sort of.'

'She didn't say anything about this group she's working with?'

'What group?'

'She's in a bad way, Eric,' Brookie told him. 'She lost her husband a year ago, and her daughter just came back east to college. Apparently she's been going through counselling with some grief group and everything sort of came down on her at once. She was going through this struggle to accept the fact that her husband was dead, and in the middle of it all, somebody from the group tried to commit suicide.'

'Suicide?' Eric's elbow came away from the refrigerator. 'You mean she might possibly be that bad, too?'

'I don't know. All I know is that her psychiatrist told her that when she starts getting depressed the best thing to do is to call old friends and talk about the old days. That's why she called us. We're her therapy.'

'Brookie, I didn't know. If I had . . . but she didn't say anything about a psychiatrist or therapy or anything. Is she in the hospital or what?'

'No, she's at home.'

'How did she seem to you? I mean, was she still depressed or . . .' His troubled gaze was fixed on Anna, who had stopped her work and stood watching him.

'I don't know. I got her laughing some, but it's hard to tell. How did she seem when you talked to her?'

'I don't know either. It's been twenty-three years, Brookie. It's pretty hard to tell from just her voice. I got her laughing, too, but . . . hell, if only she'd have said something.'

'Well, if you can spare the time, give her a call now and then. I think it'll help. I've already talked to Fish and Lisa and Tani. We're going to kind of take turns.'

'Good idea.' Eric considered for less than two seconds before making his decision. 'Have you got her number, Brookie?'

'Sure. You got a pencil?'

He caught the one hanging on the dirty string. 'Yeah, go ahead.'

With his mother watching, he wrote Maggie's phone number among the dozens scrawled on the cover of the phone book.

'206–555–3404,' he repeated. 'Thanks, Brookie.'

'Eric?'

'Yeah?'

'Tell her hi, and tell her I'm thinking about her and that I'll be calling her soon.'

'I will.'

'And say hi to your mom.'

'I'll do that. I'm at her house now. Bye, Brookie.'

'Bye.'

When he hung up, his gaze locked with Anna's. He felt like a herd of horses was galloping through his insides.

'She's in some counselling group for people who are suicidal. Her doctor told her to call old friends.' He released a tense breath and looked harried.

'Well, the poor, poor thing.'

'She never told me, Ma.'

'Can't be an easy thing to make yourself say.'

He wandered to a kitchen window, stared out, seeing Maggie as he remembered her, a gay young girl who laughed so easily. He stood for a long time, filled with a startling amount of concern, considering what was proper.

Finally he turned back to Anna. He was forty years old, but he needed her approval before doing what was on his mind. 'I've got to call her back, Ma.'

'Absolutely.'

'You care if I call from here?'

'You go right ahead. I got to take a bath.' She abandoned the percolator and coffee grounds in the sink, crossed the room to him and gave him a rare hug and several bluff thumps on the back. 'Sometimes, son, we got no choice,' she said, then left him standing in the empty room beside the waiting telephone.

Chapter 3

On the day following her conversations with Brookie and Eric, Maggie's phone made up for its usual silence. Her first call came at six A.M.

'Hi, Mom.'

Maggie shot up and checked the clock. 'Katy, are you all right?'

'I'm fine, which you would have known last night, except your phone was busy all night long.'

'Oh, Katy, I'm sorry.' Maggie stretched and settled into her pillow. 'I had two of the most wonderful conversations with old high school friends.' She filled Katy in on the highlights, asked where she was, told her to be sure to call again tonight, and said good-bye without any of the loneliness she'd expected upon ending her first long-distance conversation with her daughter.

Her next call came as she was bobbing her first tea bag of the day. It was Nelda.

'Tammi's going to make it and Dr Feldstein says it would be good for her to see us.'

Maggie put a hand to her heart, breathed, 'Oh, thank God,' and felt the day's promise brighten within her.

At 10:30 A.M. her next call came, this one wholly unexpected.

'Hello,' she answered, and a voice out of her past said, 'Hello, Maggie, this is Tani.'

Jolted by surprise, Maggie smiled and held the receiver with both hands.

'Tani. Oh, Tani, how *are* you? Gosh, it's good to hear your voice.'

Their conversation lasted forty minutes. Within an hour

after it ended, Maggie answered the phone again, this time to hear a squeaky cartoon-mouse voice that could hardly be mistaken.

'Hi, Maggie. Guess who?'

'Fish? Fish, it's you, isn't it?'

'Yup. It's the fish.'

'Oh my gosh, I can't believe this! Brookie called you, right?'

By the time Lisa called, Maggie was half expecting it. She was putting on the last of her makeup, preparing to go to the hospital and see Tammi when the phone rang yet again.

'Hello, stranger,' a sweet voice said.

'Lisa . . . oh, Lisa . . .'

'It's been a long time, hasn't it?'

'Too long. Oh, goodness . . . I'm not sure I won't break down in tears here in a minute.' She was half laughing, half crying.

'I'm a little choked up myself. How are you, Maggie?'

'How would you be if four of your dearest old friends rallied round when you put out the call? I'm overwhelmed.'

Half an hour later, when they'd reminisced and caught up, Lisa said, 'Listen, Maggie, I had an idea. Do you remember my brother, Gary?'

'Of course. He's married to Marcy Kreig.'

'Was. They've been divorced for over five years. Well, Gary is getting remarried next week and I'll be in Door for the wedding. I was thinking, if you could come home, I'm sure Tani and Fish could drive up, and we could all get together out at Brookie's house.'

'Oh, Lisa, I can't.' Disappointment coloured Maggie's voice. 'It sounds wonderful, but I'm due to start teaching in less than two weeks.'

'Just a quick trip?'

'I'm afraid it would be too quick, and at the beginning of the term like this . . . I'm sorry, Lisa.'

'Oh, shoot. That's a disappointment.'

'I know. It would have been so much fun.'

'Well, listen . . . will you think about it? Even if it's only for the weekend. It would be so great to get everybody together again.'

'All right,' Maggie promised. 'I'll think about it.'

She did, on her drive in to the hospital to visit Tammi – about Brookie calling all the girls, and each of them concerned enough to make contact after all these years, and how her own outlook had brightened in so short a time. She thought about the curious rhythms in life, and how the support she'd just been given she would now pass on to another.

At 2:55 that afternoon she sat flipping the pages of a *Good Housekeeping* magazine in the family lounge of the intensive care unit of Washington University Hospital, waiting to be summoned. A television with its volume lowered murmured from its perch on the far wall. In a corner by the window a father and two sons waited for news of a mother who had undergone bypass surgery. From a Formica niche in the wall the smell of strong coffee drifted through the room.

A nurse entered, thin, pretty, walking briskly in on her silent, white shoes.

'Mrs Stearn?'

'Yes?' Maggie dropped her magazine and jumped to her feet.

'You can go in and see Tammi now, but only for five minutes.'

'Thank you.'

Maggie wasn't prepared for the sight that greeted her upon entering Tammi's room. So much machinery. So many tubes and bottles; screens of various sizes bleeping out vital signs; and a thin, gaunt Tammi lying on the bed with a network of IVs threaded into her arms. Her eyes were closed, her hands lying wrist-up, her arms dotted by purple bruises where previous IVs had been. Her apricot-blonde hair, which she'd always kept with meticulous teenage pride and wore in a style much like Katy's, lay brittle and spiky as a bird's nest on the pillow.

Maggie stood beside the bed for some time before Tammi opened her eyes and found her there.

'Hi, little one.' Maggie leaned close and touched the girl's cheek. 'We've all been so worried about you.'

Tammi's eyes filled with tears and she rolled her face away.

Maggie brushed back Tammi's hair from her forehead. 'We're so happy you're still alive.'

'But I'm so ashamed.'

'Noooo . . . noooo.' Cupping Tammi's face, Maggie gently turned it toward herself. 'You mustn't be ashamed. Think ahead, not behind. You're going to get stronger now, and we're all going to work together to get you happy.'

Tammi's tears continued building and she tried to lift a hand to wipe them away. The hand was shaky, tethered by the IVs, and Maggie gently pushed it down, took a tissue from a nearby box and dried Tammi's eyes.

'I lost the baby, Maggie.'

'I know, honey, I know.'

Tammi turned her brimming gaze away while Maggie stayed close, brushing her temple.

'But you're alive, and it's your happiness we all care about. We want to see you up and smiling again.'

'Why should anyone care about me?'

'Because you are you, an individual, and special. Because you've touched lives in ways you didn't realize. Each of us does that, Tammi. Each of us has worth. Can I tell you something?' Tammi turned back to Maggie who went on, 'Last night I was so blue. My daughter had left for college, and you were in the hospital, and the house was so empty. Everything seemed hopeless. So I called one of my old high school friends, and do you know what happened?'

Tammi's eyes showed a spark of interest. 'What?'

'She called some others, and started this wonderful chain reaction going. Today I had calls from three of them – wonderful old friends I haven't heard from in years, people I would never have suspected cared one way or the other about whether I was happy or not. That's how it will be with you, too. You'll see. Why, by the time I was getting ready to leave the house to come and see you, I was hoping the phone would stop ringing.'

'Really?'

'Really.' Maggie smiled, and received a glimmer of a smile in return. 'Now, listen, little one . . .' She took Tammi's hand, careful not to disturb any of the plastic tubes. 'They said I could stay for only five minutes, and I think my time is up. But I'll be back. Meanwhile, you think about what you'd like me to bring when you get into your own room. Malts, magazines, nachos – whatever you want.'

'I know one thing right now.'

'Just name it.'

'Could you bring me some Nexxus shampoo and conditioner? I want my hair washed worse than anything.'

'Absolutely. And my dryer and curling iron. We'll fix you up like Tina Turner.'

Tammi almost laughed.

'That's what I like to see, those dimples showing.' She kissed Tammi's forehead and whispered, 'I've got to go. Get strong.'

Leaving the hospital, Maggie felt charged with optimism: when a twenty-year-old girl asked to have her hair done, she was rounding the corner towards recovery! She stopped at a beauty shop on the way home and bought the things Tammi had asked for. Carrying the bag, she entered her kitchen to find her phone ringing again.

She charged across the room, whisked up the receiver and answered breathlessly, 'Hello?'

'Maggie? It's Eric.'

Surprise took her aback. She held the paper sack of shampoo against her stomach and stood tongue-tied for a full five seconds before realizing she must make some response. 'Eric – well, heavens, this is a surprise.'

'Are you okay?'

'Okay? I . . . well, yes. A little breathless is all. I just came in the door.'

'I talked to Brookie and she told me the real reason you called last night.'

'The real reason?' She set the bag on the cupboard in slow motion. 'Oh, you mean my depression.'

'I should have figured it out last night. I knew you weren't calling just to say hello.'

'I'm much better today.'

'Brookie said someone in your group tried to commit suicide. I just got so scared – I mean . . .' He heaved in a deep breath and expelled it loudly. 'Christ, I don't know what I mean.'

Maggie touched the receiver with her free hand. 'Oh, Eric, you mean you thought I might be suicidal, too – that's why you're calling?'

'Well . . . I didn't know what to think. I just – hell, I couldn't get you off my mind today, wondering why you'd called. Finally, I had to call Brookie, and when she told me you'd been depressed and in therapy my gut clinched up. Maggie, you were always laughing when we were young.'

'I'm not suicidal or even close to it. Honest, I'm not, Eric. It was a young woman named Tammi, but I just got back from visiting her in the hospital and she's not only going to make it, I got her to smile and almost laugh.'

'Well, that's a relief.'

'I'm sorry I wasn't completely truthful with you last night. Maybe I should have told you that I've been in group therapy, but after you answered the phone I felt – I don't know how to describe it – self-conscious, I guess. With

Brookie it was a little easier, but with you, well . . . it seemed like an imposition after so many years, to call you up and wail about my difficulties.'

'An imposition? Hell, that's silly.'

'Maybe it was. Anyway, thanks for saying so. Listen, guess who else called today? Tani *and* Fish *and* Lisa. Brookie called every one of them. And now you. This has really been old home week.'

'How are they? What are they doing?'

Maggie filled him in on the girls and as they talked, the constraints of last night disappeared. They reminisced a little. They laughed. As the conversation lengthened, Maggie found herself bent over the kitchen cabinet propped on both elbows, wholly at ease talking with him. He told her about his family, she told him about Katy. When a lull finally fell, it was comfortable. He ended it by saying, 'I thought about you a lot today while I was out on the boat.'

She traced a blue figure on a canister and said, 'I thought about you, too.' Insulated by distance, she found it easy to say. Harmless.

'I'd look out over the water and see you in a blue-and-gold letter sweater cheering for the Gibraltar Vikings.'

'With my hair in some horrible beehive I suppose, and Cleopatra eye makeup.'

He chuckled. 'That's about it, yeah.'

'Want to know what I see when I close my eyes and think of you?'

'I'm afraid to hear it.'

She turned and braced her spine against the cabinet edge.

'I see you wearing a baby-blue sweater and dancing to the Beatles with a cigarette between your teeth.'

He laughed. 'The cigarette is gone but I'm still wearing a blue shirt, only now it says Captain Eric on the pocket.'

'*Captain* Eric?'

'The customers like it. Gives them the illusion they're going seafaring.'

'I'll bet you're good at it, aren't you? I'll bet the fishermen love you.'

'Well, I can usually make them laugh and come back next year.'

'Do you like it, what you do?'

'I love it.'

She settled more comfortably against the cabinet. 'So tell me about Door today. Was it sunny, did you catch fish, were there lots of sails on the water?'

'It was beautiful. Remember how you'd get up some mornings and the fog would be so thick you couldn't see across the harbour to Peninsula Park?'

'Mmmm . . .' she replied dreamily.

'It started out that way, with a heavy mist, then the sun came up over the trees and tinted the air red, but by the time we'd been on the water an hour the sky was as blue as a field of chicory.'

'Oh, the chicory! Is it blooming now?'

'Full bloom.'

'Mmm, I can just see it, a whole field of it, looking like the sky fell in. I loved this time of year back home. We don't have chicory here, not like in Door. Go on. Did you catch fish?'

'Eighteen today – fifteen chinook and three browns.'

'Eighteen, wow,' she breathed.

'We filled out.'

'Hooray. And were there sails?'

'Sails . . .' he teased, perpetuating the long-standing raillery between power- and sail-boaters they'd inherited when they'd been born in Door County. 'Who cares about sails?'

'I do.'

'Yeah, I seem to remember you always were a ragman.'

'And you always were a stinkpotter.'

Maggie smiled and imagined him smiling, too. After seconds, her smile became whimsical. 'I haven't been on the water for so long.'

'Living in Seattle, I thought you'd have a boat.'

'We do. A sailboat, naturally. But I haven't taken it out since Phillip died. I haven't fished either.'

'You should come home and let me take you out with your dad. We'll hook you a big twenty-four pounder or so, and you'll get your share of fishing in one catch.'

'Mmm, sounds heavenly.'

'Do it.'

'I can't.'

'Why not?'

'I'm a teacher and school begins in less than two weeks.'

'Oh, that's right. What do you teach again?'

'Home economics – food, clothing, family life, career planning. It's a mixed bag these days. We even have a unit where we turn the departments into a nursery school and bring in preschoolers so the kids can study child development.'

'Sounds noisy.'

She shrugged. 'Sometimes.'

'So . . . are *you* good at it?'

'I suppose. I get along well with the kids, I think I make class interesting for them. But . . .' She paused.

'But what?'

'Oh, I don't know.' She turned again and bent over the cabinet as before. 'I've been doing the same thing for so many years it gets rather stagnant. And since Phillip's death . . .' Maggie put a hand to her forehead. 'Oh, heavens, I get so tired of that phrase. *Since Phillip's death.* I've said it so often you'd think the calendar began that day.'

'Sounds like you need a change.'

'Maybe.'

'I made a change six years ago. It was the healthiest thing I ever did for myself.'

'What did you do?'

'Moved back to Door after living in Chicago since right after college. When I left here after high school I thought it was the last place on earth I'd come back to, but after sitting at a desk all those years, I was feeling claustrophobic. Then Dad died and Mike kept badgering me to come back and run the boat with him. He had these ideas about expanding our services, buying a second boat. So finally I said yes, and I haven't regretted it a day.'

'You sound very happy.'

'I am.'

'In your marriage, too?'

'In my marriage, too.'

'That's wonderful, Eric.'

Another silence fell. It seemed they had said all that needed saying. Maggie straightened and checked the kitchen clock. 'Listen, I'd better let you go. Gosh, we've been talking a long time.'

'Yeah, I guess so . . .' An indistinguishable sound followed, the kind accompanied by a stretch. It ended abruptly. 'I'm still up at Ma's house and Nancy's probably holding supper.'

'Eric, thank you so much for calling. It's been wonderful talking to you.'

'Same here.'

'And please don't worry about me anymore. I'm happier than I've been in weeks.'

'That's great to hear, and listen . . . call anytime. If I'm not around call out here and talk to Ma. She'd love to hear from you.'

'Maybe I will, and tell her hello again. Tell her nobody in the world ever made bread as good as hers. I remember going to your house after school and polishing off about half a loaf at a time.'

He laughed. 'She still bakes, still claims store-bought bread will kill you. She'll get smug, but I'll give her your message anyway.'

'Eric, thanks again.'

'No thanks necessary. I enjoyed it. Now you take it easy, all right?'

'I will.'

They both paused, uneasy for the first time in over thirty minutes.

'Well . . . good-bye,' he said.

'Good-bye.'

When Maggie hung up, her hand lingered on the phone, then fell away slowly. Studying the receiver, she stood motionless for a long time. The late afternoon sun slanted across the kitchen floor and from outside came the muffled sound of a neighbour mowing his lawn. From long ago came images of the same sun shining on other lawns, other trees, other water – not Puget Sound but Green Bay. In time Maggie slowly turned away from the telephone and wandered to the patio door. She rolled it open, leaned a shoulder against the casing and stood staring out, remembering. Him. Them. Door. That last year of high school. First love.

Ah, nostalgia.

But he was a happily married man. And if she saw him again he'd probably be twenty-five pounds overweight and balding and she'd be happy he was married to someone else.

Nevertheless, talking to him brought back thoughts of home, and as she stood staring at the evening yard she saw not a redwood deck surrounded by evergreens, but a sunbaked carpet of azure chicory. Nothing was as intense a blue as a field of blooming chicory stretched out beneath the August sun. And at evening it turned violet, sometimes creating the illusion that sky and earth were one. The Queen Anne's lace would be in full bloom, too, rioting in the high country fields and roadsides, sharing the rocky earth with black-eyed Susans and clumps of white yarrow. Was there another place on earth where wildflowers bloomed so profusely as in the Door?

She saw, too, gambrel-roofed red barns and rows of

green corn and century-old log cabins with white-painted caulking; split rail fences and stone walls bordered by thick spills of orange lilies. White sails on blue water and unspoiled beaches that stretched for miles. She tasted home-baked bread and heard the growl of inboard motors coming home at dusk and caught the aroma of fishboils lifting over the villages on a Saturday night such as this one, coming from the backyards of restaurants where guitars played and red-and-white checked tablecloths flitted in the evening breeze.

From two thousand miles away Maggie remembered it all and felt a surge of homesickness she had not known in years.

She thought of calling home. But Mother might answer, and if anyone could wreck a mellow mood, it was Mother.

Instead, she drew away from the door and went into the den where she took down a book called *Journeys to Door County*. For nearly half an hour she sat in Phillip's desk chair turning the full-colour pages until the glossy photos of lighthouses and log cabins and landscapes prompted her to finally pick up the phone.

Dialling her parents' phone number she hoped her father would answer.

Instead, she heard her mother's voice answer, 'Hello?'

Hiding her disappointment Maggie said, 'Hello, Mother.'

'Margaret?'

'Yes.'

'Well, it's about time you called. It's been over two weeks since we've heard from you, and you said you'd let us know when we could expect Katy. I've been waiting and waiting for you to call!'

Not, *Hello, dear, it's good to hear from you*, but *It's about time you called!* forcing Maggie to begin the conversation with an apology.

'I'm sorry, Mother, I know I should have called, but I've

been busy. And I'm afraid Katy won't be stopping there on the way. It's out of her way, and she had her roommate with her and the car was loaded to the roof so they decided they'd better go straight to school and check into their dorm.'

Maggie closed her eyes and waited for the list of grievances she was certain would follow. True to form, Vera came through with them.

'Well, I won't say I'm not disappointed. After all, I've been cooking and baking here all week. I put two apple pies in the freezer and bought a big beef roast. I don't know what I'll do with a piece of meat that big with only your dad and I to eat it up, and I cleaned your old room from top to bottom and did up the bedding and the curtains, and they're real devils to iron!'

'I know, Mother.'

'I guess young people don't have time for their grandparents like they did when I was a girl,' Vera remarked petulantly.

Maggie rested her forehead on four fingertips and felt herself getting a headache.

'She said she'll drive up from Chicago in a couple weeks, after she gets settled in school. She mentioned maybe coming up in October when the leaves are turning.'

'What is she driving? You didn't buy her that convertible, did you?'

'Yes, I did.'

'Margaret, that child is too young to own an extravagant car like that! You should have bought her something sensible or better yet made her wait until she's out of college. How is she ever going to learn to appreciate things if you give her everything on a silver platter?'

'I think Phillip would have wanted her to have it, and heaven knows I can afford it.'

'That's no reason to overdo it with her, Margaret. And speaking of money, you be careful about who you see. These divorced men are out there just looking for a rich, lonely widow. They'll take you for everything you've got and use your money to pay child support, mark my words!'

'I'll be careful, Mother,' Maggie promised tiredly, feeling the headache intensify.

'Why, I remember a few years back when that young Gearhart fellow was stepping out on his wife and who was he seeing but some summer tourist who came up here from down in Louisiana someplace on a flashy cabin cruiser. They say the two of them were seen on the deck kissing on a Saturday night, and then Sunday morning he showed up at church all pious and pure with his wife and kids. Why, if Betty Gearhart knew what –'

'Mother, I said I'll be careful. I'm not even dating anyone, so you don't have to worry.'

'Well, you can't be too careful, you know.'

'I know.'

'And speaking of divorcés, Gary Eidelbach is getting remarried next Saturday.'

'I know, I talked to Lisa.'

'You did? When?'

'Today. I've been in touch with all the girls lately.'

'You didn't tell me that.' Vera's voice held a trace of coolness, as if she expected to be told everything before it transpired.

'Lisa wants me to come home for the wedding. Well, not exactly for the wedding, but she's coming up from Atlanta so she thought all us girls could get together out at Brookie's.'

'Are you coming?'

Then you could use up your beef roast and your apple pie, couldn't you, Mother?

'No, I can't.'

'Why not? What else are you going to do with all that money? You know your father and I can't afford to travel out there on a plane and, after all, you haven't been home for three years.'

Maggie sighed, wishing she could hang up the phone without a further word. 'It isn't a question of money, Mother, it's a question of time. School will be starting soon and –'

'Well, we're not getting any younger, you know. Your dad and I would appreciate a visit from you every now and then.'

'I know. Is Daddy there?'

'He's here someplace. Just a minute.' The phone clunked down and Vera went off, shouting, 'Roy, where are you? Margaret is on the phone!' Her voice crescendoed as she returned and picked up the receiver. 'Just a minute. He's outside pottering in the garage, sharpening the mower again. It's a wonder the thing has any blades left, as much time as he spends out there. Here he is now.' As the phone exchanged hands Maggie heard Vera order, 'Keep your hands off the counter, Roy, they're filthy!'

'Maggie, honey?' Roy's voice held all the warmth Vera's didn't. Hearing him, Maggie felt her homesickness return.

'Hi, Daddy.'

'Well, this is a nice surprise. You know, I was just thinking about you today, about when you were a little girl and you'd come around asking for a nickel to buy a Dixie Cup.'

'And you always gave me one, didn't you?'

He laughed and Maggie pictured his round face and balding head, his slightly stooped shoulders and the hands that never stopped working.

'Well, my head is turned by a pretty girl, same as the next man's. It's sure good to hear your voice, Maggie.'

'I thought I'd better call and let you know Katy's not coming. She's going straight to school.'

'Well, she'll be in our neck of the woods for four years. We'll see her when she's got time.' It had always been this way – all the petty concerns Vera blew out of proportion, Roy put back into perspective. 'And how about you?' he asked. 'I suppose it's a little lonely around there with her gone.'

'It's terrible.'

'Well, honey, you get out of the house. Go to a movie or something. You shouldn't be there alone on a Saturday night.'

'I won't be. I'm going to the club for dinner,' she lied to ease his worry.

'Good . . . good. That's what I like to hear. School starting pretty soon, is it?'

'In less than two weeks.'

'Here, too. Then the streets will be quiet during the week again. You know how it is. We cuss the tourists when they're here and miss 'em when they're gone.'

She smiled. How many times in her life had she heard the equivalent of his remark? 'I remember.'

'Well, listen, honey, your mother's waiting to talk to you again.'

'Here's a kiss, Daddy.'

'And here's one for you. Be good now.'

'Bye, Daddy.'

'Good-b–'

'Margaret?' Vera had taken the receiver before Roy had a chance to finish.

'I'm here, Mother.'

'Did you get rid of that sailboat yet?'

'No, but I've still got it listed with the agent at the marina.'

'Don't you go out on it alone!'

'I won't.'

'And be careful who you invest that money with.'

'I will. Mother, I've got to go now. I'm going out to the club for dinner and I'm running a little late.'

'All right, but don't wait so long to call next time.'

'I won't.'

'You know we'd call more often if we could, but these

long-distance rates are absolutely ridiculous. Now, listen, if you talk to Katy tell her her grandpa and I are anxious for her to come up.'

'I will.'

'Well . . . good-bye then, dear.' Vera never failed to include one perfunctory endearment as their conversations ended.

'Bye, Mother.'

By the time Maggie hung up, she needed a hot drink to soothe her nerves. She made a cup of herb tea and took it into the bathroom while she brushed her hair. Viciously.

Was it too much to expect a mother to inquire about her daughter's welfare? Her happiness? Her friends? Concerns? As always, Vera had turned the focus on herself. *Vera*'s hard work. *Vera*'s disappointments. *Vera*'s demands. The entire *world* should consider Vera's wishes before it made its next move!

Return to Door County? Even for a vacation? No way on God's green earth!

Maggie was still punishing her scalp when the phone rang again. This time it was Brookie, opening without an introduction.

'We've got it all arranged. Lisa is getting in on Tuesday and she'll be spending a week or so at her mother's. Tani's right in Green Bay, and Fish's got only a three-hour drive from Brussels, so we're all getting together out here at my house on Wednesday noon and we plan on you being here, too. What do you say? Can you come?'

'Not within a hundred miles of my mother! Absolutely not!'

'Oh-oh. Sounds like I called at a bad time.'

'I was talking to her. I just hung up.'

In a conversational tone Brookie inquired, 'How is the old bat?'

A snort of laughter caught Maggie by surprise. 'Brookie, she's my *mother*!'

'Well, that's not *your* fault. And it shouldn't keep you from coming home to see your friends. Now what do you say – all five of us, a few bottles of vino, a few laughs and a good long gab session. All it takes is a plane ticket.'

'Oh, damn, it sounds good.'

'Then say you'll come.'

'But I've –'

'But shit. Just come. Drop everything and jump on a plane.'

'Damn you, Brookie!'

'I'm a devil, ain't I?'

'Yes.' Maggie thumped a foot on the floor. 'Oh, I want to come so badly.'

'Well, what's holding you back?'

Maggie's excuses tumbled out, as if she were trying to convince herself. 'It's such short notice, and I'd only have five days, and teachers have to be back in school three days before the students, and I'd have to stay at my mother's and I can't even carry on a *telephone* conversation with her without wanting to put myself up for adoption!'

'You can stay with me. I can always throw a sleeping bag on the floor and another bone in the soup. Hell, there are so many bodies around this house that one more will hardly be noticed.'

'I couldn't do that – come all the way to Wisconsin and stay at your house. I'd never hear the end of it.'

'So stay at your mother's nights and make sure you're gone all day. We'll go swimming and walk across the bar to Cana Island and poke around the antique shops. Heck, we can do anything we feel like. I've got one last week of vacation before school starts and I lose my built-in baby-sitters. God, I could use the escape. We could have a great time, Maggie. What do you say?'

'Oh, Brookie.' The words conveyed Maggie's wilting determination.

'You said that before.'

'Oh, Brookieeee!' Even as they laughed Maggie's face became distorted by frustration and longing.

'I suspect you've got plenty of money to buy a ticket,' Brookie added.

'So much that you'd gag if I told you.'

'Good for the woman. So come. Please.'

Maggie lost her struggle with temptation.

'Oh, all right, you pest, I will!'

'*Eeeyiiiiiiyow!*' Brookie broke off the banshee yell to tell someone nearby, 'Maggie's coming!' To Maggie, she said, 'I'm getting off this phone so you can call the airport. Call me as soon as you get into town, or better yet, stop here first before going to your folks'. See you Tuesday!'

Maggie hung up and said to the wall, 'I'm going to Door County.' She rose from the chair and *exclaimed* to the wall, her palms raised in amazement, 'I'm going to Door County! Day after tomorrow, I'm actually going to Door County!'

The sense of surprise remained, augmented. Maggie accomplished nothing on Sunday. She packed and unpacked five assortments of clothes, finally deciding she needed something new. She styled and restyled her hair deciding, too, on a trip to the beauty shop. She called for plane reservations and booked a seat in first class. She had almost a million and a half dollars in the bank and decided – for the first time ever – that it was time she started enjoying it.

At Gene Juarez the following day she told the unfamiliar hair designer, 'Do something state of the art. I'm going home to get together with my high school girlfriends for the first time in twenty-three years.' She came out looking like something that had been boiled and hung upside down to dry. The odd thing was, it exhilarated her as nothing had in years.

Next she stopped at Nordstrom's and asked the clerk, 'What would my daughter wear if she were going to a

Prince concert?' She came out with three pairs of acid-washed blue jeans and a selection of strappy undershirts that looked like something old man Niedzwiecki would wear selling used auto parts in his junk yard.

At Helen's Of Course she bought a couple of refined dresses – one for travel, one for any exigencies that might arise – sniffed the favourite perfumes of everyone from Elizabeth Taylor to Lady Bird Johnson, but wound up in Woolworth's dime store merrily paying $2.95 for a bottle of Emeraude which remained her perennial favourite.

On Tuesday morning she stepped out of a cab at Sea-Tac International Airport into driving rain, deplaned four hours later in Green Bay beneath a blinding sun, and rented a car in a state of disbelief. During all her years of travel with Phillip they had always planned their trips weeks, months in advance. Impulsiveness was new to Maggie; it was exhilarating. Why had she never tried it before?

She made the drive north with a renewed sense of emerging and crossed the canal at Sturgeon Bay with an onrushing feeling of home. Door County at last, and within miles her first glimpse of cherry orchards. The trees – already shorn of their bounty – marched in formation across rolling green meadows rimmed with limestone walls and green forests. Apple and plum orchards hung heavy with fruit which shone like beacons in the August sun. At intervals along the highway open-air markets displayed colourful crates of fruits, berries, vegetables, juices and jams.

And of course there were the barns, telling the nationality of those who'd built them: the Belgian barns made of brick; the English ones of frame construction with gabled roofs and side doors; the Norwegians' variety of square-cut logs; the German ones of round logs; tall Finnish barns of two storeys; German bank barns built into the earth, others half-timbered with the spaces between the timbers filled with brick or stovewood. And one grand specimen painted with a gay floral design against a red ground.

In Door County log structures were as common as frame ones. Sometimes entire farms remained as they had been a hundred years ago, their log buildings lovingly preserved, the cabins enhanced by modern bay windows and dormers, trimmed with white door- and window-frames. Yards were surrounded by split rail fences and abundant flowers – daylilies in grand, thrusting clumps of yellow and orange; petunias in puddles of pink; and hollyhocks, tipping their showy stalks at roadside culverts.

At Egg Harbor Maggie slowed to a crawl, amazed to see how it had grown. Tourists dawdled everywhere, crossing the road licking ice cream cones; on sidewalks before antique displays; in the doorways of craft shops. She passed the Blue Iris Restaurant, and the Cupola House, standing tall and white and unchanging, feeling their familiarity seep into her spirit and excite it. Then out onto the highway towards Fish Creek, between rich, tan wheat fields and more orchards and great stands of birches that stood out like chalk marks upon green velvet.

She reached the high bluff above her hometown, a last cherry orchard on the left, then the sharp downswing of the highway around the base of a sheer limestone cliff, into the town itself. Coming upon it was forever a pleasing surprise. One minute you were in the farmland above with no inkling the town lay below; the next you were sitting at a stop sign looking straight ahead at the sparkling waters of Fish Creek Harbor with Main Street stretching off to your left and right.

It was exactly as she remembered, tourists everywhere, and cars inching along while pedestrians jaywalked wherever they pleased; gaily decorated shops built in old houses along a shady Main Street whose east and west ends were both visible from where she sat. How long had it been since she'd been in a town without a traffic light or a turn lane? Or one whose Main Street needed mowing in the summer and raking in the fall? Where else did the Standard

Gas Station look like Goldilock's cottage? And the bakery have a front verandah? And the alleys between the buildings need regular watering to keep the petunias and geraniums healthy?

Across Main an old false-fronted building drew her attention: the Fish Creek General Store where her father worked. She smiled, imagining him behind the long white butcher case where he'd been cutting meat and making sandwiches for as long as she remembered.

Hi, Daddy, she thought. *I'll be right back.*

She turned west and drove at a snail's pace beneath the boulevard maples, past flowered lawns and gabled houses that had been transformed into gift shops, past the Whistling Swan, an immense white clapboard inn with its great east porch replete with wicker chairs. Past the confectionery and Founders Square, and the cottage of Asa Thorpe, the town's founder, and the community church where the doves and morning glories on the three stained-glass windows were exactly as she remembered. Out past the White Gull Inn to the end of the road where a tall stand of cedars marked the entrance to Sunset Beach Park. There the trees opened up and gave a majestic view of Green Bay, sparkling in the late afternoon sun.

She stopped the car, got out and stood in the lee of the open door, shading her eyes, admiring the sails – dozens of sails – far out on the water.

Home again.

In the car once more, she drove back the way she'd come.

The traffic crawled, and parking spots were at a premium, but she snagged one in front of a gift shop called The Dove's Nest and walked back a block and a half, past the stone retaining walls where tourists sat and sipped cool drinks.

Raising a hand to stop traffic she sneaked between two bumpers to the other side of the street.

The concrete steps of the Fish Creek General Store were

as pitted as ever, leading up to doors set in an inverted bay. Inside, the floors squeaked, the lighting was less than adequate, and the smell was rich with memory: years of fruit that had grown too old to sell, and home-cured sausage and the sweeping compound Albert Olson still used when he swept the floors at night.

At five o'clock in the afternoon the place was crowded. She passed the busy counter up front, waving to Albert's wife, Mae, who called a surprised hello, and worked her way to the rear where a knot of customers surrounded the shoulder-high meat and delicatessen counter. Behind it, her father, dressed in a long white bibbed apron, was busy charming the customers as he ran the meat slicer.

'Fresh?' he was saying, above the whine of the machine. 'Why, I went out and killed the cow myself at six o'clock this morning.' He reached down and switched off the motor, swinging into the next motion without a wasted movement. 'That's one with French mustard and Swiss. One pumpernickel with mustard and American.' He sliced a French roll, slapped down two slices of pumpernickel, slathered them with butter and mustard, clapped on two stacks of corned beef, rolled open the glass door of the display case, peeled off two slices of cheese, plopped the ingredients into stacks and snapped the finished sandwiches into plastic containers. The entire process had taken him less than thirty seconds.

'Anything else?' He stood with the butts of his hands braced on the shoulder-high counter. 'Potato salad's the best you'll find anywhere on the shores of Lake Michigan. My grandma grew the potatoes herself.' He winked at the couple who were waiting for their sandwiches.

They laughed and said, 'No, that'll be all.'

'Pay up front. Next?' Roy bellowed.

A sixty-ish man in Bermuda shorts and a terrycloth beach jacket ordered two pastrami sandwiches.

Watching her father make them, Maggie was amazed

anew at his business persona, so different from the one he displayed around home. He was amusing and startlingly efficient. People loved him on sight. He could make them laugh and come back for more.

She stood back, remaining inconspicuous, watching him work the crowd like a barker in a sideshow, scarcely appearing to glance at them as he rushed from spot to spot. She listened to the sound of the butcher paper tearing, of his hands slapping down beef roasts, of the heavy rolling doors on the meat case – the same one that had been there since she was a child. There was a wait – in summer there always was – but he kept tempers off edge with his efficiency and showmanship.

When she had watched for several minutes, she stepped up to the counter while his back was turned.

'I'll have a nickel from your pocket to buy a Dixie Cup,' she said quietly.

He glanced over his shoulder and his face went blank with surprise.

'Maggie?' He swung around, wiping his hands on his white apron. 'Maggie-honey, am I seeing things?'

She laughed, happy she'd come. 'Nope, I'm really here.' If the meat case had been any lower he might have vaulted over it. Instead he came around the end where he scooped her up in a jarring hug.

'Well, Maggie, this is a surprise.'

'To me, too.'

He held her away by both shoulders. 'What are you doing here?'

'Brookie talked me into coming.'

'Does your mother know yet?'

'No, I came straight to the store.'

'Well, I'll be.' He laughed jubilantly, hugging her again, then remembered his customers. With an arm around her shoulders, he turned to them. 'For those of you who think I'm just a dirty old man, this is my daughter, Maggie, from

Seattle. Just gave me the surprise of my life.' Releasing her, he said, 'Are you going up to the house now?'

'I guess so.'

He checked his watch. 'Well, I've got another forty-five minutes here yet. I'll be home at six. How long are you staying?'

'Five days.'

'That's all?'

'I'm afraid so. I have to go back Sunday.'

'Well, five's better than nothing. Now go on so I can take care of this crowd.' He headed back towards his duties, calling after Maggie, 'Tell your mother to call if she needs anything extra for supper.'

As Maggie started her car and headed home, her enthusiasm waned. She drove slowly, wondering as she often did whether it was her tendency to expect too much of her mother that always made homecoming a disappointment. Pulling up before the house where she'd grown up, Maggie leaned over and peered at it a moment before leaving the car. Completely unchanged. Prairie-styled, two-storeyed, with a low-pitched hipped roof and widely overhanging eaves, it would have been perfectly square were it not for the front porch with its massive native limestone supports. Sturdy and solid, with bridal wreath bushes on either side of the stone steps and matched elms in the side yards, the house looked as if it would be standing a hundred years from now.

Maggie turned off the engine and sat awhile: for as long as she could remember her mother had rushed to the front window at the sound of any action on the street. Vera would stand back from the curtains and watch neighbours unload their passengers or purchases and at supper would give a blow-by-blow, laced with aspersions. 'Elsie must have been to Sturgeon Bay today. She had bags from Piggly Wiggly. Why she'd want to shop in *that* store is beyond me. It has the worst smell! I swear things are never fresh in there. But of course you can't tell *Elsie* anything.'

Or, 'Toby Miller brought that Anderson girl home in the middle of the afternoon when I know perfectly well his mother was working. Only sixteen years old and in the house all alone for a good hour and a half – Judy Miller would have a fit if she knew!'

Maggie closed the car door with little more than a click and walked up the front sidewalk almost reluctantly. On the parapets at the foot of the steps a pair of stone urns held the same pink geraniums and vinca vines as always. The wooden porch floor gleamed with its annual coat of grey paint. The welcome mat looked as if no shoe had ever scraped over it. The aluminium screen door had the same 'P' on its grille.

She opened it quietly and stood in the front hall, listening. At the far end of the house a radio played softly and the kitchen water ran. The living room was quiet, tasteful, spotless. It had never been allowed to be otherwise, for Vera let it be known that shoes were to be left at the door, feet kept off the coffee table, and no smoking was allowed anywhere near her draperies. The fireplace had the same stack of birch logs it had had for thirty years because Vera never allowed them to be burned: fires made ashes and ashes were dirty. The andirons and fan-shaped firescreen had never been tarnished by smoke nor had the cinnamon-red bricks been discoloured by heat. The mahogany mantel and woodwork gleamed, and through a square archway the cherry dining-room table held the same lace runner and the same silver bowl as always – one of Vera and Roy's wedding gifts.

Maggie found the changelessness simultaneously comforting and stifling.

Down the strips of varnished floor beside the hall runner, reflected light gleamed from the kitchen at the rear, and to the left the mahogany stairway climbed the wall and took a right turn at the landing with a high window. A thousand times Maggie had come running down only to hear her mother's voice ordering from below, 'Margaret! *Walk* down those stairs!' Maggie was standing looking up at the landing window when Vera entered the opposite end of the hall, came up short, gasped and screamed.

'Mother, it's me, Maggie.'

'Oh my word, girl, you scared the daylights out of me!' She had fallen back against the wall with a hand on her heart.

'I'm sorry, I didn't mean to.'

'Well, what in the world are you doing here anyway?'

'I just came. Just . . .' Maggie spread her hands and shrugged. '. . . jumped on a plane and came.'

'Well, my word, you could let a person know. What in the *world* have you done to your hair?'

'I tried something new.' Maggie reached up, unconsciously trying to flatten the moussed strands that only yesterday had made her feel jaunty.

Vera looked away from the hair and took to fanning her face with a hand. 'Gracious, my heart is still in my throat. Why, a person my age could have a stroke from a shock like that – standing there in front of the screen door where a person can't even see your face. All I could see was that hair sticking up. Why, for all I know you could have been a burglar looking for something to grab and run with. These days, from the things you read in the papers you never know anymore, and this town is full of strangers. A person should almost keep their doors locked.'

Maggie moved towards Vera. 'Don't I get a hug?'

'Why, of course.'

Vera was much like her house: stout and stocky, meticulously neat and unmodish. She'd worn the same hairstyle since 1965 – a backcombed French roll with two neat crescent curls up above the corners of her forehead. The hairdo got lacquered in once a week at Bea's Beauty Nook by Bea herself, who had as little imagination as her customers. Vera wore a homogenized outfit of polyester aqua-blue double-knit slacks, a white blouse and white nurse's shoes with thick crepe soles, rimless glasses with a silver slash across the top, and an apron.

As Maggie moved towards her she gave more of a hug than she received.

'My hands are wet,' Vera explained. 'I was peeling potatoes.'

As the hug ended, Maggie experienced the vague disappointment she always felt when she reached for any affection from her mother. With her father she'd have sauntered towards the kitchen arm in arm. With her mother she walked apart.

'Mmm . . . it smells good in here.' She would try *very hard.*

'I'm making pork chops in cream of mushroom soup. Goodness, I hope I have enough for supper. I just *wish* you had called, Margaret.'

'Daddy said for you to call and he'd bring home anything you need.'

'Oh? You've seen him already?' There it was – the subtle jealous undertone Maggie always sensed at the mention of Roy.

'Just for a minute. I stopped at the store.'

'Well, it's too late to put your pork chops in with the others. They'll never get done. I guess I'll just have to fry them for you.' Vera headed directly for the kitchen phone.

'No, Mom, don't bother. I can run up and get a sandwich.'

'A sandwich, why don't be silly!'

Maggie rarely ate pork anymore and would have preferred a turkey sandwich but Vera was dutifully dialling the phone before Maggie could state a preference. While she spoke she used her apron to polish the top of the spotless telephone. 'Hello, Mac? This is Vera. Will you tell Roy to bring two pork chops home?' Next she polished the adjacent countertop. 'No, two will be fine, and tell him to get here at six or everything else will be all dried up like it was last night. Thanks, Mac.' She hung up and turned towards the sink, rushing on without a pause. 'I swear you wouldn't know that father of yours owns a watch. He's supposed to get off at six on the dot, but he doesn't give a rip if he walks in here half an hour late or not. I said to him the other day, I said, "Roy, if those customers at the store are more important than coming home to supper on time, maybe you should just move in down there." Do you know what he did?' Vera's wattle shook as she picked up a peeler and began slashing at a potato. 'He went out to the garage without so much as a word! Sometimes you wouldn't even think I lived here, for all he talks to me. He's out in the garage all the time. Now he even took a TV out there to watch his baseball games while he potters.'

Maybe he'd watch it in the house, Mother, if you'd let him set his popcorn bowl where he wants to, or put his feet up on your precious coffee table.

Returning to her mother's realm, Maggie wondered how her father had tolerated living with her for forty-odd years. Maggie herself had been in the house only five minutes and already her nerves felt frayed.

'Well, you didn't come home to hear about that,' Vera said in a tone that warned Maggie would hear plenty more in the next four days. Vera finished her peeling and put the pan of potatoes on the stove. 'You must have some suitcases in the car. Why don't you bring them in and put them upstairs while I set the table?'

How badly Maggie wanted to say, 'I'm staying out at Brookie's,' but Vera's dominance could not be shrugged off. Even at age forty, Maggie hadn't the courage to cross her.

Upstairs, she forgot and set her suitcase on the bed. A moment later she plucked it off and set it on the floor, glancing cautiously towards the door, then smoothing the spread, relieved to see she hadn't left a mark on it.

The room looked the same. When Vera bought furniture,

she bought it to last. Maggie's maple bed and dresser sat in the same spots as always. The subtle blue-flowered wallpaper through which Maggie had never been allowed to put thumbtacks would serve for years yet. Her desk was back in place; during the years when Katy had been a baby Vera had installed a crib in the spot for their convenience.

The memory brought a stab of longing. At the window Maggie held back the curtain and gazed down at the tidy backyard.

Phillip, I miss you so much. It was always easier to face Mother with you beside me.

She sighed, dropped the curtain into place and knelt to unpack.

Inside the closet some of her father's old suits hung beside a sealed plastic bag holding her formal from senior prom. Pink. Eric had asked her to wear pink and had given her a wrist corsage of pink tea roses.

Eric is married and you're acting like a middle-aged idiot, standing here staring at a musty old dress.

She changed from her linen travelling suit into a pair of new Guess jeans and two of her rib-knit tank tops, blue over white. Around her throat she tied a twisted cotton scarf and added a pair of oversized lozenge-shaped earrings.

When she entered the kitchen, Vera took one look at her ensemble and said, 'Those clothes are a little young for you, aren't they, dear?'

Maggie dropped a glance at the blotchy blue-and-white denim and answered, There was no age restriction on the tag when I bought them.'

'You know what I mean, dear. Sometimes when a woman is middle-aged she can make herself look ridiculous by trying to appear younger than she really is.'

Rage formed a lump in Maggie's throat, and she knew if she didn't get away from her mother soon she'd blow up and make the next four days intolerable.

'I'm going out to Brookie's tonight. I doubt that she'll mind what I wear.'

'Going to Brookie's! I don't see why you have to run out there the minute you get here.'

No, Mother, I'm sure you don't, Maggie thought, and headed for the back door to escape her for a few minutes.

'Need anything from the garden?' she asked with forced lightness.

'No. Supper is all ready. All we need is your dad.'

'Think I'll go out anyway.'

Maggie slipped outside and wandered around the impeccably neat backyard, past the tidy strips of marigolds bordering the house, into the garage where her dad's vice and tools were arranged with military neatness. The floor was ridiculously clean, and the television set was perched above the workbench on a newly constructed shelf.

Poor Daddy.

Closing the service door of the garage she trailed around the vegetable garden where the beans and pea vines were already pulled up and gone, the tops of the onions drying. In all of her life she never remembered her mother putting off a single job that needed doing. Why did she resent even that?

Vera called out the back door. 'On second thought, dear, pick me a couple of ripe tomatoes for slicing.'

Maggie stepped between the tomato stakes and picked two to take to the house. But when she delivered them to the kitchen and stepped off the back rug, Vera scolded, 'Take your shoes off, dear. I just waxed the floor yesterday.'

By the time Roy got home Maggie felt ready to explode. She met him halfway up the sidewalk from the garage and walked with him, arm in arm, to the house.

'It's good to see you running out here to meet me,' he said fondly.

She smiled and squeezed his arm, feeling her frayed emotions smooth.

'Ah, Daddy!' she sighed, tipping her face to the sky.

'I suppose you surprised the daylights out of your mother.'

'She nearly had a stroke, or so she claimed.'

'Your mother will never have a stroke. She wouldn't abide it.'

'You're late, Roy,' Vera interrupted from the doorway, opening the screen door and gesturing impatiently towards the white package in his hand. 'And I still have to fry those pork chops. Hurry up and bring them up here.'

He handed her the package and she disappeared. Left on the steps, Roy shrugged and smiled dolefully at his daughter.

'Come on,' she said, 'show me what's new in your workshop.'

Inside the room with its scent of fresh wood, she asked, 'Why do you let her do that to you, Daddy?'

'Aw, your mother's a good woman.'

'She's a good *cook* and a good *housekeeper*. But she drives us both crazy. I don't have to live with it anymore, but you do. Why do you put up with it?'

He considered a moment and said, 'I guess I never thought it was worth the trouble to buck her.'

'Instead, you just come out here.'

'Well, I enjoy it out here. I've been making a few birdhouses and birdfeeders to sell at the store.'

She put a hand on his arm. 'But don't you ever want to tell her to shut her mouth, to let you think for yourself? Daddy, she runs all over you.'

He picked up a piece of planed oak and rubbed it with his fingertips. 'Do you remember Grandma Pearson?'

'Yes, a little.'

'She was the same way. Ran my dad like a drill sergeant runs new recruits. It's all I ever knew.'

'But that doesn't make it right, Daddy.'

'They celebrated their golden wedding anniversary before they died.'

Their gazes caught and held for several seconds. 'That's perseverance, Daddy, not happiness. There's a difference.'

His fingers stopped rubbing the oak and he set it neatly aside. 'It's what my generation believes in.'

Perhaps he was right. Perhaps his life was peaceful enough, out here in his workshop, uptown at his job. Certainly his wife provided an immaculate home, good meals and clean clothing – the traditional wifely duties in which his generation also believed. If he accepted these as enough, who was she, Maggie, to foment dissatisfaction?

She reached for his hand. 'All right, forget I mentioned it. Let's go in and have supper.'

Chapter 4

Glenda Holbrook Kerschner lived in a ninety-year-old farmhouse surrounded by twenty acres of Montmorency cherry trees, sixty acres of untilled meadow and woods, a venerable old red barn, a less venerable steel pole barn and a network of paths worn by children, machinery, dogs, cats, horses, cows, deer, racoon and skunks.

Maggie had been here years before, but the house was larger now, with a clapboard addition jutting off the original limestone structure. The verandah, once railed in white, had been enclosed with glass and had become part of the living space. An immense vegetable garden stretched down an east-facing hill behind the house and on a clothesline (nearly as big as the garden) hung four rag rugs. Maggie drove into the yard shortly before eight o'clock that evening.

The engine was still running when the back door flew open and Brookie sailed out, shouting, 'Maggie, you're here!'

Leaving the car door open, Maggie ran. They met in the yard, off balance, hugging, glisteny-eyed.

'Brookie, it's so good to see you!'

'I can't believe it! I just can't believe it!'

'I'm here! I'm really here.'

Pulling back at last, Brookie said, 'My God, look at you! Thinner than a rake handle. Don't they feed you back in Seattle?'

'I came back here to get fattened up.'

'Well, this is the place, as you can see.'

Pirouetting, Glenda displayed her newel-post shape. Each of her pregnancies had left her five pounds heavier, but she was middle-age cute, with short brown hair curling around her face, an infectious smile and attractive hazel eyes.

She clapped both hands on her ample width and looked down at herself. 'As Gene would say – heat in the winter and shade in the summer.' Before Maggie finished laughing she was being herded to the house, tight against Brookie's side. 'Come and meet him.'

On the back step Gene Kerschner waited, tall, angular, dressed in blue jeans and a faded plaid shirt, holding the hand of a barefoot little girl in a nightgown, no taller than his hip. He looked the part of a contented farmer, a happy father, Maggie thought as he released the child's hand to give her a welcoming hug. 'So this is Maggie. It's been a long time.'

'Hello, Gene.' She smiled up at the slow-spoken man.

'Maybe now that you're here Glenda can stop fretting.'

The little girl tugged his jeans. 'Daddy, who's that?'

He lifted the child and perched her on his arm. 'This is Mommy's friend, Maggie.' And, to Maggie, 'This is our second youngest, Chrissy.'

'Hi, Chrissy,' Maggie extended a hand.

The child stuck a finger in her mouth and shyly laid her forehead against her father's jaw.

Laughing, they all moved inside while Glenda added, 'The rest of the kids are scattered around. Justin's two, he's already down for the night, thank heavens. Julie and Danny are out riding Penelope, our horse. Erica's out on a date – she's sweet sixteen and madly in love. Todd's working in town, waiting tables at The Cookery. He's nineteen and he's trying to decide whether he should join the Air Force. And Paul, our oldest, has already gone back to college.'

The house was spacious and serviceable with a farm-size kitchen dominated by a clawfoot table surrounded by eight chairs. The living room extended the kitchen, great-room style, and was furnished with worn davenports, a console TV and, at the end where the porch had been enclosed, an antique iron daybed flanked by two rocking chairs. The decor was unglamorous, a combination of Sears Roebuck, children's school art projects, and K Mart wall plaques and houseplants, but the moment Maggie walked in she felt at home.

She could tell immediately, Brookie's family was handled with a firm but loving hand.

'Kiss Mommy,' Gene told Chrissy, 'you're going to bed.'

'Nooooo!' Chrissy flailed her feet against his stomach and draped her backside over his arm in token resistance.

'Yup, 'fraid so.'

She took her father's face in both hands and tried a little female wile. 'Pleeeeze, Daddy, can't I stay up for a little while longer?'

'You're a flirt,' he said, tipping her towards her mother. 'Kiss her quick if you want one.'

Chrissy's straight long hair swayed around her mother's chin as the two exchanged a kiss and hug.

' 'Night, sweetie.'

With no further complaint the child went upstairs on her father's arm.

'There,' Glenda said, 'now we can be alone. And true to my word . . .' With a flourish she opened the refrigerator and produced a long-necked green bottle. 'I got a jug of zinfandel for the occasion. How 'bout that!'

'I'd love some. Especially after being with my mother for the last three hours.'

'How is old Sergeant Pearson?' The name went way back to the days when Brookie would step onto the Pearsons' front porch and salute crisply at the 'P' on the screen door before walking in with Maggie.

'Exasperating as ever. Brookie, I don't know how my dad lives with her. She probably watches when he goes to the bathroom to make sure he doesn't splatter the lid!'

'Too bad, because your dad's such a great guy. Everybody loves him.'

'I know.' Maggie accepted a goblet of wine and sipped. 'Mmm, thank you.' She followed Brookie to the far end of the great room where Brookie sat on a rocker and Maggie on the daybed hugging a plump throw pillow. Maggie gave Brookie a rundown of the criticism she and Roy had received in the brief time she'd been home. Gene came back downstairs, took a sip of Glenda's wine, kissed the top of her head, said, 'Enjoy yourselves,' and discreetly left the pair alone.

Within five minutes, however, Julie and Danny slammed in, smelling like horses, uncomfortable with introductions but suffering them politely before retreating to the kitchen where they began mixing up Kool-Aid. Erica and her boyfriend came in with another couple their age, boisterous and giddy, searching for the newspaper to find out what was playing at the drive-in theatre. 'Oh, hi!' Erica said when introduced to Maggie. 'We've heard lots of stories about what you and Mom did together in high school. These are my friends, Matt and Karlie and Adam. Mom, can we make some popcorn to take to the movie?'

While the popping was in progress, Todd came home, teased his siblings on his way through the kitchen, said, 'Hi, Mom, is this Maggie? She looks just like her picture in your yearbook.' He shook Maggie's hand, then appropriated his mother's wine glass and took a sip.

'That stuff'll stunt your growth. Give me that.'

'Doesn't look like it stunted yours,' he teased, and leapt aside when she took a swat at his derriere.

'Is it always like this around here?' Maggie asked when Todd had gone back to the kitchen to steal popcorn and aggravate his younger siblings.

'Most of the time.'

The contrast between Maggie's life and Brookie's was so sharp it prompted a series of comparisons, and when the house finally quieted down and the two were left alone, they talked as if the years of separation had never happened, comfortable and frank with one another.

Maggie described what it was like to have a husband die in a plane crash and learn the news when you switched on your TV in the morning; Brookie described what it was like to discover you were pregnant at thirty-eight.

Maggie told how lonely it felt having an only child go off to college, Brookie admitted the frustrations of having seven underfoot all the time.

Maggie spoke of her suppers alone in the silent, empty house with only MacNeil and Lehrer for company; Brookie described cooking for nine when it was ninety-five degrees and the house had no air conditioning.

Maggie told of her chagrin at being propositioned by a married friend of hers and Phillip's at a golf club whose greens were shaped like bear paws, complete with individual toes; Brookie said, meanwhile, she was mowing beneath twenty acres of cherry trees to keep the ground weeds under control.

Maggie described the loneliness of facing an empty bed after years of snuggling into the warmth of someone you loved. Brookie replied, 'We still sleep three in a bed – sometimes four – whenever there's a thunderstorm.'

'I envy you, Brookie,' Maggie said. 'Your house is so full of life.'

'I wouldn't trade a one of them, even though there were times I thought my uterus would drop off.'

They laughed. They had polished off the bottle of zinfandel and felt woozy and relaxed as they slumped in their chairs. The room was lit by only one floor lamp and the house was quiet, inspiring confidences.

'Phillip and I tried to have more,' Maggie admitted, her feet up-drawn on the daybed, the empty goblet swinging upside down between two fingers. 'We tried twice, but I miscarried both times, and now I've started my change.'

'Already?'

'About three months after Phillip died I was lying in bed at about eleven o'clock one night when I thought I was having a heart attack. I mean, it really felt like what I thought a heart attack must feel like, Brookie. It started in my chest and ran like electrical impulses down my arms and legs, out my fingers and toes and left my palms and soles damp. I was terrified. It happened again and I woke Katy and she drove me to the hospital. Guess what it was.'

'I don't know.'

'A hot flush.'

Brookie tried to hold back a grin but couldn't.

'Brookie, if you laugh, I'll slug you!'

'A hot flush?'

'I was sitting in an examination room waiting for a doctor when the nurse who was taking my vital signs asked me to describe what had happened. As I was describing it, it happened again. I told her, here comes one now. She watched my face and said, Mrs Stearn, how old are you? I thought she was crazy to be asking me a question like that when I was having a heart attack, but I told her thirty-nine and she said, you're not having a heart attack, you're having a hot flush. I'm watching the redness climb your chest and neck right now.'

Glenda could hold back her snickers no longer. One came out. Then another. Soon she was leaning back in her rocking chair, hooting.

Maggie stretched a stockinged foot off the daybed and kicked her.

'You think it's so funny, wait till you get one!'

Brookie quieted, caught her nape on the back of the rocking chair and crossed her hands on her belly. 'Crimeny, can you believe we're getting that old?'

'Not we. Just me. *You're* still producing babies.'

'Not anymore, I'm not! I keep a candy dish of condoms on the dining-room table.'

They laughed again, drifted into amiable silence, and Maggie reached out a hand for Brookie's. 'It's so good to be here with you. You're better than Dr Feldstein. Better than group therapy. Better than any friends I've made in Seattle. Thank you so much.'

'Aw, now we're getting sappy.'

'No, I mean it, Brookie. I wouldn't be here in Door if you hadn't called everyone and started the round of telephoning. First Tani, then Fish and Lisa, and even Eric.'

'So he *did* call you!'

'Yes. I was so surprised.'

'What did he say?'

'That he'd found out from you the real reason I'd called him. He was worried I might be suicidal, but I assured him I wasn't.'

'And?'

'And . . . the usual. We talked about his business, how the fishing had been, and about my teaching, and how long we'd both been married, and how many kids we had or didn't have, and he told me he's very happily married.'

'Wait'll you see his wife. She's a knockout. Model material.'

'I doubt that I will, or Eric either.'

'Yeah, maybe not when you're here for such a short time.'

'Why do you suppose they didn't have a family? It seems odd because when I went with Eric he always said he wouldn't mind having a half-dozen.'

'Who knows?'

'Well, it's none of my business anyway.' Maggie yawned and stretched. Her doing so seemed to trigger a yawn in Brookie. Dropping her feet to the floor, Maggie said, 'If there was ever a signal for a guest to go home . . .' Checking her watch, she exclaimed, 'Oh, my gosh, it's nearly one o'clock!'

Brookie walked Maggie to her car. The night was warm

and filled with scent from the petunia beds and the horse corral. Overhead the stars were showy on a blue-black firmament.

'It's funny about hometowns,' Maggie mused.

'They call you back, huh?'

'Mmm . . . they really do. Especially when friends are there. And tomorrow it'll be all of us.'

They hugged.

'Thank you for being here when I needed you. And for caring.'

For once Glenda made no humorous comment. 'It's good to have you back. I wish you'd stay forever.'

Forever. Maggie thought about it on her way home through the cool August night, its scent of cut grain and ripening apples reminding that autumn stood poised. Nowhere was autumn more magnificent than in Door County, and it had been over two decades since she'd been here to witness the change of leaves. She'd love to experience a Door County autumn again. But forever? With Vera in the same town? Hardly.

At home, Vera had managed to leave one last order. Propped against Maggie's dresser lamp was a note: *Turn out the nightlight in the bathroom*.

The following day at eleven A.M. four mature adults descended upon Brookie's house, reducing themselves to a quintet of giggly, giddy throwbacks.

They hugged. They bounced. They cried. They kissed. They all talked at once. They called one another by their long-unused teenage nicknames. They dropped profanities with surprising ease after years of trimming these unladylike expletives from their speech. They admired Lisa (still the prettiest), commiserated with Maggie (the widowed), teased Brookie (the most prolific) and Carolyn (already a grandmother) and Tani (the greyest).

They compared family pictures, children's dispositions,

and obstetric memories: wedding rings, husbands and jobs; travels, house styles and health setbacks; ate chicken salad and drank wine and grew giddier; caught up on extended-family history – mothers, fathers, sisters and brothers; gossiped about former classmates; relived teenage memories. They got out Brookie's yearbook and laughed at themselves in unflattering hairdos and heavy-lidded make-up; criticized the teachers they had disdained and praised those they had liked back in 1965; tried to sing the school song but couldn't remember the words (except for Brookie who still attended games). In the end they settled for a rendition of 'Three White Doves Went Seaward Flying' sung by Lisa, Brookie and Maggie in dubious three-part harmony.

They played scratchy Beatles records and danced the watusi. They walked through Brookie's meadow five abreast, arms linked, singing raunchy songs they would have punished their own children for singing, songs the boys had taught them clear back in high school.

At suppertime they went to town and ate at The Cookery where they were waited on by Brookie's son, Todd, who received the largest tip of his career. They walked along Main Street among the late summer tourists, down to the city beach where they sat on rocks and watched the sun drape itself across the water.

'Why haven't we done this before?' one of them said.

'We should make a pact to get together every year this way.'

'We should.'

'Why are you all sounding so sad all of a sudden?' Lisa asked.

'Because it *is* sad, saying good-bye. It's been such a fun day.'

'But it's not good-bye. You're all coming to Gary's wedding, aren't you?'

'We're not invited.'

'Of course you are! Oh, I almost forgot!' Lisa zipped open her handbag. 'Gary and Deb sent this for all of you.' She produced a pale grey invitation with all their names on the envelope, which she passed around.

'Gene and I will be there,' Brookie confirmed, glancing around at the circle of faces. 'Small town . . . everybody goes.'

'And Maggie's not going home until Sunday,' Lisa reasoned, 'and you two live close enough to drive down. Honest, Gary and Deb want you all to come. He made it a point to remind me. The reception's going to be out at Bailey's Harbor Yacht Club.'

They glanced at one another and shrugged, wanting to say yes.

'I'll come,' Tani agreed. 'I love the food at the yacht club.'

'So will I,' Fish seconded. 'How about you, Maggie?'

'Well, of course I'll come if all the rest of you are going to be there.'

'Great!'

They rose from the rocks, brushed off their clothing and ambled towards the street.

'What about tomorrow, Maggie?' Brookie inquired. 'Let's do something. Swim? Shop? Walk out to Cana Island? What?'

'I feel guilty, taking you away from your family again.'

'Guilty!' Brookie spouted. 'When you've had as many as I have, you learn to snatch every opportunity to get away by yourself. Gene and I do plenty for our kids, they can do this for me, give me a day to myself now and then.'

The plan was cemented and they set a time before wishing each other goodnight.

The following morning Maggie sat in the kitchen drinking tea, attempting to carry on a conversation with her mother without losing her temper.

'Brookie has a wonderful family, and I love her home.'

'It's a shame the way she let herself go to fat though,'

remarked Vera. 'And as for family, I'd say she could stand a little less of it. Why, she must have been thirty-eight when she had the last one.'

Maggie bit back her exasperation and defended her friend. 'They get along so well, though. The older ones look after the younger ones and they've been trained to pick up after themselves. They're a wonderful family.'

'Nevertheless, when a woman's near forty she should be more careful. Why, she could have had a retarded child!'

'Even after forty, pregnancies aren't nearly as rare as they used to be, Mother, and Brookie said she wanted every one of her babies. Her last one was no mistake.'

Vera's lips pruned and she raised one eyebrow.

'So what about Carolyn?' she asked.

'Carolyn seems happy being a farmer's wife. She and her husband are going to raise ginseng.'

'Ginseng! Who in the world eats ginseng?'

Once, again, Maggie had to fight down a sharp retort. Vera grew more opinionated the older she got. Whatever the subject, unless Vera used it, or owned it or approved it, the rest of the world was screwed up to do so. By the time Vera asked about Lisa, Maggie wanted to shout, Why do you even ask, Mother, when you don't care? Instead, she answered, 'Lisa's just as beautiful as ever, maybe more so. Her husband is a pilot so they've travelled all over the world. And remember Tani's bright-red hair? It's the prettiest peach colour you've ever seen. Like a silver maple leaf in the fall.'

'I heard her husband started up a machine shop of his own and lost it a few years back. Did she say anything about it?'

Just shut up and get out of here before you blow, Maggie thought.

'No, Mother, she didn't.'

'And I'll bet not a one of them has the money that you've got.'

How did you get this way, Mother? Is there no generosity in your spirit at all? Maggie rose to set her cup in the sink. 'I'm going to do some things with Brookie today, so don't plan lunch for me.'

'With Brookie . . . but you haven't spent more than a two-hour stretch at home since you've been here!'

For once Maggie refused to apologize. 'We're going to do some shopping and take a picnic out to Cana Island.'

'What in the world do you want to go out there for? You've been there a hundred times.'

'It's nostalgic.'

'It's useless. Why, that old lighthouse is going to fall right over one of these days and when it does the county will have to pay for –'

Maggie walked out in the middle of Vera's diatribe.

Maggie drove. She picked up Brookie and together they went to the Fish Creek General Store where Roy made them towering sandwiches of turkey and cheese and smilingly said, 'Have fun!'

They spent the morning poking through antique shops out on Highway 57 – restored log cabins whose charm came alive behind white shutters and hollyhock borders. One was a great red barn, its doors thrown open to immense splashes of sun which fell across painted pine floors. Its rafters were hung with clusters of herbs, and dried flowers, the loft filled with hand-tied quilts and candles with uncut wicks. They examined pitchers and bowls, tin toys, antique lace, sleds with wooden runners, crocks and rockers and urns and armoires.

Brookie found a charming blue basket filled with baby's breath and dried cornflowers with an immense pink bow on its handle.

'Oh, I love this.' She suspended it on one finger.

'Buy it,' Maggie suggested.

'Can't afford it.'

'I can.' Maggie took it from Brookie.

Brookie retrieved it and set it back on a pierced tin pie safe. 'Oh, no, you don't.'

Maggie snatched the basket again. 'Oh, yes, I do!'

'Oh, no, you don't!'

'Brookie,' Maggie scolded while they held the basket between them. 'I have so much money and nobody to spend it on. Please . . . let me.'

Their eyes met in a friendly face-off while above their heads a wind chime rang softly.

'All right. Thanks.'

An hour later when they had walked across the rocky shoal to Cana Island, had visited the lighthouse, explored the shore, swam, and eaten their picnic looking out at Lake Michigan, Maggie lay on her back on a blanket, her eyes shielded by sunglasses.

'Hey, Brookie?' Maggie said.

'Hm?'

'Can I tell you something?'

'Sure.'

Maggie pulled her sunglasses half off and peered at a cloud through them, her elbows hanging in the air. 'It's true, you know, what I said back at the antique store. I'm filthy rich and I don't even care.'

'I wouldn't mind trying it for a while.'

'It's the *reason*, Brookie.' She slammed the glasses firmly on her face. 'They gave me over a million dollars for Phillip's life, but I'd give every penny of it if I could have him back again. It's an odd feeling . . .' Maggie rolled to her side facing Brookie and propped her jaw on a hand. 'From the moment that FCC ruling came in – pilot error, the ground crew left a flap open on the plane – I knew I'd never have to worry about money again. You wouldn't believe what settlements like this cover.' She counted them on her fingers. 'Grief of the children, their support and college education, the pain and suffering of the survivors, even the suffering of the *victim* while the plane was falling out of the sky. I get paid for that, Brookie . . . me!' She touched her chest in exasperation. 'Can you imagine what it feels like to take money for Phillip's suffering?'

Brookie inquired, 'Would you rather have taken nothing?'

Maggie's mouth drooped as she stared thoughtfully at Brookie. She flopped to her back with an arm over her forehead.

'I don't know. No. It's stupid to say I would. But, don't you understand? Everything is paid for – the house in Seattle, Katy's schooling, new cars for both of us. And I'm tired of teaching tenth-graders how to roll out pie crust when they'll probably buy pre-made crusts anyway. And I'm tired of noisy preschoolers, and of teaching child development when statistics show that a third of the couples who marry these days decide against having children, and most of the rest of them will probably end up in divorce court. I have all this money and nobody to spend it with, and I'm not ready to go out on dates yet, and even if I did, any man who'd ask me out would become suspect because I'd be afraid he was after my money. Oh, God, I don't know what I'm trying to say.'

'I do. You need motivation. You need a change.' Brookie sat up.

'That's what everybody keeps telling me.'

'Who's everybody?'

'My psychiatrist. Eric Severson.'

'Well, if everybody's saying it, it must be true. All we need to do is come up with what.' Brookie scowled at the water, deep in thought.

Maggie peeked at her with one eye, then closed it, mumbling, 'Oh, this should be good.'

'Now let's see . . . all we have to do is think of what you'd be good at. Just a minute . . . just a minute . . . it's coming . . .' Brookie sprang up onto her knees. 'I've got it! The old Harding place out on Cottage Row! We were talking about it last week at supper. Did you know old man Harding died this spring and the house has been sitting empty ever since? It would make a perfect bed-and-breakfast inn. It's just waiting for –'

'Are you crazy? I'm no innkeeper!'

'. . . somebody to come along and fix the place up.'

'I don't want to be tied down.'

'Summers. You'd be tied down summers. Winters you could take your piles of money and go to the Bahamas in search of a man richer than you. You said you were lonely. You said you hate your empty house, so buy one you can put people in.'

'Absolutely not.'

'You always loved Cottage Row, and the old Harding house probably has piles of potential charm oozing from between the floorboards.'

'Along with draughts and mice and termites, more than likely.'

'You're a natural. Hell, what is home economics about anyway? Running a home economically – cooking, cleaning, decorating – I'll bet you've even taught a few charm courses to those greasy-headed little punks, haven't you?'

'Brookie, I don't want –'

'And you love antiquing. You'd go euphoric antiquing for real, to fill that place. We'd go to Chicago to the flea markets and auctions. To Green Bay to the junk dealers. Up and down Door County to all the boutiques and antique shops. With all your money you could furnish the place like the Biltmore mansion and –'

'I refuse to live within less than a thousand miles of my mother! Good heavens, Brookie, it wouldn't even be a long-distance phone call away!'

'That's right, I forgot. Your mother is a problem . . .' Brookie squeezed her lower lip thoughtfully. Abruptly she brightened. 'But we'd work that out. Put her to work cleaning, scrubbing, something like that. Nothing makes old Vera happier than when she's got a dustcloth in her hand.'

'Are you kidding? I wouldn't have my mother on the place under any circumstances.'

'Okay then, Katy can clean.' Brookie's face grew even more avid. 'Of course, it's perfect! Katy can come home summers from college and help you. And if you lived this close she could drive down weekends and holidays, which is what you want, isn't it?'

'Brookie, don't be silly. No woman without a man would be in her right mind to take on a house that old.'

'Men, hell. You can buy men. Handymen, gardeners, plasterers, carpenters, even teenagers looking for summer jobs. Even my *own* teenagers looking for summer jobs. You can leave all the dirty work to the hired help and take care of the business yourself. And the timing would be perfect. You buy it now, spend the winter getting the place fixed up, and it gives you time to advertise and open for next year's tourist season.'

'I don't want to run a bed and breakfast.'

'What a setting, right on the Bay! I'll bet the place has a view from every room. You'd have customers beating down your door to stay in a place like that.'

'I don't want customers beating down my door.'

'And if I'm not mistaken, it has a gardener's apartment above the garage, remember? Tucked back into the hill across the road. Oh, Maggie, it'd be perfect.'

'It'll have to be perfect for somebody else then. You're forgetting, I'm a home ec teacher from Seattle and I return to work on Monday.'

'Oh, yes, Seattle. The place where it rains all winter long, and where your best friends' husbands proposition you at the country club, and where you get so depressed you have to talk about it in group therapy sessions.'

'Now you're being crass.'

'Well, don't you? What friends came rushing in to help

you when you needed it? *This* is where your friends are. This is where your roots are, whether you want them to be or not. What has Seattle got to make you stay?'

Nothing. Maggie tightened her lips to keep from replying.

'What are you being so stubborn about? You're going back to a job that bores you, back to a house with no people in it, back to . . . hell, I don't know what it *is* you're going back to. Your shrink says you need a change and the problem is, what change? Well, how are you ever going to find out until you start shopping around for a new life? Maybe it's not running a bed and breakfast, but what harm can there be in checking it out? And when you get back to Seattle, who have you got there to fire you up and make you start looking? Well, what are you sitting there for? Pack up your things, we're going to see the Harding house!'

'Brookie!'

Brookie was already on her feet, wadding up a beach towel. 'Pack up, I said. What else have we got to do this afternoon? You can stay here if you want to. *I'm* going to see Harding House by myself if I have to.'

'Brookie, wait!'

But Brookie was already ten yards away with her beach towel under one arm and her empty white sack under the other, heading for the mainland. While Maggie sat up on her heels and looked after her exasperatedly, Brookie yelled back over her shoulder, 'I'll bet that place is a hundred years old or more, old enough to be on the National Register! Just think, you could be listed in *Bed-and-Breakfast Inns of America*!'

'For the last time, I don't want to be listed in *Bed-and-Break* –' Maggie thumped both fists on her thighs. 'Damn you, Brookie,' she called and scrambled up to follow.

At Homestead Realty, Althea Munne looked up while licking and sealing an envelope.

'Be right with you ladies. Oh, hello, Glenda.'

'Hi, Mrs Munne. You remember Maggie Pearson, don't you?'

'I certainly do.' Althea rose and came forward, studying Maggie through eyeglasses whose rims had more angles than the roofline of the Vatican. The lenses were tinted cranberry with exposed, polished edges, and upon the left, a tiny gold 'A' rested just above Althea's cheek. The spectacles were set with what appeared to be the crown jewels, and Althea glittered like a mirrored ballroom. The heavy glasses rested on a tiny owl-nose above a pair of lips ludicrously enlarged with Pepto-Bismol-pink lipstick that had bled into the cracks about her mouth.

A former teacher, she studied Maggie and recalled, 'Class of '64. Honour society, school choir, cheerleader.'

'All correct except the year. It was the class of '65.'

The phone rang, and while Althea excused herself to answer, Maggie glanced at Brookie who flashed a smug grin and said under her breath, 'See if you can top that with a Seattle realtor.'

Mrs Munne returned momentarily and asked, 'What can I do for you?'

'Do you have the listing on the Harding house?' Brookie asked.

'The Harding house . . .' Althea licked her lips. 'Yes. Which one of you is interested in seeing it?'

'She is.'

'She is.'

Maggie pointed at Brookie and Brookie pointed at Maggie.

Althea's lips pursed. She waited as one might expect an ex-teacher to wait for a class to silence.

Maggie sighed and lied. 'I am.'

'The house lists for ninety-six, nine. It has one and a half acres and 150 feet of shoreline.' Althea turned away to get the listing sheets and Maggie flung a withering glare at Brookie. The realtor returned and asked, 'Would that be in your price range?'

'Ah . . .' Maggie jumped. 'Yes, that's . . . that's within my price range.'

'It's vacant. It needs a little repair, but it has limitless possibilities. Would you like to take a ride over and see it?'

'Ahh . . .' Maggie balked and received a discreet thump on the knee from Brookie. 'Yes, I . . . well, of course!'

Althea drove, giving a brief history of the house as they rode towards it.

The Harding place had been built in 1901 by a Chicago shipping magnate named Throckmorton for his wife, who had died before the building was complete. Inconsolably saddened by her death, Throckmorton sold the house to one Thaddeus Harding whose descendants had occupied it until the demise of old Thad's grandson, William, last spring. William's heirs lived in scattered parts of the country and showed no interest in maintaining the white elephant. All they wanted was their share of the money from its sale.

In the backseat, Maggie rode stubbornly beside Brookie – her mind closed – to the west end of Main Street, then south up Cottage Row on a picturesque road that twisted and climbed a steep limestone bluff; through thick cedar forest between old estates that had been established in the early 1900s by Chicago's wealthy, who rode the shoreline up Lake Michigan to spend summers in the cool lake breezes of Door Peninsula. The wooded road gave glimpses of genteel homes – no two alike – behind rows of stacked stone walls. Some were perched below road level, their garages backed up against the stone cliff on the left, across the road from the houses themselves. Others lifted above dappled lawns. Many were glimpsed through tangles of old shrubbery and trellises. Occasionally the brilliant blue waters of Green Bay glittered, bringing images of panoramic views from the houses.

Maggie's first impression came not from Harding House itself, but from an abandoned tennis court nestled at the base of the cliff across the road. Moss had taken hold between the limestone paving blocks, some of which had cracked and buckled. The playing surface was covered with the slough of the infringing woods: dead leaves, twigs and pinecones and aluminium cans tossed by uncaring tourists from passing autos.

But along the south edge of the court a weathered arbour seat covered with grapevines spoke of days when the *wump* of tennis balls had resounded from the cliff wall, and players had rested on the curved wooden bench between sets. The vine had grown so heavy it had broken the wooden structure, but it evoked images of a grander day. At the opposite end of the court there was a garage with an apartment above, built in later years but still a relic itself, with cumbersome wooden doors, hinged at the sides. Maggie found her eyes drawn back to the arbour seat as she followed Althea through the break in a thick row of arborvitae that sheltered the yard and house from the road.

'We'll walk around the outside first,' Althea directed.

The house was a Queen Anne cottage, grey with age and disrepair, and from the landward side seemed to offer little save a small rear verandah with a rotting floor, gap-toothed railings, and a lot of wooden siding badly in need of painting. But as Maggie followed Althea around the structure, she looked up and saw an enchanting collection of asymmetrical shapes covered in fish-scale shingles, with tiny porches tucked at all levels, exposed cornice brackets, carved bargeboards with finials and pendants in the gable peaks, a sweeping front verandah overlooking the lake and on the second storey of the southwest corner the most fanciful verandah of all, rounded, with turned wood columns beneath a witch-hat roof.

'Oh, Brookie, look!' she exclaimed, pointing up at it.

'The belvedere,' Althea clarified. 'Off the largest bedroom. Would you like to go in and see it?'

Althea was no dummy. She took them in through the front door, across the wide front verandah whose floor was in much better shape than that of the rear; through a carved-oak door with a leaded, stained-glass window and matching sidelights; into a spacious entry hall with a staircase that brought a gasp of delight from Maggie. Looking up, she saw it turn at two landings around a shaft of open space leading to the upper hall.

Her heart began hammering even as her nostrils smelled the mould.

'The wood throughout the house is maple. It's said that Mr Throckmorton had it custom milled in Sturgeon Bay.'

From a doorway to the left Brookie said, 'Maggie, look at this.' From between the walls she rolled a pocket door, and with it came dust, spider webs and a loud creak of rusty hardware.

Althea quickly explained, 'Mr Harding lived here alone for nearly twenty years after his wife died and I'm afraid he let the place fall into disrepair. Many of the rooms he simply closed off. But anyone with a good eye will recognize the quality underneath the dirt.'

The main floor contained the formal parlour with a small stone fireplace and an adjoining 'music room'. Across the hall was the dining room which connected, through a butler's pantry, with the kitchen at the rear. Opposite the pantry was the maid's room. When Althea opened the door a chipmunk scurried down between voluminous stacks of old newspapers that appeared to have got wet and dried many times over the years.

'The place would need a little tightening up,' Althea said sheepishly, and proceeded into the kitchen.

The room was horrendous with bile-green paint flaking off the walls in one corner, giving evidence of bad plumbing. The sink was rustier than an ocean-bound tanker and the cupboards – a mere five-foot length of them – were made of tongue-and-groove beadboard, painted the same digestive hue as the walls. Two long narrow windows held shredded lace curtains that had turned the colour of an old horse's tooth, while behind them hung tattered window shades of army green. Between the two windows a battered, windowless door led to the small rotting verandah they'd first glimpsed from outside.

The kitchen brought Maggie to her senses.

'Mrs Munne, I'm afraid we're wasting your time. This is just not what I had in mind.'

Althea proceeded, undaunted. 'One has to picture it as it could be, not as it is. I'm sorry about this kitchen, but as long as we're here, we might as well take a look upstairs.'

'I don't think so.'

'Yes, let's.' Brookie commandeered Maggie's arm and forced her to comply. Climbing the stairs behind Mrs Munne, Maggie pinched Brookie's arm and whispered through clenched teeth, 'This place is a wreck and it smells like bat shit.'

'How do you know what bat shit smells like?'

'I remember from my aunt Lil's attic.'

'There are five bedrooms,' Mrs Munne said. 'Mr Harding had them all closed off but one.'

The one he'd used turned out to be the Belvedere Room and the moment Maggie stepped into it she had the sinking feeling she was lost. Not the water-stained wallpaper, nor the musty-smelling carpet, nor the obscene collection of ancient mouse-chewed furniture could hide the room's appeal. It came from the view of the lake, seen through tall, deep-silled windows and the exquisitely turned columns of the belvedere itself. As one upon whom a spell has been cast, Maggie opened the door and stepped out. She pressed her knees against the wooden railing, gazing westward as the sun jewelled the surface of Green Bay. Below, the lawn lay in neglect, a rotting wooden dock listing to one side, half in the water, half out. But the trees were maples, lacy and ancient. The belvedere was solid, graceful, evocative, a place where women perhaps had once watched for steamships to bring their husbands home.

Maggie experienced a sense of loss for her own husband who would never stride up that long lawn, would never share the room behind her or clatter down the magnificent staircase.

But she knew as surely as she knew she'd regret it dozens of times that she would do this insane thing Brookie had suggested: she would live in Harding House.

'Show me the rest of the bedrooms,' she ordered, returning inside.

They mattered not a whit. Each of the four had charms of its own, but all paled beside the belvedere room. Returning from the attic (which proved Maggie right – she'd be sharing the place with hundreds of bats) she stepped into her favourite room one more time.

I have come home, she thought unreasonably, and shivered.

Following Althea back downstairs she said, 'I'd be making it into a bed-and-breakfast inn. Would there be any zoning problems?'

Brookie grabbed Maggie from behind and spun her by an arm, presenting bulging eyes and a mouth gaping in amazement.

'Are you serious?' she whispered.

Maggie pressed a palm to her stomach, whispering, 'I'm trembling inside.'

'A bed and breakfast – hmmm . . .' Althea said, reaching the main floor. 'I'm not sure. I'd have to check into that.'

'And I'd want to have an architectural engineer look the place over to make sure it's structurally sound. Does it have a basement?'

'After a fashion. We're on bedrock here, you know, so it's really only a tiny cellar.'

The Spanish Inquisition might have taken place in the cellar, so dank and black was it. But the place had a furnace and Althea claimed it worked. A re-examination of the kitchen wall and the maid's quarters which abutted it showed that the plumbing surely had leaked. Probably the bathroom fixtures overhead were ready to drop through the ceiling. But even as Maggie quavered Brookie called from the front parlour, 'Maggie, come here! You've got to see this!'

Brookie had rolled back a moth-eaten rug and was on her hands and knees. She was rubbing the floor with a dampened Kleenex. She spat, rubbed again and exclaimed, 'It is! It's parquet!'

Maggie's emotional barometer soared once more.

Together, on their hands and knees, dressed yet in bathing suits and beach jackets, the two discovered what Althea had not guessed: the parlour was paved with inch-wide quartersawn maple strips, laid in a bird's-nest design. In the dead centre of the room they found the smallest piece; a perfect square. From it the strips telescoped to the outer edges of the room, growing longer and longer until they disappeared beneath the high, delicately-coved mopboards that languished beneath years of crust and dust.

'Glory be. Imagine this sanded and polyurethaned,' Brookie said. 'It'd gleam like a new violin.'

Maggie needed no more convincing. She was heading back upstairs to have one more look at the belvedere room before she had to bid it a temporary good-bye.

One hour from the time they had stepped foot into the Homestead Realty office Maggie and Brookie were back in the rented Toyota, gaping at each other and suppressing whoops of excitement.

'What in the name of God am I doing?' Maggie said.

'Curing yourself of your depression.'

'Oh lord, Brookie, this is insane.'

'I know! But I'm so excited I'm ready to pee my pants!'

They laughed, whooped and pounded their feet on the floorboards. 'What day is it?' Maggie asked, too exhilarated to sort out such incidentals.

'Thursday.'

'That gives me two days to do some fast footwork, one and a half if I go to that wedding. Damn, I wish I hadn't told Lisa I'd go. Do you have any idea where I'd find out what the zoning would be on a bed and breakfast?'

'We could try the town hall.'

'Does this town have ay architects or engineers?'

'There's an architect up in Sister Bay.'

'How about a lawyer?'

'Carlstrom and Nevis, same as always. My God, you're serious, Maggie. You really are serious!'

Maggie pressed a hand to her hammering heart. 'Do you know how long it's been since I felt this way? I'm hyperventilating, almost!' Brookie laughed. Maggie squeezed the steering wheel, threw her head back and forced her shoulder blades deep into the seat cushions. 'Oh, Brookie, it feels good.'

Belatedly Brookie warned, 'It'd cost a bundle to fix that relic up.'

'I'm a millionaire. I can afford it.'

'And you might not be able to buck the residential zoning out there.'

'I can try! There are B and Bs in residential areas all over America. How did they manage?'

'You'd be living in the same area code as your mother.'

'Oh,' Maggie groaned, 'don't remind me.'

'What should we do first?'

Maggie started the engine, smiling, and felt her zest for life restored. 'Go tell my dad.'

Roy beamed and said, 'I'll help you every way I can.'

Vera scowled and said, 'You're crazy, girl.'

Maggie chose to believe her dad.

During the last business hour of that day Maggie made tracks to the town hall and verified that Cottage Row was, as expected, zoned residential and that an appeal would need to be made to get that zoning changed, but the clerk said the zoning was regulated by the county, not the township. Next Maggie contacted Burt Nevis with an order to draw up papers – conditional – to accompany earnest money. She spoke with the Sister Bay architect, Eames Gillard, who said he was all tied up for two weeks, but who directed her to a Sturgeon Bay structural engineer named Thomas Chopp. Chopp said he could examine the house and would give an *opinion* on its soundness, but would give no written warranties nor did he know of any engineer or architect who *would* on a house ninety years old. Lastly, she called Althea Munne and said, 'I'll have earnest money and a conditional purchase agreement for you by five o'clock tomorrow afternoon.'

After supper Maggie sat down with Roy who worked up a generic checklist for the house: furnace, plumbing, wiring, termite condition, ground survey and water test if it was a private well, which, he said, it would be since Fish Creek had no city water.

Next he prepared a list of consultants from whom she might get estimates and advice.

All the while Vera carped, 'I don't see why you don't have a pretty new house built up on top of the bluff, or move into one of the new condominiums. They're springing up all over the county, that way you'd have close neighbours and you wouldn't have to put up with leaky pipes and termites. And taking in lodgers – for heaven's sake, Maggie – it's beneath you! Plus the fact that a woman alone has no business opening her door to strangers. Who knows what kind of weirdos might walk in? And to have them sleeping under your roof! Why, it gives me the shivers to think of it!'

To Maggie's surprise Roy lowered his chin, levelled his gaze and said, 'Why don't you find something to clean, Vera?'

Vera opened her mouth to retort, snapped it shut and spun from the room, red-faced with anger.

The next day and a half were a frantic merry-go-round of

telephoning, exacting promises and dates from contractors, comparing real estate values, meeting lawyers; contacting the chamber of commerce, Althea Munne, the county, the state . . . and the state . . . again and again and again in an effort to obtain a Wisconsin state code book regulating bed-and-breakfast inns. After being misdirected no less than nine times, Maggie finally reached the person under whose jurisdiction B and Bs fell: the state milk inspector.

The state milk inspector, for God's sake!

After exacting his promise to send the pamphlet first class to her Seattle address, she raced to pick up the purchase agreement her lawyer had drawn up, then to Althea Munne's office where she paid the earnest money in spite of the fact that she still had no answer regarding the zoning permit. As she shook hands with Althea she glanced at her watch and stifled a shriek. She had fifty minutes to get back home, bathe, dress, and be at the community church for Gary Eidelbach's wedding.

Chapter 5

There could have been no more perfect day for a wedding. The temperature was in the low eighties, the sky clear, and shade dappled the front steps of the Fish Creek Community Church where the wedding party had gathered after the ceremony.

Eric Severson knew every person in the receiving line and most of the guests. His mother and Nancy moved ahead of him while behind him came Barbara and Mike, followed by businessmen, neighbours, and friends he'd known for years. He shook hands with the parents of the groom and made introductions. 'Honey, this is Gary's mom and dad. Carl, Mary, my wife Nancy.'

While they exchanged small talk he watched their admiring eyes linger on his wife and felt proud, as always, to have her at his side. Wherever he took her people stared. Women, children, old men and young: all were susceptible. Not even at a wedding did the bride receive more admiring glances.

Moving through the line, he kissed the bride's cheek. 'You look beautiful, Deborah. Think you can keep this rounder in line?' he teased, cocking a grin at the groom who was ten years older than the woman in white beside him. The smiling groom drew his new wife firmly against his side and laughed into her eyes.

'No problem,' he replied.

Eric shook Gary's hand. 'Congratulations, fella, you deserve it.' Everyone in town knew Gary's first wife had abandoned him with two children five years ago to run off with a cinematographer from LA who'd been in Door County on a shoot. The children were now eleven and thirteen and stood beside their father, dressed in their first formal wear.

'Sheila,' Eric teased, taking the girl's hands. 'Don't you know it's not polite to be prettier than the bride?' He kissed her cheek and made it turn the same bright pink as her first ankle-length dress.

She smiled, revealing a mouth full of braces, and replied shyly, 'Your wife is prettier than all the brides in the world.'

Eric grinned, dropped a hand on Nancy's neck and let his appreciative gaze touch her face. 'Why, thank you, Sheila, I think so, too.'

Next came Brett, the eleven-year-old. Eric fingered the silk lapel of Brett's tuxedo and whistled through his teeth. 'Would you look at those threads! Michael Jackson, *sit down!*'

'I'd rather be wearing my football jersey,' Brett grumbled, reaching inside his tux jacket to tug up his cummerbund. 'This thing keeps fallin' down all the time.'

They laughed and moved on to the end of the line where Eric broke into a wide smile at the sight of a familiar face he hadn't seen in years. 'Well, I'll be darned. Lisa . . . hello!'

'Eric!'

He hugged the pretty, dark-haired woman, then backed away to make introductions. 'Nancy, this is Gary's sister, Lisa. Homecoming queen, class of '65. You can see why. She and I were friends way back when Gary was just a little punk who always wanted us guys to throw him some passes or tag along on the boat. Lisa, this is my wife, Nancy.'

The two women greeted one another and Eric added, 'Lisa, I mean it. You look sensational.' The line edged forward behind him and he was forced to move on, adding, 'We'll talk more later, okay?'

'Yes, let's. Oh, Eric . . .' Lisa caught his arm. 'Did you see Maggie?'

'Maggie?' His bearing snapped alert.

'She's here someplace.'

Eric scanned the wedding guests milling about the sidewalk and boulevard.

'Over there . . .' Lisa pointed. 'With Brookie and Gene. And that's my husband, Lyle, with them, too.'

'Thanks, Lisa. I'll go over and say hi.' To Nancy he said, 'You don't mind, do you, honey?'

She did but refrained from saying so. He touched her shoulder and left her with his mother, saying, 'Excuse me, honey, I'll be right back.'

Watching him go, Nancy felt a shot of trepidation, realizing he was walking towards his old high school steady. The woman was a rich widow who'd recently called him in the dead of night, and Eric was an attractive man in a new grey suit and white shirt that accented his trimness and his healthy summer tan. As he moved through the crowd two teenagers and one woman a good seventy years old let their eyes follow him as he passed. If they looked twice, what would his old girlfriend do?

Eric saw Maggie for the first time from behind, dressed in white with a splash of watermelon pink thrown around her neck and over one shoulder, still dark-haired, still thin. She was involved in an animated exchange with the others, raising both hands, clapping once, then settling her weight on one foot and tilting the opposite high heel against the sidewalk.

Approaching her, he felt a smack of tension – anticipation and curiosity. She poked Brookie in the chest, still apparently talking, and the group laughed. As he reached her she was exclaiming, '. . . the Wisconsin state milk inspector, of all people!'

He touched her shoulder. 'Maggie?'

She glanced back and went motionless. They both stared. Years had gone by, but past intimacy held them trapped in a moment's beat while neither knew quite what to do or say next.

'Eric . . .' she said, recovering first, smiling.

'I thought it was you.'

'Well, Eric Severson, it's so good to see you.' Anyone else

she would have hugged, but to Eric she only extended her hands.

He took them, squeezing hard. 'How are you?'

'Fine. Much better.' She shrugged and smiled broadly. 'Happy.'

She was wand thin. The cleft still gave her chin the shape of a heart but had been joined by two deep grooves that parenthesized her mouth when she smiled. Her eyebrows were thinner and at the corners of her eyes crow's feet had appeared. Her clothing was chic and her hair – still auburn – a study in stylish indifference.

'Happy – well, that's a relief. And looking wonderful.'

'So do you,' she replied.

The blue of Lake Michigan still tinted his eyes, and his skin was smooth and dark. His hair, once nearly yellow and well past his collar, had darkened to the hue of apple cider, and was now trimmed short and neat. He had matured beyond the boyish good looks of his teenage years into a honed, handsome man. His trunk had broadened; his face had filled out; his hands were hard and wide.

She dropped them discreetly.

'I didn't know you'd be here,' Eric said.

'I didn't know myself. Brookie talked me into coming home, and Lisa insisted I attend the wedding. But you . . .' She laughed as if in happy surprise. 'I didn't expect to see you here either.'

'Gary and I are members of the Fish Creek Civic Association. We worked together to save the old town hall from being demolished. When you stick with a project that long you either become friends or enemies. Gary and I became friends.'

At that moment Brookie stepped forward and interrupted. 'And what about the rest of your friends, Severson – not even a hello for us?'

Belatedly Eric turned to greet them. 'Hi, Brookie. Gene.'

'And this is Lisa's husband, Lyle.'

The two shook hands. 'I'm an old school friend, Eric Severson.'

'Tell him your news, Maggie,' Brookie demanded smugly.

Eric glanced down as Maggie smiled up at him. 'I'm buying the old Harding house.'

'You're kidding!'

'No. I just put earnest money on it today and signed a conditional purchase agreement.'

'That big old monstrosity?'

'If all goes well it'll be Fish Creek's first bed-and-breakfast inn.'

'That was fast.'

'Brookie coerced me into looking at it.' She touched her forehead as if dizzy. 'I still can't believe I've done it . . . I *am doing* it!'

'That old place looks like it's ready to crumble.'

'You could be perfectly right. I'm having an architectural engineer take a look at it next week, and if it's anything less than structurally sound, the deal's off. But for now, I'm excited.'

'Well, I don't blame you. So, how long have you been home?'

'I got here Tuesday. I'm going back tomorrow.'

'Short trip.'

'But fateful.'

'Yes.' They found themselves studying each other again – two old friends, slightly more, realizing they would always be slightly more.

'Listen,' he said abruptly, glancing over his shoulder. 'Come and say hello to my mother. I know she'd love to see you.'

'She's here?' Maggie asked eagerly.

A grin climbed Eric's left cheek. 'Got her hair all kinked up for the occasion.'

Maggie laughed as they turned towards a group several

feet away. She picked out Anna Severson immediately, curly-headed, grey, and stacked like a double-decker ice cream cone. She stood with Eric's brother, Mike, and his wife, Barbara, whom Maggie remembered as an upperclassman who'd played a murderer in the class play. With them, too, was a beautiful woman Maggie immediately took to be Eric's wife.

Eric ushered Maggie forward with a touch on her elbow. 'Ma, look who's here.'

Anna cut herself off in mid-sentence, turned, and threw her hands up. 'Well, for the cry-eye!'

'Hi, Mrs Severson.'

'Margaret Pearson, come here!'

Anna took Maggie in a gruff hug and thwacked her on the back three times before pushing her away and holding her in place. 'You don't look much different than when you'd come in my kitchen and clean me out of a batch of warm bread. A little skinnier is all.'

'And a little older.'

'Yeah, well, who ain't? Every winter I say I ain't going to run the business again next spring, but every spring at ice-out I start getting itchy to see those tourists come in all excited over the big one they caught, and to see the boats coming and going. You watch for them boats your whole life, you don't know what you'd do if you didn't have to anymore. The boys got two of them now, you know. Mike, he runs one. You remember Mike, don't you? And Barb.'

'Yes, hello.'

'And this,' Eric interrupted, resting a proprietorial hand on the nape of the most awesomely beautiful woman Maggie had ever seen, '. . . is my wife, Nancy.' Her features had a natural symmetry almost startling in their perfection, enhanced by flawlessly applied makeup whose shadings blended like air-brushed art. Her hairstyle was chosen for its simplicity so as not to distract from her beauty. Added to what nature had provided was a carefully-honed thinness enhanced by costly clothing worn with an insouciant flair.

'Nancy . . .' Maggie extended a warm, lingering handshake, looking square into the woman's eyes, noting the hair-fine lashes drawn on her lower eyelids. 'I've been told by a good half-dozen people how beautiful you are, and they were certainly right.'

'Why, thank you.' Nancy withdrew her hand. Her nails were garnet, sculptured, the length of almonds.

'And I want to immediately apologize for waking you up the other night when I called. I should have checked the time first.'

Nancy tipped up her lips but the smile stopped short of her eyes. Neither did she offer any conciliatory nicety, leaving an unpleasant void in the conversation.

'Maggie's got some news,' Eric announced, filling the gap. 'She tell's me she's put in a bid on the old Harding place. Wants to be an innkeeper. What do you think, Mike, will that old house stand up long enough to make it worth her while?'

Anna answered. 'Why of course it'll stand! They built that house back when they knew how to build houses. Milled the lumber down in Sturgeon Bay and hired a Polish carver from Chicago to come and live here while it was going up, to hand-carve all the newel posts and spandrels and fireplace mantels and what not. Why, the floors in the place alone are worth their weight in gold.' Anna interrupted herself to peer at Maggie. 'An innkeeper, huh?'

'If I can get a zoning permit. So far I haven't been able to find out where I have to go to apply for one.'

'That's easy,' put in Eric. 'The Door County Planning Board. They meet once a month at the courthouse in Sturgeon Bay. I know because I used to be on it.'

Elated to learn this much at last, Maggie turned eagerly to Eric. 'What do I have to do?'

'Go before them and appeal for a conditional use permit and tell them what it's for.'

'Do you think I'll have any trouble?'

'Well . . .' Eric's expression turned dubious as he reached up and ran a hand down the back of his head. 'I hope not, but I may as well warn you, it's possible.'

'Oh, no.' Maggie looked crestfallen. 'But Door County's economy depends on tourism, doesn't it? And what better facility to attract tourists than a B and B?'

'Well, I agree, but unfortunately I'm not on the board any longer. Five years ago I was, and we had a situation where –'

Brookie interrupted at that moment. 'We're taking off for the reception now, Maggie. Are you riding with us? Hi, everybody. Hi, Mrs Severson. Anyone mind if I haul Maggie away?'

'Yes, but –' Maggie glanced between Brookie and Eric who ended her consternation by saying, 'Go ahead. We'll be at the reception, too. We can talk more there.'

The yacht club was on the Lake Michigan side of the peninsula, a twenty-minute drive away. All the way there Maggie talked animatedly with Brookie and Gene, formulating plans, projecting into next spring and summer when she hoped to be open for business, worrying about her teaching contract and what difficulties she might have getting out of it, and the sale of her home in Seattle. Reaching the yacht club and marina where dozens of sailboats were moored, she exclaimed, 'And my boat! I forgot about my boat! I've got to get that sold, too!'

'Easy, honey-child, easy,' Brookie advised with a crooked smile. 'First we're going in here and have us a wedding feast, *then* you can start worrying about your new business and making the move.'

Bailey's Harbor Yacht Club had always been one of Maggie's favourite places, and entering it again she felt its familiarity impose itself upon her. Ceiling-to-floor windows wrapped around the broad, low-slung building giving a captivating view of the marina and docks where cabin cruisers, down from Chicago for the weekend, shared the slips with more modest sailboats. Beside the bleached-grey planking of the docks their white decks gleamed like a string of pearls floating upon the crystal-blue water. Between the club and the docks, pampered lawns inclined gently to the water's edge.

Inside, the carpet was plush and the air filled with the odour of freshly-ignited Sterno from a twenty-foot stretch of buffet tables placed against the windows. Blue flames swayed beneath gleaming silver chafing dishes. A line of cooks in tall, white mushroom hats waited with their hands crossed behind their backs, nodding to the arriving guests. In the adjacent lounge a three-piece combo played lazy jazz which filtered into the dining room, adding to the ambience. The tables were draped with white linen; coral napkins stood, pleated, upon each white plate; and crystal goblets awaited filling.

As the wedding guests meandered in, Maggie recognized many familiar faces – a little older now, but unmistakable. Old Mrs Huntington, who years ago had been a cook at the high school, approached Maggie for a fond hello and offered an expression of condolence over her recent widowhood. Dave Thripton, who pumped gas at the Fish Creek docks, came up and said, 'I remember you – you're Roy Pearson's daughter. You used to sing for the PTA meetings, didn't you?' Mrs Marvella Peterson, one of the members of her mother's ladies' aid group, offered, 'We live up on the top of the bluff now just two houses off the highway. Stop in sometime.' Clinton Stromberg and his wife, Tina, who ran a resort near Sister Bay, already knew about Maggie's bid on the Harding place and wished her luck with her undertaking.

She was standing discussing the Door County lodging situation with the Strombergs when from the corner of her eye she saw Eric and his party arrive. With one ear on what Clinton was saying she watched Eric exchange handshakes and accept a glass of champagne from a circulating waitress, seat his wife, his mother and himself on the opposite side of the room.

There had been little mistaking Nancy Severson's cool reception of her, and though Maggie was eager to resume her conversation with Eric, she felt it expedient to refrain from approaching him again. She found a seat with her own group clear across the dining room from Eric.

Their eyes met once, during the course of the dinner. Eric flashed an impersonal smile, and Maggie broke the contact by turning to say something to Brookie, on her left.

They dined on the yacht club's renowned seafood extravaganza –scallops Mornay, stuffed flounder, Cajun catfish, marinated shrimp and steamed crab claws. Afterward, when the mingling and socializing resumed, Maggie found a moment alone. The dancing had begun as she stood at the immense window, watching the westering sun glint upon the blue water of the bay. A pair of sailboats appeared, white and nonchalant as gulls. The waiters had carried off their dripping silver pans and extinguished the blue flames. The strong smell of the Sterno, so peculiar to posh restaurants, reminded Maggie of the Bear Creek Country Club where she had last attended a wedding reception. Phillip had been alive then, and they had sat with friends, talked, laughed, danced. Six months after his death she had declined the invitation to another wedding, unwilling to face it alone. Now here she was, having an enjoyable day, another barrier of widowhood broken. Perhaps, as she'd been told in her classes on grief, she had been the one to withdraw from her friends. At the time she had adamantly argued, 'No, *they've* abandoned *me*!'

Here, among familiar surroundings and remembered faces, and exhilarated by the imminent changes in her life, she finally admitted to herself a truth that had been a full year coming.

If I'd reached out earlier, I'd have been less lonely and miserable.

The sun had relaxed. It sat atop the water like a great golden coin. Across its path the pair of sailboats gave the illusory appearance of hovering inches above the water. Nearer, about the moored boats, the undisturbed water lay like cerulean silk, wrinkled only by a pair of mallards out for a last evening swim.

'It's beautiful, isn't it?' Eric remarked quietly at Maggie's shoulder.

She controlled the impulse to glance back at him, realizing his wife was in the room somewhere, probably watching them. 'Beautiful and familiar, which is even better.'

'You really needed this trip home.'

'Yes. I didn't realize how badly until I got back. I've been standing here admitting that during the past year I pushed a lot of people away. I don't understand why, but it happens. All the time I thought they had abandoned me when actually it was the other way around. What made me finally see it was coming here, doing the reaching out myself. Do you know that this is the first sizeable social function I've attended since Phillip's death?'

'And you're enjoying it?'

'Oh, very much. If I'd had time to consider the invitation I probably wouldn't have come. As it happened, I was caught off guard by Lisa. And here I am, suddenly not feeling sorry for myself anymore. Do you know what else I've discovered?'

'What?'

She turned to find him near, holding his glass without drinking, watching her. 'That I don't feel like a fifth wheel the way I thought I would without a man at my side.'

'Progress,' he said simply.

'Yes, definite progress.'

A lull fell. They studied each other while he stirred his drink with an olive-studded toothpick, took a sip and lowered the glass.

'You look good, Maggie.' The words emerged quietly, as if he could not keep himself from saying them.

'So do you.'

They stood close, tallying the changes in one another, pleased, suddenly, that they had aged gracefully. In their eyes were memories which would more wisely have been veiled.

He was the one to pull them out of their absorption with one another, shifting to put additional distance between them. 'After you called, Ma dug out our yearbook and we laughed at how skinny and long-haired I look. Then I tried to imagine you at thirty-nine . . .'

'Forty.'

'That's right. Forty. I don't know what I imagined. An old wrinkled grey-haired dowager in orthopaedic shoes and a shawl or something.'

She laughed, released by his frankness to admit, 'I did some wondering, too – if you'd gone bald or fat or had developed boils on your neck.'

He tipped back his head and laughed.

'I'd say we've both weathered well.'

She smiled and held his gaze. 'Your wife is very beautiful.'

'I know.'

'Will she mind our talking like this?'

'She might. I don't know. I don't talk to many single women anymore.'

Maggie glanced across the room to find Nancy watching them. 'I don't want to cause any friction between you but I have dozens of questions to ask.'

'Ask away. May I get you a drink?'

'No, thank you.'

'A glass of white wine, maybe, or something soft?'

'On second thought, wine would be nice.'

While he was gone she made a decision to make it unquestionably clear to Nancy Severson that she had no designs on her husband. She skirted the dancers, made her way to Eric's table and said, 'Excuse me, Mrs Severson?'

Nancy looked up, regarding Maggie with lukewarm detachment and replied, 'It's Macaffee.'

'I beg your pardon?'

'My *name* is Nancy Macaffee. I kept it when I married Eric.'

'Oh,' Maggie returned, nonplussed. 'Ms Macaffee. May I sit down?'

'Of course.' Nancy removed her small beaded bag from the seat of a chair but added no welcoming smile.

'I hope you don't mind if I pick Eric's brain for a while. I have so very little time before I have to fly back to Seattle, and so much I need to learn.'

Flourishing the flat of her hand and giving her returning husband a trenchant glare, Nancy said, 'He's all yours.'

'Here you are.' Handing Maggie a glass of chilled wine, he looked at his wife, amazed at her undisguised brittleness, which fell just short of outright rudeness. What he'd told Maggie was true – he seldom socialized with single women. He was a married man and the thought never entered his mind. Furthermore, it felt peculiar to be the one observing jealous reactions instead of squelching them. Given Nancy's traffic-stopping face, he had to do little more than appear in public with her to witness males following her with beguiled glances, sometimes saluting her silently with a raised glass across a dining room. He had come to accept it without feeling threatened, to take it as a compliment to his good taste in choosing her for his wife.

But here he was, on the receiving end of a cool draught of jealousy, and he was male enough – and faithful enough – to appreciate its origins and regard them as healthy in a marriage of eighteen years.

He chose a seat beside Nancy and draped a wrist over the back of her chair.

'So you're really going to go for it, huh?' he said to Maggie, reopening the topic of earlier.

'Do you think it's a crazy idea? Opening a bed and breakfast in the Harding place?'

'No, not at all. If the house is sound.'

'If it is, and if I came back to get a business established, tell me what I'd have to face when I come up against the planning board.'

'They may grant your permit immediately or there may be outright hostility.'

'But why?'

He leaned forward and propped both elbows on the table. 'Five years ago a big conglomerate called Northridge Development came in and started secretly dealing on land, using what was later called "kid-glove tactics" to persuade the owners to sell, even though they at first resisted. They applied for a conditional use permit and after we granted it, Northridge put up a thirty-two-unit condominium on a half-acre site, creating problems right and left, starting with parking. Fish Creek's barely got enough room for tourist parking, crowded against the bluff as it is, and we're trying damned hard to avoid paved lots, which would ruin the Grandma Moses atmosphere. When the new units were occupied the businesses nearby claimed their foot traffic had fallen off because people couldn't find a place to park. They claimed the conglomerate had intentionally ignored our density requirements, and raised particular hell with the board over the appearance of the place, which has a few too many skylights and sheer walls for local taste. We had the environmentalists on our backs, too, yelling about flora and fauna and sprawl and preservation of our shoreline. And they're right, they're all right. Door County's appeal lies in its provincialism. It's the board's duty to preserve not only what space we have left, but the rural atmosphere of the entire peninsula. That's what you'll be up against when you go in there and ask for rezoning to open another tourist facility.'

'But I wouldn't be putting up thirty-two units. I'd only be opening four or five rooms to the public.'

'And you'd be dealing with a cross-section of Door citizens that only hear the word "motel".'

'But a bed and breakfast isn't a motel! Why, it's . . . it's . . .'

'It's sprawl, some of them would say.'

'And I have adequate parking! There's an old tennis court across the road that'll make the perfect parking lot.'

'The board would take that into consideration, I'm sure.'

'And I'm not some . . . some sly eastern conglomerate trying to buy up valuable property and make a killing selling condo units. I'm a home-town girl.'

'Which would work in your favour, too. But you have to remember –' Eric was pointing a toothpick at Maggie's nose when Nancy grew tired of the animated conversation and drolly pushed his hand aside. 'Excuse me. I think I'll go listen to the music awhile.'

Pausing with a half-drawn breath, obviously stimulated by the conversation, he let her go, then pointed the toothpick again. 'You have to remember, you're appealing to a group of Door residents who've been entrusted to look out for all interests. Right now sitting on the board there's a farmer from Sevastopol, a teacher from the high school, a newspaper reporter, a restaurant owner, a commercial fisherman and Loretta McConnell. Do you remember Loretta McConnell?'

Maggie's optimism flagged. 'I'm afraid I do.'

'What she didn't own in Fish Creek she coveted. Her people have been here since Asa Thorpe built his cabin. If she decides to vote against your zoning permit, you'll have a battle on your hands. She's got money and power, and unless I miss my guess, eighty or not, she gets off on wielding them both.'

'What'll I do if they refuse me?'

'Re-appeal. But the best way to avoid that is to come before them armed with as many facts and figures as you can. Tell them how much you're willing to spend to renovate the place. Bring in the actual quotes. Get statistics on the number of lodging units that are filled here at peak seasons, and how many potential tourists get turned away for lack of lodging. Reassure them about the parking. Get local residents to speak up for you and talk to the board.'

'Would you?'

'Would I what?'

'Speak up for me?'

'Me?'

'You were a board member. They know you, respect you. If I can make you believe I'll blend my business into the environment with as few changes as possible, and that I won't crowd Cottage Row with cars, would you come before the board with me and encourage them to give me the zoning change I'd need?'

'Well, I don't see why not. I might want to be reassured myself about what you're going to do to the place.'

'Absolutely. As soon as I have estimates and plans, you'll be the first to see them.'

'One other thing.'

'What?'

'I'm not trying to pry, and you don't have to answer if you'd rather not, but have you got the money to carry this thing through? When Northridge came applying, the thing that convinced the board was the amount of money they had allotted for the project.'

'Money is no problem, Eric. When an airliner that size goes down the survivors are paid well.'

'Good. Now tell me who you've got lined up to give you estimates on the work.'

The talk moved on to engineers, workmen, architecture, nothing more personal. She told him she'd get in touch with him when the time came that she'd need his help again, thanked him and they bade good-bye with a very proper handshake.

Shortly after midnight that night, Eric and Nancy were undressing on opposite sides of their bedroom when she remarked, 'Well, Maggie whatever-her-name-is didn't waste any time coming on to you, did she?'

Eric paused with his tie half-loosened. 'I figured this was coming.'

'I'll bet you figured!' Nancy glared at him in the mirror while removing her earrings. 'I could have curled up with mortification. My husband flirting with his old flame and half the town looking on!'

'I wasn't flirting any more than she was.'

'Well, what would you call it then?' She threw the earrings into a cut glass dish and yanked a bangle bracelet off her wrist.

'You were there, you heard. We were talking about the business she wants to open up.'

'And what were you talking about over by the window? Don't tell me that was business, too!'

Eric turned to her, holding up both palms to forestall her. 'Listen, I've had a couple of martinis and so have you. Why don't we just shelve this discussion until morning?'

'Oh, you'd like that, wouldn't you!' She pulled her dress over her head and flung it aside. 'Then you could run off to your precious boat in the middle of it and not have to answer me at all!'

Eric yanked his tie from under his collar and hung it on the closet door, followed by his suit jacket. 'We were friends in high school. What did you expect me to do? Ignore her?'

'I didn't expect you to fawn over her right out in front of

the damned church and to leave me alone in the middle of a wedding reception to go make calf eyes at her!'

'Calf eyes!' His head thrust forward. He stood still with his shirttails half-out of his trousers.

'Don't lie, Eric, I saw you! I never took my eyes off the pair of you!'

'She was telling me about how she missed her husband and that it was the first time she's been able to face going out without him.'

'She didn't seem to be missing him very badly when she made calf eyes back at you!'

'Nancy, what the hell's got into you! In all the years we've been married, when have I ever so much as looked at another woman?' With his shoulders atilt, he propped both hands on his hips and faced her.

'Never. But then you didn't have any old flames around till now, did you?'

'She's not my old flame.' He returned to undressing.

'You could've fooled me. Were you lovers in high school?' Nancy asked brittlely, dropping to the bed to remove her nylons.

'Nancy, for God's sake, drop it.'

'You were, weren't you? I knew it the minute I saw you walk over to her on the church steps. When she turned around and saw you it was as plain as the dent in her chin.' Dressed in a pair of brief navy-blue satin undergarments Nancy moved to the vanity mirror, raised her chin and ran four fingertips up her throat. 'Well, I'll say one thing for you, you've got good taste. You pick 'em pretty.'

It struck him as he watched her that she was too beautiful for her own good. The idea of his paying even minimal attention to another woman became a disproportionate threat. As he watched, she went on reassuring herself, running her fingertips up her taut throat, admiring her reflection.

Apparently finding her beauty intact, she dropped her

chin and reached to her nape to free the gold barrette, then began brushing her hair violently.

'I don't want you helping that woman.'

'I already told her I would.'

'That's it then? You'll do it whether I object or not?'

'You're blowing this thing out of all proportion, Nancy.'

She threw down the brush and spun to face him. 'Oh, am I? I'm on the road five days a week and I should leave you here to squire your old lover around to committee meetings while I'm gone?'

'You're on the road five days a week by choice, my dear!' Angrily, he pointed a finger at her.

'Oh, now we're going to start that old whining, are we?'

'Not we. You! You started the whole thing, so let's finish it once and for all. Let's get it nice and clear that I'd like my wife to *live* with me, not just drop in on weekends!'

'And what about what *I* want!' She spread a hand on her chest. 'I married a man who said he wanted to be a corporate executive and live in Chicago, and all of a sudden he announces that he's going to pitch it all and become a . . . a *fisherman*!' She threw up her hands. 'A *fisherman*, for Chrissake! Did you ask me if I wanted to be a fisherman's wife?' She splayed a hand on her chest and leaned forward from the waist. 'Did you ask me if *I* wanted to live in this godforsaken no-man's land, eighty miles from civilization and –'

'Your idea of civilization and mine are two different things, Nancy. That's our trouble.'

'Our trouble, Mr Severson, is that you changed course in the middle of our marriage, and all of a sudden it no longer mattered to you that I had a blossoming career that mattered as much to me as your precious fishing mattered to you!'

'If you'll strain your memory, my dear, you'll recall that we did talk about your career, which, at the time, we thought would only last a couple more years and then we'd start a family.'

'No, that was what *you* thought, Eric, not me. *You* were the one who outlined the five year plan, not me. Anytime I indicated that I wasn't interested in having a family you turned a deaf ear.'

'And obviously that's what you expect me to keep doing. Well, time's running out, Nancy. I'm already forty years old.'

She turned away. 'You knew it when we got married.'

'No.' He grabbed her by the arm and made her stay. 'No, I never knew it. I assumed –'

'Well, you assumed wrong! I *never* said I wanted children! Never!'

'Why, Nancy?'

'You know why.'

'Yes, I do, but I'd like to hear you say it.'

'Make sense, Eric. What do you think we've been talking about here? I've got a job I love, with perks a thousand women would kill to have – trips to New York, a red-air travel card, sales meetings at Boca Raton. I've worked hard to get every one of them and you're asking me to give that up to stick myself here in this . . . this cracker box and raise babies?'

Her chosen phrasing cut deep. As if they'd be just anybody's babies, as if it scarcely mattered to her the babies would be his and hers. He sighed and gave up. He could throw her narcissism in her face, but what purpose would it serve? He loved her and he had no desire to hurt her. To be truthful, he, too, had loved her beauty. But as the years went by that physical pulchritude mattered less and less. Long ago, he had realized he would love her as much – perhaps even more – if her hips widened and she lost the ultra-chic thinness she so carefully safeguarded by dieting. He'd love her as much if she appeared in the kitchen at seven in the morning with a squalling infant on her shoulder and her makeup still in the pots on her vanity. If she dressed in jeans and a sweatshirt instead of couturier creations from Saks and Neiman-Marcus.

'Let's go to bed,' he said disconsolately, scraping down the covers, then dropping heavily to the edge of the mattress to pull his socks off. He flung them aside and sat staring at them, slump-shouldered.

She watched him for a long time from across the room, feeling the framework of their marriage cracking, wondering what, short of children, would hold it together. She padded to him barefoot and knelt between his knees. 'Eric, please understand.' She circled him with both arms and pressed her face to his chest. 'A woman has no business conceiving a baby she'd resent.'

Put your arms around her, Severson, she's your wife and you love her and she's trying to make peace between you. But he couldn't. Or wouldn't. He sat with his hands folded over the edge of the mattress, feeling the awful weight of finality settle in his vitals. In the past when they'd had this same argument it had had no succinct end, but had taken days petering out while she nursed her displeasure with him. But that very open-endedness had always left him feeling they'd talk – argue – about it again before the issue was settled.

Tonight, however, Nancy presented a calm, reasonable defence against which there was no arguing. For he would no more wish his child onto a resentful mother than she would.

Chapter 6

Upon Maggie's return to Seattle her life became a frenzy. The school principal said he was sorry to see her leave, but he'd have no trouble hiring another full-time teacher to replace her. Before she left the building she had cleaned out her desk. At home she raked the dead pine needles, trimmed the shrubs, called an acquaintance and realtor, Elliott Tipton, and before he left the house a lockbox hung on her door. At Elliott's suggestion, she contacted workers to repaint the trim on the outside of the house, and repaper one bathroom. She called Waterways Marina and told them to shear two thousand dollars off the price of the boat: she wanted to unload it fast. She called Allied Van Lines and got a moving estimate. She heard from Thomas Chopp who informed her Harding House had dry rot in the porch floors, wet rot in one of the walls (the maid's room corner where the plumbing had leaked and carpenter ants had been busy), no insulation, inadequate wiring, too small a furnace, and would need new flashings and roof vents. The roof, however, he said, was in surprisingly good shape, as were the floor stringers and interior-bearing walls, therefore it was his opinion the place could be renovated but it would be costly.

She received the Health and Social Services pamphlet governing bed-and-breakfast establishments for the state of Wisconsin, and discovered she would need one additional bathroom and a fire exit upstairs to meet code, but found no other glaring reasons she would be denied a licence.

She called Althea Munne and gave her the order to have papers prepared for the final purchase and hold them until further notice.

She contacted three Door County contractors and arranged for them to submit drawings and bids on the remodelling.

She called her father who said she was welcome at their house for as long as it took to make her own liveable.

She spoke to her mother who gave her a string of orders, including the warning not to cross those mountains by herself if there was snow.

And finally, she called Katy.

'You're going to what!'

'Move back to Door County.'

'And sell the house in Seattle?' Katy's voice rose with dismay.

'Yes.'

'Mother, how could you!'

'What do you mean, how could I? It would be senseless to keep two houses.'

'But it's the house where I was born and raised! It's been my home for as long as I remember! You mean I'll never have a chance to see it again?'

'You'll be able to come to my house in Fish Creek anytime.'

'But it's not the same! My friends are in Seattle. And my old room will be gone, and . . . and . . . well, just everything!'

'Katy, *I'll* still be there for you, no matter where I live.'

Katy's voice grew angry. 'Don't pull your parental psychology on me, Mother. I think it's a lousy thing to do, sell the house right out from under me the minute I'm gone. You wouldn't like it either.'

Maggie hid her dismay at Katy's anger. 'Katy, I thought you'd be happy to have me closer, so you could come home more often. Why, it's close enough that you can even drive up on weekends, and on holidays we can be with Grandpa and Grandma, too.'

'Grandpa and Grandma. I hardly even know them.'

For the first time Maggie's voice grew sharp. 'Well, perhaps it's time you got to! It seems to me, Katy, that you're being rather selfish about this whole thing.'

At the other end of the line an astonished silence hummed. After moments Katy said tightly, 'I gotta go, Mom. I've got a class in ten minutes.'

'All right. Call anytime,' Maggie ended coolly.

When she'd hung up she stood beside the phone pressing her stomach. Inside, it trembled. She could count on one hand the number of times she had put her own wishes before those of Katy, and she couldn't remember the last time the two of them had snapped at each other. She felt a sharp disappointment. How incredibly selfish one's children could be at times. As far as Katy was concerned Maggie might do whatever was necessary to bring happiness back into her life . . . as long as it didn't inconvenience Katy.

I was there for you your whole life, Katy. I was a good, attentive mother who made sure quality time with you was never sacrificed to my career. And now, when I need your approval to make my excitement complete you withhold it. Well, young woman, whether you like it or not, the time has come for me to please myself and not you.

Maggie's resoluteness startled even herself. Standing in the kitchen where Katy had sat in a high chair and been spoon-fed, where years later she had left muffin crumbs for her mother to wipe up, Maggie felt like a moth emerging from a chrysalis.

My goodness, she thought, *I'm forty years old and I'm still growing up*. She realized something else in that moment, something Dr Feldstein had said on numerous occasions: she had within herself the power of either creating or defeating happiness by choice. *She* had done it. *She* had gone to Door County, *she* had renewed old friendships, *she* had explored an old house and put anticipation back into her life. And anticipation made the difference. A life without it made a parent lean too hard on her children, a patient lean too hard on her psychiatrist, and a widow lean too hard on herself.

She walked into the family room and stood in the centre of it, turning a slow circle, studying the room that held hundreds of memories. *I'll leave here without regrets, looking back only in fondness. You won't mind, Phillip, I know you won't. You would not have wanted me to keep the house as a shrine in exchange for my own happiness. Katy will come to realize this in time.*

She made the move to Door County in mid-September. The Seattle house had not sold so she left the furnishings behind and took along only what personal possessions her car would hold.

She had never been an alert long-distance driver and amazed herself again by remaining wide awake through ten-hour stretches without anyone to spell her. In the past she had been the relief driver and even as such had become mesmerized during the first hour behind the wheel. Now, knowing she had to do it on her own, she did.

Neither had she ever stayed in a motel alone. Always, Phillip had been there to lift the suitcases out of the trunk, a partner with whom to scout out a place for dinner, and afterward, a warm familiar body in a cold, strange bed. She settled the dinner issue by going through the drive-in window of a McDonald's and eating her hamburger and fries in her motel room. Exhausted after her day of driving, she fell asleep almost before the last French fry was eaten, and slept like a newborn, scarcely missing Phillip.

Idaho was rugged, Montana beautiful, North Dakota endless, and Minnesota exciting, for she was nearing home. But the moment she crossed the St Croix River into Hudson, she felt the difference. *This* was Wisconsin! The clean, rolling farms with immense herds of black and white holsteins. The proud old two-storey farmhouses beside red gambrel-roofed barns. Vast tracts of yellow field corn meeting vast tracts of green woods. Cheese shops and antique shops, and a tavern at every country crossroad. Once, near Neillsville she saw a farmer–Amish, no doubt–harvesting behind a team of draught horses. And farther east, the ginseng farms with their shade frames stretched out like patchwork quilts.

She rounded Green Bay and headed north, feeling the same surge of elation as the last time she'd entered Door County, appreciating its changelessness, understanding the need to preserve it. It looked like a bit of Vermont misplaced. The wild sumac – harbinger of autumn –had begun to turn scarlet. The first apples of the season were being picked. The woodpiles were high and straight beside cottage doors.

Approaching Fish Creek, she decided to drive past *her* house first. A left turn off the highway led her onto a road known as the switchback which dropped in a series of tight curves to Cottage Row and her new neighbourhood. She rolled down the window and savoured the smells – the pungent scent of cedars and the herbal perfume of poplars at certain times of year when their sap is moving. Her heart plunged as she rounded a curve and caught sight of her own row of arborvitae. She pulled off onto the tennis court beside the rickety arbour seat and looked down towards the house. Little more than its roof showed beyond the untended shrubbery, but a mere glimpse of it charged her with fresh anticipation. Beside the road a sold board had been added to the Homestead Realty sign.

Sold . . . to Maggie Stearn, the start of her new life.

She settled temporarily – very temporarily, she promised herself – into her parents' house and called Katy to let her know she'd arrived safely. Katy's response was, 'Yeah, good, Mom. Listen, I can't talk right now, the girls are waiting to go down to the dining room.' Hanging up, she thought, *Wise up, Maggie, kids don't worry about parents the way parents worry about kids.*

Vera bore out the fact by hounding Maggie incessantly. 'Now make sure your lawyer looks over all the fine print so you know what you're getting into. Whatever you do, don't hire that Hardenspeer bunch to do the remodelling. They'll come to work half drunk and fall off a ladder and sue you for every cent you've got. Maggie, are you sure you're doing the right thing? It just seems to me a woman alone could get taken twenty ways trying to remodel a house that big. I almost wish you'd stayed in Seattle, much as I like having you here! I don't know what your father was thinking to encourage you!'

Maggie tolerated Vera's needling by keeping busy. She drove to Sturgeon Bay and filled out an application for a conditional use permit to open a bed-and-breakfast establishment in Fish Creek. She arranged for a water inspection which was required by law before the resale of any home that had its own well; she opened a cheque account in the Fish Creek Bank, arranged for phone and electric service, and a box at the post office, since Fish Creek had no home mail delivery within its township limits. She met each of the three contractors she'd contacted by phone and collected their estimates, the lower of which hovered just below the $60,000 mark.

Common sense said, wait until the county board gives you the permit before proceeding with the purchase of the house, but weather became a primary consideration: frost would be coming soon. Given the amount of plumbing that would have to be reworked, and the fact that an entire wall would have to be torn out and the furnace replaced, Maggie made a decision to go ahead with the purchase and hope for the best.

The closing took place during the last week of September, and two days later, the Lavitsky brothers – Bert and Joe – knocked a hole in the maid's room wall big enough to drive their truck through: the refurbishing had begun.

Maggie received the call from the Door County Board of Adjustments – commonly called the planning board – that same week, instructing her to appear before them the following Tuesday night.

Which meant she must contact Eric.

She had neither seen nor talked to him since she'd been back, and felt a distinct ambivalence about dialling his number. On a chilly Friday morning with the maples outside her window tinged with frost, she stood in her noisy kitchen dressed in a thick red sweater with her hand on the phone. Inside, Bert Lavitsky was tearing the cupboards off the wall. Outside, his brother was replacing the back verandah floor. KL5-3500. For some strange reason, she knew his number by heart but she withdrew her hand without dialling and crossed her arms tightly, frowning at the phone. *Don't be silly, Maggie, remember what Brookie said. It's no big deal, so don't make it one. And anyway, Anna will probably answer.*

She grabbed the receiver and punched out the number before she could change her mind. The voice that greeted hers was definitely not Anna's.

'Severson Charters.'

'Oh . . . hello . . . Eric?'

'Maggie?'

'Yes.'

'Well, hello! I heard you were back and you closed the deal on the house.'

She plugged one ear. 'Could you talk a little louder, Eric? I'm at the house and there's a lot of hammering going on here.'

'I said, I heard you were back and that you closed the deal on the house.'

'Sooner than might have been wise, but the snow could

be flying in four weeks so I thought I'd better get the Lavitsky boys tearing into the walls without delay.'

'The Lavitskys, huh?'

'That's who's making all the racket here. I checked around. They seem to have a good reputation,' she said above the pounding of hammers.

'They're honest and they do good work. How fast they do it is another matter.'

'Forewarned is forearmed. I'll keep that in mind and see what I can do to light a fire under them.' At that moment Bert slipped his hammer into a loop on his overalls and went out to sit with Joe on the verandah step and have their morning coffee.

'Oh, what a relief,' Maggie said as the welcome silence fell. 'It's break time so you can stop shouting at me.'

She heard Eric laugh.

After a pause, she added, 'I've heard from the county board. They want me to be at their meeting this Tuesday night.'

'Would you still like me to come with you?'

'If it's not too much trouble.'

'No. No trouble at all. I'll be happy to.'

She released a breath slowly, forcing herself to relax. 'Good. I really appreciate it, Eric. Well, I'll see you there then. Seven-thirty at the courthouse.'

'Wait a minute, Maggie. Are you driving down alone?'

'I'd planned on it.'

'Well, there's no sense in two of us driving. Do you want to ride with me?'

Unprepared for the suggestion, Maggie stammered. 'Well . . . I . . . sure, I guess so.'

'Should I pick you up at your parents' house?'

Vera would have a fit, but what could Maggie say? 'That'll be fine.'

On Tuesday night she left the mousse out of her hair and

chose her clothing carefully in hope of favourably impressing the board. She wanted to appear mature, tasteful and – admittedly – well off enough to have the funds to restore a place the size of Harding House. Yet not too flashy. She chose a softly-pleated challis skirt in a mixture of autumn hues from rust to ruby, an ivory blouse with a tucked bodice and embroidery trim, a soft leather belt with an oversized buckle and, at her throat, an oval pin set with an amethyst crystal. Over the ensemble she wore a cropped-waisted jacket of burgundy suede.

When she came downstairs her mother gave her a cursory glance and remarked, 'Dressing rather fancy for a town meeting, aren't you?'

'It's not a town meeting, Mother, it's an appearance before a board who'll pass judgement on me as much as on the business I'm proposing. I wanted to hint that I'd know how to make a decrepit old house attractive again. I thought the oval pin was a nice quaint touch, wouldn't you say?'

'It's quaint, all right,' Vera replied. 'I don't know what the world's coming to when a single woman runs all over the countryside with a married man, and right under her mother's nose.'

Maggie felt herself blushing. 'Mother!'

'Now, Vera,' put in Roy, but she ignored him.

'Well, that's what you're doing, isn't it?'

'Eric is going to try to convince the board in my favour, nothing more!'

'Well, you know what people will say. His wife gone more than she's home, and him squiring a new widow around.'

'He is not *squiring* me around! And I resent your implications!'

'You might very well resent them, Margaret, but I'm your mother, and as long as you're in this house –'

The doorbell interrupted Vera and she hurried forward to answer it before anyone else could. To Maggie's chagrin it was Eric, standing on the porch in a blue windbreaker that said SEVERSON'S CHARTERS on the breast. Had he only pulled up at the kerb and honked the horn Maggie would have felt less culpable. But there he stood, smiling and congenial, much as he had in the days when he'd come to pick her up for a date. 'Hello, Mrs Pearson. How're you?'

'Hello,' Vera replied without a smile.

'Maggie's riding down to Sturgeon with me.'

'Yes, I know.'

Maggie picked up her purse and brushed past Vera. 'I'm all ready, Eric. We'd better hurry or we'll be late.' She passed him like a streak and trotted down the porch steps at full steam. She was standing at the truck door, pulling fruitlessly on the handle when he reached around her and pushed her hand aside. 'This old beater is a little spunky. Sometimes you've got to talk to 'er and coax 'er a little.' Putting his body into it, he opened the door. Climbing in, Maggie could feel her mother's eyes dissecting every move from the living room window. Eric slammed the door, walked around and got in.

'Sorry about the truck,' he said, putting the vehicle in gear. 'It's kind of like an old family pet – you know you ought to put it to sleep, but it's hard to make yourself do it.'

Maggie remained stiff and silent, glaring out the windshield.

As the truck began rolling, Eric glanced at her and said, 'What's the matter?'

'My mother!' she answered in a voice tight with indignation. 'She's a shrew.'

'It's hard to live with them, once you've been away.'

'It was hard to live with her *before* I went away!'

'I'll admit, I've received warmer receptions in my life than I did tonight. Is she upset about us riding to Sturgeon together?' At her stubborn silence, he realized he'd guessed right. 'Maggie, you should have said something, you should have called and we could have gone down separately. I just thought as long as we were both going to the same place –'

'Why should I say something? Why should I let her cast aspersions on a perfectly innocent meeting? We're riding to the courthouse together and I *refuse* to let her make me feel guilty about it! Damn it, I *have* nothing to feel guilty about! It's just her mind, her nosiness – she thinks everybody in town is like her, anxious to think the worst about people.'

Eric looked at her intently. 'The trouble is, they probably are and I never considered it until this moment. Do you want to go back, Maggie, and get your own car?'

'Absolutely not!'

'Everybody in the county knows this old truck. Hell, my name is right on the door.'

'I wouldn't give my mother the satisfaction. And besides, like Brookie said, can't two adults be friends? I need your help tonight. I'm happy to have it. Let's leave it at that and let my mother work out her own hang-ups.' Anxious to change the subject, Maggie glanced around curiously. 'So this is your old truck.' She took in the worn seats, the cracked side window, the dusty dash.

'I have a name for her, but I'd better not tell you what it is. It's not very polite.'

Maggie grinned and said, 'I can just about imagine.'

'I didn't stop to think about your being all dressed up. Maybe you *would* have preferred to take your own car.'

'My own car's got no character. This does.'

Their banter eased the tension between them, and as they rolled south out of town beneath the great dome of evening, where the first bright star hung in the southwest sky, they spoke of other subjects: the autumn weather; the tourist trade which would reach its peak along with the autumn colours within two weeks; how the salmon were tougher to catch now that fall was here, but the brown trout were hot at Portage Park and Lily Bay; when Eric and Mike would take their boats out of the water, and how the Lavitsky boys were doing.

Then Eric said, 'Maggie, I've been thinking a lot about Loretta McConnell and her . . . shall we call it conservatism. If anyone on the board raises objections to your permit, she'll be the one. I've thought of a way to soften her up.'

'How?'

'Have you come up with a name for your inn yet?'

'A name? No.'

'Well, I was talking to Ma, and it came out that Loretta McConnell is a shirttail relative of the original Harding who owned the place. As close as we can figure it, her mother's side of the family would have been the third generation removed from Thaddeus Harding, though the lineage is somewhat obscured by married names. But my guess is, Loretta would know exactly, and if there's anyone who's rabid to preserve heritage, it's Loretta McConnell. She's an active member of the historical society, and gives them a good chunk of money every year. Supposing we appeal to her family pride. We tell her you've decided to keep the name Harding House to preserve as much of the place's heritage as possible.'

'Oh, Eric, that's a wonderful idea! Harding House . . . I love it. And it's so common sense. After all, everyone in town has called it that for years, so why change it now?'

'I thought you might want your name on it.'

'Stearn House . . .' She pondered, then shook her head. 'Uh-uh. It doesn't have the ring that Harding House has. I can see it now, done in graceful copperplate on a swinging sign at the top of the walk. A wooden sign, I think, on a single post with a finial at the top.' She gestured in the air as if the sign hung before her. 'Harding House. A Bed-and-Breakfast Inn. Maggie Stearn, Proprietress.'

He chuckled, charmed by her enthusiasm.

'You love it all, don't you – planning it, working on it?'

'Absolutely. I owe so much to Brookie for talking me into going there in the first place. I find myself fantasizing more and more about the day the first guest signs in. If this board says no tonight I'll probably burst into tears.'

'I have a feeling you'll come out of that courthouse smiling.'

The courthouse at Sturgeon Bay was a combination of old and new – the old Victorian building surrounded by the newer one of beige brick and grey stone. They parked on 4th Street and walked along the sidewalk beneath a row of mountain ash whose red berries had dropped onto the walkway. Between a pair of round red maples and green front lawns, into a doorway flanked by stone planters in which the marigolds and salvias lay black and wilted after the previous week's frosts.

Inside, Eric knew his way to the correct room. Entering it, Maggie felt nervous and expectant. She recognized Loretta McConnell immediately, a singularly unattractive woman with two missing bottom teeth, crooked eyeglasses and straight undressed hair, crudely cropped like that of an Elizabethan page boy. 'There she is,' she whispered, taking a seat in a wooden folding chair beside Eric.

'Don't be misled by her looks. She's a brilliant woman, privy to the doings of more politicians, musicians and artists than you've probably ever heard of. She's a great supporter of the arts and gives enormous endowments to everything from violin prodigies to our own Ridges Nature Sanctuary. Her name is as familiar in Washington as it is in Door County. But for all her power, she's a reasonable woman. Just remember that if she challenges you.'

They waited through a variety of appeals – a landowner unwilling to move his new fence although it would cause problems for the county snowplough; the owner of lake-shore property seeking a variance to have a new well drilled; a woman applying for a permit to open an antique shop in one of the county's original log cabins; a restaurant owner seeking a liquor licence; a seedy, emaciated young man demanding that the county buy him a new pair of glasses because his had been sat on by the operator of the county bookmobile. (The latter was advised by Lorretta McConnell that he was barking up the wrong county tree.)

Then it was Maggie's turn.

'Margaret Stearn,' the chairman read off her application. 'Wants to open a bed-and-breakfast inn on Cottage Row in Fish Creek.'

Maggie rose and moved to the front of the room. The chairman lifted his eyes from the paper. He was a rawboned man who appeared much more suited to riding a tractor than sitting on a board such as the one he chaired. Obviously, he was the farmer from Sevastopol. He had large ears with tufts of hair springing from them. His suit – apparently a concession – was liver brown and dated; the knot in his tie, beneath a crinkled yellowy collar, skewed to one side. Maggie took one look at him and thanked herself for wearing her hair in a tidy downsweep.

'You're Maggie Stearn?' he asked.

'Yes, sir. My maiden name was Pearson. My father is Leroy Pearson. He's been a butcher at the Fish Creek General Store for forty-two years. I was born and raised in Fish Creek.'

'Yes, of course. I know Roy Pearson.' His glance passed over her suede jacket and returned to the paper.

'You've been living elsewhere?'

'In Seattle for eighteen years. My husband died a year ago and my daughter is a freshman at Northwestern College in Chicago, so I decided to move back to Door County.'

'It says here you've already bought the property in question.'

'That's right.' Since homes in Fish Creek had no street addresses, only fire numbers, she identified the house by its common name. 'The old Harding house. I hired an architectural engineer to assess the house for soundness.

Here is his report.' On the table before the chairman she laid the letter from Thomas Chopp. 'I'm investing sixty thousand dollars in refurbishing the house, and the work is already under way. Here's a copy of the contract between myself and the Lavitsky Brothers of Ephraim, who are doing the renovation on the structure itself. Here's another from Workman Electric who'll be replacing the furnace and bringing the electrical up to code. And this one is from Kunst Plumbing who'll be putting in an extra bathroom to meet state lodging codes for bed and breakfasts. This is a copy of the legal survey showing that the property covers one and a half acres, which would mean, if my rooms were full, and if I had one hired hand and myself, we would more than meet the density requirements. The ratio, as you can see, would be one person to every point-one-five-zero acres. I also have an estimate from J & B Blacktopping for tarring the tennis court on the opposite side of the road, which will provide ample parking for my guests. And here, from the Door County Chamber of Commerce, I have figures on the number of inquiries for lodging which they cannot accommodate – you'll notice it works out to approximately ten per cent annually, which represents a significant loss of revenue not only for the hotel- and motel-keepers but for other retail businesses as well. Next I have a letter from the office of the county health inspector outlining what requirements I'd have to meet to pass inspection – not all of them are met at this point, but I assure you, they will be. Next – fire code regulations. You'll note in the estimate from the Lavitsky Brothers that an additional exit and exterior stairway is planned on the second floor to meet fire code. Here I have a room by room estimate for wallpaper, towels, bed linens, curtains and furnishings. And I've done a breakdown of daily costs for laundry services which would be provided by Evenson's at Sturgeon Bay – they'll do the sheets only. We'll do the towels ourselves. And a much rougher estimate on supplies such as soaps, toilet paper, paper cups, cleaning supplies and the like, although I'm still shopping for a better bargain on those items. I've also done a breakdown of the cost per serving of certain foods I'd be serving such as muffins, coffee cakes, coffee and juice. With those foods which could be homemade, you'll notice I've done a comparison between using the services of a bakery and making them myself. And lastly, I have a copy of my last six months' Merrill Lynch statement and I've circled in red the telephone number where you can verify my investments and average monthly balance, which I trust you'll hold in confidence. All this to show you that I'm very much in earnest, that I know very closely what it will cost to open and run this place, and that I can afford it. I want to assure you, ladies and gentlemen, that I won't be opening one season and closing the next. I think my inn would be a great asset to Fish Creek and Door County.'

Maggie retreated one step and stood waiting. The courtroom was so silent you could have heard the hair growing in the board chairman's ears. A titter sounded at the rear of the room. The chairman blinked once and seemed to draw himself out of a daze.

'How long did you say you've been back in Door County?'

'A little less than three weeks.'

He angled a wry grin to his constituents, both left and right, then said with a glint of humour in his eyes, 'I imagine by now you know whether any of the members of this board have had a parking ticket in the last year.'

Maggie smiled. 'No, sir, I don't. But I know how much you make for sitting on the board. Since I'm a taxpayer here now, I thought it prudent to find out.'

Laughter broke out throughout the room, even at the front table.

'Do you mind my asking, Mrs Stearn, what you did in Seattle?'

'I was a home economics teacher, which I consider an additional advantage. I know how to cook and sew and decorate – all prerequisites for running an inn, and I think I'd have little trouble learning to manage the business end of things.'

'There's no doubt in my mind.' He glanced at the application form, then back to Maggie. 'I imagine there's a question of zoning out there.'

'I thought so, too, sir, until I received the Health and Social Services regulations for B-and-B establishments which state clearly that if I were to have five guest rooms or more I'd be considered a hotel, and I could only operate in an area that's zoned commercial. But as long as I stick to four guest rooms or less I'll be considered a bed and breakfast, and they are allowed in residential zones. There's a copy of the pamphlet there for you, too, somewhere. You'll find the ruling in paragraph three under HSS 197.03, the section called Definitions.'

The leader of the group looked as if he'd been poleaxed. His eyebrows nearly touched his hairline, and his lips hung open. 'I'm almost afraid to ask . . . is there anything else you'd like to add?'

'Only that I have a former member of this board, Eric Severson, here with me tonight to give me a character reference.'

'Yes, I noticed him sitting next to you. Hello, Eric.'

Eric lifted a palm in hello.

At last Loretta McConnell spoke up. 'I have a few questions for Mrs Stearn.'

'Yes, ma'am.' For the first time Maggie faced the woman whose gaze was shrewd and intimidating.

'Where would you advertise?'

'Primarily in the Chamber of Commerce publications, and I intend to make an appeal to Norman Simsons, the author of *Country Inns and Backroads*, in the hope that my inn will be included in the next edition of his book. And, of course, I'd have a discreet sign in front of the house itself.'

'No road signs?'

'Cluttering up Door County? Absolutely not. I'm a native, Miss McConnell. I want to see it kept as unspoiled as possible. I can live without billboards.'

'And the exterior of the house – are there any changes planned there?'

'The one stairway, which I mentioned, to meet fire code. And a new rear verandah because the original one was falling off, but the new one will be an exact replica of the old. The exterior painting has already begun, and the house will be restored to its original colours, which, as you know, is being required by law in some areas of the country. The house will be the same colours chosen by Thaddeus Harding – saffron yellow with tarnished-gold window trim, Prussian blue cornice brackets and a paler China blue on the bargeboards. The fretwork and porch rails will be all white. Those are the only changes I have planned. When I hang out the sign that says Harding House, the people who've known it all these years will find it just as they remember it in its early days.'

Loretta McConnell took the subtly-dangled bait. 'Harding House?'

'I intend to keep the name, yes. It's every bit as much a landmark as this courthouse is. Landmarks ought not to be renamed, don't you think?'

Five minutes later Maggie and Eric left the courthouse with the Conditional Use Permit in hand.

They held in their hallelujahs as they moved down the echoey halls, but once outside, they both bellowed at once. She rejoiced while he let out a war whoop, picked her up and swung her off her feet.

'Holy balls, woman, did you have 'em bulldozed! Where in God's name did you get all that information so fast?'

She laughed, still amazed, and exclaimed, 'Well, you told me to present them with facts!'

He set her down and smiled into her face. 'Facts, yes – but they weren't expecting the World Almanac, and neither was I! Maggie, you were magnificent!'

'Was I?' She chuckled and felt her knees beginning to wobble. 'Oh, Eric, I was so scared.'

'You didn't look scared. You looked like Donald Trump putting up another building in New York, or Iacocca announcing a new model.'

'I did?' she asked disbelievingly.

'You should have seen yourself.'

'I think I have to sit down. I'm shaking.' She fell back onto the edge of the concrete planter beside the front door and pressed a hand to her belly.

He perched beside her.

'You didn't have a thing to worry about, not from minute one. I've sat on that board, Maggie. Do you know how many people come in there asking for permits to build this or that, and they don't know wild honey from baby shit about what it would take to open it up, the cost of operating it, its chances for success, nothing! You knocked 'em right off their pins, Maggie. Hell, you didn't need me there at all.'

'But I'm so happy you were. When I turned around and saw you smiling, I . . .' She interrupted herself and ended, 'I'm so glad you're here to help me celebrate.'

'So am I.' He extended a hand. 'Congratulations, Maggie M'girl.'

She gave him her hand and he squeezed it. And held it. A little longer than prudent. The name had come out of nowhere, an echo of a bygone time. Their eyes met and held while the October night pressed near, and beside them the light fell through the window of the courthouse door. It felt too good, having her narrow hand in his much wider one.

She sensibly withdrew hers.

'So you're an innkeeper now,' Eric remarked.

'I still can't believe it.'

'Believe it.'

She rose, joined her hands and hung them over the top of her head and turned a slow circle, looking at the stars. 'Wow,' she breathed.

'Did you see Loretta McConnell's face when you were slapping all those papers on the table?'

'Lord, no. I was afraid to look at her.'

'Well, I did, and I could count her missing teeth, her mouth was open so wide. And then when you laid that colour scheme on her – Maggie, how in the hell did you find out what colour the place was?'

'I read an article in the *New York Times* on paint restoration and analysis. It named paint manufacturers who specialize in analysing the old paint on buildings and producing authentic Victorian colours. I contacted one in Green Bay. What I didn't tell Loretta McConnell is that I didn't accomplish all this in the last three weeks. I started the moment I got back to Seattle. I ran up a long-distance bill that would make you quiver and wince.'

He chuckled and grinned at the stars. 'Harding House Bed-and-Breakfast Inn,' he mused. 'I can see it already.'

'You want to?' The question popped out of nowhere, prompted by Maggie's excitement.

'Now?'

'Now. I've just *got* to go see it now that I know it's really going to happen! Want to go with me?'

'Absolutely. I've been waiting for you to ask.'

He had to stretch his legs to keep up with her on their way to the truck. 'I'm going to run the classiest inn you ever saw!' she proclaimed as they hurried along. 'Sour cream scones and Battenberg lace and eyelet bedding and antiques everywhere! Just you wait and see, Eric Severson!'

He laughed. 'Maggie, slow down, you'll break your neck in those high heels.'

'Not tonight. Tonight I'm charmed!'

She chattered all the way back to Fish Creek, spilling plans, from the most major such as where the laundry facilities would be, to the most minor – a dish of candy always available in the parlour, and cordials for the guests at bedtime. Amaretto, perhaps, or crème de cacao with cream floated on top. She had always been partial to crème de cacao and cream, she told him, and loved to watch the two colours swirl together after taking the first sip.

At her house he parked beside the thick wall of arborvitaes and followed her down a set of broad steps to the newly-restored back verandah where she unlocked the door and led the way inside.

'Stay there till I find the lightswitch.'

Eric heard a click, but all remained black. The switch sounded again, four times in rapid succession. 'Oh, damn, they must have disconnected something. The Lavitskys were using their electric tools when I left today, but . . . just a minute – wait here while I go try another light.' A moment later he heard a dull thud and the scrape of wood on wood. 'Ouch!'

'Maggie, you all right?'

'It's just a little bruise.' More clicking. 'Oh, shoot, I guess nothing's working.'

'I've got a flashlight in the truck. Wait, I'll get it.'

He returned in a minute, shining a light into the kitchen, catching Maggie in its beam. She looked incongruous, wearing high heels and suede, standing beside a sawhorse with a pile of broken plaster at her feet.

They stood in the dark room, their features highlighted by the dim flashlight, much as they'd been highlighted by dash lights years ago when they'd parked until the wee hours.

He thought, *You shouldn't be here, Severson.*

And she thought, *You'd better move. Fast.*

'Come on, let's go look at the house.'

He handed her the flashlight. 'Lead on.'

She showed him the kitchen where there would soon be white cabinets with glass doors; the maid's room where the exterior wall had already been replaced; the tiny bathroom which would be for her private use, tucked beneath a stairway just off the kitchen, with its angled ceiling and beadboard wainscot; the main parlour with its fine quarter-sawn maple floor which she would use for her guests, and the music room which would become her own parlour; the pocket doors which could close to divide the two; the dining room where she would serve hot scones and coffee at breakfast time; the main stairway with its dramatic banister and newels; three upstairs guest bedrooms, and a fourth, which would be divided to create the new exit and an additional guest bath.

'I saved the best for last,' Maggie told Eric, leading him through one last doorway. 'This . . .' She stepped inside. '. . . is the Belvedere Room.' She flashed the light around the walls and crossed to a door on the opposite wall. 'Look.' She opened it and stepped out into the cool night air. 'This is the belvedere. Isn't it lovely? In the daytime you can see the bay and the boats and Chambers Island from here.'

'I've seen this from the water many times and always imagined it must have an impressive view.'

'It'll be my best room. I'd love to have it for my own but I've come to realize that doesn't make a whole lot of sense. Not when I can use the maid's room downstairs, and have my own small bathroom, with access to the kitchen and second parlour. So, I've decided to make the Belvedere Room the honeymoon suite.' She led the way back inside. 'I'm going to put in a big brass bed and pile it with mountains of lacy pillows. Maybe an armoire on that wall, and over there a cheval mirror, and white lace on the windows so the view is never completely cut off. Of course, all the hardwood floors and woodwork will have to be refinished. Well, what do you think?'

'I think you're going to have a busy winter.'

She laughed. 'I don't mind. I'm looking forward to it.'

'And . . .' He glanced at the illuminated face of his watch. 'I think it's time I got you back home before your mother has a fit.'

'I guess you're right. She'll probably be waiting up, ready to treat me as if I were fourteen years old again.'

'Ah, mothers – they're all a thorn in the side at times.'

They headed downstairs together with the light bobbing before them. 'I can't imagine yours being one.'

'Not often, but she has her moments. She gets on my case about Nancy working and being gone all the time. She thinks that's no way for a marriage to run.' Reaching the bottom of the steps, Eric added, 'The trouble is, neither do I.'

In the dark, Maggie halted. It was the first time Eric had hinted at anything being amiss with his marriage, and it left Maggie searching for a graceful reply.

'Listen, Maggie, forget I said that. I'm sorry.'

'No . . . no, it's all right, Eric. I just didn't know what to say.'

'I love Nancy, honest to God, I do. It's just that we seem to have become so remote from one another since we moved back here. She's gone five days a week, and when she's home I'm out on the boat. She resents the boat and I resent her job. It's something we have to work out, that's all.'

'Every marriage has its troubles.'

'Did yours?'

'Of course.'

'What? If you don't mind my asking.'

They remained where they'd stopped, with Maggie aiming the flashlight at the floor between them.

'He liked gambling and I resented it. I still go on resenting it because it's what finally killed him. The plane he was on when he died was heading for a gambling junket in Reno. He went there once a year with a group from Boeing.'

'And you never went with him?'
'Once. But I didn't like it.'
'So he went without you.'
'Yes.'
'Was he addicted to it?'
'No, which left a lot of grey area between the two of us. It was simply a getaway for him, something he enjoyed that I didn't. He was always quick to point out that the money he gambled with was his own. Money he'd saved for that purpose. And he'd say, is there anything you want that you don't have? There wasn't, of course, so what could I say? But I always felt it was money we could have used together – to travel more, or . . . or . . .'

Silence fell around them. Seconds passed while they stood close enough to touch, but didn't. At last Maggie drew a shaky breath. 'God, I loved him,' she whispered. 'And we did have everything. We *did* travel, and we *did* have luxuries – a sailboat, membership in an exclusive country club. And we'd still have all that – together – if he only hadn't gone on that last trip. You can't imagine the guilt I carry for still being angry with him when *he's* the one who's dead.'

Eric reached out and squeezed her arm. 'I'm sorry, Maggie. I didn't mean to dredge up unwanted memories.'

She moved and he knew she'd wiped her eyes in the dark. 'It's all right,' she said. 'I learned in my grief group that it's perfectly normal for me to feel angry with Phillip. Just as it's probably perfectly normal for you to feel angry with Nancy.'

'I *do* feel angry with her, but guilty, too, because I know she loves her job, and she's so damned good at it. And she works so hard. When she's flying all over the country she sometimes doesn't get into her hotel before nine or ten at night, and when she's home on weekends there's a horrendous amount of paperwork for her to do. But I find myself resenting that, too. Especially in the winter when we could be together on Saturdays. Instead, she's doing sales reports.' He sighed and added despondently, 'Oh, Christ . . . I don't know.'

Silence returned and with it came a peculiar intimacy.

'Maggie, I never talked to anyone about this before,' he admitted.

'Neither have I. Except in my group.'

'My timing stinks – I'm sorry. You were so happy and excited before I started turning over stones.'

'Oh, Eric, don't be silly. What are friends for? And I'm still happy and excited . . . underneath.'

'Good.'

In unison they turned and followed the beam of light toward the kitchen verandah door where they paused while Maggie flashed the light around the room once more.

'I like your house, Maggie.'

'So do I.'

'I'd like to see it when it's all done, sometime.'

In an effort to buoy their deflated mood, she said, 'I'll make sure I have you in for high tea in the parlour.'

They stepped out onto the back verandah and Maggie locked the door. On their way to the truck Eric asked, 'Will you be here tomorrow?'

'And the next day, and the next. I've started painting the upstairs woodwork and after that it's wallpapering and curtains.'

'I'll sound the air horn when I go by in the boat.'

'And I'll wave from the belvedere if I hear you.'

'It's a deal.'

They rode the short distance to her parents' house in silence, aware that a subtle change had taken place during the course of the evening. The attraction was back. Curbed, but back. They told themselves it did not matter because tonight was an isolated dot of time which would not be repeated. She would go about the opening of her business and he about the continuation of his own, and if they occasionally met on the street they would pass each other with a friendly hello, and neither would admit how good it had felt being together one October night, how close they had felt celebrating her victory outside a courthouse. They would forget that he had unwittingly called her Maggie M'girl, and admitted things could be better with his marriage.

At her parents' house he pulled to the kerb and shifted into neutral. The sea shimmied beneath them. Maggie sat as far away from him as possible, her right hip touching the door. In the living room the draperies were closed but the light was on.

'Thank you so much, Eric.'

'My pleasure,' he said softly.

They studied each other in the meagre light from the dashboard, she with a portfolio against her side, he with his hands draped over the wheel.

She thought, it would be so easy.

He thought, get out, Maggie, quick.

'Good-bye,' she said.

'Good-bye . . . and good luck.'

She looked down, found the door handle and pulled, but the door stuck as it always did. He leaned across her lap and for that one brief moment while he opened the door, his shoulder grazed her breast.

The door swung open and Eric pushed himself upright. 'There you go.'

'Thanks again . . . goodnight,' she said, clambering out, slamming the door before he could reply.

The truck changed gears and rolled away without delay, and she walked up the porch steps touching her hot face, thinking, Mother will know! Mother will know! She'll be waiting on the other side of this door.

She was.

'Well?' was all Vera said.

'I'll tell you in a minute, Mother. I have to go up to the bathroom first.'

Maggie hurried upstairs, closed the bathroom door and leaned against it with her eyes closed. She walked to the medicine chest and studied her reflection in the mirror. It remained remarkably normal and unflushed, considering the charged emotions that had filled the truck only moments ago.

He's married, Maggie.

I know.

So that's the end of it.

I know.

You'll stay away from him.

I'll stay away.

But even as she made the promise she realized it should not have been necessary.

Chapter 7

The air horn of the *Mary Deare* sounded the following afternoon, a great resonating bellow worthy of an antebellum riverboat.

Awoooooooozhhhhhh!

Even from a distance, it made the floors and windows vibrate.

Maggie's head came up. She sat back on her heels with a paintbrush in her hand, alert and tingling. It sounded again and she scrambled to her feet and ran along the upstairs hall, through the southwest bedroom and out onto the belvedere. But her view of the water was obstructed by the maples, still in full leaf. She stood in the thick shade, her hips pressed against the railing as her pulse slowed and disappointment settled in.

What are you doing, Maggie?

She backed up a step, composing herself.

What are you doing, running at the sound of his boat whistle?

As if someone had scolded her aloud, she turned sedately and went back inside.

After that, once each day, the air horn beckoned, always startling her, making her stop what she was doing and glance towards the front of the house. But she never ran again, as she had that first day. She told herself her fixation with Eric was simply a reaction to being back on familiar ground again. He was part of her past, Door County was part of her past, the two went together. She told herself she had no right to be thinking of him, to feel a jolt of reaction at the idea that he was thinking of her. She reminded herself of the low opinion she'd always held for single women who picked up married men.

Chasers, her mother had called them.

'That Sally Bruer is a chaser,' Vera had said years ago of a young woman Maggie remembered as red-haired and blowzy, a chatterbox who worked behind the ice cream counter at the corner store. She had always been particularly nice to the kids, though, giving them extra big scoops.

When Maggie was seven years old she overheard her mother talking with some ladies from her sewing circle about Sally Bruer. 'That's what you get when you chase,' Vera had said. 'Pee-gee. And no telling whose baby it is because she runs with every Tom, Dick and Harry in the county. But they're saying it's Curve Rooney's.' Curve Rooney was the town's baseball pitcher whose nickname was derived from his wicked curveball. Curve's pretty young wife came to every home game with their three apple-cheeked children and Maggie had seen them many times when she'd gone to games with her father. Sometimes she played with the oldest Rooney boy under the bleachers. Not until Maggie was twelve did she learn what pee-gee meant, and ever after she felt sorry for Curveball Rooney's children and for his pretty wife.

No, Maggie did not want to be a chaser. But the boat whistle called her every day, and she felt a pang of guilt at her reaction to it.

In mid-October she got away for two days. She drove to Chicago to choose furnishings for the house. At the Old House Store she bought a pedestal sink, clawfoot tub and brass hardware for the new bathroom. At Heritage Antiques she found a magnificent hand-carved oak bed for one of the bedrooms, and at Bell, Book and Candle, a mahogany marble-topped table and a pair of high-button shoes as unmarked as the day they'd been made, which she bought on a whim – period flavour for one of the guest rooms, she thought, picturing them side by side on the floor beside a cheval glass.

That evening, she took Katy out to dinner. Katy chose

the spot – a small pub down on Asbury, frequented by the college crowd – and acted remote all the way there. When they were seated across the booth from one another she immediately immersed herself in the menu.

Maggie said, 'Could we talk about it, Katy?'

Katy looked up, her brows sharply arched. 'Talk about what?'

'My leaving Seattle. I take it that's what's kept you silent ever since I picked you up.'

'I'd rather not, Mother.'

'You're still angry.'

'Wouldn't you be?'

The discussion started antagonistically on Katy's part, and resolved nothing. When the meal ended Maggie's emotions were a mixture of guilt and repressed exasperation at Katy's refusal to give her blessings to Maggie's move to Door County. As they said good-bye in front of Katy's dorm Maggie said, 'You're coming home for Thanksgiving, aren't you?'

'Home?' Katy repeated sardonically.

'Yes. Home.'

Katy glanced away. 'I guess so. Where else would I go?'

'I'll make sure I have a room ready for you by then.'

'Thanks.' There was no warmth in the word as Katy reached for the door handle.

'Don't I get a hug?'

It was perfunctory, at best, perhaps even reluctant, and when they said good-bye Maggie headed away experiencing again an obscure guilt that she knew perfectly well she should not be feeling.

She returned to Door County the following day to the news that her Seattle house had sold. There was a message to call Elliot Tipton immediately. Dialling him, she expected to hear the news that there would be another delay while the buyers waited for their loan to be approved. Instead he told her the buyers had cash and were living out of a rented motel room, having undergone a company transfer from Omaha. They wanted to close as soon as possible.

She flew to Seattle within the week.

Leaving the Seattle house proved as unemotional as she had predicted, largely because it happened so fast. Upon her arrival she worked in the house for two frantic days, throwing away half-filled ketchup and mayonnaise bottles from the refrigerator, disposing of the turpentine and other combustibles the movers could not transport, dumping dirt and dead houseplants out of planters, giving away several pieces of furniture and cursorily sorting castoffs for the Salvation Army. On the third day the movers came and began packing. On the fourth, Maggie signed her name twenty-four times and turned over her house keys to the new owners. On the fifth she flew back to Door County to find a remarkable transformation had taken place at Harding House.

The exterior painting was finished, the scaffolding gone. In its new coat of original Victorian colours, Harding House dazzled. Maggie set her suitcase on the back sidewalk and walked clear around it, smiling, sometimes touching her mouth, wishing someone were with her to share her excitement. She looked up at the belvedere, down at the window ledges, up at the gingerbread gables, back down at the wide front porch. The painters had been forced to cut down the bridal-wreath bushes to get at the foundation, revealing the latticework wrapping the base of the porch. She imagined a cat slipping under there to sleep on the cool dirt on a hot summer day. She retreated to the lakeshore to view the house through the half-denuded maples whose brilliant orange leaves littered the lawn in a rustling carpet. She completed the circle and entered via the kitchen where the sheet rocking was finished, the walls smooth, white and empty, waiting for cabinets.

She set down her suitcase and listened.

From somewhere in the depths of the house came the sound of a radio playing a George Strait song, accompanied by the rhythmic swish of sandpaper on a plastered wall. She followed the sound along the front hall where the sun, enriched by its journey through stained glass, streamed across the entry and music room floors.

Tilting her head, she called up the stairs, 'Hello?'

'Hello!' a man returned, 'I'm up here!'

She found him in one of the smaller bedrooms, his clothes dusted with white, standing on a plank between two stepladders, sanding a replastered wall.

'Hello,' she repeated from the doorway in a tone of surprise. 'Where are the Lavitsky brothers?'

'Gone to do a short job somewhere else. I'm Nordvik, the plasterer.'

'I'm Maggie Stearn, the owner.'

He motioned with the sandpaper. 'House is coming along fine.'

'It certainly is. When I left there was no heat in here, and no kitchen walls. And, my goodness, the bathroom and fire exit are all in!'

'Yup, it's comin' right along. Plumber got the furnace in first of the week and the rockers started hanging the same day. Oh, by the way, there was a delivery came this morning from Chicago. We told 'em to put it in the living room. Hope that's okay.'

'Fine, thank you.'

Maggie rushed downstairs to find her antique furniture in the main parlour, and experienced one of those minutes where everything seemed so right, and the future so rosy, she simply had to be with somebody.

She called Brookie.

'Brookie, you've got to come and see my house! It's all painted outside and nearly ready for paint on the inside, and I've just come back from Seattle and the house there is all sold and my first pieces of antique furniture just arrived from Chicago and . . .' She paused for a breath. 'Will you come, Brookie?'

Brookie came to share her excitement, bringing – out of necessity –Chrissy and Justin, who explored the vast, empty rooms and played hide-and-seek in the closets while Maggie gave their mother a brief tour. Nordvik left for the day. The place became quiet, permeated by the cardboardy smell of new plaster and the sharper tang of glue from the tiles in the new bathroom. Maggie and Brookie walked through all the upstairs rooms, pausing finally in the Belvedere Room where they stood in a warm patch of sunlight while the voices of the children drifted in from down the hall.

'It's a great house, Maggie.'

'It is, isn't it? I think I'm going to love living here. I'm so glad you forced me to come and look at it.'

Brookie sauntered to the window, turned and perched on its low sill. 'I hear you saw Eric a couple weeks ago.'

'Oh, Brookie, not you, too.'

'What do you mean, not me, too?'

'My mother nearly freaked out because we rode to Sturgeon Bay together for that board meeting.'

'Oh . . . I *didn't* hear that. Did anything happen?' Brookie grinned impishly.

'Oh, Brookie, honestly! You're the one who told *me* to grow up.'

Brookie shrugged. 'Just thought I'd ask.'

'Yes, something did happen. I got my permit to open a bed and breakfast.'

'I already found that out, even though my *best friend* didn't bother to call and tell me.'

'I'm sorry. Everything got crazy – the trip to Chicago, then to Seattle. I can't tell you how happy I'll be to get my own belongings back. As soon as I have so much as a frying pan and a bucket to dip lake water I intend to move out of my mother's house.'

'It's been bad, huh?'

'We don't get along any better now than we did when I was in school. Do you know she hasn't even come to see the house?'

'Oh, Maggie, I'm sorry.'

'What is it with my mother and me? I'm her only daughter. We're supposed to be close, but sometimes I swear, Brookie, she acts like she's jealous of me.'

'Of what?'

'I don't know. My relationship with Dad. My money, this house. The fact that I'm younger than she. Who knows? She's a hard woman to figure out.'

'I'm sure she'll come to see the house soon. Everyone else has, that's for sure! This place is the talk of Fish Creek. Loretta McConnell's been bragging hither and yon that you intend to name it after *her* forefathers, and about how you restored it to its original colours. You can't talk to a soul who hasn't driven past to look at it. It really looks beautiful, Maggie.'

'Thanks.' Maggie crossed to the wide window and sat down beside Brookie. 'But you know what, Brookie?' Maggie studied the new plaster while the sound of the children's play echoed from the distance. 'When I see it changing – something new finished, like today when I got here – I get this . . .' Maggie pressed a fist beneath her breast. '. . . this big lump of emptiness because there's nobody to share it with. If Phillip were alive . . .' She dropped her fist and sighed. 'But he's not, is he?'

'No.' Brookie got to her feet. 'And you're going to do it all alone, and everyone in town including your mother is going to admire you for it.' She hooked an elbow through Maggie's and drew her up.

Maggie's lip lifted into a grateful smile. 'Thanks so much for coming. I don't know what I'd do without you.' Arm in arm, the two sauntered toward an adjacent room to scout up the children.

In the days that followed, as Maggie watched the house take shape, the lump of dejection appeared sporadically, particularly at the end of the day when the workers left and she'd wander the rooms alone, wishing for someone to share her sense of accomplishment. She couldn't call Brookie every day; Brookie had her own family responsibilities to keep her busy. Roy came often, but his enthusiasm was always counterposed by the fact that Vera never came with him.

The kitchen cabinets were hung, the Formica countertops set, the new bathroom fitted with its antique fixtures and the water turned on at last. Maggie's furniture arrived from Seattle and she moved out of her parents' house with a sense of great relief. On her first night in Harding House she slept in the Belvedere Room, though it contained only Katy's twin bed, a table and a lamp. The bulk of her belongings were piled into the crowded garage and the apartment above it until the floors in the main house could be refinished. An antique door for the new upstairs exit was located; Maggie stripped and varnished it, watched Joe Lavitsky hang it and as the light fell through its etched window for the first time she wished anew for someone with whom to share such moments.

October, viewed from the deck of the *Mary Deare*, was a season without rival, the sky-blue water reflecting the change in colour that intensified daily as the trees turned in familiar sequence – first the butternuts, then the black walnuts, green ash, basswood, sugar maples, and finally the Norway maples. As the days progressed, Eric watched the breathtaking spectacle with a veneration that returned each year on cue. No matter how many times he witnessed it, autumn's impact never dulled.

This year Eric watched the season's change with an added interest, for each descending leaf exposed another bit of Maggie's house. It became anathema, this misplaced preoccupation with a woman not his wife. Yet he found himself passing Harding House daily, watching it appear section by section behind the maple trees, and he sounded his horn wondering if she ever stepped to a window to watch him pass, or onto the belvedere after he had.

Often he thought about the night they'd moused around in the blackness of her house with only a cone of light between them. It had been unwise, the kind of thing which, if discovered, could start tongues wagging. Yet it had been wholly innocent. Or had it? There had been a nostalgic feeling about the entire night, picking her up at her house just as he had when they were in high school, the hug on the courthouse steps, the ride back to Fish Creek and the confidences they'd exchanged in that black, black house.

In moments of greater clarity, he recognized the danger of putting himself anywhere near her, but at other times he'd ask himself what harm could come from sounding a whistle clear out on the bay.

By the last week of October the branches of her maples were nearly bare and he thought he saw her once, in a window of the Belvedere Room, but he wasn't sure if it was she or only a bright reflection off the glass.

November arrived, the waters of Green Bay turned cold and bare, its flotilla of autumn leaves sunk like shipwrecked treasures. There came that dreaded and anticipated day when the last of the fishermen had come and gone, and it was time to lay up the *Mary Deare* for the winter. Every year it was the same, looking forward to the slack time yet feeling forlorn when it arrived. Hedgehog Harbor, too, seemed forlorn, quiet with inactivity – no boat trailers unloading, no fishermen in misshapen caps posing for snapshots, no engines, horns, or shouting anywhere. Even the gulls – fickle birds – had disappeared now that their ready supply of food had stopped. Jerry Joe and Nicholas were back in school, and Ma had shut off the two-way radio till spring. She spent her days watching soap operas and shaping pieces of coloured foam rubber into butterflies with magnetic bellies that perched on refrigerator doors. In those silent, crisp days that preceded snow, Eric cleaned the *Mary Deare* for the last time, winterized her engine, swaddled her up in canvas, lifted her from the water and blocked her up on a cradle. Mike laid up *The Dove* then disappeared into his back twenty to put up next winter's stovewood. The sound of the engine on his log-splitter sometimes drifted through the quiet from a half-mile away, revving and idling, revving and idling with monotonous regularity, adding to the melancholy.

Eric had told him to go; he'd finish the rest. When the fish-cleaning shed was scoured, and the docks out of the water, the rods and reels stored for the winter and all the outbuildings padlocked, Eric spent a few restless days at home, eating doughnuts and drinking coffee alone, doing what little laundry had accumulated, straightening spice cans in the kitchen cupboards. The coming winter loomed long and lonely, and he imagined Nancy at home with him, or the two of them going south, to Florida maybe, as so many of the other Door fishermen did in the winter.

Then one day when the house got too lonely, he went out to the woods to help Mike.

He found his brother beside the log-splitter, working alone over the noisy gasoline engine mounted on a knee-high trailer. Eric waited through the crescendo of sound while the powerful pneumatic ram slowly pushed the log against the wedge. The log creaked, tore, and finally fell to the earth in two pieces.

As Mike leaned over to pick up one, Eric called, 'Yo, brother!'

Mike straightened, tossing the firewood aside. 'Hey, what're you doing here?'

'Thought you might like a little help.' Tugging worn leather gloves more tightly on his hands, Eric stepped to the far side of the rig. He tossed aside the other half of the log, then reached for a whole one and placed it on the splitter.

'I'd never turn that down. It takes a mountain of wood to heat that house all winter.' Mike engaged the clutch and the sound swelled as the log began moving. Above it, Eric shouted, 'Thought you were going to put in a gas furnace this year.'

'So did I but Jerry Joe decided to go to college so it'll have to wait.'

'You need extra, Mike? I'd do damn near anything for that kid, you know.'

'Thanks, Eric, but it's not just Jerry Joe. There's something else.'

'Oh?'

Another log split, fell, and the engine quieted.

Mike picked up a piece of oak and said, 'Barbara is pregnant again.' He gave the wood a ferocious heave, then stood glowering at it.

Eric stood motionless, letting the news settle, feeling a wad of jealousy lodge in his chest: another one for Mike and Barb when they already had five scattered in ages from six to eighteen while he and Nancy had none. As quickly as it came, the jealousy fled. He picked up the piece of oak from his side of the splitter and tossed it onto the pile, grinning. 'Well, smile, man.'

'Smile! Would you smile if you'd just found out you were expecting your sixth one?'

'Damn right, especially if they were all like Jerry Joe.'

'In case you hadn't heard, they don't come out that way, all raised and wearing size-ten shoes. First they need shots and they get ear infections and colic and measles and they go through about two thousand damned expensive diapers. Besides, Barb's forty-two already.' He stared morosely at the naked trees nearby, then muttered, 'Christ.'

Between the two men the engine idled, forgotten.

'We're too damn old,' Mike said at last. 'Hell, we thought we were too old last time, when Lisa was born.'

Eric leaned down and killed the engine, then stepped over it to grip Mike's shoulder.

'Listen, don't worry. You read all the time about how people are younger at forty than ever before, how women are having babies later and later in life, and everything's turning out fine. Hell, a couple years ago I remember reading about a woman in South Africa fifty-five years old who had a baby.'

Mike laughed ruefully and dropped down to sit on a log. He sighed and mumbled 'Aw, shit . . .' then stared a long time before raising a look of dismay to Eric. 'You know how old I'll be when that kid graduates from high school? Retirement age, that's how old. Barb and I were looking forward to having a little time to ourselves before then.'

Eric dropped to a squat, inquiring, 'So, if you didn't want it, how did it happen?'

'Hell, I don't know. I guess we're just one of those statistics. What is it? Ten out of a thousand, even *with* birth control?'

'I don't know if it'll help, but I think you and Barb are the best parents I've ever known. The way your kids turned out – why, hell, the world ought to be grateful to have one more.'

The remark finally raised a partial grin on Mike's face. 'Thanks.'

The two brothers sat in silence for some time before Eric spoke again. 'You want to know something ironic?'

'What?'

'While you're sitting there upset about having another baby, I'm sitting here envying the hell out of you because you're going to. I *know* how damned old you are because I'm only two years behind you and my time's running out.'

'Well, what's holding you up?'

'Nancy.'

'I thought so.'

'She doesn't want one.'

After several seconds of silence, Mike admitted, 'Everyone in the family guessed as much. She doesn't want to give up her job, does she?'

'Nope.' Eric let that settle before adding, 'I don't think she's too crazy about the idea of losing her shape either. That's always been so important to Nancy.'

'Have you talked to her about it, told her you wanted a family?'

'Yeah, for about six years now. I just kept waiting, thinking she'd say yes one of these times, but it's not going to happen. I know that now and it's got to the point where we fight about it.'

Again the two sat ruminating while a noisy flock of sparrows settled in a nearby sumac copse. 'Aw, hell, it's more than that. It's Fish Creek. She hates it here. She's happier when she's out on the road travelling than when she's home.'

'You could be imagining that.'

'Yeah, I could be, but I don't think so. She never wanted to move here.'

'That might be so, but that doesn't mean she hates coming home.'

'She always used to say how she hated leaving on Mondays, but I don't hear that anymore.' Eric studied the sparrows awhile. They were pecking on the ground beneath the sumac, murmuring soft *cheep-cheeps*. He'd grown up with lots of birds around, both water and land birds. The first Christmas after they were married, Nancy had given him a beautiful Audubon book and had written on the flyleaf, *because you miss them*. Before moving here from Chicago she'd boxed up the book with a bunch of others and had given it to the Goodwill without his knowledge. Watching the sparrows on the chill autumn day he grieved not over the loss of the book but over the loss of affection it represented.

'You know what I think happened?'

'What?'

Eric turned to look at his brother. 'I think we stopped giving.' After a stretch of profound silence, Eric went on. 'I think it started when we moved here. She was deadset against it and I wouldn't have it any other way. I wanted a family and she wanted a career, and it started this cold war between us. On the surface everything appears fine, but underneath it's all turned sour.'

The flock of sparrows flew away. Off in the distance a pair of crows called. In the clearing all was still beneath a steely grey sky that seemed to reflect Eric's morose mood.

'Hey, Mike,' he said after some moments of silence, 'do you think people without kids get sort of selfish after a while?'

'That's a pretty broad generalization.'

'I think it happens though. When you've got kids you're forced to think about them first, and sometimes, even though you're bone tired, you get up and you relieve the other one. When kids are sick, or whiny, or when they need you for one thing or the other. But when there are just the two of you . . . aw, hell, I don't know how to say it.' Eric picked up a piece of bark and started flaking off bits with his thumbnail. After some time he forgot his preoccupation and gazed into the distance.

'Remember how it was with Ma and the old man? How at the end of a busy day after she'd manned the office all day long and washed clothes in that old wringer washer and hung them on the line between customers and fed us kids and probably acted as referee in about a dozen fights, she'd go out there and help scour down the fish shed? And the next thing you know they'd be laughing down there. I used to lay in my bed and wonder what they found to laugh about in the fish-cleaning shack at ten-thirty at night. The crickets would be squawking, and the water would be lapping down by the boats, and I'd lay there and listen to them laugh and feel so damned good. Secure, I guess. And one time – I remember this so clearly, it's as if it just happened yesterday – I came into the kitchen late at night when all of us kids were supposed to be asleep and you know what he was doing?'

'What?'

'He was washing her feet.'

The two brothers exchanged a long, silent glance before Eric continued. 'She was sitting on a kitchen chair and he was on his knees in front of her washing her feet. She had her head back and her eyes were closed and neither one of them said a word. He was just holding her soapy foot above a wash basin and rubbing it real slow with his hands.' Eric paused thoughtfully. 'I'll never forget that. Her lumpy old feet that always hurt so much, and the way the old man was doing that for her.'

Once more the two brothers sat in silence, bound by the memory. In time Eric went on quietly, 'That's the kind of marriage I want, and I don't have it.'

Mike settled his elbows on his knees. 'Maybe you're too idealistic.'

'Maybe.'

'Different marriages work for different reasons.'

'Ours isn't working at all, not since I forced her to move back here to Fish Creek. I realize now, that's when our trouble really started.'

'So what are you going to do about it?'

'I don't know.'

'You going to give up fishing?'

'I can't do that. I love it too much.'

'Is she going to give up her job?'

Disconsolately, Eric shook his head.

Mike scooped up two twigs and began snapping them into pieces.

'So . . . you scared?'

'Yeah . . .' Eric glanced over his shoulder. 'It's scary as hell the first time you bring it out into the open.' He chuckled ruefully. 'As long as you don't admit your marriage is falling apart, maybe it isn't . . . right?'

'Do you love her?'

'I should. She's still got a lot of the qualities I married her for. She's beautiful, and smart, and hard-working. She's really made something of herself at Orlane.'

'But do you love her?'

'I don't know anymore.'

'Things okay in bed?'

Eric cursed softly and threw away the bark. He propped his elbows on his knees and shook his head at the ground. 'Hell, I don't know.'

'What do you mean, you don't know. Does she play around?'

'No, I don't think so.'

'Do you?'

'No.'

'Then what is it?'

'It all harks back to the same old problem. When we're making love . . .' It was hard to say.

Mike waited.

'When we're making love everything is okay until she gets out of bed to use that goddamned contraceptive foam, then I feel like . . .' Eric's lips narrowed and his jaw tensed. 'Like taking the can and throwing it through the goddamned wall. And when she comes back, I want to push her away.'

Mike sighed. He considered at length before advising, 'The two of you ought to talk to somebody – a doctor or a marriage counsellor.'

'When? She's gone five days a week. Besides, she doesn't know how I feel about the sex part.'

'Don't you think you should tell her?'

'It'd kill her.'

'It's killing you.'

'Yeah . . .' Eric replied despondently, staring off

through the skeletal trees at the tarnished silver sky. He sat for a long time, hunched like a cowboy before a campfire. Finally he sighed, stretched out his legs and studied the buckled knees of his blue jeans. 'Hell of a deal, isn't it? You with more kids than you want and me without any?'

'Yeah. Hell of a deal.'

'Does Ma know yet?' Eric glanced at Mike.

'That Barb's pregnant? No. She'll have something to say, I'm sure.'

'She's never said anything about our not having any. But she says plenty about Nancy being gone all the time, so I suppose it's the same thing.'

'Well, she was raised on old-fashioned ways, and since she worked beside the old man her whole life long she thinks that's the way it ought to be.'

They pondered awhile, thinking about their lives as they were now and as they were when they were younger. Presently, Eric said, 'You want to know something, Mike?'

'What?'

'Sometimes I wonder if Ma is right.'

Three days later, on a Saturday night after a late supper at home, Nancy sat back, toying with a glass of Chablis and eating the last of her green grapes. The atmosphere was intimate, the mood lazy. Outside the wind plucked at the shingles and sent the cedars swaying against the metal rain gutters, sending out a muted screech that filtered through the walls. Inside, candlelight reflected off the surface of the teakwood table and enriched the texture of the cutwork linen place mats.

She studied her husband appreciatively. He'd showered before supper and had come to the table uncombed. With his hair loose and unstyled, he made an arresting sight. He was dressed in jeans and a new designer sweatshirt she'd brought him from Neiman-Marcus, an oversized pewter grey slop-top with a rolled collar and immense raglan sleeves that made him look rugged and negligent as he sat slant-shouldered, drinking Irish coffee.

He was a handsome thing, as handsome as any man she'd ever seen, and she'd seen many. In her job, she bumped shoulders with them in every town, in the best department stores, dressed like fashion plates and smelling good enough to stuff into a dresser drawer with your lingerie. They had haircuts like girls and wore wool scarves over their suit-jackets and dressed in flat Italian slippers of exquisitely thin leather, without socks. Some were gay, but some were overtly heterosexual and made it no secret.

She had grown accustomed to parrying their advances, and on the few occasions when she returned them, she made sure the *tête-à-tête* lasted only one night; for, once in bed, those men never quite measured up to Eric. Their bodies were small where his was large, their hands soft where his were hard, their skin white where his was brown, and with none of them could she achieve the sexual harmony it had taken her and Eric eighteen years to achieve together.

She studied him, relaxed and appealing across the table, and hated to mar the mood she had so carefully cultured with the candlelight, linens and wine. But she had cultured it for a purpose, and the time had come to test its effectiveness.

She slipped one nylon-covered foot onto Eric's chair. 'Honey?' she murmured, rubbing the inside of his knee.

'Hm?'

'Why don't you put the boat up for sale?'

He studied her impassively for some moments, tipped up and emptied his cup of coffee and silently turned to study a woven wood shade.

'Please, honey.' She leaned forward provocatively with her forearms lining the table edge. 'Advertise it now, and by spring you'll have it sold and we can move back to Chicago. Or any other major city you like. How about Minneapolis? It's a beautiful town, lakes everywhere and it's a mecca for the arts. You'd love Minneapolis. Eric . . . please, can't we discuss it?' She watched a muscle tic in his jaw while he continued avoiding her eyes. Finally he faced her, speaking with careful control.

'Tell me something. What do you want out of this marriage?'

Her foot stopped caressing his knee. This was not going at all as she'd hoped. 'What do I want?'

'Yes, want. Besides me, or . . . or having sex with me on the Saturdays and Sundays when you don't have your period. What do you want, Nancy? You don't want this house, you don't want this town, you don't want me to be a fisherman. And you've made it perfectly clear you don't want a family. So what *do* you want?'

Instead of answering, she demanded sharply, 'When are you going to get over this?'

'Get over what?'

'You know what I mean, Eric. Playing the Old Man and the Sea. When we left Chicago I thought you'd play fisherman with your brother for a couple of years and get it out of your system, then we'd move back to the city so we could spend more time together.'

'When we left Chicago I thought you'd want to give up your job with Orlane and stay here with me to start a family.'

'I make a lot of money. I love my work.'

'So do I.'

'And you're wasting a perfectly good college degree, Eric. What about your business degree, don't you intend to use it again?'

'I use it every day.

'You're being stubborn.'

'What will change if we live in Chicago or Minneapolis? Tell me.'

'We'd have a city – art galleries, orchestra halls, theatres, department stores, new –'

'Department stores, ha! You spend five days out of seven in department stores as it is! How the *hell* can you want to spend any more time there!'

'It's not the department stores alone and you know it. It's urbanity! Civilization! I want to live where things happen!'

He studied her a long time, his expression arctic and unapproachable. 'All right, Nancy, I'll make you a deal.' He pushed back his cup, crossed his forearms on the table edge and fixed her with unrelenting eyes. 'You have a baby and we'll move to the city of your choice.'

She drew back as if he'd swung at her. Her face grew white, then red as she struggled with a compromise she was incapable of accepting. 'You're not being fair!' Her anger flared and she rapped a fist on the table. 'I don't *want* a damn baby, and you know it!'

'And I don't want to leave Door County, and you know it. If you're going to be gone five days a week at least I want to be near my family.'

'I'm your family!' She pressed her chest.

'No, you're my wife. A family includes progeny.'

'So we're at the same old impasse.'

'Apparently so, and it's been on my mind so much since our last argument that I finally talked to Mike about it the other day.'

'To Mike!'

'Yes.'

'Our personal problems are no business of Mike's, and I resent your spilling them to him!'

'It just came up. We were talking about babies. They're going to have another one.'

Nancy's expression became one of distaste. 'Oh, Christ, that's obscene.'

'Is it?' he retorted sharply.

'Don't you think it is? Those two spawn as regularly as salmon! My God, they're old enough to be grandparents!

Why in heaven's name would they want another baby at their age?'

Eric threw his napkin onto the table and lurched to his feet. 'Nancy, sometimes you really piss me off!'

'And you run right to your brother and tell him so, don't you? So, naturally the world's best father has some choice opinions about a wife who'd *choose* not to have babies.'

'Mike has never said *one* negative thing about you!' He pointed a finger at her nose. 'Not one!'

'So what did he say when he found out the reason we don't have a family?'

'He advised us to see a marriage counsellor.'

Nancy stared at Eric as if she had not heard.

'Would you?' he asked, watching her closely.

'Sure,' she replied sarcastically, sitting back in her chair with her hands joined at her midriff. 'Tuesday nights are usually reasonably free when I'm in St Louis.' Her tone changed, became exacting. 'What's going on here, Eric? All of a sudden this talk about marriage counsellors and malcontent. What's wrong? What's changed?'

He picked up his coffee cup, spoon and napkin and took them into the kitchen. She followed, standing behind him as he set the dishes in the sink and stood staring down at them, afraid to answer her question and start the tumult he knew he must start if he was ever to make his life happier.

'Eric,' she appealed softly, touching his back.

He drew a deep breath and, with his insides trembling, stated the thing that had been eating at him for months. 'I need more out of this marriage than I'm getting, Nancy.'

'Eric, please . . . no, don't . . . Eric, I love you.' She coiled her arms around his trunk and rested her face on his back. He stood unyielding, facing the sink.

'I love you, too,' he told her quietly. 'That's why this hurts so much.'

They stood awhile, wondering what to say or do next, neither of them prepared for the heartbreak already setting in.

'Let's go to bed, Eric,' she whispered.

He closed his eyes and felt a wave of emptiness that terrified him worse than anything thus far.

'You just don't understand, do you, Nancy?'

'Understand what? That part has always been good. Please . . . come upstairs.'

He sighed and for the first time ever, turned her down.

Chapter 8

Nancy left for work again on Monday. Their parting kiss was filled with uncertainty and he watched her drive away with a sense of desolation. When she was gone, he spent the days on winter work, tallying the number of feet of fishing line used during the season, the number of lures lost, searching through the hundreds of suppliers' catalogues for the best replacement prices. He sent in preregistration fees for display booths at the Minneapolis, Chicago and Milwaukee Sportsmen's Shows and ordered brochures to pass out there. He tallied up the number of Styrofoam coolers they'd sold out of the office and contracted to buy an entire truckload of them for the next year's season.

In between times, he wondered what to do about his marriage.

He ate alone, slept alone, worked alone, and asked himself how many more years it would be this way. How many more years could he tolerate this solo existence?

He went uptown for a haircut before he actually needed one because the house was so quiet and there was always pleasant company at the barbershop.

He called Ma every day and went out to check her fuel oil barrel well before he knew it was empty, because he knew she'd ask him to stay for supper.

He changed the oil in the pickup and tried to fix the sticking passenger door but couldn't. It reminded him of Maggie, of leaning across her lap the night he'd dropped her off at her mom and dad's. He thought of her often. How was she doing, how was her house progressing, had she found all those antiques she talked about? Rumour had it the outside paint job was done and her house looked like a showplace. Then one day he decided to drive by himself, just to take a look.

Just to take a look.

The leaves were all down, lying in battered windrows along the edge of Cottage Row as his pickup climbed the hill. The evergreens appeared shaggy and black against a late afternoon sun. It had turned cold, the sky taking on a haze almost like sun dogs, warning it would be colder tomorrow. Most of the houses along the Row were deserted now, their wealthy owners gone back to the southern cities where they wintered. As he approached Maggie's place he noted a Lincoln Town Car with a Washington licence plate parked beside her garage – undoubtedly hers. The cedars at the edge of her property were still untrimmed and cut off much of the view; he rolled by slowly, glancing down the break between them, catching a glimpse of the gaily coloured house. They'd been right: it was a showplace.

That night, at home, he turned on the television and sat before it for nearly an hour before realizing he hadn't heard a word. He'd been sitting motionless, staring at the shifting figures on the screen, thinking of Maggie.

The second time he drove past her place he was armed with a registration form from the chamber of commerce and a copy of their summer tourist booklet. Her car was parked in the same place as before as he pulled up beside the cedars, killed the engine and stared at the booklet on the seat. For sixty seconds he stared, then started the engine and tore up the hill without glancing at her house.

The next time he drove by, a green panel truck was parked at the top of her walk, its rear doors open and an aluminium ladder hanging from its side. If the truck hadn't been there he might have driven right by again, but it would be okay with a workman in the house.

It was late afternoon again, chilly with a cutting wind that snapped at the papers he carried as he slammed his truck door. Rolling them into a cylinder, he passed the panel truck and peered inside – conduit, coils of wire and tools – good, he was right. He loped down the broad steps toward the house and knocked on the back door.

Whistling softly through his teeth, he waited, eyeing the back verandah. A cluster of Indian corn and orange ribbon hanging on the wall; an oval brass plaque announcing, HARDING HOUSE; white lace curtains covering the window of an antique door; a new spooled railing painted yellow and blue; a new floor painted grey; a braided rug; and a crock in the corner holding a clump of cattails and Indian tobacco. Rumour had it Maggie wasn't afraid to spend money to dress up the place, and if the outside was any indication, she'd been busy at it. Even the tiny verandah had charm.

Eric knocked again, harder, and a male voice shouted, 'Yeah, come on in!'

He stepped into the kitchen and found it empty, bright and transformed. His glance took in white cabinets with mullioned glass panes, rose-coloured countertops, gleaming hardwood floors, a long, narrow drop-leaf table with a scarred top, a long lace runner, and a knobby basket of pinecones with a fat pink bow on its handle.

From another room a voice called, 'Hullo, you lookin' for the missus?'

Eric followed the sound and found an electrician who looked like Charles Bronson hanging a chandelier in the ceiling of the empty dining room.

'Hi,' Eric greeted, pausing in the doorway.

'Hi.' The man glanced back over his shoulder, his arms upraised. 'If you're looking for the missus, she's upstairs working. You can go on up.'

'Thanks.' Eric headed across the dining room to the entry hall. By daylight it was impressive: newly refinished floors still smelling of polyurethane and freshly plastered walls giving the impression of wide white space anchored by unbroken stretches of lustrous wood. A massive banister dropped from above and from somewhere up there, a radio was playing.

He started up, paused at the top and glanced down the hall with all its doors open. He moved toward the music. In the second doorway on the left, he stopped.

Maggie knelt on the floor, painting the wide baseboard moulding on the opposite side of the room. She and the tunebox and the paint can were the only three things in it. No other distractions. Just Maggie, on all fours, looking refreshingly artless. He smiled at the soles of her bare feet, the paint smears on her sacky blue jeans and the tail of her sloppy shirt trailing on the lip of the paint can.

'Hi, Maggie,' he said.

She started and yelped as if he'd sounded his boat horn at her ear.

'Oh my God,' she breathed, sinking back on her heels, pressing a hand to her heart. 'You scared the daylights out of me.'

'I didn't mean to. The guy downstairs said I should come right up.' He gestured with a roll of papers toward the hall behind him.

What was he *doing* here? Maggie knelt before him with her heart still erratic as he stood in the doorway dressed in loafers, jeans and a puffy black-leather bomber jacket with the collar turned up against his pale hair, just as he'd turned it up years ago. A little too fetching and a lot too welcome.

'I can come back some other time if –'

'Oh, no, that's fine . . . that's . . . the radio was on so loud . . .' Still on her knees, she stretched toward it and lowered the volume. 'I was just thinking of you, that's all, and all of a sudden you said my name and I . . . you were . . .'

You're babbling, Maggie. Be careful.

'And here I am,' he finished for her.

She got control of herself and smiled. 'Welcome to

Harding House.' She spread her arms wide and looked down at her apparel. 'As you can see, I'm dressed for guests.'

To Eric, she looked utterly engaging, dappled with white paint, her hair tied away from her face with a dirty shoestring. He couldn't stop smiling at her.

'As you can see . . .' He held out his hands, too. 'I'm not a guest. I just brought you some information about joining the chamber of commerce.'

'Oh . . . great!' She laid her paintbrush across the can and with a rag from her back pocket scrubbed her knuckles as she got to her feet. 'You want a tour while you're here? I have lights now.'

He stepped further into the room and gave it an appreciative glance. 'I'd love a tour.'

'At least, I think I have lights. Just a minute.' She hurried out into the hall and called downstairs, 'Can I turn on the lights, Mr Deitz?'

'Just a minute and I'll have this hooked up!' he called back.

She turned to Eric. 'We'll have lights in a minute. Well, this is a guest room . . .' She gave another flourish. '. . . one of the four. As you can see, I'm using the original light fixtures because they're made of solid brass. I found out, after I started examining them closer, that they were all originally gas lights – did you know this town didn't get electricity until the 1930s?'

'Really?'

'So everything's been converted. I love the old fixtures because they're authentic. When Mr Deitz gets the electricity back on, you'll see how pretty they look, even in daylight.'

They stood beneath the gas fixture, looking up, close enough to smell each other. He smelled like crisp air and leather. She smelled like turpentine.

'And didn't my floors turn out beautifully? Wait till I show you the one downstairs in the main parlour.'

He glanced down. Her feet were bare below baggy

denims rolled to mid-calf, familiar feet he'd seen tens of times aboard the *Mary Deare* that summer when they had practically lived in bathing suits.

'They look just like new,' he said of the floors, then glanced around the bare room. 'The decorating's a little austere though.'

Maggie chuckled and buried her hands in her front pockets. 'All in due time.'

'I heard you'd moved back. You sold your Seattle house?'

'Yup.'

'Where are your things?'

'In the garage. So far I've only taken out the kitchen furnishings and one bed for me to sleep on.'

'The kitchen looks great, by the way. I can see you have a touch.'

'Thanks. I'm anxious to get all the woodwork redone so I can move the rest of the furniture inside.' She lifted her gaze to the wide cove moulding overhead and he found himself studying the curve of her throat. 'I decided to paint all the upstairs mopboards and ceiling mouldings white, and leave those downstairs natural wood. As soon as I get them finished I can start the wallpapering, but everything takes so long to get. Three weeks for most of the paper out of Sturgeon Bay. When I've finished the painting I've decided to give myself a break and go to Chicago. I can get wallpaper there in one day.'

'You're going to do the papering yourself?'

'Uh-huh.'

'Who taught you how?' he asked, following her into the next bedroom.

'Taught me?' She glanced back and shrugged. 'Trial and error, I guess. I'm a home economics teacher. Need I tell you how non-economical it is to hire paperers? Besides, I enjoy it, and I have all winter, so why not do it myself?'

He thought about coming over sometime in the dreary days of mid-winter and helping her. Stupid thought.

'You know what I've decided?' Maggie asked.

'What?'

'To name each bedroom after Thaddeus Harding's children. This one will be the Franklin, that one the Sarah, and that one the Victoria. I'll get a little brass plaque for each door. Fortunately for me, Thaddeus only had three children, so this last room will get the name it deserves.' She led Eric into the fourth room. 'The Belvedere Room. How could it be anything else?' He stood beside her, surveying the room by daylight. Bright, white, furnished only with her bed which sat dead centre in the room. It had neither been neatened this morning nor overly mussed last night. She slept – he noted – facing the window and the water. In one corner of the room a pair of vintage high-button shoes sat primly on the floor.

He grinned, glanced from her bare feet to the shoes and remarked, 'Ah, so this is where you lost them.'

Maggie laughed and looked down, swishing a bare sole across the smooth floor. 'These floors feel like satin. I can't get enough of them.'

Their eyes met and memories bedevilled again – both of them, this time – of summer days aboard the *Mary Deare*, barefoot and in love.

She looked away first, towards the window, and breathed, 'Oh, look . . . snow!'

Outside great downy flakes had begun to fall, lining the maple branches and disappearing as they touched the water. The sky was hueless, sunless, a great blending of white-on-white.

'I've missed it,' Maggie said, moving towards the window. 'In Seattle it snowed up in the mountains, of course, but I missed watching it change the yard like this, or waking up that first morning when your bedroom would be so bright even the ceiling was lit and you'd know it had snowed overnight.'

He trailed towards her and stood at her shoulder, watching

the snow, wishing just once he and Nancy could enjoy it together this way. For Nancy, snow always signalled the beginning of the difficult travelling season, so she found little in it to appreciate, not even aesthetically. When she was home it seemed they never took time for the quiet things like this.

What are you doing here, Severson, making comparisons between Maggie and your wife? Give her the damned papers and get out!

But he stood at the window beside Maggie, watching the rough tweed of winter disappear beneath a powdery blanket of white.

'You know what it reminds me of?' Maggie asked.

'What?'

'A linen tablecloth the world puts on for Thanksgiving. It should be snowy for Thanksgiving, don't you think?'

She glanced up and found him very close, studying her instead of the snow.

'Absolutely,' he answered quietly, and for a moment they forgot the view, and the presence of the electrician downstairs, and the reasons they should not be standing so close.

Maggie recovered first and moved away discreetly. 'Should we go downstairs?'

On their way down she explained, 'I found the high-button shoes in an antique shop in Chicago and I couldn't resist them. They'll add a quaint touch to one of the bedrooms, don't you think?'

Her sensible chatter ended the threat they had felt upstairs, and if for a moment they'd been tempted, and if for that moment they'd recognized it as mutual, they moved on through her house pretending it had not happened. She kept up a lively dialogue while guiding him from room to room, showing him her walls and her windows and her floors, especially in the downstairs parlour.

'I discovered this marvellous craftsmanship underneath

an old musty rug.' She knelt and ran a hand over the exquisite wood. 'It's quarter-sawn maple. Look how it's laid, isn't it a lovely design?'

He squatted, too, knees snapping, and touched it. 'It's beautiful. Is this the room where you intend to have the candy bowl and the cordials?'

'Yes. We could have some now,' she remarked gaily, 'if I had any candy or cordials in the house. Unfortunately, I haven't put in a supply. Would a cup of coffee do?'

'I'd love one.'

Leading the way to the kitchen she detoured through the dining room where the electrician was working with a screwdriver at a wall switch. With the power still off and twilight settling in, the room was dusky. 'Do you know Patrick Deitz?'

'I don't believe I do.'

'Patrick Deitz, this is Eric Severson. He runs a charter boat out of Gills Rock. We're going to have some coffee. Would you like some?'

'Don't mind if I do, Mrs Stearn.' Patrick slipped the screwdriver into his pocket and shook hands with Eric. 'But wait right here while I get the power back on.'

He was gone only momentarily, leaving Maggie and Eric standing in the gloaming facing a wide bay window. It was all right this time: Deitz was nearby and they had weathered the moment of captivation upstairs. They watched the snow, drawn together by the emptiness of the house and the change of season which was happening before their eyes, and by the very coming of twilight.

'I'm going to love it here,' Maggie said.

'I can see why.'

Deitz returned, experimented with a dimmer switch on the wall, and said, 'How's that, Mrs Stearn?'

Maggie smiled up at the ornate fixture which gleamed from a recent polishing. 'Perfect, Mr Deitz. You were absolutely right about which bulbs to choose. The candle-shaped ones add exactly the right touch. It's a grand chandelier. Isn't it a grand chandelier, Eric?'

Actually, it was a rather ugly piece of metal, but the longer Eric studied it, the more he was able to appreciate its antique charm. First the snow, then the floor, now the chandelier. Though he'd warned himself against making comparisons, it was impossible not to, for he realized while walking through this house how little time Nancy took to appreciate things – little things, simple things. Maggie, on the other hand, managed to make the mere coming of dusk into an occasion.

'Well, how about that coffee?' she said.

The three of them sat at the table where she served coffee in mansized mugs, tea for herself, and a plate of cinnamon cookies, which she replenished twice. They talked about the Green Bay Packers' season; and how you couldn't buy fuzzy peaches anymore because hybridization had made them smooth; and which was the best way to cook salmon; and about Maggie's kitchen table which she'd found beneath the tools in her father's garage. They had a lively discussion about which were the best antique stores in Door County and Maggie had numerous anecdotes about the people who owned them.

After thirty minutes Patrick Deitz checked his watch, clasped his knees and said he'd better pick up his tools, it was five-thirty already.

As soon as he got up, so did Eric. 'I'd better go, too,' he said while Deitz went into the dining room.

'Aren't you going to show me what you brought for me?' Maggie asked, pointing to the papers Eric had dropped on an empty chair.

'Oh, I almost forgot.' He handed them across the table to her. 'It's just some information about registering with the chamber of commerce. I'm a member, and we try to get around to all the new businesses as soon as possible. I guess you can consider this your formal invitation to join.'

'Why, thank you.' She glanced at the magazine. *The Key to the Door Peninsula*. On the cover was a summer lakescape. Inside was a gathering of tourist information and ads for food, lodging and shopping in Door County.

'That's a copy of last summer's *Key* and the extra sheet has information about what it costs to register. It would be impossible to run an inn in Door County without belonging. Most of your referrals will come from the chamber so you'll find it's the best advertising money you'll spend.'

'Thanks. I'll look it over right away.'

'I'd guess we'll probably be going to the printer in February or March with next summer's copy, so you'll have plenty of time to have an ad laid out. I have mine done in Sturgeon Bay at Barker's. They have a pretty good graphic arts department.'

'I'll remember that, thanks.'

They moved to the door and paused. 'The members of the chamber meet once a month for breakfast at different restaurants around town. Nothing formal, just a way of touching base with the other business-people. Next month – on the fourth, I think – we're meeting at The Cookery. You're welcome to come.'

'I may do that.'

Deitz came through the kitchen with his toolbox. 'Well, goodnight, Mrs Stearn. Thanks for the coffee and cookies. They were real good.'

'You're welcome.'

'Nice to meet you, Eric.' Deitz nodded.

'Same here.'

Deitz moved between them and Maggie opened the door to let him out. When he was gone she stood in the cold air with the door still open.

'Well, think about the breakfast,' Eric encouraged.

'I will.'

'And thanks for the tour of the house.'

'You're welcome.'

'I really love it.'

'So do I.' The air continued blowing inside. She crossed her arms.

'Well . . .' He reached in a pocket for his gloves and drew them on slowly. 'Good-bye, then.'

Neither of them moved, only their eyes, to each other. She hadn't intended to say the words but they came out of nowhere. 'Let me get my jacket and I'll walk you up the hill.'

He closed the door and waited while she disappeared into the maid's room and returned wearing a pair of Reeboks without socks, shrugging into a fat pink jacket. She dropped to one knee in the middle of the kitchen floor, rolled down her pants legs, then stood, zipping her jacket.

'Ready?'

She looked up and flashed a smile.

'Aha.'

He opened the door, let her pass before him into the five-thirty dark where the softly falling snow created a halo around the back verandah light. The air smelled fresh, of first winter as they moved side by side in Deitz's tracks.

'Be careful,' he warned. 'It's slippery.' Instead of taking her elbow he let his arm buffer hers, a touch of nothing more than insulated clothing, yet through two winter sleeves they were aware of one another as flesh and blood. Somewhere above them Deitz slammed his truck door, started the engine and drove away. When he was gone, they moved slower, up the broad steps that climbed to the road.

The snow fell in great weightless flakes, straight down, in air so still the contact of sky with earth could be heard like the soft tick of a thousand beetles on a warm June night. Reaching the second step, Maggie stopped. 'Shh, listen.' She tilted her head back.

He lifted his face to the milky sky . . . listening . . . listening . . .

'Hear that?' she whispered. 'You can actually hear the snow falling.'

He closed his eyes and listened, and felt the flakes striking his eyelids and cheeks, melting there.

You go on home now, Eric Severson, and forget about standing in the snow with Maggie Pearson. He never thought of her as Maggie Stearn.

He opened his eyes and felt momentarily dizzy watching the perpetual motion above him. A flake plopped on his upper lip. He licked it off and forced himself to move on.

She moved with him, close by his elbow.

'What are you doing for Thanksgiving?' he inquired, suddenly certain she'd be on his mind that day.

'Katy is coming home. We'll be at Mom and Dad's. How about you?'

'Everybody will be at Mike and Barb's. Ma makes the stuffing though. She's scared to death Barb might put a little store-bought bread in it and kill off the whole family.'

They laughed, reaching his truck where they stopped and turned toward one another, suddenly taken by the snow between their feet.

'It'll be the first time Katy sees the house.'

'She's in for a treat.'

'I'm not so sure. Katy and I had a difference of opinion about my selling the house in Seattle.' Holding a prolonged shrug, Maggie continued as if vexed with herself. 'Oh, damn, I may as well be honest. We argued about it, and she hasn't exactly been cordial to me since. I'm a little uneasy about her coming. She thinks it's a mother's duty to keep the home fires burning, as long as the home is the one the kids grew up in. I went to Chicago a couple of weeks ago and took her out for dinner but the atmosphere was a little chilly, to say the least.' She sighed. 'Oh, kids . . .'

'My mother always says all kids go through a selfish streak somewhere between puberty and common sense, when they think their parents are damned fools who don't dress right, talk right or think right. I remember going through that stage myself.'

Maggie innocently widened her eyes. 'Did *I*?'

He laughed. 'I don't know. Did you?'

'I suppose. I couldn't wait to get away from my mother.'

'Well . . . there you go.'

'Eric Severson, you're not the least bit sympathetic!' she scolded with mock petulance.

Again he laughed, and when it ended he turned thoughtful. 'Count your blessings, Maggie,' he remarked, suddenly serious. 'You have a daughter coming home for Thanksgiving. I'd give anything to have one, too.'

His admission brought a jolt of surprise followed by a discomfited sense of having been told a confidence to which she was not altogether sure she wanted to be privy. Something changed, knowing there was such a chink in his marriage.

'You know, Eric, you can't make a remark like that without leaving one obvious question in a person's mind. I won't ask it, though, because it's none of my business.'

'Is it all right if I answer it anyway?' When she refrained from replying he went on. 'Nancy never wanted any.' He studied the distance as he said it.

After a moment of silence she offered quietly, 'I'm sorry.'

He moved restlessly, shovelling snow with his feet. 'Aww . . . well . . . I probably shouldn't have said anything. It's my problem and I'm sorry if I made you uncomfortable bringing it up.'

'No . . . no, you didn't.'

'Yes, I did, and I'm sorry.'

She lifted her eyes and resisted the urge to touch his sleeve and say, I'm the one who's sorry, I remember how you wanted children. To do so would have been unpardonable, for in spite of the rifts between Eric and his wife, the fact remained he was married. For moments only the snow spoke, ticking to earth all around them. She remembered kissing him, long ago, on a night such as this, on his snowmobile in the ravine below the bluff, tasting him and the snow and winter on his skin. He had stopped the machine and they'd sat in the sudden silence, faces lifted to the dark night sky. Then he'd turned and swung his leg over the seat and said, softly, 'Maggie . . .'

'I'd better go,' he said now, opening the truck door.

'I'm glad you came.'

He glanced toward the house. 'I'd like to see it sometime when the furniture is all in.'

'Sure,' she said.

But they both knew the prudent course would be his never coming back here again.

'Have a nice Thanksgiving,' he wished, climbing into the truck.

'Same to you. Say hello to your family.'

'I'll do that.' But he realized he couldn't pass along her message, for what reason could he give for having been here?

The truck door slammed and Maggie stepped back while the starter growled . . . and growled . . . and growled. From inside the cab she heard a dull thump as Eric gave the vehicle a little encouragement, presumably with a fist to the dash. Then more growling and the sound of the window being rolled down.

'This damned old whore,' he said affectionately.

While Maggie laughed, the engine caught and roared. He worked the foot feed, turned on the wipers and shouted above the sound, 'So long, Maggie!'

'Bye. Drive carefully!'

A moment later his tyre tracks funnelled away into the darkness. She stood a long time, studying them, feeling sensitized and restless.

On Thanksgiving Day twenty people gathered around the Severson table, eleven of them Anna's grandchildren. Mike and Barb were there with their five. Ruth, the baby of the family, had come from Duluth with her husband, Dan, and their three. Larry, the second youngest, and his wife, Fran, had come from Milwaukee with three more, one of them still young enough to need a high chair.

When the carving knife was sharpened and the roast turkey sat before Mike at the head of the table, he quieted the group and said, 'Let's all hold hands now.'

When the ring of contact created an unbroken circuit, Mike began the prayer.

'Dear Lord, we thank you for another year of good health and prosperity. We thank you for this food and for letting us all be around the table again to enjoy it. We're especially grateful to have Ma who has seen to it one more time that none of us suffers from eating store-bought bread. And for having Ruth and Larry's families here this year, too, though we ask you to remind little Trish when she's had enough pumpkin pie and whipped cream, bearing in mind what happened last year after she had her third piece. And of course we thank you for this sturdy bunch of kids who are all going to pitch in after dinner and wash the dishes for their mothers. And one more thing, Lord, from both Barb and I. Sorry it's taken us so long to be properly grateful, but we finally saw the light and we trust you're doing the right thing when you give us one more to oversee. Next year, when we hold hands around this table again and there are twenty-one of us, let us all be as healthy and happy as we are today. Amen.'

The youngest children repeated, 'Amen.'

Nancy shot a glance at Eric.

The others stared at Mike and Barbara.

Nicholas finally found his tongue. 'Another one?'

'Yup,' replied Mike, picking up the carving knife. 'In May. Just in time for your graduation.'

As Mike cut into the turkey all eyes swerved to Anna. She unceremoniously helped her nearest grandchild mash a candied yam and remarked, 'There's something nice and round and satisfying about an even dozen grandchildren.

Barbara, you gonna get those potatoes and gravy started down there or are we gonna sit here staring till the food gets cold?'

One could see the visible relaxing of tension around the table.

The day left Eric feeling quietly despondent. Being with his brothers and sister again brought back lush, picturesque recollections of his boyhood in a family of six – the noise, the commotion, the bandying. He had assumed his whole life long that he would re-create the same scene with his own offspring. Accepting that it would never happen took some acclimatizing; it took, too, the punch of unfettered happiness out of this year's festivities.

Surrounded by noise and celebration, Eric lapsed often into periods of silence. Sometimes he'd stare at the TV screen without registering the touchdowns being made there. The others would cheer and rouse him from his reverie, tease him about napping. But he hadn't been napping, only brooding. Sometimes he'd gaze out the window at the snow and remember Maggie turning to say over her shoulder, 'Thanksgiving should have snow, don't you think?' He pictured her at her parents' house having her Thanksgiving dinner and wondered if she'd settled the discord with her daughter. He recalled the hour spent in her house and realized he had been happier there than he was today, surrounded by people he loved.

He found Nancy studying him across the room and reminded himself of the true meaning behind today's observation. Taking his cue from Mike, he set firmly in his mind the things for which he should be grateful: this family surrounding him, the continuing good health of them all, his livelihood, the boat, the house, a hard-working, beautiful wife.

Arriving home at eight o'clock that night, he made a resolution to stop thinking about Maggie Stearn and to keep away from her house. As Nancy opened the front closet door he caught her and from behind, doubling his arms around her ribs, buried his face in her neck. The collar of her white wool coat smelled like a spicy garden. Her neck was warm and supple as she tipped her head aside and covered his arms with her own.

'I love you,' he murmured, meaning it.

'I love you, too.'

'And I'm sorry.'

'For what?'

'For saying no the last time you wanted to make love. For shutting you out these last couple weeks. It was wrong of me.'

'Oh, Eric.' She swung around and came hard against him, clasping her arms around his neck. 'Please don't let this baby thing come between us.'

It already has.

He kissed her and tried to put the realization from his mind. But it remained, and the kiss – for Eric – became bleak. He buried his face against her, feeling bereaved and very frightened. 'I'm so damned jealous of Mike and Barb.'

'I know,' she said. 'I saw it on your face today.' She held him, petting the back of his head. 'Please . . . don't. I've got four days at home. Let's make them happy.'

He would try, he vowed. He would try. But he recognized something he carried deep inside him, something new and disturbing and destructive. That something was the first seed of bitterness.

Katy Stearn left Chicago after her one o'clock class the day before Thanksgiving. She drove alone, giving her ample time to fret and build offences against her mother.

I should be flying back to Seattle with Smitty. I should be meeting the gang down at The Lighthouse and checking out who's getting fat on cafeteria cooking at college and who's fallen in love already and who's still a nerd. I should be showing off my Northwestern sweatshirt and my new haircut and checking out old

Lenny – find out if he's dating anybody at UCLA yet, or if I broke his heart for good. I should be driving down familiar streets and waiting for friends to call and sleeping in my old room.

She was newly eighteen and typical and considered herself not selfish, but wronged by her mother's sudden decision to move to Door County.

She had purposely avoided asking the location of Maggie's new house and drove instead directly to her grandparents', arriving shortly before seven.

Vera answered the door. 'Katy, hello!'

'Hi, Grandma.'

Vera accepted a hug while glancing at the empty porch. 'Where's your mother?'

'I haven't been there yet. I decided to stop here first.'

Pulling back she scolded, 'Good gracious, child, where are your rubbers? You mean to tell me you drove all the way from Chicago without any rubbers in the car? Why, you'd catch pneumonia if you broke down and had to walk.'

'I have a brand new car, Grandma.'

'That's no excuse. New cars break down, too. Roy, look who's here, and without rubbers!'

'Hi, Grandpa.'

'Well, little Katy.' He came from the kitchen and gave her a bear hug. 'Imagine you being old enough to drive up here clear from Chicago. How's school?'

They chatted as they ambled back toward the kitchen. Vera asked if Katy had had supper, and when she said no, opened the refrigerator door. 'Well, I have some leftover soup I'll warm up for you. Roy, move your junk aside. You've got it strewn all over the table.' She began warming soup while Katy and Roy sat at the table and he asked her about Chicago and school.

When she had first made plans to go away to college, this was the scene she had imagined happening with her mother when she returned home. If she'd gone to her mother's first, it *would* be happening there. But that *strange* house in this *strange* little town! How could her mother have done this to her? How? Her mother accused her, Katy, of being selfish when Katy viewed Maggie's move as a rash act of selfishness.

Vera came with the soup, crackers, cheese and lunch meat and joined them while Katy ate. Afterwards she began cleaning up the kitchen and Roy drew his work back to the centre of the table.

'What are you making, Grandpa?'

'A whole Victorian town. I make a couple of buildings each year. The first year I did the church, and I've done nine since then.'

'What are you doing this year?'

'A house. A model of your mother's actually.' Watching him piece together two delicate pieces of wood she became filled with a mixture of longings she did not understand. To be with her mother; to be free of her. To see the house; never to see it. To love it; to despise it. 'She's bought herself quite a beautiful place, you know.'

Vera spoke up from the sink. 'I told her she was crazy to buy a place that big. And that *old*, for heaven's sake, but she wouldn't listen to me. What a single woman wants with a house that size is beyond . . .'

Vera went on and on. Katy stared at the replica and tried to understand her complex emotions. Roy spread glue on a miniature window-frame and applied it to the house. What would the finished house look like? The upper half, the roof?

'. . . hasn't got a stick of furniture in the place, so I don't know *where* you're going to sleep if you *do* go over there,' Vera finally ended.

The scent of the glue filled the room. At the sink, Vera shined the faucets. Without glancing up from his work, Roy told his granddaughter, 'I wouldn't be surprised if your mother is waiting for you right now to show it to you.'

Katy's eyes began stinging. The tears blurred Roy's

hands as she watched him spread glue along another piece and hold it in place. She thought of Seattle and the house she knew so well. She thought of a house across town where not a single memory dwelled. She must go to this place she resented, to this mother with whom she'd fought, whom she missed so hard it hurt her chest.

She waited until Vera went upstairs to the bathroom.

In the quiet kitchen Roy continued piecing his model.

'Grandpa?' Katy said quietly.

'Hm?' he replied, giving the impression his only concern was completing another building for his Victorian town.

'I need some directions to find it.'

He looked up, smiled like a tired Santa Claus and reached across the table to give her hand a squeeze. 'Good girl,' he said.

The road was steep and curved. She remembered it vaguely from years ago when they'd occasionally come here for a summer vacation and would drive up the hill to look at the summer homes of the 'rich people'. The cliff, on the left, and the overhanging trees on the right hemmed in the road itself. No streetlights lit it, only an occasional light from a back porch, and in places even these were held back by walls of thick evergreens. The car lights picked out stone walls, frosted with snow, and the steep gabled roofs of garages that appeared to have more character than many modern homes.

She spotted her mother's car easily and pulled up across from it beside a tall wall of evergreens. Shifting to neutral, she stared at the vehicle with its cap of snow, at the strange garage, the flat white surface of the tennis court and the dilapidated arbour seat about which her mother's letters had been filled. She felt strangely remote, confronting these things that already meant something to her mother. Again came the sense of abandonment for she, Katy, was no part of anything around her.

A glance to the right revealed the thick hedge that cut off her view of the house. Reluctantly, Katy switched off the lights, killed the engine and left the car.

She stood for moments at the top of the walk between the pungent shrubs, looking down on the backside of a house where the light on a small rear verandah beamed a welcome. There was a door with a window, and beside it another window, long and skinny, throwing a slash of gold across the snow. She glanced up at the looming roofline, but made out only great bulk with no detail visible in the shadows.

At last she started down the steps.

On the verandah she paused, her hands pushed deep into her pockets, staring at the lace on the window and the unclear images beyond. She felt as if her own needs, like the image seen through the coarse lace, had become obscure. She did not need her mother, yet her absence hurt. She did not need to come here for the holiday, yet going to Seattle without family was unthinkable. She glanced at the Indian corn and the brass plaque, prepared to dislike the place, cataloguing instead its welcoming charm.

She rapped on the door and stood back, waiting. Her heart hammered with both expectation and trepidation as she saw, through the lace, a figure move deep in the room. The door opened and there stood Maggie, smiling, wearing a pair of modish grey acid-washed bib overalls and a shirt styled like pink underwear.

'Katy, you're here.'

'Hello, Mother,' Katy replied coolly.

'Well, come inside.' Embracing Katy, who more or less allowed it, Maggie thought, *Oh, Katy, don't be like Mother. Please don't turn out like her.* Released, Katy stood with her hands in her pockets, behind a barrier as palpable as a steel wall, leaving Maggie to search for enough social graces for two.

'So, how was your ride up?'

'Fine.'

'I expected you much earlier.'

'I stopped at Grandma and Grandpa's. I had supper with them.'

'Oh.' Maggie carefully concealed her disappointment. She had prepared spaghetti and meatballs, cheese bread and apple crisp – all Katy's favourites. 'Well, I'm sure they loved that. They've really been looking forward to your coming.'

Pulling her wool scarf from around her neck, Katy glanced at the kitchen. 'So this is the house.' A room with warmth and hospitality but so different from the house in which she'd grown up. Where was their old kitchen table? Where had this new one come from? And when had her mother begun dressing like a coed? So many changes. They gave Katy the impression she'd been away for years instead of weeks, that her mother had been perfectly happy without her.

'Yes, this is it. This was the first room I had redone. That's an old table of Grandpa's, the cabinets are new, but the floor is original. Would you like to see the rest of it?'

'I suppose.'

'Well, here . . . take your jacket off and we'll walk through.'

As they moved through the empty rooms Katy asked, 'Where's all our furniture?'

'Stored in the garage. When it arrived I hadn't had the floors refinished yet.'

It became apparent, as Katy was led through the house, that her mother had no intention of unearthing the relics of their past, that she would furnish the entire house with strange pieces. Katy's resentment prickled once again, although even she was forced to admit their traditional furniture would look puny and out of place in this house with its ten-foot ceilings and generous rooms. The structure demanded pieces with bulk and character and a long history.

They reached the Belvedere Room, and there at last was

the familiarity for which Katy so longed: her own bed and dresser, looking ridiculously dwarfed in the immense space. The bed was covered with her familiar blue daisy spread, looking faded and ill chosen, and Maggie had unearthed several giant stuffed toys to set beside it. On the dresser were a jewellery box Katy had received as a Christmas gift when she was nine and a basket holding the mementoes of recent years: beads and perfume bottles and the pom-poms from her roller skates.

She stared at it, feeling a lump form in her throat. How childish everything suddenly looked.

Behind her Maggie spoke quietly. 'I wasn't sure what you'd like put out.'

The blue daisies grew wavery and the awful weight of change pressed upon Katy. She felt her throat constrict. She wanted to be twelve again, and have Daddy alive, and not have to grow accustomed to changes. Simultaneously she liked being a college freshman, taking her first step in the world and being free of parental constraints. Abruptly she spun and threw herself into Maggie's arms.

'Oh, Mother, it's s . . . so hard gr . . . growing up.'

Maggie's heart swelled with love and understanding. 'I know, darling, I know. For me, too.'

'I'm sorry.'

'So am I.'

'But I miss the old house and Seattle so m . . . much.'

'I know you do.' Maggie rubbed Katy's back. 'But it, and all the memories associated with it are part of the past. I had to leave them and make room for something new in my life, otherwise I would have withered away, don't you understand?'

'I do, really I do.'

'Leaving there doesn't mean I've forgotten your father, or what he meant to both of us. I loved him, Katy, and we had the best life I could imagine, the kind I'd wish for you and your own husband someday. But I discovered that when he died, I'd died, too, for all practical purposes. I sealed myself away and mourned him and stopped caring about things it's not healthy to stop caring about. Since I've been here, I've felt so . . . so *alive* again! I have purpose, don't you see? I have the house to work on, and spring to look forward to, and a business to get on its feet.'

Katy saw it all, this new side of her mother, a woman of tremendous resilience who could lay aside the straits of widowhood and bloom anew, immersed in fresh interests. A woman of eclectic tastes who could store away a houseful of traditional furniture and, eager-eyed, thrust herself into the gathering of antiques. A businesswoman who greeted new challenges with surprising confidence. A mother who was facing a catharsis as consequential as that which Katy herself was feeling. Accepting this new side of Maggie meant saying good-bye to the old one, but Katy realized she must do so.

She pulled back, still sniffling. 'I love the house, Mom. I didn't want to, but I can't help it.'

Maggie smiled. 'You didn't want to?'

Mopping her eyes, Katy complained, 'Well, damn it, I hate antiques! I've *always* hated antiques! And you start writing to me about armoires and brass beds and I start getting curious, and now here I am, picturing them and getting excited!'

Laughing, Maggie drew Katy into her arms again and the two rocked from side to side. 'That's called growth, dear – learning to accept new things.'

Katy pulled back. 'And what is this called . . .' She plucked at Maggie's shirt sleeve. '. . . my forty-year-old mother dressed like a teeny-bopper. Is this growth, too?'

Maggie buried her hands in her deep overalls pockets, rolled back on her heels and looked down at her clothes. 'You like them?'

'No. Yes.' Katy threw her hands in the air. 'Cripes, I don't know! You don't look like Mom anymore. You look like one of the girls in the dorm! It's scary.'

'Just because I'm a mother doesn't mean I have to dress like Harriet Nelson, does it?'

'Who's Harriet Nelson?'

'Ozzie's Harriet, and by the way, I like being forty.'

'Oh, Mom . . .' Katy smiled and hooked Maggie's arm with her own, turning her toward the stairs. 'I'm happy for you, really I am. I doubt that this will ever feel like home to me, but if you're happy, I guess I should be glad for you.'

Later, when they were getting Katy settled in the Belvedere Room, she observed, 'Grandma's not too happy about your buying this place, is she?'

'What has Grandma ever been happy about?'

'Not much that I can remember. How did you end up so different from her?'

'With a conscious effort,' Maggie replied. 'Sometimes I pity her, but other times she absolutely infuriates me. Since I've moved out of her house and into this one I've only gone over there once a week, that's the only way we can get along.'

'Grandpa is sweet though.'

'Yes, he is, and I regret that I don't see him more. But he stops over here quite often. He loves the house, too.'

'What about Grandma?'

'She hasn't seen it yet.'

Katy halted in surprise. 'What!'

'She hasn't seen it yet.'

'Haven't you invited her?'

'Oh, I've invited her, but she always finds some excuse not to come. I said she infuriates me, didn't I?'

'But why? I don't understand.'

'Neither do I. We've never gotten along. I've been trying to puzzle it out lately and it's almost as if she doesn't want others to be happy . . . I don't know. No matter what it is that anyone mentions, if it makes them happy, she has to either put it down or scold them for something that's totally unrelated.'

'She scolded me the minute I came in the house, because I didn't have my boots on.'

'That's the kind of thing I mean. Why does she do that? Is she jealous? It sounds ridiculous, but sometimes she acts as if she is, though I don't know of what. In my case, maybe it's my relationship with Dad – he and I have always gotten along fabulously. Maybe about the fact that I *can* be happy, even in spite of your dad's death. There's certainly *some*thing bothering her about my buying this house.'

'So I take it we're eating Thanksgiving dinner at her house?'

'Yes.'

'And you're disappointed?'

Maggie summoned a bright smile. 'Next year we'll eat here. How about that?'

'It's a date. Without any grief from me.'

Maggie put her mother from her mind. 'And when summer comes, if you want to, you can come and work for me cleaning rooms. You'd have the beach right here and I know some young people I can introduce you to. Would you consider doing that?'

Katy smiled. 'I might.'

'Good. Then how about some apple crisp?'

Katy grinned. 'I thought I smelled it when I walked in.'

Maggie linked an arm around Katy's waist. It had been three months of antagonism between them. Having the weight of it lifted was the only thing Maggie had needed to make her Thanksgiving happy. Side by side the two of them ambled toward the kitchen.

Chapter 9

They had withstood Thanksgiving day with Vera. Katy stayed four days and promised to return to spend at least the first half of her winter break with her mother, after which she planned to fly to Seattle and stay with Smitty.

December arrived, bringing more snow and virtually no tourists until after the holidays when the cross-country skiers and snowmobilers would begin invading Door County once more. The Door changed colours – blue shadows on white land; black draping hemlocks and here and there the scarlet berries of the sumac bushes like plumes of fire above the snow. The birds of autumn stayed – the jay and chickadee and kinglets; the nuthatches, hanging upside down and racing around the tree trunks. The lake began to freeze.

Maggie drove uptown one day shortly before noon to pick up her mail. The streets had ample parking now so she pulled up to the kerb halfway between the post office and the general store. She was just stepping up onto the sidewalk when somebody called, 'Maggie! Hey, Maggie!'

She looked around but saw no one.

'Up here!'

She raised her head and shaded her eyes against a piercing noon sun. A man stood in the bucket of a boom truck, high overhead, waving.

'Hi, Maggie!'

He was dressed in a parka and held a giant red Christmas bell in one hand. The sun caught in the tinselled greenery which cascaded over the edge of the bucket to a light pole on the opposite side of the street.

'Eric, is that you?'

'Hello! How are you?'

'Fine! What are you doing up there?'

'Putting up Christmas decorations. I volunteer every year.'

She smiled, and squinted and felt improperly glad to see him again. 'They look good!' She glanced along Main Street where swags of garland already created a canopy effect above the street and red bells decorated the poles clear to the curve at the east end. 'My. Such impressive civic pride!' she teased, glancing up again.

'I've got plenty of time on my hands. Besides, I enjoy it. Puts me in the holiday mood.'

'Me, too!'

They smiled at each other several seconds before he called, 'How was your Thanksgiving?'

'Fine, and yours?'

'Okay. Did your daughter come home?'

'Yes.'

From the sidewalk below the boom another man yelled, 'Hey, Severson, you gonna hang that thing or should I go take a lunch break while you decide?'

'Oh, sorry. Hey, Dutch, you know Maggie?'

The man peered at Maggie from across the steet. 'Don't believe I do.'

'This is Maggie Stearn. She's the one who bought Harding House. Maggie, Dutch Winkler. He fishes.'

'Hi, Dutch!' she called, waving. Dutch returned the wave as a red Ford drove past, veering to avoid the boom truck that was blocking one traffic lane. The driver of the Ford waved to Dutch and touched his horn.

When the truck had passed, Maggie craned to look at Eric again. 'Don't you get dizzy up there?'

'Who me? A fisherman who stands on a rocking deck all day long?'

'Oh, of course. Well, it's nice of you to volunteer and make the town festive for the rest of us.'

'You get to see all the pretty girls from up here and they don't know you're watching,' he teased.

Had he not been shouting so anyone on the street could hear, she'd have guessed he was flirting. She felt her cheeks grow warm and decided she'd dallied long enough.

'Well, nice to see you. I'd better go get my mail and my milk. Bye!'

'Bye!' He watched her from above, following her dark head and her pink jacket.

Pink jacket!

It struck him at that moment how she'd always favoured pink. He'd forgotten. Now it came back, how he'd teased her, and given her small pink things. Once a pink teddy bear he'd won at a carnival. Once a pink peony from one of his mother's bushes, which he'd stuck in the vents of her school locker. Another time, pink tassels for her ice skates. But the time he remembered best was that spring they were seniors. The orchards had been in full bloom, and he'd borrowed Mike's car to take her to a drive-in movie. On his way, he'd stopped out in the country and picked pink apple blossoms, whorls of them, and had stuck them behind the visors and in the handles of the wing windows, and behind the clothes hooks and even in the ashtray. When he'd gone to pick her up he'd parked two houses away from hers, afraid her mother would see and think he was crazy; Vera was always gawking out the window when he came to get Maggie. When Maggie saw the blossoms she'd covered her mouth with both hands and got all flustered. He remembered hugging her – or she hugging him – in the car on her street before he'd started the engine, and the smell of the blossoms heady around them, and the spring evening pale at the windows, and being in love for the first and most wondrous time in his life. They'd never made it to the movie that night. Instead they'd parked out in Easley's orchard, beneath the trees, and they'd opened the car doors to let their blossoms mingle with those crowding the roof of the car, and there, for the first time, they'd gone all the way.

Standing in a manlift twenty feet above Maggie on a frigid winter day, Eric watched her pink jacket disappear into the post office and remembered.

When she was gone, he returned to work, distracted, keeping one eye on the post office door. Momentarily, she reappeared, shuffling through her mail as she walked toward the general store a half-block away. When she drew abreast of him she waved again – a waggle of two fingers – and he lifted a gloved hand, wordlessly. She disappeared into the store and he finished hanging the plastic bell, then peered down over the edge of the bucket. 'Hey, Dutch, you getting hungry?'

Dutch checked his watch. 'By golly, it's nearly twelve o'clock. Want to break for lunch?'

'Yeah, I'm ready.'

Riding down, to the hum and shudder of the bucket, Eric kept his eyes on the door of the general store.

You're chasing her, Severson.

What do you mean? Everybody eats lunch.

The store was busy. Busy for Fish Creek in December. Everyone in town knew what time the mail came in: between eleven and twelve each day. And with no home delivery within the city limits, noon brought a daily deluge of people who walked uptown to get their mail and pick up whatever they might need at the store. If there was a social time in Fish Creek, mail time was it.

When Maggie entered the general store, most of the customers were up front. At the rear meat counter, nobody waited. She peeked around the high deli case.

'Hey, what's going on back here?' she inquired teasingly.

Roy looked up and broke into a smile. 'Well, this is the nicest thing that's happened today. How're you, angel?' He left his chopping block and came to bestow a hug.

'Mmm . . . good.' She kissed his cheek. 'Thought I'd have you make me a sandwich as long as I'm here.'

'What kind?'

'Pastrami. And make it thick, I'm hungry as a bear.'

'Wheat?'

'No, rye.' He pulled out a rye bun while she investigated the contents of the display case. 'What've you got good in here? Oh, the herring barrel's in!' She rolled back the heavy glass door, lifted a chunk of herring on a slotted spoon and popped it into her mouth with her fingers. 'Mmm . . . now I *know* Christmas is coming!' she mumbled with her mouth full.

'You want to get me fired, picking in there with your fingers?'

'They're clean,' she declared, licking off her fingertips. 'I only scratched my armpit once.'

He laughed and shook a huge French chef knife at her. 'You're taking liberties with my livelihood, young lady.'

She pranced over, kissed his forehead, and leaned saucily against the butcher block. 'Nobody'd fire you. You're too sweet.'

On the other side of the deli case someone remarked dryly, 'Well, I *was* going to order some herring.'

Maggie swung around at the sound of Eric's voice.

'Hello, Eric,' Roy greeted.

'It's hard to keep a Scandinavian's fingers out of the herring barrel, isn't it?'

'I told her she's going to get me fired.'

'Whatever you're making there, make two,' Eric ordered.

'Pastrami on rye.'

'Fine.'

Maggie moved back to the meat case, crooked a finger and said in a stage whisper, 'Hey, Eric, come here.' After a stealthy glance toward the front of the store, she appropriated another chunk of herring and handed it to him over the top of the tall, old-fashioned cooler. 'Don't tell anybody.'

He ate it with relish, tipping his head back and grinning, then licking his fingers.

'All right, you two, take your sandwiches and get out of my herring!' Roy scolded good-naturedly just as Elsie Childs, the town librarian, came around the corner. 'I got business to tend to. What can I do for you today, Elsie?'

'Hi, Elsie,' Maggie and Eric greeted in unison, taking their sandwiches and making a quick escape. Maggie grabbed a carton of milk and they paid up front, then left together. Outside, Eric asked, 'Where were you planning to eat?'

She glanced at the long wooden bench against the store wall, where in summer tourists sat licking ice cream cones. 'How about right here?'

'Mind if I join you?'

'Please do.'

They sat on the frigid bench with their backs against the white wooden wall, facing south, warming in the radiant rays of sun pelting their faces. Wearing thick-fingered gloves they unwrapped toppling sandwiches containing an inch-high layer of meat, struggling to open their mouths wide enough to accommodate the first bites.

'Mmm . . .' she praised through her first mouthful.

'Mmm-hmmm!' he seconded.

She swallowed and asked, 'Where's Dutch?'

'He went home to eat with his wife.'

They continued their meal, conversing between bites. 'So did you get your disagreement settled with your daughter?'

'Yes. She loves the house and wants to come and work with me this summer.'

'Wonderful.'

She reached in the brown paper bag for the milk carton, opened it and took a swig.

'Want some milk?' she offered, handing him the carton.

'Thanks.' He tipped his head back and she watched his Adam's apple bob as he drank. He lowered the carton and backhanded his mouth with a gloved hand. 'It's good.'

They smiled at one another and she shimmied aside so he could set the carton between them.

With their legs stretched out, their booted feet crossed, they ate on, leaning back lazily against the wall. Elsie Childs came out of the store and Eric drew back his feet as she passed in front of them.

'Hello again,' he said.

'You two look comfortable,' she commented.

They replied in unison.

'The sun is warm.'

'Yes we are.'

'Enjoy yourselves.' Elsie continued toward the post office.

They finished their sandwiches while townspeople came and went before them. They drank last gulps of milk and Maggie put the half-empty carton back in the sack.

'Well, I should go home.'

'Yeah, Dutch will be back soon. We have about six more swags to hang.'

But neither of them moved, only sat with their napes to the wall, soaking sun like a pair of lizards on a warm rock. In the bare locust tree across the street a pair of chickadees sang their two-note song. Occasionally a car would pass, its tyres singing *shhhh* in the slushy street. The wood beneath them grew as warm as the sun on their faces.

'Hey, Maggie?' Eric murmured, as if preoccupied with his thoughts. 'Can I tell you something?'

'Sure.'

He remained silent for so long she looked over to see if he'd fallen asleep. But his squinted eyes were fixed on something across the street, his interlaced, gloved fingers draped across his belly.

'I never did anything like this with Nancy,' he said at last, rolling his head to face her. 'She would no more sit on an icy bench and eat a sandwich than wear Reeboks without socks. It just isn't in her.'

For moments they studied one another, the sun beating so brightly upon their faces it paled their very eyelashes.

'Did you do things like this with your husband?' Eric asked.

'All the time. Spontaneous, silly things.'

'I envy you,' he said, rolling his face once more to the sun, letting his eyes drift closed. 'I think Ma and the old man used to sneak away and find things like this to do, too. I remember when they'd go out on the boat sometimes after dark, and they'd never let us kids come with them.' He opened his eyes and watched the chickadees. 'When they'd come home, her hair would be wet and Mike and I used to giggle because we knew she never took a bathing suit. Now I think it's like that for Mike and Barb. Why is it some people find the secret and some people don't?'

She took a moment to reply. 'You know what I think?'

'What?' He glanced at her again.

She allowed several beats of silence before giving her opinion. 'I think you're allowing one dissatisfaction to magnify others. We all do that sometimes. We're upset with someone about one specific thing, and it makes us dwell on all the other insignificant or irksome things the other person does. We blow them up out of proportion. What you have to do when you're unhappy about one thing is to remember the good. Nancy has dozens of attributes that you're letting yourself forget right now. I know she does.'

He sighed, slumped forward, elbows to knees, and studied the sidewalk between his boots.

'I suppose you're right,' he decided after some thought.

'May I offer a suggestion?'

Still hunkered forward, he glanced back over his shoulder. 'By all means.'

'Invite her.' Maggie's eyes and voice turned earnest as she sat forward, shoulder to shoulder with Eric. 'Let her know it's the kind of thing you'd love to do with her. Get out her warmest jacket, bundle her in it and order two sandwiches from Daddy, then take her to your favourite spot and let her know that the joy you get from it is as much from being there with her as it is from the novelty of eating a picnic in the snow.'

For several beats of silence, he studied her face, the face he was coming to appreciate far too much. Often at night, between lights-out and sleep, it visited him in the dark. At length he asked, 'So, how'd you learn all this?'

'I read a lot. I had a wonderful husband who was willing to try things with me, and I've taught a Family Life unit in home ec, which means taking a lot of psych classes.'

'My mother didn't read a lot, or take psych classes.'

'No. But I'd be willing to bet she overlooked a lot of minor shortcomings in your dad and worked damned hard at her marriage.'

He looked away and his voice grew brittle. 'Saying you don't want a family is more than a minor shortcoming, Maggie. It's a monumental deficiency.'

'Did you talk about it before you and Nancy got married?'

'No.'

'Why not?'

'I don't know. I just assumed we'd have kids.'

'But if you didn't talk about it, whose fault is it that it's come between you now?'

'I know. I know.' He jumped to his feet and went to the edge of the sidewalk where he hung from the kerb by his heels, staring at the empty lot across the street. She'd put her finger on the thought that had rankled him countless times.

She studied his back, picked up her sack of milk and rose from the bench to stand behind him.

'I think you need a marriage counsellor, Eric.'

'I suggested that. She said no.'

How sad he looked, even from behind. She had never realized how sad stillness can seem.

'Do you have any friends you could both talk to who might help? Sometimes having a mediator helps.'

'That's another thing that's struck me lately. We don't have any friends, not as a couple. How the hell can we make friends when we scarcely have time to ourselves? I have friends, and I can talk to Mike – I already have. But Nancy would never open up to him or to any of the rest of my family. She doesn't know them well enough, probably doesn't even *like* them well enough.'

'Then I don't know what else to suggest.'

He turned to face her. 'I'm some cheery company, huh? Every time we're together I manage to dampen your spirits.'

'Don't be silly. My spirits are resilient. But what about yours?'

'I'll be okay. Don't worry about me.'

'I probably will, the way I used to worry about my students when they'd come to me with some family problems from home.'

They walked towards her car.

'I'll bet you were a damned good teacher, weren't you, Maggie?'

She gave some thought to her reply. 'I cared a lot. The kids responded to that.'

He found her modesty becoming, but suspected he'd guessed right. She was bright, insightful and unbiased. People like Maggie taught others without even being aware they were doing so.

They reached her car and stepped onto the street together.

'Well, the lunch was fun anyway,' he said, trying to sound cheerier.

'Yes, it was.'

He opened her car door and she set the milk on the seat.

'And your dad makes a walloping delicious sandwich. Tell him I said so.'

'I will.'

She got into the Lincoln and he stood with his hands curled over the top of the open door.

She looked up at him and for a moment neither of them could think of a thing to say.

He still had the most beautiful eyes of any man she'd ever met.

She still looked wonderful in pink.

'Here comes Dutch. You'd better get back to work.'

'Yeah. Well . . . take care of yourself.'

'You, too.'

'So long.' He slammed the door and stepped back as she put her key into the ignition, then stood in the street until the car began moving, and raised a gloved hand in farewell.

That night, alone in her kitchen, Maggie took out a carton of milk to pour a glass. She popped open the pouring spout and Eric's image came back as he had looked that day – his chin tipped up sharply, blond hair flattened against the store wall, his eyes nearly closed and his Adam's apple marking each swallow as his lips cupped the carton. She ran a fingertip over the edge of the pouring spout.

Resolutely, she forced the image from her mind, filled a tumbler and slammed the carton away in the refrigerator.

He's married.

And unhappy.

That's justifying, Maggie, and you know it!

What kind of wife would refuse to have her husband's babies?

You're making judgements, and you've only heard one side of the story.

But I feel sorry for him.

Fine. Feel sorry for him. But stay on your own side of the street.

The warning stayed with her while she counted down the days until the chamber of commerce breakfast, making her ambivalent about attending. As a woman, she thought it wisest to avoid further meetings with Eric Severson, while as a businesswoman she recognized the importance of not only joining the organization, but of taking an active interest in the group and getting to know the other members. In a town the size of Fish Creek, their referrals could bring in a lot of business. From a social point of view, if this was to be her home, she had to start building friendships someplace. What better place than at such a breakfast? And as for seeing Eric again, who could fault them if they both just happened to be at a breakfast attended by nearly every businessman in the county?

The Tuesday morning of the breakfast she arose early, bathed and dressed in trousers of hunter-green wool and a winter-white sweater with a jewellery neckline, patch pocket and shoulder pads. She put on a string of pearls, replaced it with a gold chain and discarded the chain in favour of a gold pendant watch which she pinned over her left breast. In her ears she wore tiny gold loops.

When her hair was arranged and her makeup applied she caught herself spritzing perfume for the second time and glanced up sharply at her own consternated eyes in the mirror.

You know what you're doing, don't you, Maggie?

I'm going to a businessmen's breakfast.

You're dressing for Eric Severson.

I am not!

How many times have you put on mascara and eye shadow since you've lived in Fish Creek? And perfume? Twice, yet!

But I'm not dressed in pink, am I?

Oh, big deal.

Irritated, she slammed off the lightswitch and hurried from the bathroom.

She drove to the breakfast realizing that already things around town reminded her of Eric Severson. In the steel-grey morning Main Street appeared to have a brightly lit cathedral ceiling, the one he had hung. The front steps of the community church brought to mind their first surprised perusal of one another the day of Gary Eidelbach's wedding. The white bench before the general store brought back the memory of them sitting there at high noon, sharing lunch.

His pickup was parked on Main Street and Maggie could not deny her reaction to seeing it there – the full-body flush and the speeding pulse so like when she was first falling in love with him years ago. Only a fool would declare it was anything but anticipation.

Stepping into The Cookery, she picked him out immediately, from a good two dozen people in the room, and her heart gave a leap that warned she must consciously avoid seeking him out. He stood across the room, talking with a group of men and women, dressed in grey trousers and a dusty blue sports coat over an open-collared white shirt. His blond hair was neatly combed and he held a paper in his hand as if they'd been discussing something written on it. He glanced up immediately, as if her entry had activated some sensor warning him of her presence. He smiled and came to her directly.

'Maggie, I'm so glad you came.'

He shook her hand – a firm, hard handshake, absolutely correct, not even a trifle lingering, yet she felt stunned by his touch.

'You have new glasses,' she remarked, smiling. They made him seem the faintest bit a stranger and for a moment she indulged in the fantasy that she was meeting him for the first time.

'Oh, these . . .' A mere strip of gold held up the rimless lenses that set off his clear, blue eyes. 'I need them for reading. And you have a new coat,' he noted, stepping behind her as she unbuttoned the winter-white Chesterfield.

'No, it's not new.'

'I was watching for the pink jacket,' he admitted as he

stepped behind her and took the coat as it slipped from her shoulders. 'You always did look best in pink.'

She threw a sharp glance over her shoulder and in the instant their eyes met she discovered that a room full of businesspeople was no protection at all, for his words resurrected memories she'd thought only *she* had fostered, and gave the lie to any pretended indifference she might have assumed. No, he was no stranger. He was the same person who had given her pink trinkets when they were young, who had once said their first baby would be a girl and that they would paint her room pink.

'I thought you had forgotten that.'

'I had, until the other day when I stood twenty feet above your head and watched you walk into the post office wearing a pink jacket. It started a lot of old memories rolling back.'

'Eric –'

'I'll hang this up and be right back.'

He turned, leaving her rattled and trying to hide it, leaving her clinging to the subtle essence of his after-shave and admiring his shoulders and the line of his head as he carried her coat away.

Momentarily he returned, touched her elbow. 'Come on, I'll introduce you.'

If she had expected any false displays of indifference from him she had done him an injustice, for he was alarmingly straightforward in playing her personal host. Before the meal he kept her circulating, meeting members, then he seated her beside himself at a round table for six. He asked the waitress to bring a pot of tea without inquiring if she preferred it to coffee. He inquired whether her wallpaper had come yet. He said, 'I have something for you,' and belled out the front of his sports jacket, reaching for the inside pocket.

'Here.' He handed her a newspaper clipping. 'I thought you might be interested in this. There should be a lot of antiques.'

It was an ad for an estate sale. Reading it, her eyes grew bright and avid.

'Eric, this sounds wonderful! Where did you find this?' She flipped it over and back.

'In the *Advocate*.'

'How did I miss it?'

'I don't know, but it says there's a brass bed. Isn't that what you want for the Belvedere Room?'

'And a Belter settee upholstered with French tapestry!' she exclaimed, reading on. '. . . and antique china, and bevelled mirrors, and a pair of matched rosewood chairs . . . I'm going for sure!' THURSDAY NINE TO FIVE, 714 JAMES STREET, STURGEON BAY, the ad said. She looked up, beaming, excited. 'Oh, thank you, Eric.'

'You're welcome. Do you need a truck?'

'I might.'

'The old whore is temperamental, but she's yours if you want her.'

'Thank you, I just might.'

'Excuse me,' a male voice interrupted.

Eric looked up. 'Oh . . . Mark, hello.' He pushed back his chair.

'I take it this is the new owner of Harding House,' the man said, 'and since I'll be introducing her today, I thought I should meet her first.' He was already extending his hand to Maggie. She looked up into a long, slim fortyish face framed by brown, wavy hair. The face might have been attractive but Maggie was distracted by the fact that he immediately brought it too close to hers, and wore a cologne so overpoweringly sweet it caused a tickle in her throat.

'Maggie Stearn, this is Mark Brodie, president of the chamber. Mark . . . Maggie.'

'Welcome back to Fish Creek,' Mark said, shaking her hand. 'I understand you graduated from Gibraltar High.'

'Yes, I did.'

He held her hand too long, squeezed it too hard, and she

guessed within ten seconds of their introduction that he was unattached and scouting the new female in town. He effectively monopolized her for the next five minutes, giving vibes of interest as unmistakable as his geraniumy-smelling cologne. During those five minutes he managed to confirm the fact that he was a divorcé by choice, that he owned a local dinner club called the Edgewater Inn, and that he was more than a little interested in seeing both her and her house sometime in the near future.

When he left to assume his duties as the head of the group, Maggie turned back to the table and took a drink of water to clear the taste of his cologne out of her throat. The others at her table were listening to a woman named Norma tell an anecdote about her nine-year-old son. While they were preoccupied with the story, Eric leaned back in his chair and glanced at Maggie.

'Brodie's a real go-getter,' he remarked.

'Hm.'

'And unattached.'

'Hm.'

'Runs a successful business, too.'

'Yes, he made sure I knew.'

Their eyes met and Eric's remained absolutely expressionless. He sat back with one finger hooked in the handle of his coffee cup while Maggie wondered what to make of his remarks. The waitress arrived and stepped between them to set their plates on the table.

After breakfast Mark Brodie called for quiet and took care of a couple of business items before introducing Maggie.

'Ladies and gentlemen, we have a new member with us today. She was born and raised right here in Fish Creek, graduated from Gibraltar High School and is back with us opening our newest bed and breakfast.' Mark leaned closer to the microphone. 'She's mighty pretty, too, I might add. Everybody, say hello to the new owner of Harding House, Maggie Stearn.'

She rose, feeling her face colour. How dare Brodie put his mark on her before the entire town! The entire county for that matter! Her introduction signalled the end of the breakfast and she was immediately surrounded by members who reinforced Mark's official welcome, wished her well, and invited her to call on them for any help or advice she might need. In the congenial exchange, Maggie became separated from Eric, and looked up some minutes later to see him with a group of others, donning his coat and gloves near the exit. Someone was talking to her, and someone was speaking to him as he pushed open the plate-glass door and headed outside. Just before the door closed he glanced back at Maggie, but his only farewell was a slight delay in allowing the door to close behind him.

Mark Brodie wasted no time confirming Maggie's first impression of him. He called that evening.

'Mrs Stearn? Mark Brodie.'

'Oh, hello.'

'Did you enjoy the breakfast?'

'Yes, everyone was very cordial.'

'I wanted to talk to you before you left, but you were surrounded by people. I was wondering if you'd be interested in going on a sleigh ride on Sunday evening. It's for the young people's group from Community Church and they've asked for volunteers to act as chaperones.'

Was he asking her for a date or not? How cagey of him to put it in such a way that she couldn't be sure. She decided to hedge.

'A sleigh ride – you mean there's enough snow for a sleigh ride?'

'Barely. If not, Art Swenson will take the runners off his rig and put the rubber tyres on. It starts at seven and we'll be out about two hours. What do you say?'

Maggie weighed the possibilities and decided Mark

Brodie was not her style, whether he intended the invitation as a date or not.

'I'm really sorry, but I have plans for Sunday night.'

'Oh, well, maybe some other time then,' he replied brightly, sounding not the least bit nonplussed.

'Maybe.'

'Well . . . if there's anything I can do to help you settle in here, just let me know.'

'Thank you, Mr Brodie.'

She hung up and stood beside the phone recalling his overbearing smell and his overbearing mien, and thought, *No* thank you, Mr Brodie.

He called again the next morning, his voice overtly cheerful and loud in her ear.

'Mrs Stern, it's Mark Brodie. How are you today?' He sounded like an over-zealous used-car salesman on a TV commercial.

'Fine,' she replied automatically.

'Are you busy Monday night?'

Caught off-guard, she answered truthfully, 'No.'

'There's a theatre in Sturgeon Bay. Could I take you to a movie?'

She frantically groped for a reply. 'I thought you owned a supper club. How can you get all these nights off?'

'It's closed Sundays and Mondays.'

'Oh.'

Undaunted by her sidestepping, Brodie repeated, 'So, how about the movie?'

'Ah . . . Monday?' No excuse popped into her mind. None!

'I could pick you up at six-thirty.'

'Well . . .' She felt embarrassed at her lack of excuses, but her mind remained blank.

'Six-thirty. Say yes.'

She released a nervous laugh.

'If you don't, I'll only call again.'

'Mr Brodie, I don't date.'

'All right. I'll show up at your door with supper in a brown paper bag some night. That won't be a date.'

'Mr Brod –'

'Mark.'

'Mark. I said I don't date.'

'So, pay your own admission to the movie.'

'You're very persistent, aren't you?'

'Yes, ma'am, I am. Now how about Monday?'

'Thank you, but no,' she replied firmly.

'All right. But don't be surprised when you hear from me again.'

The man had hubris enough to fill a hayloft, she thought, as she hung up.

The phone rang again on Wednesday afternoon and she answered it with an excuse all prepared. But instead of Mark Brodie, it was Eric who opened the conversation without identifying himself, 'Hi, how are you?'

She smiled broadly. 'Oh, Eric, it's you.'

'Who were you expecting?'

'Mark Brodie. He's called twice already.'

'I told you he was a go-getter.'

'He's becoming a pest.'

'You have to expect that in a town of this size that hasn't got many single women, much less pretty, rich ones.'

'Mr Severson, you're embarrassing me.'

He laughed and she felt totally at ease with him. 'Can you hold on a minute while I wash my hands?'

'Sure.'

She returned in moments, saying, 'There, that's better. I was a little pasty.'

'You're wallpapering?'

'Yes.'

'How does it look?'

'Absolutely great. Wait till you see the Belvedere Room,

it . . .' She interrupted the thought, realizing the implications of such familiarities.

'It – ?' he encouraged.

It's a dusty shade of pink and you'll never see it. We must both make sure of that. 'It's nearly finished, and the paper is going up like a dream.'

'Wonderful. So what did you decide about the truck?'

The truck. The truck. She hadn't given it another thought, but she had no other means of transporting furniture.

'If you're sure you don't mind, I'll take it.'

'Could you use a little company?'

She'd expected to simply borrow the truck and drive it herself. She stood in the kitchen feeling undermined, wondering how to answer, staring at the handle on the refrigerator door and picturing his face. When she failed to reply, he added, 'I thought, if you bought anything big you could probably use some help unloading it.'

How awkward. To object on the grounds of impropriety put motives in his mind of which he was perhaps not guilty, yet to accept might give him reason for believing something of that sort had possibilities. She decided to do the honourable thing, no matter how indelicate it sounded.

'Eric, do you think that's wise?'

'My day is free, and if it's all right with you I'll stop by Bead & Ricker and pick up something I ordered for Nancy for Christmas. They called to say it's in.'

The mere mention of Nancy acquitted them both. 'Oh . . . well, fine then.'

'What time should I be there?'

'Early, so I don't miss any of the good stuff.'

'Are you a breakfast eater?'

'Yes, but –'

'I'll pick you up at seven and we'll eat on the way. And, Maggie?'

'Yes?'

'You'd better wear boots. The heater in the old whore could be a little more efficient.'

'I will.'

'See you in the morning.'

She hung up and propped her forehead in her hands, her elbows on her knees and sat there hunched over, staring at the kitchen floor. For a full two minutes, just staring, waiting for common sense to take over, thinking stupid things about widowed women making fools of themselves.

She leapt to her feet, cursed under her breath and picked up the phone to call him back and cancel.

She slammed it back down and sat on her stool again.

You know what you're getting into here.

I'm getting into nothing. This is the last time I'll see him. Honest.

She awakened the following morning with the thought singing through her mind: I'll see him today, I'll see him! She rolled to one side, snuggling her jaw deep in the feather pillow, wondering exactly how much contact with a married man constituted a friendly liaison. She lay thinking of him – his hair, eyes, mouth – and rolled to her back with her eyes closed and her arms curled tightly over her stomach.

She dressed in the most unattractive clothes she could find – blue jeans and a grotesque gold sweatshirt that made her a walking ad for Ziebart — then ruined it all by fussing with her makeup and doing the gel routine with her hair.

His truck pulled up precisely at seven and she met him halfway down the sidewalk, bundled in boots and her pink jacket, carrying four folded blankets over her arms.

'Good morning,' he said.

'Good morning. I brought some blankets to pad the furniture with, in case I buy any.'

'Here, I'll take them.'

He took the blankets as they walked side by side to the truck.

'All set to find some buys?'

'I hope so.'

Everything so platonic on the outside, while a forbidden glow was kindled by his very presence.

He stowed the blankets in the bed of the pickup and they got under way. The sun had not risen. Inside the cab the dash lights created a dim glow and on the radio Barbra Streisand sang 'Have Yourself a Merry Little Christmas'.

'Remember the time . . .'

They talked – had there ever been a person with whom she could talk with such ease? – about favourite Christmases of the past and a particular one, in the sixth grade, when they'd both been in a Christmas pageant and had had to sing a carol in Norwegian; about making snow forts as children; about how candles are made; how many varieties of cheeses come out of Wisconsin; how giving away cheese at Christmastime had become a tradition. When they grew tired of talk, they found equal ease in silence. They listened to the music and the weather forecast – cloudy with a sixty-per cent chance of snow – and laughed together at a joke made by the deejay. They rode on in companionable silence as a new song began to play. They felt the rumble of occasional ice patches beneath the tyres, and watched ruby taillights sparkle on the highway ahead, and observed the coming of dawn – a grey, sombre dawn that made the interior of the truck feel insular and cosy.

A red-and-green neon sign appeared on their right, announcing, THE DONUT HOLE. Eric slowed the truck and turned on the blinker.

'You like doughnuts?' he asked.

'At this hour of the morning?' She pretended disgust.

He angled her a grin as he made a right-hand turn and the truck bumped into an unpaved parking lot. 'It's the best time, when they're fresh out of the grease.' A tyre dropped into a pothole and Maggie slapped the seat to keep from tipping over.

She laughed and said, 'I hope their food is better than their parking lot.'

'Trust me.'

Inside, plastic Santas and plastic wreaths decorated fake brick walls; plastic poinsettias in plastic bud vases adorned each plastic-covered booth. Eric directed Maggie to a booth against the right wall, then slid in the opposite side and unsnapped his jacket all in one motion, the way he had unsnapped his leather jacket a hundred times in days gone by.

A buxom waitress with coal-black hair came over and thumped down two thick white saucerless mugs, then splashed them full of coffee. 'It's a cold one out there this morning,' she said, leaving the thermal pot. 'You're gonna need this.'

She was gone before the coffee stopped swirling in the mugs.

Maggie smiled at the woman's retreating back, glanced at their drinks and remarked, 'I guess we ordered coffee, huh?'

'I guess so.' Picking up his mug for a first drink, Eric added, ' "The Hole" isn't classy, but it's got good country cooking.' The menus stood between the sugar jar and the napkin dispenser. Eric handed her one and suggested, 'Check out the Everything-in-the-World Omelette. It's more than enough for two if you'd like to share.'

It took Maggie a full thirty seconds to read the list of ingredients in the omelette, and by the time she finished she was bug-eyed.

'They're serious? They put all *that* in one omelette?'

'Yes, ma'am. And when it comes, it's drooping over the edge of the platter.'

'All right, you've sold me. We'll share one.'

While they waited they reminisced about Snowdays dances in high school and the time the principal dressed up like Santa Claus and Brookie had taken a dare to hold a piece of mistletoe over his head and kiss him. They refilled their coffee cups and laughed about the fact that no pieces of silverware on their table matched. When their omelette arrived they laughed even more, at its sheer size. Eric cut it and Maggie served – a delectable concoction filled with three kinds of meat, two cheeses, potatoes, onions, mushrooms, green peppers, tomatoes, broccoli and cauliflower. He ate his with two enormous homemade doughnuts, and she with toast, and neither of them heeded the fact that they were again building memories.

Back in the truck, Maggie groaned and held her stomach as the pickup jounced out of its parking spot. 'Oh, easy, please!'

'You just need tamping down,' he teased, and, doing a speed shift, tromped on the gas and fishtailed across the parking lot, bouncing both of them around like corn in a popper. Maggie's head hit the roof and she shrieked, laughing. He gunned the engine, cranked the wheel in the opposite direction and she flew from the door against his shoulder, and back again before he finally lurched to a stop at the approach to the highway.

'S . . . Severson, you're cr . . . crazy!' She was laughing so hard she could scarcely get the words out.

He was laughing, too. 'The old whore's still got some spunk in 'er yet. We'll have to take her out on the ice someday and do doughnuts.'

In their younger days all the boys had 'done doughnuts' by the dozens: driven their cars out onto the frozen lake and spun in controlled circles, leaving 'doughnuts' in the snow. Then, as now, the girls had shrieked and loved every minute of it.

Sitting in Eric's truck, laughing with him while they waited for an oncoming car from the left, Maggie experienced a flash of *déjà vu* so profound it rocked her.

Maggie, Maggie, be careful.

But Eric turned and flashed her a wide, happy smile, and she ignored the voice, teasing, 'You have a doughnut fetish, you know?'

'Yeah? So sue me.'

In her younger days she would have slid across the seat and tucked herself under his arm, and felt its weight on her girlish breast, and they would have ridden that way, with the contact ripening their want for one another.

Today, they remained apart, linked only by their eyes, knowing what was happening, feeling helpless to stop it. A car rushed by from the left, leaving a gust of sound that faded away. Eric's smile diminished to a grin and he shifted lazily to first, still with his eyes upon Maggie, then turned his attention to the road and entered the highway at a respectable speed.

They rode on for some time, sorting through a welter of feelings, wondering what to do about them. Maggie stared out her window, listening to the hum of the snow tyres on the blacktop, watching tan weeds and snowbanks pass in a blur.

'Maggie?'

She turned to find his eyes on her as they rolled down the highway. He returned his attention to the road and said, 'It just struck me how seldom I've laughed in the last few years.'

There were tens of replies Maggie might have made, but she chose to remain silent, digesting the unspoken along with the spoken. She was getting a clearer and clearer picture of his marriage, his loneliness, the loosening mortar between the bricks of his relationship with Nancy. Already he was comparing, and Maggie was clear-sighted enough to understand the implications.

In Sturgeon Bay he found the address with no trouble and they were waiting when the attendant unlocked the front door of an immense nineteenth-century house overlooking Sawyer Harbor. It had been built by a wealthy shipbuilder nearly a hundred years ago, and many of his original furnishings were still in it. With the death of a recent heir, the property had passed to those remaining who were scattered across America and had decided to sell the estate and divide the moneys.

The antiques were eclectic and well preserved. Eric watched Maggie as she moved through the rooms, making discoveries, exclaiming, 'Look at this!' She'd grab his sleeve and haul him towards a find. 'It's bird's-eye maple!' she'd exclaim, or, 'It has a burled inlay!' She touched, admired, examined, questioned, sometimes dropped to her knees to look underneath a piece. Through it all she showed an enthusiasm upon which he doted.

Nancy admired fine things, too, but in a wholly different way. She maintained a certain reserve that held her just short of animation over the small excitements of life. At times that reserve bordered on hauteur.

Then Maggie found the bed, a grand old thing made of golden oak, with a serpentine-designed headboard seven feet high, replete with scrollwork and lush bas-relief carving.

'Oh, look, Eric,' she breathed, touching it reverently, staring at its intricacies as if mesmerized. 'Oh my . . .' She ran her fingertips over the oak-leaf detailing on the footboard. 'This is why I came, isn't it?' She neither expected nor received an answer, did not even draw her eyes from the piece. From the doorway he watched her caress the wood, his thoughts trailing back years and years, to a night in Easley's orchard when she had first touched him that way. 'This is a wonderful bed. Old, sturdy, solid oak. Who do you imagine did all this carving? I can never see a piece like this without wondering about the craftsman who made it. Look, there's not a mark on it.'

'The other pieces match,' he pointed out, meandering into the room with his hands in his pockets.

'Oh, a washstand and a cheval dresser!'

'Is that what you call it? My grandma used to have furniture like this.'

He stood beside her, watching her open the doors and drawers of the other pieces.

'See here? Dovetailed drawers.'

'They won't come apart for a while.'

She knelt, opened a door and poked her head inside. Her voice trailed out hollowly, like a note from a woodwind.

'Solid oak.' She emerged and looked up at him high above her. 'See?'

He squatted beside her, adulating as expected, enjoying her more with each passing minute.

'On this piece I would set a pitcher and bowl, and I'd hang huck towels on the bar. Did I tell you I've been doing huck towelling?'

'No, you didn't,' he replied, grinning indulgently, still squatting beside her with one elbow on a knee. He had no idea what huck towelling was, but when she smiled about it the dimple in her chin became as pronounced as if carved by the same artist who'd done the bedroom suite.

'I had a devil of a time finding patterns. Oh, won't they look lovely hanging on that bar?' On her knees, with eyes agleam, she turned to face him. 'I want the whole set. Let's find the man.'

'You didn't check the price.'

'I don't need to. I'd want it if it were ten thousand dollars.'

'And it's not a four-poster or a brass bed.'

'It's better than a four-poster or a brass bed.' She fixed her eyes on his. 'Sometimes when a thing is right you simply must have it.'

He did not look away.

The rose in her cheeks matched that in his. Their hearts experienced a beat of disquiet. In that unwary moment they let their susceptibilities show, then he gathered his common sense and said, 'All right. I'll get the man.'

As he began to rise she grabbed his arm. 'But, Eric?' Her brow furrowed. 'Will the old whore hold it all?'

He burst out laughing. The vulgar name was so inappropriate coming from her.

'What's so funny?' she demanded.

'Just you.' He covered her hand on his arm and gave it a squeeze. 'You're a delightful lady, Maggie Stearn.'

She bought more than a truckful. They arranged for delivery of the pieces they could not take and hauled away only the three she most prized. Maggie supervised the loading with amusing zealousness. 'Be careful of that knob! Don't rest the drawer up against the side of the truck. Are you sure it's tied tightly enough?'

Eric glanced over at her and grinned. 'Just because you're a ragman and I'm a stinkpotter doesn't mean I can't tie a decent knot. I've sailed a boat, too, in my time.'

From the opposite side of the truck she gave a mock nod, and replied, 'I beg your pardon, Mr Severson.'

One final yank on the knot and he said, 'Come on, let's go.'

They had spent the hours at the estate sale blithely forgetting his marital status, but their next stop would be at Bead & Ricker, and his mission there brought back reality with a sharp sting. By the time they pulled up at the kerb before the store a sombreness had fallen upon them both. He shifted to neutral and sat for a moment with his hands on the wheel, as if about to say something, then seemed to change his mind.

'I'll be right back,' he said, opening the truck door. 'It shouldn't take me long.'

She watched him move away – the one she could not have – loving his stride, the way his hair brushed his upturned leather collar, the way his clothing fitted, the colours he chose to wear. He entered the jewellery store and she sat with her gaze fixed on the window display – scarlet velvet and gems beneath bright window lights, trimmed with holly leaves. He had ordered his wife something custom-made for Christmas. She, Maggie, had no business feeling despondent knowing this, yet she did. What was he buying Nancy? A woman that beautiful was made to wear things that glistened and shone.

Maggie sighed and turned her attention across the street, to the entrance of a hardware store where two old women chatted. One of them wore an old-fashioned woollen scarf and the other carried a cloth shopping bag with handles. One pointed up the street and the other turned to look in that direction.

Maggie closed her eyes and dropped her head back. *You shouldn't be here.* She lifted her head and caught sight of Eric's black leather gloves lying beside her. Gloves – shaped like his hands, the fingers curled, the fleece lining undoubtedly flattened from the contours of his palms.

Only a very foolish woman would have the urge to touch them, to slip them on her own hands.

A very foolish woman did. She picked them up and put them on, surrounding her hands with the worn leather that had surrounded his. Her hands felt dwarfed; she closed her fists, savouring the contact, in lieu of that which was forbidden her.

Eric came out of the jewellery store, and she put the gloves back where he'd left them. He climbed into the truck and tossed a silver foil bag on the seat. Maggie's eyes involuntarily followed it and glimpsed inside a small box wrapped in identical foil, trimmed with a red ribbon. She looked away, at a starburst in the side window where a rock had hit it long ago. She waited for the truck to begin rolling. When it didn't, she glanced back at Eric. His bare hands rested on the steering wheel and he stared straight ahead. The expression on his face resembled that of a man who's just heard a doctor say, all we can do now is wait. For a full minute he sat, unmoving. Finally he said, 'I got her an emerald ring. She's crazy about emeralds.'

He turned his head and their eyes locked.

'I didn't ask,' Maggie replied quietly.

'I know you didn't.'

In the silence that followed neither of them seemed able to summon the wherewithal to look away.

It was back, as strong as before. Stronger. And they were courting disaster here.

He turned to stare out the windshield again until the silence grew unbearable, then, letting the breath rush out between his teeth, he fell back into the corner of the seat. He propped an elbow on the window ledge and put the pad of his thumb against his lips, his face turned away from her. There he sat, staring at the sidewalk with the unvoiced admission jangling between them.

She didn't know what to say, do, think. As long as neither of them had voiced or displayed their attraction overtly, they'd been safe. But they were safe no longer, though not a definitive word had been spoken, not a touch exchanged.

Finally he sighed, centred himself behind the wheel and put the truck in gear.

'I'd better get you home,' he said resignedly.

Chapter 10

They drove back to Fish Creek in constrained silence. She understood clearly: his displeasure lay with himself, not with her. He was the picture of a man torn. He drove the entire twenty-five miles scarcely moving a muscle, angling a shoulder into his corner of the seat, frowning at the highway. Not until they turned onto the switchback did he finally square his shoulders and settle himself behind the wheel. He parked the truck at the top of her walk, grabbed his gloves and got out without a word. She did likewise and joined him at the rear of the truck, waiting while he dropped the tailgate.

'Would you mind helping me carry it upstairs?' she asked, breaking their lengthy silence.

'It's heavy for a woman.'

'I can handle it.'

'All right, but if it's too heavy, say so.'

She would not have said so had her discs slipped, although she couldn't have said why. A return to business between them, perhaps. Two delivery persons hauling freight, putting it in place with the impersonal demeanour of United Parcel Service employees.

They hauled up the washstand first, then the cheval dresser, marching back downstairs in dual silence – hers careful, his testy. She knew instinctively she would not see him again after today. His decision had been made in the truck in front of Bead & Ricker with an emerald ring between them. They took the bed up last, the headboard and footboard bolted together onto a pair of two-by-eights. When they'd set it down, he said, 'If you've got some tools I'll put it together for you.'

'That's not necessary. I can do it myself.'

He confronted her head-on for the first time since their miserable ride back. 'Maggie, the damned headboard weighs sixty pounds by itself!' he snapped. 'If it falls over and splits you can kiss your antique value good-bye. Now get me a wrench and a screwdriver.'

She got him a wrench and a screwdriver, then stood back and watched him bend on one knee and use the tools to separate the pieces of the bed. He worked at it with singular intensity, his collar turned up, head bent, shoulders hunched within the black leather jacket.

He freed one set of bolts, moved to the other and applied the screwdriver again.

'Here, hold this or it'll fall,' he ordered without a glance in her direction.

She held the pieces upright as they came free of their support block. He rose, knees cracking, slipped the screwdriver into his rear pocket and moved about the room, laying the wooden side rails in place on the hardwood floor and coming finally to relieve her of the footboard, carrying it six feet away before kneeling again to hook the pieces together.

She tried not to watch him, to dismiss the attraction of his form as he bent and knelt while performing the peculiarly masculine task.

When the frame was assembled, he stood in the middle of it. 'Well . . . that's it. How about the mattresses?' He glanced briefly at her single bed at the edge of the room.

'They're stored in the garage. Daddy can help me with them.'

'You're sure?'

'Yes. He won't mind.'

'Well then . . .' He drew his gloves from his jacket pockets, making no second offers. 'I guess I'd better go.'

'Thank you, Eric. I really appreciate the use of the truck and all your help.'

'You got a good buy,' he stated with finality as they left the room.

'Yes, I did.'

They descended the steps side by side, rounded the newel and headed for the rear kitchen in an awkward emotional void. He moved toward the door straightaway, and she opened it politely, saying, 'Thanks again.'

'Yup,' he replied, clipped, impersonal. 'See you around.'

She closed the door firmly, and thought, well, that's that. The decision has been made. *Have some tea, Maggie. Go up and admire your new furniture. Wipe today from your mind.*

But the house seemed gloomy and she suddenly had little taste for the antiques that had been so exhilarating earlier in the day. She wandered to the kitchen sink, turned on the hot water and clacked a kettle beneath it, switched on the stove burner and put the water on to heat; got down the teapot from the top of the cupboards and desultorily stared into a canister of tea bags, caring little what flavour they were.

Outside, Eric mounted the steps at a jog, vehemently slammed the tailgate shut, strode around to the driver's side, flung himself behind the wheel and heard the seatcover rip. He rolled to one buttock, reached behind himself and muttered, 'Shit.'

He skewed at the waist to look. Maggie's screwdriver had torn a three-corner rip in the vinyl.

'Shit!' – more exasperatedly, thumping the butts of both hands on the steering wheel. So angry. So trapped by his own emotions.

He sat for a long minute, his forearms on the wheel, gloved thumbs pressed to the corners of his eyes, admitting to himself what he was really angry about.

You're acting like a damned heel, taking it out on her when it isn't her fault! If you're going to walk out of here and never come back you can at least do it gracefully.

He lifted his head. The wind had picked up. It rattled the

loose blade of a windshield wiper and spun last week's snow across the road. He scarcely noticed as he stared straight ahead, loath to go back to her door, yet spoiling for one last glimpse of her.

What do you want, Severson?

What does it matter what I want? All that matters is what I have to do.

Abruptly he started the truck engine and left it running: assurance that he'd be back up this hill in sixty seconds or less, heading home where he belonged.

At her door he knocked hard, as hard as his heart seemed to be knocking in his chest. She opened it with a tea bag in her hand and they stood like a pair of cardboard cutouts with their gazes locked.

'This is yours,' he said finally, handing her the screwdriver.

'Oh . . .' She took it. 'Thank you.'

She spoke so quietly he could scarcely hear the words, then stood with her head hanging while he studied her downturned face.

'Maggie, I'm sorry.' His voice held a note of tenderness now.

'It's all right. I understand.' She wound the tea bag string around the screwdriver, her eyes still downcast.

'No, it's not all right. I treated you as if you've done something wrong, and you haven't. It's me. It's . . .' At his hips his gloved fingers closed, then opened. 'I'm going through some troubled times and I have no right to drag you into them. I just wanted you to know I won't bother you again.'

She nodded disconsolately and dropped her hands to her sides. 'Yes, I think that's best.'

'I'm going to . . .' He gestured vaguely toward the truck. 'I'm going to go home and do what you said. I'm going to concentrate on the good. What I mean to say is, I want my marriage to work.'

'I know you do,' she whispered.

He watched her struggle to hide her emotions, but her cheeks took on a flush. The sight of it made his throat and chest feel as they had one time when the *Mary Deare* had got caught in a sudden summer gale and he thought she was going down. He spread his gloved fingers wide and pressed them to his thighs to keep from touching her.

'Well, I just wanted you to know that. I didn't feel right, leaving the way I did.'

She nodded again and tried to hide the fact that tears were springing to her eyes.

'Well, listen . . .' He took one step back and said huskily, 'You . . . you have a nice Christmas, and I hope everything works out with this place and your new business.'

She lifted her head and he saw the tears glimmering in the corners of her eyes. 'Thanks,' she said, forcing a timorous smile. 'You have a wonderful Christmas, too.'

He backed to the edge of the steps and for a heart-wrenching moment their gazes spoke clearly of the want and need they were feeling. Her brown eyes appeared magnified by the tears that trembled on her lashes. His blue ones showed the depth of restraint he placed upon himself to keep from taking her in his arms. He closed and opened his hands once more.

'Good-bye.' His lips moved, but no sound came out, then he turned and walked resolutely from her life.

During the days that followed, he avoided the post office at noon, bought his groceries anywhere but at the Fish Creek General Store and ate his lunches at home. Mornings, however, he continued his trips to the bakery and on his way down the hill often fantasized about walking in and finding her there, picking out a morning sweet, turning at the sound of the bell on the door and smiling when she saw him enter.

But she preferred eggs for breakfast; he knew that now.

The bay froze over completely and he rode his snowmobile out to go ice fishing every day. Often, sitting on a folding stool on the ice, staring down the hole at the deep water, he thought of Maggie, wondered if she liked fried fish and remembered her stealing a piece of the silvery herring from the wooden barrel in her father's cooler. He thought about taking her a fresh lake trout; after all, he caught more than he could use. But that would only be an excuse to see her, he admitted, and took the trout to his mother and Barb instead.

He made a toboggan for Mike and Barb's kids for Christmas and gave it six coats of marine varnish. When it was done and he showed it to Nancy, she pushed her glasses down her nose, gave it a far shorter perusal than she gave her finished makeup each morning, and said, 'Mmm . . . nice, dear,' before returning to her bookwork.

He cut down two spruce trees on Mike's property, put one in a stand for Ma and hauled the other one home. When it was standing in the corner of the living room, aromatic and pungent, he stood before it with his hands in his pockets, wishing someone were there to share it with. On the weekend, when Nancy came home, they trimmed the tree together with clear, plain twinkle lights, clear blown-glass balls and clear glass icicles – the same decorations they used every year. The year she had come home with them – purchased in some fancy store at The Plaza in Kansas City – he had withheld his misgivings all the while they decorated the tree. When it was done, he'd studied it in dismay and said, 'It's a little colourless, isn't it?'

'Don't be déclassé, darling,' Nancy had chided. 'It's elegant.'

He didn't want an elegant tree. He wanted one like Ma's, hung with multicoloured lights and trimmings he and his brothers and sister had made in elementary school; and some that had been on Ma's tree when she was a little girl; and others that had been given to the family by friends over the years. Instead he had a tree that left him as cold as the teakwood fruit Nancy kept in the middle of the kitchen table. So, often on weekday evenings he went out to Ma's or to Mike's and enjoyed their trees, and ate popcorn and home-smoked fish and pulled taffy and teased the little ones and held them on his lap in their feet pyjamas and watched the tree lights tint their faces many colours and listened to them speak with awe about Santa Claus.

Staring at the tree lights, Eric thought of Maggie and wondered what Christmas would have been like if he'd married her instead of Nancy. Would he have children of his own? Would they be together now near their own Christmas tree? He pictured Maggie in the big house with its bay windows and gleaming floors and the kitchen with the old, scarred table, and recalled the day he and Deitz had had coffee with her, and he missed her terribly.

During those same days and nights, she thought of him, too, and her sense of loss lingered, unaccountable though it was, for how could one lose what one had not possessed? She had lost nothing except the daily longing for Phillip which had magically dissipated since her return to Fish Creek. With some shock Maggie realized it was true – the feelings of self-pity and deprivation had mellowed into velvet memories of their happier times together. Yes, the loss of Phillip hurt less and less, but the one she missed now was Eric.

As the holidays approached she spent many bittersweet evenings recalling the recent occasions they'd shared: the first night in the dark, poking through the house with a flashlight; the day he found her painting in the Belvedere Room, and the snow had begun outside; the day they'd eaten their sandwiches on the bench on Main Street; their trip to Sturgeon Bay. When had it begun, this insidious building of memories? And was he remembering, too? She had only to recall their last minutes together to feel certain he was.

But Eric Severson was spoken for, and she tried to bear that in mind as she filled her days and prepared for Christmas.

She called her father, and Roy came to help her carry in the mattresses from the garage, and move the twin bed down to the maid's room, and to rejoice with her over the new furniture for the Belvedere Room, and to praise her wallpapering efforts.

She made up the great hand-carved bed for the first time with eyelet sheets and puffy down comforter, then fell across it to stare at the ceiling and miss a man she had no right to miss.

Mark Brodie called and invited her out to his club for dinner and she declined his invitation once again. He persisted, and she finally said, 'All right. I'll go.'

He did his best to impress her. A very private booth in a remote corner with discreet and gracious servers, linens, candlelight, crystal, champagne, escargots, Caesar salad mixed tableside, hot popovers, fresh abalone (which he'd had flown in especially for the occasion since it was not on the regular menu), and afterward Bananas Foster, again flamed tableside and served in fluted-stem glasses.

The entire meal, however, seemed flavoured by his cologne.

He was attentive to a fault and a brisk conversationalist, but he liked to talk about his own success. He drove a Buick Park Avenue that smelled inside exactly like him – spicy sweet and suffocating. When he took her home she almost leapt from it in relief and gulped the cold night air like a person coming up for the third time.

At her door he took her shoulders and kissed her. French-kissed her. For damn near half a minute while she tested herself, resisting the impulse to shove him away, spit and wipe her lips. He wasn't a masher. He wasn't bad-looking, unkempt, obnoxious or ill-mannered.

But he wasn't Eric.

When the kiss ended he said, 'I want to see you again.'

'I'm sorry, Mark, but I don't think so.'

'Why?' He sounded exasperated.

'I'm not ready for this.'

'When will you be? I'll wait.'

'Mark, please . . .' She drew away and he released her without further coercion.

'If I may be so gauche, I'm not a fortune hunter, Maggie.'

'I never thought you were.'

'Then why not have some fun together? You're single. I'm single. This town doesn't have a lot of others like us.'

'Mark, I have to go in now. It was a lovely dinner, and you have a lovely restaurant and a great future, I'm sure. But I have to go in now.'

'I'm going to break you down, Maggie. I'm not giving up.'

'Goodnight, Mark. Thank you for tonight.'

She called Brookie the next day and they made a trip to Green Bay to shop for lace curtains and Christmas presents, and to have lunch.

She admitted, 'Brookie, I'm lonely. Do you know any single men?'

Brookie said, 'What about Mark Brodie?'

Maggie replied, 'I let him kiss me last night.'

'And?'

'Did you ever eat a mouthful of geraniums?'

Brookie choked on her soup and ended up doubled over the bowl with laughter and tears and split peas nearly doing her in.

Maggie ended up laughing, too.

When Brookie could speak again she asked, 'Well, did you go in afterward and make meatballs?'

'No.'

'Then maybe you ought to ask him to change cologne.'

Maggie thought about it the next time he called and she turned him down. And the next . . . and the next.

* * *

Katy called and said she'd be heading home on December 20, right after her morning classes. Maggie put up her tree in the parlour and made fancy cookies and a rum-soaked fruitcake, and wrapped gifts and told herself it didn't matter that she had no man of her own to buy for this year. There were her father and mother and Katy and Brookie. Four people who loved her. She should thank her blessings.

The weather warnings began on Tuesday morning but sceptics, meeting on the street, grinned and reminded one another, 'They said the last two blizzards were headed our way, but we barely got enough snow to keep the winterkill off the shrubs.'

The snow began at noon, sweeping out of Canada across Green Bay, fine shards that skittered like live things across ice-slicked roads and grew into a biting force mothered by fearsome thirty-mile-an-hour winds. By two o'clock schools closed. By four o'clock businesses followed suit. By seven o'clock maintenance crews had been pulled off the roads.

Eric retired at ten P.M. but was awakened an hour later by the shrill of his bedside telephone.

'Hello?' he mumbled, still half-asleep.

'Eric?'

'Yeah?'

'Bruce Thorson at the sheriff's office in Sturgeon Bay. We've got a critical situation on our hands, travellers stranded on the roads all over the county and we've had to pull the ploughs off. We could use every able-bodied snowmobiler we can get.'

Eric squinted at the clock, sat up and ran a hand through his hair in the dark. 'Sure. Where do you want me?'

'We'll be dispatching Fish Creek volunteers through the Gibraltar Fire Station. Bring any emergency equipment you can spare.'

'Right. I'll be down there in fifteen minutes.'

He hit the floor hurrying. On his way downstairs he

buttoned his shirt and zipped his pants. He put water in the microwave for instant coffee, found a large black garbage bag and threw in candles, matches, flashlight, newspapers, a bobcap, Nancy's snowmobile suit and helmet (which she'd worn exactly once), a sack containing two leftover doughnuts, a bag of miniature Butterfinger candy bars and an apple. He pulled on his own silver snowmobile suit, boots, gloves, ski mask and helmet. A quick fill for the thermos, topped off by two glugs of brandy and he stepped outside looking like an astronaut ready for a moonwalk.

In the shelter of the house the storm appeared overestimated. Then he moved off the back steps and sank into a drift to his hips. Halfway to the garage, the maelstrom hit him full in the face and he floundered, falling sideways as he struggled on. He shivered and waded to the garage door where he was forced to shovel with his feet and hands to find the handles. Inside, the building was frigid – always more frigid on concrete than in the insulating snow. The sound of his own felt-lined boots on the icy floor reverberated in his covered ears. He filled the gas tank on his machine, tied a shovel and the bag of emergency supplies on the passenger seat, started the engine, and pulled outside. Already it was a relief to put his back to the wind while closing the overhead door. Shrugging and shivering, he faced the wind once more, boarded his machine and lowered his Plexiglas face shield, realizing it would be a long time before he climbed back into a warm bed.

The winds had escalated to near gale force, driving the snow in sheets that obliterated everything. Even from a block away, the red-and-blue Christmas lights on Main Street were invisible. Not until he was directly below them did Eric make out the eerily illuminated rings of blue and green in the swirling haze overhead. He drove down the middle of a Main Street which had disappeared, using the Christmas lights to guide him. Occasionally, on either side, a blob of white light would pierce the haze – a sign for a shop, or a streetlight.

Halfway to the fire station he heard the roar of an engine off to his left and glanced over his shoulder at a spectre looking much like himself, only dressed in black and riding a Polaris. He raised one hand and the other driver saluted back, then the two drove side by side until out of the swirling white maze the red light of the fire station guided them in.

Two other snowmobiles were parked out front. Eric left his machine idling. He threw a leg over the seat, raised his face shield and called, 'Hell of a time to be rolled out of bed, 'ey, Dutch?'

'God, you said it!' Dutch's muffled voice came from behind his face shield before he flipped it up. 'She's a real piss-cutter, ain't she?' Dutch ploughed his way to Eric and the men slogged toward the brick building together.

Inside, Einer Seaquist was parcelling out emergency supplies to two other drivers. To one of them, he ordered, 'Get over to Doc Braith's as quick as possible. He's got insulin for you to take out to Walt McClusky on County Road A. And you, Brian,' he ordered the second driver, 'take County Road F down to Highway 57. They closed it at the other end, but as close as we can figure there are three cars out there that never reached their destinations. Dutch, Eric, glad you boys could help out. You can take your pick – County Road EE or Highway 42. Damn drivers don't know when to pull into a motel. We think we've got stalled cars still out there. If you find anybody, do the best you can. Take 'em anywhere – motel lobbies, private homes, or bring 'em back here. You need any supplies?'

'Nope, got what I need,' Eric replied.

'So do I,' Dutch seconded. 'I'll take EE.'

'I'll take 42,' Eric said.

They left the fire hall together, ploughing down the steps where the wind had already obliterated the tracks they'd made coming in. Straddling the seat of his machine Eric felt the reassuring vibrations of the engine rise up to meet him and thought of how much faith men put in machinery. Dutch, too, straddled his seat, reached for his faceguard and shouted, 'Steer clear of barbed wire, Severson!'

'You, too, Winkler!' Eric returned, pulling his ski mask down and dropping his own faceguard.

They put their machines in gear and drove side by side, westward, along the length of Main Street, beneath the murky Christmas lights, then through the break in the bluff where Highway 42 climbed out of town. Up above, in open country, they followed the telephone poles, and sometimes the tops of fence posts, the dip and rise of their headlights piercing only a limited distance ahead. In spots they glimpsed the highway, swept clean by the merciless winds; on other stretches they'd not have known the blacktop was beneath them without the posts and poles to mark it. Once their headlights picked out a mound they thought was a car. Eric spotted it first and pointed. But when they pulled up and started digging, they found it was only the boulder dubbed 'the Lord's Rock', upon which the message, *Jesus Saves*, had created a landmark along Highway 42 for as long as Eric could remember.

On their machines again they drove as a pair until reaching the spot where Highway 42 intersected with County Road EE. There, with a salute of farewell, Dutch veered off to the left and disappeared into the storm.

After Dutch's departure, the temperature seemed colder, the wind keener, the snow sharper as it struck Eric's face mask. His lone headlight, beaming first high, then low, like that of a train engine, seemed to be searching for the mate that had been beside it until now. The snowmobile rocked, sometimes bumped, sometimes flew, and he gripped the throttle harder, welcoming the shimmy of motion that climbed his arms and vibrated beneath his thighs – the only other sign of life in the vast, swirling night.

In time his limbs grew weary of shifting and balancing.

The thumb of his left hand began to freeze. His eyes began to hurt and he grew dizzy from squinting into the kaleidoscopic motion before him. Monotony dulled his senses, and he feared he might have passed a stalled car without observing it. A stretch of blacktop swept along his left flank and he swerved toward it, realigning himself with the centre of the road. Deep in his mind, beyond conscious thought, echoed Dutch's warning, 'Steer clear of barbed wire!' Unwary snowmobilers had been decapitated hitting barbed-wire fences. Others who lived through it wore a red necklace of scars for the rest of their lives.

He wondered where Nancy was. She hadn't called tonight. Fargo, if he remembered right. Did the storm system stretch that far?

He hoped Ma was all right, that her fuel oil barrel was full. Damn ornery woman wouldn't let Mike and him put in a new furnace for her. *The oil burner heats as good as ever*, she insisted stubbornly. Well, when this was over, he was going to buy her a furnace whether she liked it or not. She was getting too old to live in one hot room and five cold ones.

He hoped everything was okay with the baby Barb was carrying. This would be one hell of a time to sprout any trouble along those lines with only one hospital in the whole county, and it clear down in Sturgeon Bay.

And Maggie . . . all alone in that big house with the wind howling in off the lake and the old rafters creaking beneath the weight of the snow. Was she sleeping in that carved bed they'd carried in together? Did she still miss her husband on nights like this?

Eric might have missed the car altogether, had the driver not been wise enough to tie a red scarf onto a ski and ram it upright into a snowdrift. The wind snapped the scarf out at a right angle to the earth, it and the pole the only visible clues that a vehicle lay submerged nearby. Speeding toward it, Eric rose anxiously on one knee, his heart hammering. People died of asphyxiation in stalled cars. Or of exposure when they panicked and left them. He could not tell hood from trunk; it was all one smooth mound. No engine ran, no door had sliced off the top of a snowdrift. No snow had been cleared from around the tailpipe.

He had once pulled a drowning child out of the water at Stalling's Beach, and the feelings of that day came back – controlled terror, fear of being too late, adrenalin forming a stricture around his chest. He experienced a sense of phantasm, as if he were moving through molasses when he was actually covering distance like a cyclone, jumping off his machine before it had quite stopped moving, fumbling to free the shovel, wading through waist-deep snow in the beam of his headlight, fighting the elements with demonic passion.

'Hello!' he shouted as he gouged shovelfuls of snow and speared through with one hand to ascertain it was, indeed, a car underneath.

He thought he heard a muffled, 'Hello,' but it might have been the wind.

'Hold on! I'm coming! Don't open the window!' Impatiently he threw back his faceguard, scooped five times, hit metal, scooped some more.

This time he heard the voice more clearly. Crying. Distressed. Wailing muffled words he couldn't make out.

The shovel struck a window, and he shouted again, 'Don't open anything yet!' With a gloved hand he scraped the snow from a small square of glass and peered through at a blurred face and heard a woman's voice crying, 'Oh, God, you found me . . .'

'Okay, just crack the window to let some air in while I free the rest of the door,' he ordered.

Seconds later he opened the car door, leaned in and found a panicky young woman with tears streaming down her face, dressed in a jean jacket, with a leg warmer tied around her head, a pair of grey socks covering her hands, and various sweaters and shirts tucked around her lap and legs.

'Are you all right?' He removed his helmet and ski mask so she could see his face.

She was sobbing and could hardly speak, 'Oh God . . . I w . . . was . . . so . . . scared.'

'Did you have any heat?'

'Until I r . . . ran out of g . . . gas.'

'How are your feet and hands? Can you move your fingers?' He bit off his gloves, unzipped a pocket of his snowmobile suit and pulled out a small orange plastic packet. He opened it with his teeth and slipped out a white paper pouch. 'Here, this is a chemical hand warmer.' He scrubbed it between his knuckles as if it were a dirty sock. 'All you have to do is agitate it to get it warm.' Kneeling, he reached for her hand, pulled off the sock and a thin wool glove underneath. He put the pouch in her palm, folded her hand between his own much larger ones, and brought them to his lips to blow on her fingers. 'Move your fingers for me so I know you can.' She wiggled them and he smiled into her teary eyes. 'Good. Feel that heat starting?' She nodded miserably and sniffed, childlike, while tears continued streaking down her cheeks.

'Keep it in your glove and keep squishing it around. In a minute your hands will be toasty.' After finding a pouch for her other hand he inquired, 'Now, how about those feet?'

'I can't f . . . feel them any m . . . more.'

'I've got warmers for them, too.'

She had pulled two pairs of leg warmers over her thin leather flats. Removing them, he asked, 'Where are your boots?'

'I . . . left them at sch . . . school.'

'In Wisconsin, in December?'

'You s . . . sound like my g . . . grandma,' she replied, making a feeble attempt at rescuing her humour.

He grinned, finding two larger pouches, agitating them to generate the chemical heat. 'Well, sometimes grandmas know best.' In moments he had the pouches against her feet, and a pair of thick wool socks holding them in place, and had forced her to drink a good shot of brandy-laced coffee, which made her choke and cough.

'Ugh, that stuff's awful!' she exclaimed, wiping her mouth.

'I have a spare snowmobile suit. Can you get it on alone?'

'Yes, I th . . . think so. I'll try.'

'Good girl.'

He produced a snowmobile suit, boots, mitts, mask and helmet, but she moved so slowly he helped her. 'Young lady,' he chided while doing so, 'next time you go out on the highway in the middle of winter I hope you'll be better prepared.'

Her sniffles had stopped and she'd warmed enough to become slightly defensive. 'How was I supposed to know it got this bad? I've lived in Seattle my whole life.'

'Seattle?' he repeated, pulling the woollen mask onto her head and snapping a helmet strap under her chin. 'You drove all the way from Seattle?'

'No, just from Chicago. I go to Northwestern. I'm on my way home for Christmas.'

'To where?'

'Fish Creek. My mother runs an inn there.'

Seattle, Chicago, Fish Creek? Standing beside the stranded automobile with the wind whipping whirlwinds of snow about them, he peered at what was visible of the girl's face behind the mask and helmet.

'Well, I'll be damned,' he murmured.

'What?'

'You wouldn't be Katy Stearn, would you?'

Her surprise was evident even behind the ski mask. Her eyes opened wide and stared at him.

'You know me?'

'I know your mother. By the way, I'm Eric.'

'You're Eric? Eric Severson?'

It was his turn to be surprised that Maggie's daughter would know his last name.

'She went to the prom with you!'

He laughed. 'Yes, as a matter of fact, she did.'

'Wow . . .' Katy said, awed at the coincidence.

He laughed again and said, 'Well, Katy, let's get you home.'

He slammed her car door and led her towards the snowmobile, blazing a trail for her. Before boarding, he asked, 'You ever ridden one of these things before?'

'No.'

'Well, it's a little more fun when the windchill isn't fifty-five below zero, but we'll get there as fast and warm as we can. By the way, are you hungry?'

'Famished.'

'Apple or candy bar?' he asked, digging in his emergency bag.

'Candy bar,' she replied.

He produced the Butterfinger and started the engine while she bit into it, then straddled the seat and ordered, 'Get on behind me and put your arms around my waist. All you have to do is lean to the inside when we go into a turn. That way we'll stay on the skis, okay?'

'Okay.' She climbed on board and wrapped her arms around his waist.

'And stay awake!'

'I will.'

'All set?' he called over his shoulder.

'All set. But Eric?'

'What?'

'Thank you. Thanks a lot. I don't think I've ever been so scared in my life.'

He thumped her mittened hands in reply. 'Hang on!' he ordered, putting the machine in gear and heading for Maggie's house.

The name thrummed through his head – Maggie. Maggie. Maggie – while he gripped the throttle and felt her daughter's firm hold around his waist. Supposing they'd been a little less lucky in Easley's orchard, the girl behind him could have been theirs.

He pictured Maggie in her kitchen, lifting aside the lace curtain on the door and peering out into the storm. Pacing the room with a sweater wrapped over her shoulders. Checking the window again. Calling Chicago to inquire about Katy's departure time. Making tea which probably went undrunk. Calling the state highway patrol office to learn the ploughs had been pulled off the road and trying not to panic. Pacing again with nobody to share her burden of worry.

Maggie, honey, she's okay. I'm bringing her to you, so keep the faith.

The wind was an enemy blowing straight at their faces. Eric hunkered behind the windshield, rode the drifts with his leg muscles burning. But he didn't care – he was heading for Maggie's house.

The snow fell heavier, thicker, more disorienting. He followed the telephone poles and gripped the throttle and knew he'd find the way. He was heading for Maggie's house.

He put the cold from his mind, concentrated instead on a warm kitchen with a long scarred table, and a woman with auburn hair waiting behind a white lace curtain, throwing open the door and her arms when she saw them coming. He had vowed to stay away from her, but fate had dictated otherwise, and his heart filled with sweet exhilaration at the thought of seeing her again.

Maggie had expected Katy around five or six o'clock, seven at the latest. By nine she'd called Chicago. By ten she'd called the highway patrol. By eleven she'd called her dad who could do little to ease her concern. By midnight, still alone and pacing, she was near tears.

At one o'clock, she gave in and went to bed in the maid's room – the closest one to the kitchen door. The attempt at sleep proved futile, and she got up after less than an hour, put on a quilted robe, made tea and sat at the table with the window curtain thrown up over the rod. She propped her feet on a chair seat and stared out at the white vortex whirling around the verandah light.

Please let her be all right. I can't lose her, too.

Eventually she dozed, her head propped on a swaying arm. She awakened at 1:20 to a faint faraway sound, a dull rumble approaching on the road above. A snowmobile! She put her face to the window, cupping a hand around her eyes as the sound grew louder. A headlight scanned her arborvitaes, then swept the sky like a searchlight as the machine seemed to climb the opposite side of the drift. Suddenly the light became real. A machine appeared atop the great curl of snow, then took a steep downward plunge and headed straight for the back door.

Maggie was up and running before the engine stopped.

She threw open the door as a rider swung off the rear of the seat and a muffled voice called, 'Mother!'

'Katy?' Maggie stepped out into snow up to her knees. The creature ploughing towards her was covered in silver and black from head to foot, her face hidden by a plastic shield, but her voice was unmistakable.

'Oh, Mom, I made it!'

'Katy, darling, I've been so worried.' Tears of relief stung Maggie's eyes as the two exchanged an awkward hug, hampered by Katy's bulky clothing.

'My car skidded off the road . . . I was so scared . . . but Eric found me.'

'Eric?'

Maggie pulled back and looked at the driver who'd cut the engine and was swinging off the seat of the sled. He was clad in silver from head to foot, his face shielded as he moved towards the verandah steps. Reaching them, he pushed up his face shield, revealing three holes in a black ski mask. But there was no mistaking those eyes, those beautiful blue eyes, and the mouth she had recently watched at close range, drinking from a milk carton.

'She's okay, Maggie. You'd better go inside.'

She stared at the unearthly creature and felt her heartbeat grow erratic. 'Eric . . . you? . . . why? . . . how? . . .'

'Go on inside, Maggie, you're freezing.'

They all thumped inside and Eric closed the door. He pulled off his helmet and mask while Katy talked nonstop. 'The drifting got so bad, and it was blowing so hard you couldn't see anything, and then the car spun out and I hit the ditch, and I sat there with only a tablespoon of gas left and . . .' While Katy prattled she futilely tried to remove her helmet, still wearing thick gloves. Finally she cut herself short and demanded, 'Damn it! Will *somebody* help me get this thing off!' Eric stepped forward to help, laying his own helmet on the table before unsnapping hers and pulling it off her head along with her mask.

Katy's face emerged beneath a mop of flattened hair. Her lips were cold-burned, her nose red, her eyes snapping with excitement now that the danger was over. She flung herself into her mother's arms.

'Gol, Mom, I've never been so happy to be home in my whole life!'

'Katy . . .' Maggie's eyes closed as she hugged Katy close. 'It's been the longest night of my life.' Breast to breast, they rocked, until Katy said, 'But, Mom?'

'What?'

'I gotta go to the bathroom so bad, if I don't get out of this moonsuit pretty soon I'm going to embarrass myself.'

Maggie laughed and stepped back, reaching to help her daughter with the trio of zippers on the one-piece suit. They seemed to be everywhere, down the front and up both ankles.

'Here, I'll do that,' Eric said, nudging Maggie aside. 'You've got snow in your slippers. You'd better get it out.'

He went down on one knee and helped Katy negotiate the

ankle zippers and untie her thick boots, while Maggie went to the kitchen sink and dumped the snow from her slippers. She dried her feet on a hand towel while Eric helped Katy strip off the ungainly snowmobile suit.

'Hurry!' she pleaded, dancing in place. The suit came off and she hit for the bathroom, stocking-footed.

Eric and Maggie watched her go, amused.

Around the corner the door slammed and Katy yelled, '*You* can laugh! He wasn't feeding you coffee and brandy for the last hour!'

At the kitchen sink, Maggie turned to face Eric, the laughter melting away gradually to be replaced by a caring glow as she studied him with her lips tipped up softly.

'You didn't just happen to be out for a ride in this blizzard.'

'No. The sheriff's office called for volunteer rescuers.'

'How long have you been out?'

'A couple of hours.'

She moved towards him while he stood before the door looking twice his size in the silver suit and the felt-lined boots. His hair was dishevelled, he needed a shave, and into his ruddy cheeks was pressed the knit weave of his face mask. Even rumpled, he was her ideal.

He watched her cross the room to him, a mother who had kept vigil through the wee hours, barefooted, wearing a quilted rose-coloured robe, her face devoid of makeup, her hair hanging lank and curlless, and he thought, *Sweet Jesus, how did this happen? I love her again.*

She stopped very close to him and looked up into his eyes. 'Thank you for bringing her home to me, Eric,' she said softly and lifting up on tiptoe took him in an embrace.

He folded his arms around her, held her firmly against the sleek silver surface of his snowmobile suit. They closed their eyes and remained where they had wanted to be for weeks, padded full-length, unmoving.

'You're welcome,' he whispered and continued holding

her while his heart thundered. He spread his hand on her back and let his feeling for her swell while they remained motionless, listening to one another breathe, and to their own pulses hammering in their ears; smelling one another – fresh air, cold cream, a hint of exhaust fumes, and orange pekoe tea.

Don't move . . . not yet!

'I knew you'd be up, worrying,' he whispered.

'I was. I didn't know whether to cry or pray or both.'

'I pictured you here . . . in the kitchen . . . waiting for Katy while we rode back.'

Still the embrace continued, safeguarded by the presence of another person a mere room away.

'She never wears boots.'

'She will after this.'

'You've given me the only Christmas present I want.'

'Maggie . . .'

In the bathroom the toilet flushed and they reluctantly parted, standing close, studying one another's eyes while Eric gripped Maggie's elbows and wondered at the ambiguity of her statement.

The bathroom door opened and Maggie bent to pick up the snowmobile suit, mask and gloves, hiding her flushed cheeks.

'Whew! What time is it anyway?' Katy asked breathily, returning to the kitchen, scratching her head.

'It's going on two,' Maggie replied, keeping her face averted.

'And I'd better be going,' added Eric.

Maggie turned back to him. 'Would you like something hot to drink first? Something to eat?'

'No, I'd better not. But if I could use your phone I'll call the dispatcher at the fire station and see if they still need me.'

'Of course. It's right over there.'

While Eric made the call, Maggie stacked the extra clothing on the table. Then she got out a variety of holiday-coloured tins and began filling a plastic bag with an assortment of cookies. Katy followed her back and forth along the cabinets – an eternally hungry college student, sampling from each tin as it came open. 'Mmm . . . I'm starved. All I had was a candy bar Eric gave me.'

Maggie gave her a squeeze in passing, and said, 'I've got soup and cold ham for slicing, and meatballs and herring and cheese and fruitcake. Take your pick. The refrigerator's loaded.'

Eric's phone call ended and he turned back to the women.

'They want me to make one more run.'

'Oh, no.' Maggie turned to face him, distraught. 'It's unfit for humans out there.'

'Not when you're dressed right. And I warmed up while I was in here.'

'Are you sure you wouldn't like some coffee first? Or soup? Anything?' Anything to keep him a while longer.

'No, I'd better go. A minute can seem like an hour when you're stranded in a cold car.' He picked up his ski mask and slipped it on, followed by his helmet. He zipped his suit to the throat, donned his gloves and she watched him disappear beneath the disguise.

When he looked up, she felt a sharp thrill at the sight of his eyes and mouth so prominently highlighted while the rest of his face was hidden. His eyes – as blue as cornflowers – were unqualifiedly beautiful, and his mouth – ah, that mouth that had taught her to kiss, how badly she wanted to kiss it again. He resembled a burglar . . . a burglar who'd crept into her life and stolen her heart.

He picked up the extra clothing and she went to him with her offering – the only bit of herself she could think to send into the storm with him.

'Some cookies. For the road.'

He took the bag in his clumsy glove, then glanced into her eyes one last time. 'Thank you.'

'Keep safe,' she said quietly.

'I will.'

'Will you . . .' Maggie's consternation showed in her eyes. 'Will you call and let me know you got in safely?'

He was astounded that she'd request such a thing with her daughter listening.

'Sure. But, don't worry, Maggie. I've been helping the sheriff's office for years. I take every precaution and I carry emergency supplies.' He glanced again at the cookies. 'Well, I've got to go.'

'Eric, wait!' Katy interjected, her mouth full of cookies as she bounced across the room to commandeer him for a swift, impersonal hug, hampered by his heavy outerwear. 'Thanks a lot. I think you might have saved my life.'

He smiled at Maggie over Katy's shoulder as he leaned down in accommodation. 'Just promise me you'll carry emergency supplies from now on.'

'I promise.' She backed away, smiled, and stuffed another cookie into her mouth. 'Just imagine that – me being rescued by the guy my mom went to prom with. Wait'll I tell the girls about this.'

Eric's glance passed between the two women. 'Well . . .' He gestured with the cookies. 'Thanks, Maggie. And Merry Christmas. You too, Katy.'

'Merry Christmas to you.'

Call, Maggie mouthed for his benefit alone.

He nodded and went out into the storm.

They watched him from the window, their arms around each other, holding the curtain aside while beyond the glass the snow engulfed him. He secured the emergency clothes in the bag on the rear of the sled, straddled the seat and started the engine. Through the wall they heard it rattle to life, felt the floor vibrate, and saw the exhaust stream away in a white cloud. He lowered his face shield, raised a hand, threw his weight to one side and circled away from the house. With a sudden burst of speed, the machine shot across the yard, climbed the bank and shot through the air like Santa's sleigh, then disappeared, leaving only a whorl of white.

'What a nice man,' Katy remarked.

'Yes, he is.'

Maggie dropped the curtain into place and changed the subject. 'Now how about getting some hot food into you?'

Chapter 11

In the morning, Maggie awakened to a world of white, the wind still keening, the snow plastered to the screens. A sheet of it fell and she lay motionless, studying the shape that remained, its edge like delicate tatted lace. *Did Eric make it home safely? Will he call today as I asked?*

The house was silent, the bed cosy with the wind whistling along the eaves. She remained in her warm nest, reliving the moments in Eric's arms: his cold, stiff snowmobile suit against her face; his warm hand on her back; his breath on her ear and hers on his neck; the smell of him – ah, the smell of a man with winter on his skin.

What had they said during those few precious seconds? Only the permissible things, though their bodies had said more. So what was to happen?

Somewhere in a neighbouring state Eric's wife waited to board a plane that would bring her home for Christmas. And sometime over the holiday he would hand her a small silver box and she would pluck from it an emerald ring. Would she slip it on her own finger? Would he? What return gift would she give? And afterward would they make love?

Maggie squeezed her eyes shut and held them so a long time. Until the image of Eric and Nancy faded. Until she had chastised herself for some wishes she had no right to be making. Until her scruples were securely back in place.

She flung aside the covers, donned her quilted floor-length robe and went to the kitchen to mix up waffles.

Around 9:30 Katy came scuffing into the room, wearing one of Maggie's nightgowns and a pair of leg warmers flopping over the ends of her feet like elephant trunks.

'Mmm . . . smells good in here. What are you making?' She hugged Maggie and wandered to the window.

'Waffles. How did you sleep?'

'Like a baby.' She pushed back a curtain and squinted. 'Jeez, it's so bright!'

'It'll be your first white Christmas.'

The sun was out and the snow had stopped falling, but still swirled before a powerful wind. Up above, the bank was as high and curled as a Big Sur breaker.

'What about my things? If it's still blowing this hard, when will I get my suitcases?'

'I don't know. We can call and check with the highway patrol.'

'I've never seen so much snow at one time in my life!'

Maggie followed Katy to the window. What a sight. Not a manmade mark anywhere, only unbroken white carved into caricatures of the sea. Mounds and swales below while above the trees were so whipped and bent by the wind that no shred of snow clung to them.

'Looks like we're still isolated. It'll probably be a while before you see your suitcases.'

It was precisely thirty-five minutes before Katy saw her suitcases. They had finished their bacon and waffles and sat over tea and coffee in the kitchen, still in their nightwear with their heels propped on empty chairs, when, like a replay of last night, a snowmobile climbed the snowbank beside the road, plunged into the yard and roared to a stop six feet from the back door.

'It's Eric!' Katy rejoiced, bounding from her chair. 'He's brought my clothes!'

Maggie leapt up and hit for the bathroom, her heart already pounding. Last night, with concern for Katy uppermost in her mind, she hadn't given her appearance a thought. This morning she frantically dragged a brush through her hair and snapped a rubber band around it. She heard the door open and Katy exclaimed, 'Oh, Eric, you angel! You brought my suitcases!' She heard him stamp inside, then the kitchen door closing.

'I figured you'd want them, and the way this wind is blowing, it might be a while before the tow trucks can get out there to haul your car out of the ditch.'

Maggie slashed lipstick on her mouth and wet some stray hairs above her ears.

'Oh, thank you *sooo* much,' Katy replied ecstatically. 'I just said to Mom . . . Mom?' After a pause, Katy's puzzled voice repeated, 'Mom? Where are you?' Then, to Eric, 'She was just here a second ago.'

Maggie tightened the belt on her robe, drew a deep breath, pressed her hands to her flushed cheeks and stepped around the corner into the kitchen.

'Well, good morning!' she greeted brightly.

'Good morning.'

He seemed to fill the room, dressed in his silver snowmobile suit, looking half again his size, bringing the smell of winter inside. While they smiled at each other she tried valiantly to appear collected, but it was altogether obvious what she'd been doing in the bathroom: her lipstick was bright, the sides of her hair wet, and she was breathing with a trace of difficulty.

'Goodness, did you get any sleep at all?' she asked to cover her self-consciousness.

'Enough.'

'Well, sit down. I'll heat up the coffee. Have you had breakfast?'

'No.'

'I don't keep doughnuts around the place, but I have waffles.'

'Waffles sound wonderful.'

Katy's glance darted between the two of them and Maggie turned towards the stove to hide her pink cheeks.

'Bacon?'

'Bacon would be good, if you're sure it's not too much trouble.'

'It's no trouble at all.' No trouble at all when you're falling in love with a man. He unzipped his snowmobile suit and pulled up to her table while she busied herself at the cupboard, afraid to turn around, afraid Katy would detect more than she already had.

'How are you this morning?' he asked Katy.

'Fine. I slept like the dead.'

Maggie recognized a new wariness in her daughter's voice. Obviously, Katy was trying to puzzle out the underlying vibrations in the room.

By the time she turned around, she had managed to compose herself but, bending before Eric to set a cup of coffee on the table, her heart seized up again. His face was still ruddy from the cold, his hair plastered down from the helmet. He flattened one shoulder back against the chair and smiled up at her, leaving Maggie with the startling impression that, had Katy not been there, he would have wrapped an arm around her thighs and held her beside him for a moment. She left the coffee and retreated to the stove.

She felt wifely, cooking for him. Unforgivable, but true. Sometimes she had fantasized about it.

He put away two waffles, four strips of bacon and four cups of coffee while she sat across from him in her rose-coloured robe and tried not to study his mouth whenever he spoke.

'So you used to date my mother,' Katy remarked while he ate.

'Yup.'

'Prom, too,' Katy prodded.

'Uh-huh. With Brookie and Arnie.'

'I've heard about Brookie, but who's Arnie?'

'Arnie and I were friends in high school. We were part of a group that all hung around together.'

'The ones who set fire to a barn one time?'

Eric's surprised gaze swerved to Maggie. 'You told her about that?'

Maggie gaped at her daughter. 'When did I tell you about that?'

'One time when I was little.'

Maggie confessed to Eric, 'I don't remember telling her about that.'

'It was an accident,' Eric explained. 'Somebody must've dropped a cigarette butt, but don't get the idea that we were intentionally destructive. We weren't. We did a lot of things that were just innocent fun. Did she ever tell you about how we used to get all the girls out in some abandoned house and scare the devil out of them?'

'And get cats drunk,' Maggie reminded him.

'Maggie, *I* never got a cat drunk. That was Arnie.'

'And who shot the chimney off Old Man Boelz's chicken coop?' she inquired, holding a grin in check.

'Well . . . that was just . . .' He gestured dismissingly with his fork.

'And rolled about fifty cream cans down the hill by the creamery at one o'clock in the morning and woke darn near the entire town of Ephraim.'

Eric laughed and choked on his coffee. When he had stopped coughing, he said, 'Now, damn it, Maggie, nobody's supposed to know about that.'

They had forgotten Katy was there, and by the time they remembered, she'd glanced back and forth between them a dozen times, listening to their good-humoured interchange with growing interest. When he'd finished eating, he bundled up again and stood on the rug smiling at Maggie.

'You're a good cook. Thank you for the breakfast.'

'You're welcome. Thank you for bringing Katy's things.'

He gripped the doorknob and said, 'Have a nice Christmas.'

'You, too.'

Finally he remembered to add, 'You, too, Katy.'

'Thanks.'

When he was gone, Katy came at Maggie head first. '*Motherrrr!* What's going *on* between you two!'

'Nothing,' Maggie declared, turning away, carrying Eric's plate to the sink.

'Nothing? When you rush into the bathroom and comb your hair and put lipstick on? Come on.'

Maggie felt the beginning of a telltale blush and kept her back turned.

'We've become friends again, and he's helped me get my zoning permit for the inn, that's all.'

'So what was all that about the doughnuts?'

Maggie shrugged and rinsed off a plate. 'He likes doughnuts. I've known that for years.'

Suddenly Katy was beside Maggie, taking her by an arm and studying her face minutely.

'Mother, you've got a *thing* for him, haven't you?'

'He's married, Katy.' Maggie resumed rinsing the dishes.

'I know he's married. Oh God, Mom, you wouldn't fall for a married man, would you? It's so tacky. I mean, you're a widow and you know how . . . well . . . you know what I mean.'

Maggie looked up sharply, her mouth pinched. 'And you know what they say about widows, is that what you were about to say?'

'Well, they do.'

Maggie felt a spark of temper. 'What *do* they say, Katy?'

'Jeez, Mom, you don't have to get so mad.'

'Well, I think I have a right! How dare you accuse me –'

'I didn't accuse you.'

'It sounded that way to me.'

Katy, too, grew suddenly irate. 'I have a right to my feelings, too, and after all, Dad's only been dead a little over a year.'

Maggie rolled her eyes and grumbled as if to a third party, 'Oh, I don't believe this.'

'Mother, I *saw* how you looked at that man, and you were blushing!'

Drying her hands on a towel, Maggie faced her daughter angrily. 'You know, for a young woman who plans to work in the field of psychology you've got a lot to learn about human relations and the manipulation of feelings. I loved your dad, don't you *ever* accuse me of not loving him! But he's dead and I'm alive, and if I should *choose* to fall in love with another man, or even to have an *affair* with one, I certainly wouldn't feel obliged to ask for your approval first! Now I'm going upstairs to take a bath and get dressed, and while I do I'd appreciate it if you'd clean up the kitchen. And while you're doing so, you might give some thought to whether or not you owe me an apology!'

Maggie marched out of the room leaving Katy, gaping, behind her.

Her outburst put a strain on the rest of the holiday. Katy offered no apology, and thereafter the two women moved about the house with stiff formality. When Maggie went outside later in the day to shovel the sidewalk, Katy made no offer to help. When Katy rode off in a tow truck to retrieve her car, she didn't say good-bye. At suppertime they spoke only when necessary, and afterward Katy put her nose in a book and kept it there until bedtime. The following day she announced that she had changed her airline reservations and would be returning to Chicago the day after Christmas and from there flying to Seattle.

By the time Christmas Eve arrived, Maggie felt the stress culminating in an ache that spread from her shoulders up her neck. Compounding it was the fact that Vera had grudgingly agreed to come to the house for the first time.

She and Roy arrived at 5:00 P.M. on Christmas Eve, and Vera entered complaining, bearing a moulded jello on a covered cake dish.

'I hope this isn't ruined. I used my tallest mould, and I told your father to take it easy around the corners, but when we were starting up the hill the cover slid to one side and it probably ruined the whipped cream. I hope you have room in your refrigerator.' She sailed straight to it, opened the door and reared back. 'Judas priest, what a mess! How in the world do you find anything in here? Roy, come here and hold this while I try to make room.'

Roy followed her orders.

Vexed by Vera's autocratic attitude, Roy's blind submissiveness, and the whole wrong mood of the holiday, Maggie stepped forward and ordered, 'Katy, take the jello from Grandma and put it out on the porch. Daddy, you can put the gifts in the parlour. There's a fire in there, and Katy can bring you a glass of wine while I show Mother the house.'

The tour started off badly from the beginning. Vera had wanted them to gather at *her* house for Christmas Eve, and since they hadn't she made it abundantly clear she was here under duress. She glanced around the kitchen and remarked caustically, 'Good lord, what do you want to look at that beat-up old table of your dad's for? That thing should have been burned years ago.'

And in the new bathroom: 'Why would you ever put in one of those old clawfoot tubs? You'll be sorry when you have to get on your hands and knees to clean under it.'

And in the Belvedere Room, after boldly asking what the furniture had cost, she declared, 'You paid too much for it.'

In the parlour, only recently furnished, she made a few positive comments, but they were embarrassingly paltry. By the time Maggie left her mother with the others, she felt like there was TNT running through her veins. Vera found her minutes later, in the kitchen, slicing ham with enough vengeance to sever the breadboard. Vera came close, her wine glass in hand.

'Margaret, I hate to bring up unpleasantness on

Christmas Eve, but I *am* your mother, and if I don't talk to you about it, who will?'

Maggie glanced up, bristling, thinking, *You love to bring up unpleasantness anytime, Mother.*

'Talk about what?'

'Whatever's going on between you and Eric Severson. People are talking about it, Margaret.'

'Nothing's going on between me and Eric Severson.'

'You aren't living in a big city anymore, and you're a widow now. You have to be careful about your reputation.'

Maggie began slicing again. Rabidly. This was the second time she'd been warned about widows' reputations by people who were supposed to love her.

'I *said* nothing is going on between us.'

'You call flirting on Main Street nothing? Eating lunch together on a park bench, where the whole town can see you, nothing? Margaret, I'd have thought you'd use better sense than that.'

Maggie became so angry she didn't trust herself to speak.

'You're forgetting, dear,' Vera went on, 'that you were at my house the night he picked you up to go to that county board meeting. I saw how you dressed and how you acted when he came to the door. I tried to warn you then, but . . .'

'But you waited until Christmas Eve, didn't you, Mother?' Maggie stopped slicing to glare at her mother.

'You have no reason to be cross with me. I'm merely trying to warn you that people are talking.'

The knife started whacking again. 'Well, let them talk!'

'They say his truck has been spotted in front of your house, and that the two of you were seen early in the morning having breakfast in Sturgeon Bay. And now Katy tells me he came here during the blizzard on his snowmobile!'

Maggie threw down the knife and flung her hands up in exasperation. 'Oh, for Christ sake! He offered me the use of his truck to get the furniture!'

'I don't care for that kind of language, Margaret!'

'And he rescued Katy. You know that!'

Vera sniffed and raised one eyebrow. 'Frankly, I'd rather not hear the details. Just remember, you're not a teenager anymore, and people have long memories. They haven't forgotten that the two of you used to date in high school.'

'So what!'

Vera pressed closer. 'He has a wife, Margaret.'

'I know that.'

'One who's gone all week long.'

'I know that, too.'

After a moment's hesitation, Vera straightened and said, 'Why, you don't care, do you?'

'Not about shabby gossip, I don't.' Maggie started slapping ham slices onto a plate. 'He's a friend, nothing more. And if people are going to make something of it they must not have enough in their lives to keep them busy.' She shot a flat-eyed challenge at Vera: *that means you, Mother!*

Vera's shoulders slumped. 'Oh, Margaret, I'm so disappointed in you.'

Standing before her mother, holding the platter of Christmas ham, Maggie felt a grave disappointment of her own. The fight suddenly left her and tears sprang into her eyes. 'Yes, I know, Mother,' she replied resignedly, 'I don't seem to be able to do anything to please you. I never have.'

Only when she'd finally drawn tears did Vera step forward and place a hand on Maggie's shoulder.

'Margaret, you know I'm only concerned about your happiness.'

When had Vera ever been concerned about anyone's happiness? What drove the woman? She actually seemed unable to tolerate the happiness of others. But why? Because she was so unhappy herself? Because over the years she'd forced her own husband's emotional and physical withdrawal to the point where they lived nearly separate lives – hers in the house, his in the garage? Or was it, as

Maggie had often suspected, jealousy? Was her own mother jealous of Maggie's very happy marriage to Phillip? Of her career? Her life-style? The change she'd made in that life-style? Of the money she'd received after Phillip's death, and the independence that money had brought? Of this house? Was Vera so small that she rued her daughter having anything better than herself? Or was it nothing more complicated than her ceaseless compulsion to give orders and be obeyed?

Whatever the reason, the exchange in the kitchen cast a pall over the remainder of the night. They ate their meal wishing it were already over. They opened their gifts with animosities roiling beneath the veneer of politeness. They bade good-bye with Vera and Maggie lifting their faces but never quite touching one another.

On Christmas Day, Maggie accepted an invitation to go to Brookie's, but Katy said she'd rather not be with a bunch of strangers and went to Roy and Vera's alone.

The following day, when Katy's car was loaded, Maggie walked her up the hill.

'Katy, I'm sorry it was such a crummy Christmas.'

'Yeah . . . well . . .'

'And I'm sorry we fought.'

'I am, too, but Mother, *please* don't see him again.'

'I told you, I'm not seeing him.'

'But I heard what Grandma said on Christmas Eve. And I have eyes. I can see how good-looking he is, and how you looked at each other, and how the two of you enjoy being together. It could happen, Mother, and you know it.'

'It won't.'

During the dreary, anticlimactic days following Christmas, Maggie kept that promise firmly in mind. She turned her attention once more towards the house and the business, throwing herself into preparations for spring. She hung more wallpaper, attended two auctions, ordered an iron bed from Spiegel's, shopped by mail for bedspreads and rugs. The state health inspector came and inspected her bathrooms, dishwasher, food storage and laundry facilities. The fire inspector came and inspected the furnace, fireplaces, smoke alarms and fire exits. Her official bed-and-breakfast licence arrived and she had it framed, then hung it in the parlour above the secretary where her guests would register. She received spring catalogues from suppliers and placed orders for blankets, sheets and towels from the American Hotel Supply; made a trip to Sturgeon Bay and set up a charge account with Warner Wholesale who would supply her with soap, toilet paper, disposable drinking glasses and cleaning supplies. She scoured books for muffin and quick-bread recipes, tried some and ate them alone or with Brookie, who stopped by often when she came to town. Or with Roy, who had made it a practice to have lunch with her at least twice a week.

While her mind and hands were occupied, she found it easy to exorcize thoughts of Eric Severson. Often, however, when she paused between tasks for a cup of tea she'd find herself standing motionless, staring out a window, seeing his face in the snow. At night, in those vulnerable minutes before sleep, he would appear again, and she would recall the surge of elation she'd felt upon seeing him at her door, the giddy sensation of stepping into his arms and feeling his hand spread wide upon her back.

Then, remembering Katy's warning, she would curl up like a shrimp and force the images from her mind.

Mark Brodie invited her out to his restaurant for New Year's Eve, but she went to a party at Brookie's instead and met a dozen new people, played canasta, ate tacos, drank margaritas and stayed overnight and most of the next day.

During the second week of January, Mark invited her to an art gallery in Green Bay. Again she declined and also passed up the January chamber of commerce breakfast, daunted by the thought of encountering either Mark or Eric there.

Then one night in the third week of January, she was sitting at the kitchen table in her red Pepsi sweats designing a business brochure when someone knocked on her door.

She switched on the outside light, lifted the curtains aside and came face to face with Eric Severson.

She dropped the curtain and opened the door. No beaming smiles this time, no boundless joy. Only a reserved woman looking up into a man's troubled face, waiting with her hand on the doorknob.

They took fifteen wordless, weighted seconds to look into each other's eyes before he said, 'Hi.' Resignedly, as if his being here was the outcome of a lost battle with himself.

'Hi,' she said, making no move to grant him entry.

Sombrely, he studied her, in oversized red-and-white sweats and stockinged feet, with her hair pulled into a scraggly tail off one side of her head, with ragtail sprigs spraying away from it like fireworks. He had stayed away purposely, giving himself time to sort through his feelings, giving her the same. Guilt, desire, dread and hope. He supposed she'd run the same gamut and he had expected her cool behaviour, the forced detachment so like his own.

'May I come in?'

'No,' she replied, still barring the way.

'Why?' he asked very quietly.

She wanted to let her shoulders droop, to huddle into a ball, to cry. Instead, she answered levelly, 'Because you're married.'

His chin dropped to his chest and his eyes closed. He stood motionless for an eternity while she waited for him to leave, to release her from this yoke of guilt she'd been wearing since her daughter's and mother's accusations. To take himself beyond temptation, beyond memory, if possible.

She waited. And waited.

Finally he pulled in a deep breath and raised his head. His eyes were troubled, his mouth downturned. His pose was so familiar – feet planted firmly, hands in the pockets of his bomber jacket, the collar turned up. 'I need to talk to you, please. In the kitchen – you sit on your side of the table and I'll sit on mine. Please, Maggie.'

She glanced at his truck, parked at the top of the hill in the break between the snowbanks, his name and telephone number listed on the door as clearly as a newspaper headline.

'Do you realize I could tell you precisely how many days and hours it's been since you were here last? You aren't making it any easier on me.'

'Four weeks, two days and ten hours. And who said it would be easy?'

She shuddered involuntarily, as if he had physically touched her, pulled in a shaky breath and rubbed her arms. 'I find it difficult to deal with the fact that we're talking about this . . . this –' She flipped up her palms, then caught her arms again. '– I don't even know what to call it – as if it's foregone. What are we doing, Eric?'

'I think we both know what we're doing, and we both know what it's called, and I don't know about you, but it scares the goddamned hell out of me, Maggie.'

She was quaking inside, and freezing outside. The temperature was three degrees, and they couldn't stand in the open door forever. Stepping back, she surrendered to the awesome gravity he exerted over her. 'Come in.'

Once given permission, he hesitated. 'Are you sure, Maggie?'

'Yes, come in,' she repeated. 'I guess we both need to talk.'

He followed her inside, closed the door, unzipped his jacket, hung it on the back of a chair and sat down, still wearing the look of weary resignation with which he'd arrived. She began making coffee without asking if he wanted any – she knew he did – and a new pot of tea for herself.

'What were you doing?' he asked, glancing over the rulers, vellum and cut-and-paste books strewn over the table.

'Laying out an ad for the chamber of commerce booklet.'

He turned her work to face him, studying the neat lettering and bordering, the pen-and-ink sketch of Harding House as it looked from the lake. He felt empty and lost and very unsure of himself. 'You didn't come to the last breakfast.' He forgot the paper in his hand and followed her with his eyes as she moved along the cabinets, running water, scooping coffee.

'No.'

'Does that mean you were avoiding me?'

'Yes.'

So he was right. She'd been through the same hell as he.

She turned on the burner beneath the coffeepot and returned to the table to push aside her papers, steering well clear of him. She put muffins on a plate, found butter and a knife and brought them to him; got down a cup and saucer and refilled her sugar bowl and brought these, too, to the table. The coffee began to perk, and she turned the burner down. Finishing her busywork, she turned to find him still watching her, looking tormented.

Finally she resumed her seat, linked her fingers on the tabletop and met his gaze steadily.

'So, how was your Christmas?' she asked.

'Horseshit. How was yours?'

'Horseshit, too.'

'You want to tell me about yours first?'

'All right.' She took a deep breath, fitted her thumbnails together and gave it to him straight. 'My mother and my daughter both accused me of having an affair with you, and after a couple of pretty awful fights, they both left here very upset with me. I haven't seen either of them since.'

'Oh, Maggie, I'm sorry.' On the tabletop he took her hands.

'Don't be.' She withdrew them. 'Believe it or not, the battles between us were less about you than about my growing away from them, becoming independent. Neither one of them likes it. As a matter of fact, I'm slowly coming to realize that my mother doesn't like much of anything about me, particularly my being happy. She's a very shallow person, and I'm learning to overcome my guilt for realizing this. And as for Katy – well, she's not over her father's death yet, and she's going through a selfish stage. She'll outgrow it in time. So tell me about your Christmas. How did Nancy like her ring?'

'She loved it.'

'Then what went wrong?'

'Everything. Nothing. Christ, I don't know.' He clasped his nape with one hand and tipped back his head to its limits, closing his eyes, sucking in a deep breath and blowing it out slowly. Abruptly he snapped from the pose, leaning his forearms on the table, and settled his eyes on hers. 'It's just that everything's collapsing in my mind, the whole marriage, the relationship, the future. It's all meaningless. I look at Barb and Mike and I think, that's how it's supposed to be. Only it isn't, and I realize it's never going to be.'

In silence he studied Maggie, the lines of worry still dragging at the corners of his eyes and lips. On the stove the coffee perked and the aroma filled the room but neither of them noticed. They sat on opposite sides of the table, their gazes locked, realizing their relationship was taking an irreversible turn and frightened by how it would shake their lives and those of others.

'I just don't have any feelings for her anymore,' he admitted quietly.

So this is how it happens, Maggie thought, this is how a marriage breaks up and an affair begins. Discomfited, she rose and turned off the burners, poured water in her teapot and filled his coffee cup. When she was seated again, he stared into his cup a long time before raising his eyes.

'I have to ask you something,' he said.

'Ask.'

'What was that at the door the night I brought Katy home?'

She felt a warmth in her chest at the memory that it was she who'd broken the taboo. 'A mistake,' she replied, 'and I'm sorry. I . . . I had no right.'

With his eyes steady on hers, he remarked, 'Isn't it funny, it felt like you did.'

'I was tired, and I'd been so worried about Katy, and then you brought her home to me all safe and sound, and I was grateful.'

'Grateful? That's all?'

'What do you want me to say?'

'I want you to say what you started to say when I walked in here a few minutes ago, that what we're talking about here is that we're falling in love.'

The shock went through her like an electrical current, leaving her shaken and staring at him with her chest tight and her heart knocking. 'Love?'

'We've been through it together once before. We should be pretty good at recognizing it by now.'

'I thought we were talking about . . . about having an affair.'

'An affair? Is that what you want?'

'I don't *want* anything. I mean, I . . .' She suddenly covered her face with both hands, pressing her elbows to the tabletop. 'Oh God, this is the most bizarre conversation.'

'You're scared, Maggie, is that it?'

She slid her hands down far enough to look at him, her nose and mouth still covered. Scared? She was terrified. She bobbed her head yes.

'I told you, I am, too.'

She clutched her teacup – anything to hang on to. 'It's so . . . so civilized! Sitting here discussing it as if no one else were involved. But others are, and I feel so guilty even though we've done nothing wrong.'

'You want something to feel guilty about? I've got a few things in mind.'

'Eric, be serious,' she scolded because she was bursting with desire for him and this was the damnedest face-to-face confrontation to which she'd ever been subjected.

'You think this isn't serious?' He held out one trembling hand. 'Look at me shake.' He gripped his thighs. 'It took me damned near five weeks to come back here, and I didn't know what I was coming to do. You should have seen me at home an hour ago, getting showered and shaved and picking out a shirt as if I were going courting, but I can't do that, can I? And the other alternative makes me slightly less than honourable, so here I sit, talking about it – my God, look at me, Maggie, so I know what you're thinking.'

She lifted a face that was brilliant scarlet and encountered his blue, blue eyes, as troubled as before. She said what she knew she must say. 'I'm thinking that the proper thing for me to do right now would be to ask you to leave.'

'If you'd ask me, I would. You know that, don't you?'

She studied him for one pained moment, then whispered, 'But I can't, and you know that, too, don't you?'

Their forearms rested on the table, fingertips inches apart. He dropped his eyes to her hand, then took it loosely in his own – her right hand, bearing a gold wedding band. He ran his thumb over it and her knuckles, then raised his gaze again.

'I want you to know this is not something I do all the time. That hug five weeks ago is the closest thing to unfaithful I've ever been to Nancy.'

Maggie was human; she'd wondered. And because she had, she dropped her eyes guiltily to their joined hands.

'Let me say this once, then never again.' He spoke solemnly. 'I'm sorry, Maggie. For whatever pain this brings you, I'm sorry.'

He leaned forward and kissed her palm, a long, lingering kiss that kept him doubled over as if awaiting benediction. She remembered him at seventeen, often expressing himself in dear, touching ways such as this, and she pitied the woman who knew him so little she'd somehow failed to tap this wealth of emotion. With her free hand she touched the back of his head, the hair that had darkened to a tarnished gold since the last time she had caressed it.

'Eric,' she said softly.

He lifted his head and their eyes met. 'Come over here . . . please,' she whispered.

He left his chair and circled the end of the table, still holding her hand. She rose as he reached her, and looked up at his face, realizing he was right; they'd begun falling in love months ago.

She rested her hands on his chest and lifted her face as his descended, then his soft, open lips touched hers. Ah, that kiss, that long-awaited kiss, fragile as a new bloom, exquisite in its intentional reserve. They brought to it the charmed recollection of first times, of their timorous explorations of one another in years long past, and of a night in Easley's orchard. They let the bloom open slowly, let the stirring build, and the breathlessness mount until their lips opened wider, their tongues joined.

In time he lifted his head and their eyes met; they read it in one another's gazes – this is not going to be a simple affair; hearts are involved here.

Their eyelids began closing before their mouths met a second time. In one motion he gathered her close and her arms circled his neck. The kiss became wide, lush, and flavoured with remembrance, a taking of one another on any terms. Their tongues met and welcomed a new fervour as they clung hard, his hands stroking her back, hers his shoulders. When at last they drew apart their breathing was laboured, their mouths wet.

'Ah, Maggie, I've thought about this.'

'So have I.'

'That night I brought Katy home . . . I wanted to kiss you then.'

'I lay in bed that night and worried about you out in the storm . . . riding away from me . . . and I was sorry I hadn't kissed you. I thought, what if you died without knowing how I felt.'

He kissed her throat, her jaw. 'Oh, Maggie, you didn't have to worry.'

'A woman worries when she feels this way.'

He kissed her mouth – warm, mobile mouth waiting eagerly for his return. The fervour built, took them on a swell of feelings that set their hands in motion and made them avid for more. They tasted and tested, their lips moist and supple and impatient. He bit her lower lip, licked it and spoke into her open mouth. 'You taste exactly the way I remember.'

'How do I taste?' she murmured.

He drew back and smiled into her eyes. 'Like Easley's orchard when the apples bloom.'

She smiled, too. 'You remembered.'

'Of course I remembered.'

Struck suddenly by a sluice of happiness, she fitted herself tightly against him, wherever and however she would fit – her face to his neck, her arms around his trunk, her breasts flattened, giving herself licence to love being body to body with him at last. 'We were so young, Eric.'

'And it hurt so much to leave you.' His hands roamed down her spine and came up beneath her sweatshirt, scanning her warm back.

'I thought we'd eventually get married.'

'So did I.'

'And when we didn't, the years passed and I thought I'd forgotten all about you. Then I saw you again and it was like a kick in the gut. I just wasn't prepared for it.'

'Neither was I.'

She simply had to see his face. Had to. She pulled back, looking up, still flush against his hips. 'It's pretty stunning, isn't it?'

'Yeah . . . pretty stunning.' It was then he touched her breasts, as their eyes communicated all they felt, as she leaned back at the waist and felt him hard against her. Beneath the oversized sweatshirt he had unclasped her bra, ran his hands around her ribs and took her in hand. Both breasts at once . . . warm and erect. Gently . . . lovingly . . . stroking her . . . all the while watching her face.

Her lips dropped open and her eyes closed.

It was spring again, and they were young and raring, and he had come to pick her up with apple blossoms bedecking his car, and the same wondrous urges they had felt then, they felt now. She swayed pliantly as he stroked her, and smiled with her eyes still closed. From her throat came a sound of delight, neither word nor moan, a mingling of the two.

He dropped to one knee and she lifted her shirt, watching from above as his warm, wet mouth opened upon her, renewing memories. His head swayed, his tongue stroked, then his teeth closed lightly upon her. She gasped and her stomach muscles contracted.

'Mmm . . . you taste good.'

'Mmm . . . I feel good. It's been so long and I've missed this.'

He moved to her other breast, washed it as he had the first, then rubbed it with his hair. She cradled his head, drifting in sensation. In time he lifted his face and said in a gravelly voice, 'Maggie, M'girl, I think we're framed in your lace curtains, and they don't hide much.'

Cupping his jaws she urged him to his feet. 'Then come with me to the bed we bought together. I've wanted you in it since the night you set it up for me.'

His knees cracked as he rose and tucked her securely against his side. With their arms around each other they snapped off the kitchen light and climbed the stairs, their lazy steps giving lie to the anticipation coursing through them.

In the Belvedere Room she switched on a bedside lamp. The shadow from its silk-fringed shade swayed against the wall as she turned and found him close behind her. He reached for her hips, set them lightly against his own and asked, 'You nervous?'

'Dying.'

'Me, too.'

With a smile he released her and began freeing the buttons of his pastel-blue shirt, tugging its tails out of his jeans. When she reached for the hem of her sweatshirt he caught her hand.

'Wait a minute.' He grinned charmingly. 'Could I do that? I don't think I ever did it before, except in the dark, fumbling around.'

'You did it on the *Mary Deare* the day after prom, and it wasn't dark and you weren't fumbling.'

'Did I?'

'Yes, and you were very good at it, actually.'

He smiled crookedly and reached out, murmuring, 'Let me refresh my memory.'

He slid the baggy shirt over her head taking the bra with it, and flung them aside, looking down at her in the lamplight.

'You're beautiful, Maggie.' He brushed his knuckles along the sides of her breasts and over their uptilted nipples.

'No, I'm not.'

'Yes you are. I thought so then, and I think so now.'

'You haven't changed, do you know that? You always had a way of saying and doing sweet, tender things, like downstairs when you kissed my hand, and now when you touched me as if . . .'

'As if . . . ?' His gossamer caresses sent goose bumps up the backs of her legs.

'As if I were Dresden.'

'Dresden is cold,' he murmured, enfolding her breasts in his wide hands. 'You're warm. Take my shirt off, Maggie, please.'

What a heady pleasure it was, divesting him of the blue shirt, then the white one underneath, tugging it over his head, further dishevelling his hair. When he was naked to the waist, she held his clothes like a nest in her hands, lowered her face to them, breathing in his scent, calling back another memory.

He touched her head, stirred unbelievably by her simple gesture.

She lifted her face to him. 'You smell the same. A person doesn't forget smells.'

His belt came next. She had removed the belt of another man countless times during their years of marriage, but had forgotten the impact of doing so illicitly. Reaching for Eric's waist, she felt heat pounding everywhere in her body. She freed his buckle and the heavy metal snap at his waist, watching his eyes as she laid her hand flat upon him and caressed him for the first time through faded blue denim. Soft old denim over hard, warm man. Her first stroke closed his eyes. Her second brought him leaning forward, hard against her, reaching behind her, running his palms down deep inside her red sweat pants.

'You have a mole,' he whispered, running one warm palm against her belly. 'Right . . . here.'

She smiled. 'How could you remember?'

'I always wanted to kiss it but I was too chicken.'

She unzipped his jeans and murmured against his lips, 'Kiss it now.'

They finished undressing each other in a rush. That first moment of nakedness might have been strained but he put self-consciousness to rout by catching her hands, spreading them wide and boldly assessing her length.

'Wow,' he praised softly, meeting her eyes, grinning appreciatively.

'Yeah . . . wow,' she returned, admiring him in kind.

He dropped their hands. His expression turned grave. 'I'm not going to stretch the truth and say that I always loved you, but I did then, and I do now, and I think it's important to say so before we do this.'

'Oh, Eric . . .' she replied wistfully. 'I love you, too. I tried very hard not to, but I couldn't help myself.'

He caught her beneath the knees and arms, and laid her across the bed, touched her in the places he'd touched years ago – breasts, hips and inside, where she was liquid and warm. She touched him, too, stroked and studied him in the amber lamplight and made him tremble and feel strong one minute and weak the next. He kissed her in all the places he'd been too shy to kiss in their younger days, along her ribs and her limbs, stained golden by the lamplight while she lay lissom beneath his touch.

She tasted him in return, revelling in his textures and responses, each passing moment trying their patience.

When the limits of desire had been tested, he braced above her and asked, 'Do we have to be careful not to get you pregnant?'

'No.'

'Are you sure, Maggie?'

'I'm forty years old, and luckily for both of us, I'm beyond that particular worry.'

Their reunion was slow and supple, a mating of spirits as well as bodies. He took his time easing into her, all below billowing with feelings while the moment became prolonged pleasure. When they were wholly bound at last, they poised, motionless, making of the moment a prayer.

After so many years, lovers again.

How delicious their fit. How incredible their heat.

Momentarily he pressed back, found her eyes wide and gleaming. She girded his hips with her hands and set him in motion, silken and strong within her. He found her hands and clasped them against the bedding while she watched his face.

'You're smiling,' he said huskily.

'So are you.'

'What are you thinking?'

'That your shoulders are wider.'

'So are your hips.'

'I've had a baby.'

'I wish it were mine.'

In time she drew his head down and their smiles faded, drawn away by the wondrous gravity of sensuality. They shared some lust and some fine driven moments before he wrapped her close and took her with him, rolling to their sides. Squeezing his eyes shut he held himself deep within her. 'It's so good,' he said.

'Because we were first for each other.'

'It feels like coming full circle, like this is where I should have been all the time.'

'Have you wondered what it would have been like if we'd got married the way we planned?'

'Constantly. Have you?'

'Yes,' she admitted.

He turned her beneath him and the rhythm resumed. She watched his hair tap his forehead, and his arms tremble as they bore his weight. She rose to meet him, thrust for thrust, and murmured pleasured sounds that he echoed.

He climaxed first, and she watched it happen upon his face, watched his eyes close, his throat arch, and his muscles tense; watched beads of sweat appear upon his brow in the moment before the wondrous distress shook and shattered him.

When his body had calmed he opened his eyes, still leaning above her. 'Maggie, I'm sorry,' he whispered, as if there were some preset order.

'Don't be sorry,' she whispered, touching his damp brow, his temple. 'You were beautiful to watch.'

'Was I?'

'Absolutely. And besides,' she added guilelessly, 'I'm next.'

And she was.
Next.
And next.
And next again.

Chapter 12

At 1:20 A.M. Maggie and Eric sat in the clawfoot tub, in nipple-high bubbles, drinking root beer and trying to yodel. He took a swig, backhanded his mouth, and said, 'Here, I got one!' Raising his face like a baying hound, he broke into song.

'Mockingbird singing, yodel-o-yodel-o-do-hoo . . .'

While he howled, Maggie rocked like an Irishman in a pub and thrust her mug in the air. He howled so loud she expected the mirror to shatter, and ended with a long, mournful note that stretched his lips toward the ceiling.

'There, how was that?'

She set her mug on the floor and applauded. 'Remarkable! Now I've got one. Just a minute.' She retrieved her mug, took a swig and wiped her mouth. After clearing her throat she tried a chorus of the 'Cattle Call'.

Woo-woo-woo-oo-oo-oo! Woo-woo-woo-up! A-woo-oo-oo . . .

When the chorus ended, he yelled, 'Bravo! Bravo!' and applauded while she bowed over her updrawn knees and spread her arms wide, dropping suds on the floor.

'Let's see . . .' He squinted at the ceiling, took a drink and hummed thoughtfully above his mug. 'Mmm . . . mmmmmmmm . . . yuh! I got it! An old Cowboy Kopus tune.'

'Cowboy who?'

'Cowboy Kopus. You mean you never heard of Cowboy Kopus?'

'Nobody ever heard of Cowboy Kopus.'

'Shows how much *you* know. When I was little we used to put on shows on the back porch. Larry was Tex Ritter.

Ruth was Dale Evans and I wanted to be Roy Rogers, but Mike said *he* was Roy Rogers, I had to be Cowboy Kopus. So I stood there and bawled. Had my little six-shooters strapped on, and my red felt cowboy hat with the string pulled up tight under my chin with a little wooden ball, and my Red Rider cowboy boots, bawlin' fit to kill 'cause I had to be Cowboy Kopus. So don't tell me nobody ever heard of Cowboy Kopus.'

She was laughing long before he cut loose with his pitiful rendition of 'Shy Little Ann from Cheyenne'.

When he finished, she suggested, 'How about if we do one together?'

'Okay. You know "Ghost Riders in the Sky" by Vaughn Monroe?'

'Vaughn Monroe?'

'You don't remember him either?'

'Can't say that I do.'

'Then how about "Tumbling Tumbleweed" by The Sons of the Pioneers.'

'That I know.'

'I'll lead off.'

He drew a deep breath and began.

See them tumbling down . . .

They sang three verses, humming the parts where they'd forgotten the words, managing some dubious harmony and ending with a pair of notes rendered like a pack of yowling coyotes.

Drifting along with the tumbling tum-bul-weeeeeeeeeeeeeeeeds!

When the last note died, they collapsed into gales of laughter.

'I think we missed our calling.'

'I think we cracked your new plaster.'

They fell back weakly and Maggie caught a faucet between the shoulder blades.

'*Ow-woooo!*' she howled, coyote-fashion again. 'That huuuuuuurts!'

He grinned. 'C'm'ere. I got a place that won't hurt.'

'No spouts and knobs?' she inquired, setting her mug on the floor.

'Well, maybe a couple,' he replied, settling her between his silky thighs. 'But you're gonna like 'em, Miss Maggie, I can promise you that.'

'Mmmmm . . .' she purred, resting her forearms on his chest. 'You're right. I do.'

They kissed, growing aroused beneath the bubbles, his hands gliding over her naked rump.

After some time she opened her eyes and inquired lazily, 'Hey, cowboy?'

'Ma'am?' he drawled, arranging his mouth in a triangular grin.

'You wouldn't want to kiss my mole again, would you?'

'Well now,' he replied in his best sagebrush accent. 'A gentleman ought not to refuse a lady when she asks so sweet-like. I think we can take care of that little matter with no problem at all.'

They took care of that little matter and a couple of others, and by the time they had done so it was after three o'clock in the morning. They lay on the rumpled bed in the Belvedere Room with their tired limbs twined. His stomach rumbled and he inquired, 'What've you got to eat, Miss Maggie? I'm damn near stove in.'

Hooking her heel on the far side of his leg, she asked, 'What do you want? Fruit? A sandwich? An omelette?'

He turned up his nose. 'Too sensible.'

'What then?'

'Doughnuts,' he declared, slapping his belly. 'Big, fat, warm, yummy doughnuts.'

'Well, you've come to the right place. Let's go.' She grabbed his hand and hauled him off the bed.

'You're kidding!' he exclaimed. 'You really have doughnuts?'

'No, I don't, but we can make them.'

'You'd start making doughnuts at 3:15 in the morning?'

'Why not? I've been collecting quick bread recipes till they're sticking out of the drawers. I'm sure in some of those books we'll find doughnuts. Come on. I'll let you choose.'

He chose orange drop doughnuts, and they built them together, she wearing her rose quilted housecoat, exclusively, he wearing blue jeans, also exclusively. It took them longer than warranted: she put him to work squeezing an orange and he tried to do so against some unorthodox places that brought about a good-natured scuffle, ending with the two of them rolling and giggling on the floor. While he was grating a rind, he scraped the end of a knuckle, and its doctoring included enough kisses to delay the making of doughnuts for a good ten minutes. When the batter was finally mixed, it had to be tasted, resulting in an arousing round of finger sucking from which Maggie surfaced with the lazy warning, 'If you don't let me go my grease is going to catch fire.' His reply rocked them both with laughter that dwindled eventually and left them leaning against cupboards like a pair of surfboards stored in a corner. He planted his feet, locked his hands over her spine and studied her face with a growing sense of wonder. The laughter fell away.

'My God, but I love you,' he said. 'I'm halfway through my life and it took me till now to find out how it really ought to be. I do . . . I love you, Maggie, more than I planned on.'

'I love you, too.' She felt full with it, reborn. 'During the past couple of months I've imagined this night finally happening, but I never imagined this part of it. This is special, the laughter, the sheer happiness. Do you suppose if we'd got married when we were fresh out of school we'd still be this way?'

'I don't know. It feels like it.'

'Mmm . . . yes it does.' She smiled up at him. 'Isn't it

nice? We not only love each other, we like each other as well.'

'I think we've found the secret,' he replied.

He studied her face, tipped up at an acute angle, her delicate chin with its distinctive dimple, her adoring brown eyes and softly smiling mouth. Upon it he placed a lingering, unurgent kiss.

When it ended she murmured, 'Let's finish our doughnuts so I can curl up next to you and turn over while I sleep and feel you there behind me.'

At 4:05 they fell into bed exhausted, with orange doughnuts on their breath. Eric curled behind Maggie, his face in her hair, his knees cupped behind hers, one hand on her breast.

He sighed.

She sighed.

'You wore me out.'

'I think it's the other way around.'

'Fun though.'

'Mm-hmm.'

'Love you.'

'Love you, too. Don't leave without waking me.'

'I won't.'

And like two who'd been together for years, they slept in utter peace.

He awakened to the feel of their moist skins joined and his hand lying lax on her belly, lifting and falling with each breath she took. He lay still, filling his senses: her rhythmic breathing on the pillow; rumpled eyelet sheet covering their shoulders; her naked rump sealed to his thighs. The smell of her hair and something flowery somewhere nearby; sun and snow indirectly lighting the room; dusty-rose paper covering the walls; the noiseless motion of white lace curtains in the forced air from the furnace. Warmth. Contentment.

I don't want to leave here. I want to stay with this woman, laugh and love with her and share the thousands of mundane tasks that bind lives. Carry the things that are too heavy for her, reach the things that are too high, shovel her walk, shave in her bathroom and use the same hairbrush. Stand in a doorway in the morning and watch her dress, and in the same doorway in the evening and watch her undress. Call home to say, I'm on my way. Share unshaven Sundays and rainy Mondays and the last glass of milk in the carton.

I want her with me when I put the boat in the water for the first time, to understand spring as a season of the heart as much as of the calendar. And in summer when I pass by on the water, to watch her turn with a trowel in her hand and wave from the yard at the sound of my horn. And in autumn to understand my sadness when I lay up the Mary Deare *for the winter. I want for us some fine things – an occasional Dom Perignon, two weeks in Acapulco, chateaubriand by candlelight; and some less than fine – greying hair and lost keys and spring colds.*

No, I don't want to leave this woman.

He knew the precise moment she awakened by the change in rhythm of her breathing, and the slight tensing of muscles that fell just short of a stretch. He spread his hand on her stomach and touched her back with his nose. She reached behind and slipped her hand between his legs. Stroked him – once, twice – tight, deft, certain, and his flesh sprang alive in her hand. She smiled – he knew it as certainly as if he could see her face – and curled forward, tucking him inside her, then reaching around with an arm and drawing him flush against her. He gripped her hips and said good-morning-I-love-you in an age-old, wordless way.

When they had shuddered and stilled, and the moisture lay drying upon their skins, she turned, their bodies still precariously linked, and hooked her legs over his thighs.

The smile he had earlier divined, he saw and met with one of his own. He crooked an elbow beneath his ear and fitted the fingers of his free hand between hers. They lay studying one another's eyes while morning brightened the sills of the room. His thumb drew lazy circles around hers. The furnace clicked off and the curtains stopped fluttering. She reached to smooth a tuft of hair on his head, then linked her hand with his as before and resumed the lazy stirring of thumbs. No word was spoken, no promises lent, but during that silence they both said the most meaningful things of all.

A half hour later they sat at the table, holding hands, wishing useless wishes. He emptied his coffee cup and rose reluctantly, drawing his jacket from the back of the chair. He slipped it on slowly, delaying the inevitable, his head hanging as he reached for the bottom snap. She came to him and brushed his hands aside, usurping the task. One snap. Another. Another. Each drawing them closer and closer to parting. When all but the top snap were closed, she raised his collar and held it against his jaws with both hands, drew his face down and tenderly kissed his mouth.

'I would not have traded last night for Aladdin's lamp,' she told him softly.

Closing his eyes, he wrapped both arms around her.

'It was much better than when we were kids.'

'Much better.' She smiled. 'Thank you.'

They drifted into the sombre silence of pre-parting.

'I don't know what's going to happen,' Eric told her. 'What I feel is strong, though. It'll need some kind of resolution.'

'Yes, I suppose it will.'

'I don't think I'll live too easily with guilt.'

She spread her hands on the supple leather covering of his shoulder-blades and felt the need to make of this parting not a mere good-bye but a valediction.

'Let's not feel we must make promises to one another. Instead, let's believe this was predestined, like our first time in Easley's orchard. A lovely, unexpected gift.'

He drew back, studied her serene brown eyes and thought, you're not going to ask, are you, Maggie? Not when you'll see me again, or if I'll call, or any of the questions I have no answers for.

'Maggie M'girl . . .' he said lovingly. 'It's going to be very hard for me to walk out of that door.'

'Isn't that the way it should be when two people become lovers?'

'Yes.' He smiled and brushed her jaw with his knuckles. 'That's the way it should be.'

They said good-bye with their eyes, with the lingering touch of his fingertips on her throat, and hers on his jacket front, then he bent, kissed her lightly, and whispered, 'I'll call you.'

She moved through the day vacillating between gladness and gloom. Sometimes she felt as if she radiated a halo of well-being, something shining and discernible. If a deliveryman were to come to the door, surely he would raise his eyebrows in surprise and ask, 'What's that?' and she would reply, 'Why, that's happiness.'

Other times she was struck by a wave of melancholy. It would stop her in the middle of a task and leave her with her eyes fixed on some inanimate object on the opposite side of the room. *What have you done? What's going to happen? Where will this lead?* To certain heartbreak, she was convinced, not for two people, but for three.

Do you want him to come back?

Yes.

No.

Yes, God help me, yes.

He moved through the day experiencing intermittent flashes of grievousness and guilt that would stop him cold and draw the corners of his mouth down. He'd expected it, but nothing this heavy. If he were to drive out to Mike's, his brother would frown and ask, 'What's the matter?' and Eric would undoubtedly confess his wrongdoing. He had broken his marriage vows, had wronged a wife who, in spite of her shortcomings, deserved better, and a mistress who, given the grief she'd recently suffered, also deserved better.

Are you going back there?

No.

Yes.

No.

By noon he missed her so badly he called simply to hear her voice.

'Hello,' she answered, and his heart thrust harder in his chest.

'Hello.'

For moments neither of them spoke, only pictured each other and ached.

'What are you doing?' he asked at last.

'Brookie is here. She's helping me hang a wallpaper border strip in the dining room.'

'Oh.' Disappointment seemed to crush him. 'Well, I'd better let you go then.'

'Yes.'

'I just wanted to tell you that I don't think I'd better come over tonight.'

'Oh . . . well . . .' Her pause told him little of what she felt. 'That's okay. I understand.'

'It isn't fair to you, Maggie.'

'Yes, I understand,' she said quietly. 'Well, just call whenever you can.'

'Maggie, I'm sorry.'

'Good-bye, then.'

She hung up before he could explain further.

For the remainder of the afternoon he walked around hurting. Listless. Staring. Torn. It was Wednesday. Nancy would be home on Friday around four; the two days stretched before him like a bleak, featureless desert, though her arrival would bring him face to face with what kind of man he was.

He went upstairs and lay down on the bed with his hands stacked under his head, his insides quivering. He thought about going out to Mike's. Or Ma's. Talk to somebody. Yeah, he'd go out to Ma's. Fill her fuel oil barrel.

He rose and took a shower, shaved and put after-shave on his face. And his chest. And on his genitals.

What're you doing, Severson?

I'm getting ready to go out to Ma's.

With after-shave on your pecker?

Goddamn you!

Come on, man, who're you kidding?

He slammed the bottle down and muttered a curse, but when his eyes lifted, the same alter ego regarded him from the mirror.

Go there one more time and you'll go there a hundred, then you'll have a full-blown affair on your hands. Is that what you want?

I want to be happy.

You think you'll be happy married to one woman and consorting with another?

No.

Then go to Ma's.

He went to Ma's and stalked in without knocking. She turned from the kitchen sink, wearing maroon double-knit slacks and a yellow sweatshirt sporting a green pickerel leaping after a lure.

'Well, look who's here,' she said.

'Hi, Ma.'

'You musta smelled my Swiss steak clear in town.'

'I just stopped for a minute.'

'Yeah, sure, and a snake's got toenails. I'll peel another couple of potatoes.'

He filled her fuel oil burner. And ate a chunk of Swiss

steak and a mound of mashed potatoes and some detestable green beans (these as penance). Then he sat on her lumpy sofa and watched one game show and an hour and a half of championship wrestling (an even greater penance) and one detective show, which brought him safely to ten o'clock.

Only then did he stretch and rise and wake Ma, who sat slumped in her favourite rocker with the pickerel folded in half across her flaccid breasts.

'Hey, Ma, wake up and go to bed.'

'Whuh? . . .' she muttered, the corners of her lips wet. 'Mmm . . . You going?'

'Yeah. It's ten o'clock. Thanks for the supper.'

'Yeah, yeah . . .'

'Goodnight.'

'Yeah, g'night.'

He got into the old whore and drove at the speed of a glacier, telling himself if he burned up another half hour, by the time he reached Fish Creek it would be too late to drop by Maggie's house.

When he got to town he told himself he'd only head up Cottage Row to see if her lights were on.

When he drew abreast of her snowbanks he told himself he was only crawling along so he could peer down the path as he flashed past, make sure she was all right.

When he caught a quick glimpse of lights in the lower level, he ordered himself, keep going, Severson! Just keep your ass going!

Twenty feet beyond her house he braked and sat motionlessly in the middle of the road staring at the tip of someone's roof and a dark dormer window.

Don't do it.

I've got to.

The hell you do.

'Son of a bitch,' he muttered as he slammed the truck into reverse, flung an arm along the back of the seat and careened backward at thirty miles an hour. He swerved to a halt at the top of her sidewalk, killed the engine and sat studying Maggie's kitchen windows between the high snowbanks – pale gold ingots of light drifting from somewhere deeper in the house. Why wasn't she asleep by now? It was going on eleven, and any woman with a lick of sense would have stopped waiting for a man by this time of night. And any man with an ounce of respect would leave her alone.

He threw open the truck door and slammed it vehemently behind himself, bounded down the steps and arrived breathless at her back door. Angrily, he knocked, then waited on the dark verandah feeling as if someone had driven a wedge into his larynx, watching for her approach through the darkened kitchen.

The door opened and she stood in a veil of night shadows wearing a long quilted robe.

He tried to speak, but couldn't – apology and appeal trapped in his throat. In silence they confronted one another, their own vulnerability and this terrible, magnificent greed they felt for one another. Then she moved, hurtling against him with a faint, lost cry, throwing her arms around his neck and kissing him as women kiss men who have returned from war.

'You came.'

'I came,' he repeated, lifting her free of the verandah floor with her feet trailing inches above his as he hauled her over the threshold. He elbowed the door shut with such force the lace curtain caught in the weather stripping. In the semi-darkness they kissed, openmouthed and ravenous, abandoning grace and reserve, clawing at clothing and dropping it where it fell. Their impatience was a lightning bolt carrying them from one forbidden pleasure to the next – a puddle of clothing upon a kitchen floor; untrammelled seeking; an almost manic compulsion to find, touch, taste everywhere; his mouth upon her breast, belly and mons; hers upon him; her back against the kitchen door; his arm clamping her waist and hauling her down to her knees atop their discarded clothing, a frantic coupling and the racking of limbs, accompanied by the baring of teeth and their rasping cries of release.

Then two people panting and wilted, waiting for their breath to return.

It ended where it had begun, beside the kitchen door, with both of them astounded by their own abandon, still trying to sort through the maelstrom of emotions.

He fell to his back, watched her roll away and sit beside him running a shaky hand through her hair. The only light in the kitchen came from the opposite end of the house, barely illuminating her silhouette. A lump of clothing bored into his waist and a cold draught threaded in beneath the door.

'You said you weren't going to come over tonight,' she said, almost defensively.

'And you said, "okay," as if it didn't matter one way or another.'

'It mattered. I was afraid to let you know how much.'

'Now I know, don't I?'

She felt like weeping. Instead she got up and padded to the small lavatory around the corner.

He lay where she'd left him while the light snapped on. The water ran. He sighed, then got up and followed. He stopped in the open doorway and found her standing naked, staring at the sink. It was a tiny room with an angled ceiling, papered in dusty blue with a border strip following the ceiling. It contained only the sink and the toilet, on opposite walls. He spied a box of tissues and moved inside to stand back to back with her, tending to necessities. 'I didn't want to come back tonight. I went out to Ma's and stayed there late enough that I thought you'd be in bed. If the house had been dark I never would have stopped.'

'I didn't really want you to come over either.'

She turned on the water and cupped some against her face. He flushed the toilet, then turned to study her rounded back bent over the sink. She reached up blindly, found a towel and buried her face in it while he stroked the hollow between her shoulder blades and asked, 'Maggie, what's wrong?'

She straightened and drew the towel to her chin, meeting his eyes in the mirror, an oval mirror mounted high on the wall, cutting off their reflections at shoulder level. 'I didn't want it to be this way.'

'What way?'

'Just . . . just lust.'

'It's not just lust.'

'Then why did I think about it so much today? Why did that just happen in the kitchen, just what I thought would happen if you came back?'

'You didn't enjoy it?'

'I loved it. That's what scares me. Where was the spiritual element?'

He fitted his body close behind hers, slipped both arms below her breasts and dropped his lips to her shoulder.

'Maggie, I love you.'

She aligned her arms with his. 'I love you, too.'

'And what happened in the kitchen was the result of frustration.'

'I don't think I'll be very good at this . . . having an affair. I'm already an emotional wreck.'

He lifted his head. For moments they studied one another's troubled eyes.

'May I stay here tonight?'

'Do you think that's wise?'

'You didn't question wisdom last night.'

'I've done some thinking since then.'

'So have I. That's why I went out to Ma's.'

'And I'm sure we came up with the same conclusions.'

'Nevertheless, I want to stay.'

He spent that night and the next in her bed, and on Friday morning when he prepared to leave, the same pall fell upon them. They stood at the back door, his hands on her upper arms, hers at her sides. She had armoured herself by assuming a mood of dispassion.

'I'll see you next week,' he told her.

'All right.'

'Maggie, I . . .' He struggled again with his great inner conflict. 'I don't want to go back to her.'

'I know.'

He felt some confusion at her lack of clinging. She remained cool, almost remote, lifting tearless brown eyes, while he was the one who felt like crying.

'Maggie, I need to know what you're feeling.'

'I love you.'

'Yes, I know that, but have you thought about the rest of your life? About ever marrying again?'

'Sometimes.'

'About marrying me?' he asked simply.

'Sometimes.'

'Would you? If I were free?'

She paused, afraid to answer, because in the last three days she'd had time to consider how rash this had all been, and where it was taking her life.

'Maggie, I'm very new at this. I've never had an affair before, and if I seem unsure it's because I am. I don't know what comes first. I can't be intimate with two women at the same time, and she's coming home, and it's decision time. Oh, hell, this is awkward.'

'For both of us, because I've never had an affair either. Eric, please understand. I *have* thought about what it would be like to be married to you. But it's been . . .' She paused, seeking honesty. 'It's been more fantasy than anything else. Because we were first for each other, and if things had gone differently we might have been married all these years. I suppose it was natural that I idealized you, and fantasized about you. And then suddenly you came sweeping back into my life like a . . . a knight on a steed, a sailor at the helm, blowing your air horn and making my heart plunge. My first love.'

She rested her hands on his leather jacket at the level of his heart. 'But I don't want us to make commitments we can't keep, or demands we have no right to make. We've been together only three days, and – let's be honest – the way the sex has been, we may be reasoning with our glands right now.'

He drew a deep breath and let his shoulders sag. 'I've told myself the same thing at least a dozen times a day, and to tell the truth, I was afraid to bring up marriage for exactly the same reasons. Everything is happening so fast. But I wanted you to know before I left here that I've made a decision and I'm sticking to it. I'm going to tell Nancy tonight that I can't live with her anymore. I won't be one of those men who keeps stringing two women along.'

'Eric, listen to me.' She took his face in her hands. 'There's a part of me that loves hearing you say that, but there's another part that sees very clearly how people in this situation do the thing that's ultimately wrong for them. Eric, think. Think very hard about your reasons for leaving her. They must be because of your relationship with her, not because of your relationship with me.'

He studied her brown eyes, thinking how wise she was and how unclassic their responses: he supposed in most cases such as theirs, the single one would be clinging, the married one evasive.

'I told you before this started, I don't love her anymore. I haven't for months. I even talked to my brother, Mike, about it last fall.'

'But if you've made the decision to leave her and you did it impulsively, there's a good possibility you're reacting to the last three nights instead of the last eighteen years, and which should bear more weight?'

'I said I've made my decision, and I'll stick to it.'

'All right. You do what you must, but do it understanding that I have just embarked upon a new phase of my life. I have this house, and a business I've barely begun, and some things to accomplish on my own.' More quietly, she added, 'And I still have some healing to do.'

For some time they stood separately, untouching.

'All right,' he said at length. 'Thanks for being honest with me.'

'I've read,' she told him, 'that in order to buy a handgun you must fill out an application and wait three days. The lawmakers think it eliminates a lot of shootings. Perhaps they ought to make a similar law about leaving wives when affairs begin.' Their eyes met, Eric's dismayed, Maggie's drawn with concern. 'Eric, I've never considered myself a potential homewrecker, but I've got my guilts over what happened, too.'

'So what do you want to do?'

'Would you agree to put off doing anything for a while, and during that time, staying away from me? From here?'

He studied her, beleaguered. 'For how long?'

'Let's not set a time limit. Let's just consider it a commonsense time.'

'Could I call you?' he asked, looking like a little boy chastised.

'If you think it's wise.'

'You're putting it all on me.'

'No. I'll only call you if I think it's wise, too.'

He looked sad.

'Now smile for me once, before you go,' she requested.

Instead, he clutched her close against him. 'Aw, Maggie . . .'

'I know . . . I know . . .' she soothed, rubbing his back.

But she didn't know. She had no more answers than he.

'I'll miss you,' he whispered. His voice sounded tortured.

'I'll miss you, too.'

A moment later he spun away, the door opened and he was gone.

Chapter 13

Nancy had had a trying trip up from Chicago and arrived irritable. The roads had been icy, the weather frigid and the store clerks temperamental. When she opened the kitchen door and stepped inside, burdened by luggage, Eric was there to meet her. The aroma in the room immediately took the edge off her temper.

'Hi,' she said, catching the door with her heel while he reached for her suitcase and garment bag.

'Hi.'

She lifted her face toward his but he grabbed her things and carried them away without the customary kiss. When he returned to the kitchen, he moved straight to the refrigerator and reached inside for a bottle of lime water.

'It smells good in here. What have you got in the oven?'

'Cornish game hens with wild-rice stuffing.'

'Cornish game hens . . . what's the occasion?'

Guilt, he thought, but answered, 'I know they're your favourites.' He closed the refrigerator, twisted off the bottle cap and opened a lower cabinet door to drop it into the garbage. She was close behind him when he turned.

'Mmm . . . what a nice homecoming,' she said invitingly.

He raised the bottle and took a swig.

She caught him in the circle of her arms, pinning his elbows to his sides. 'No kiss?'

He hesitated before giving her a quick one. The look on his face set off an alarm bell in Nancy.

'Hey, wait a minute . . . is that all I get?'

He eased free. 'I've got to check the birds,' he said, and picked up a pair of pot holders off the countertop before shouldering around her to reach the stove. 'Excuse me, I have to open the oven.'

Within Nancy the alarm bell sounded again, more insistently. Whatever was bothering him, it was serious. So many excuses to avoid a kiss, a glance. He checked the birds, drank his bottle of lime water, set the table, served her favourite foods, inquired about her week, and maintained eye contact for a grand total of perhaps ten seconds through the entire meal. His replies were distant, his sense of humour nonexistent, and he left half the food on his plate.

'What's wrong?' she asked at meal's end.

He picked up his plate, carried it to the sink and turned on the water. 'It's just these winter doldrums.'

It's more, she thought as a frisson of panic ricocheted through her body. It's a woman. The truth struck her like a broadside: he had begun changing the day his old girlfriend came back to town. Nancy added it up again – his distraction, his uncharacteristic quietness, the way he'd suddenly begun avoiding physical contact.

Do something, she thought, say something that will forestall him.

'Honey, I've been thinking,' she said, leaving her chair, fitting her body behind his and twining her arms around his belt. 'Maybe I'll ask to have my territory split so I could have a couple more days a week at home.' It was a lie. She hadn't considered it for a moment, but, driven by desperation, she said what she hoped he'd want to hear.

Beneath her cheek she felt his back muscles working as he scrubbed a plate.

'What do you think?' she asked.

He continued moving. The water ran.

'If you want to.'

'I've also been doing a little more thinking about having a baby.'

He went still as a threatened spider. With her ear against his back she heard him swallow.

'Maybe one wouldn't be so bad.'

The water stopped running. In the silence, neither of them moved.

'Why the sudden change of heart?' he asked.

She improvised as fast as her thoughts could race. 'I was thinking since you don't work during the winter you could take care of it then. If I went back to work we'd only need a baby-sitter for half the year.'

She ran a hand down his jeans and curled it against the warmth of his compressed genitals. He draped the butts of his hands against the edge of the sink and said nothing.

'Eric?' she whispered, beginning to stroke him.

He swung around and seized her against him, wetting the back of her silk dress, clutching her with the desperation of a mourner. She sensed she had stumbled upon some moment of crisis and felt certain she knew what it was: guilt.

He was rough with her, giving her no chance to resist, stripping her from the waist down as if afraid she – or he – might change their minds. There was a small sofa in the living room around the corner. He hauled her to it and without giving her the opportunity to take precautions, made short order of putting sperm within her: without kisses or tenderness their coupling could be called little else.

When it was over, Nancy was angry.

'Let me up,' she said.

In silence they moved to separate parts of the house to put themselves in order.

In their bedroom upstairs she stood a long time in the dim light from the hall, staring at a knob on a chest of drawers, thinking, if he made me pregnant, so help me God, I'll kill him!

In the kitchen he stood for minutes. At length he sighed, resumed cleaning off the table, abandoned the job midway and returned to the living room to sit in the gloom on the edge of a chair with his elbows on his knees and reflect upon his life. He was so damned confused. What was he trying to prove by manhandling Nancy that way? He felt like a pervert, guiltier than ever after what he'd done. Did he really want her pregnant now? If he walked into the bedroom at this moment and said, I want a divorce, and she said okay, wouldn't he walk right out of this house and go to Maggie without a second thought?

No. Because he, not his wife, was the guilty party here.

The house remained so quiet he could hear the kitchen faucet dripping. He sat in the gloom until his eyes discerned the outline of the sofa where the cushions remained askew in one corner where he'd thrown her.

He rose disconsolately and straightened them. Went upstairs, climbing with heavy steps. In the doorway of their bedroom he stopped and looked into the darkened room. She was sitting on the foot of the bed beside the garment bag he'd brought up earlier. On the floor nearby sat her suitcase. He thought he would not blame her if she picked them up and walked out.

He shuffled in and stopped beside her.

'I'm sorry, Nancy,' he said.

She remained motionless, as if she had not heard him.

He touched her head heavily.

'I'm sorry,' he whispered.

Still sitting, she pivoted to face the far wall and crossed her arms tightly. 'You should be,' she said.

He let his hand slip off her head and drop to his side.

He waited, but she said no more. He searched for something further to offer her, but felt like a drained vessel without a single droplet left to offer her for sustenance. After some time he walked from the room and isolated himself downstairs.

On Monday forenoon he went out to Mike's, driven by the need for a confessor.

Barb answered his knock; round as a dirigible and wholesomely happy. She took one look at his glum face and said, 'He's down in the garage changing the oil in his truck.'

Eric found Mike dressed in greasy coveralls, lying on a creeper beneath his Ford pickup.

'Heya, Mike,' he said cheerlessly, closing the door.

'That you, little bro?'

'It's me.'

'Just a minute, let me get this oil draining.' There followed several grunts, a metallic grating, then the ping of liquid hitting an empty pan. The creeper bumped along the concrete floor and Mike emerged, wearing a red bill-cap turned backward.

'You out slumming?'

'You guessed it,' Eric obliged with a halfhearted grin.

'Looking like a whipped spaniel, too,' Mike observed, rising, wiping his hands on a rag.

'I need to talk to you.'

'Woa! This *is* serious.'

'Yes, it is.'

'Well, hang on. Let me stick a couple chunks of wood in the stove.' In one corner of the garage a barrel-sized cast-iron stove gave off warmth. Mike opened its squeaky door, thrust in two pieces of maple, returned to Eric, and overturned a green plastic bucket. 'Sit,' he ordered, dropping onto the creeper with his legs outstretched and his ankles crossed. 'I've got the whole damn day,' he invited, 'so shoot.'

Eric sat still as a rock, his eyes on a toolbox, wondering how to begin. Finally his troubled gaze shifted to Mike.

'Remember when we were little and the old man would whip our asses when we did something wrong?'

'Yup. Whip 'em good.'

'I've been wishing he was around to do it again.'

'What have you done that you need whipping for?'

Eric drew a deep breath and said it plain. 'I'm having an affair with Maggie Pearson.'

Mike's hairline rose and his ears seemed to flatten. He took the news without comment at first, then turned the bill of his cap to the front and remarked, 'Well, I see why you wish the old man were here, but I don't think a licking would do much good.'

'No, probably not. I just had to tell someone because I feel like such a lowlife.'

'How long has it been going on?'

'Last week, that's all.'

'And it's over?'

'I don't know.'

'Oh-oh.'

'Yeah. Oh-oh.'

They mulled awhile before Mike asked, 'So you intend to see her again?'

'I don't know. We agreed to stay away from each other for a while. Cool off a little and see.'

'Does Nancy know?'

'She probably suspects. It was a hell of a weekend.'

Mike blew out a long breath, removed his cap, scratched his head and replaced the cap with the bill low over his eyes.

Eric spread his hands. 'Mike, I'm so damned mixed up. I think I love Maggie.'

Mike studied his brother thoughtfully. 'I figured this was going to happen, the minute I heard she was moving back to town. I know how you were with her in high school. I knew you two were getting it on back then.'

'You knew?' Eric's face registered surprise. 'Like hell you knew.'

'Don't look so surprised. It was my car you were borrowing, remember? And Barb and I were getting a little ourselves, so we guessed about you and Maggie.'

'Damn it, you're so lucky. Do you know how lucky you two are? I look at you and Barb, and your family, and how you turned out together and I think, why didn't I grab Maggie back then, and maybe I'd have what you've got.'

'It's more than luck, and you know it. It's damned hard work and a lot of compromise.'

'Yeah, I know,' Eric replied disconsolately.

'So what about you and Nancy?'

Eric shook his head. 'That's a mess.'

'How so?'

'In the middle of all this she comes home and says, *maybe* she'll have a baby after all. *Maybe* one wouldn't be so bad. So I put her to the test. I jumped her then and there without giving her a chance to take any precautions, and she hasn't talked to me since.'

'You mean you forced her?'

'I guess that's what you'd call it, yeah.'

Mike peered at his brother from beneath his bill-cap and said quietly, 'Not good, man.'

'I know.'

'What the hell were you thinking?'

'I don't know. I felt guilty about Maggie, and scared and angry that Nancy waited all this time to finally consider having a family.'

'Can I ask you something?'

Eric glanced at his brother, waiting.

'Do you love her?'

Eric sighed.

Mike waited.

Beneath the pickup the oil gurgled once and stopped running. The smell of it filled the place, mixed with the smokehouse scent of burning maple.

'Sometimes I get flashes of feeling, but it's mostly wishing for what might have been. When I first met her it was all physical attraction. I thought she was the greatest-looking woman on the face of the earth. Then after I got to know her I realized how bright she was, and how much ambition she had, and I figured someday she'd succeed at something in a big way. Back then all of that mattered as much as her looks. But you want to know something ironic?'

'What?'

'It's the very things I admired her for that are driving me away. Her business success somehow came to matter more to her than the success of our marriage. And, hell, we don't share anything anymore. We used to like the same music, now she puts those headphones on and listens to self-motivation tapes. When we were first married we'd take clothes to the laundromat together and now she has her dry cleaning done overnight while she's in hotels. We don't even like the same kinds of food anymore. She eats health food and carps at me about eating doughnuts all the time. We don't use the same cheque book, or the same doctors, or even the same bar of soap! She hates my snowmobile, my pickup, our house – Christ, Mike, I thought when people were married they were supposed to grow *together*!'

Mike crooked his arms around his updrawn knees.

'If you don't love her you have no business trying to persuade her to have a baby, much less jumping her without a condom.'

'I know.' Eric hung his head. In time he shook it forlornly. 'Aw hell . . .' He stared at the stove. 'Falling out of love is a bitch. It really hurts.'

Mike rose and went to his brother, clapping an arm around Eric's shoulders. 'Yeah.' They remained that way awhile listening to the snap of the fire, surrounded by its warmth and the familiar smells of hot cast iron and motor oil. Years ago they had shared the same bedroom and an old iron bed. They had shared both the praises and punishments of their parents, and sometimes – when it was dark and neither of them could sleep – their hopes and dreams. They felt as close now at the crumbling of one of their dreams as they had upon disclosing them as lads.

'So what do you want to do?' Mike asked.

'I want to marry Maggie, but she says I'm probably thinking with my glands right now.'

Mike laughed.

'Besides, she's not ready to get married again. She wants to be a businesswoman for a while, and I guess I can't blame her for that. Hell, she hasn't even taken in her first customer yet, and after all the money she sank into that house, she wants a chance to see it go.'

'So you came to me asking what you ought to do about Nancy, but I can't answer. Would it bother you to let it ride for a while?'

'It just seems so damned dishonest. I had a hell of a time keeping from telling her this weekend and making a clean break, but Maggie made me promise I'd give it some time.'

After a moment's thought, Mike squeezed Eric's shoulder. 'Tell you what let's do.' He turned Eric towards the truck. 'Let's get this oil changed and take the snow-mobiles out for a ride. That always clears the head.'

They were men who'd been born in the north where winter makes up nearly half the year. They'd learned young how to appreciate the bright blues and stark whites of it, the sturdiness of skeletal trees, the beauty of snow-draped branches, of purple shadows and red barns against the white landscape.

They drove south, to Newport State Park, and along the shoreline of Rowley's Bay where the harbour appeared as a jigsaw puzzle of ice, the beach a crescent of white. Swells of water had surged beneath the frozen lake and raised great windows, which eventually fell beneath their own weight, and cracked into great sheets that shifted back and forth, the cracks enlarging to ponds where goldeneyes, mergansers and buffleheads consorted. The ice hit upon itself and chimed in the empty bay. White-winged scoters swam along the ice-edge and dived for food beneath the glass. From the distance came a garbled yodel. '*O-owaowa-wa-wa*.' A flock of birds lifted from the water, their long, thin tails trailing behind like giant stingers – old squaws, summer residents of the Arctic Circle on southern holiday in Door County.

Inland, the riders passed sumac and dogwood whose red berries shone like jewels against the snow, then on beneath a cathedral of hemlock and white pine branches, and into a copse of yellow birch laden with seed catkins where redpolls were having a repast. They followed a deer trail of dainty footprints where the animals had been dallying, and eventually came upon great pock marks where the deer had broken into a run and plunged down a steep dune where their bounding hooves had left great explosions of white, like giant doilies, upon the snow.

Blue jays swooped before them, scolding in their unpretty voices, and for a time a pileated woodpecker led them from one bend to the next. They found craters where deer had slept, a running spring where mink, mouse and squirrel had drunk.

They drove on to an ice-covered reservoir near Mud Lake where a beaver lodge rose like an untidy hairdo wearing a hat of white.

They sat for a time on a bluff above Cana Island with the forest at their backs and the horizon flat as a blue string in the distance, broken only by the spire of the island lighthouse. Nearby, a nuthatch sang its tuneless note while the ice below shifted and belched. A woodpecker hammered in a dead birch. Somewhere on the south end of Door County the frantic pace of the winter shipyards signalled their busiest season, but here, only calm prevailed. In it, Eric felt the essence of winter salve his soul.

'I'll wait,' he decided quietly.

'I think that's wise.'

'Maggie doesn't know what she wants either.'

'But if you take up with her again you should make the break with Nancy right away.'

'I will. I promise.'

'Okay, then, let's go home.'

January advanced. He said nothing to Nancy and kept his

promise not to call or see Maggie, though he missed her with a hollow-bellied intensity. In early February he and Mike attended the Sports Show in Chicago where they rented a display booth, passed out literature, pitched prospective customers and booked charters for the upcoming fishing season. They were long, tiring days when they talked until their throats were sore, stood until their feet hurt, lived primarily on hot dogs available from vendors on the showroom floor, and slept poorly in strange hotel rooms.

He returned to Fish Creek to an empty house, a note from Nancy outlining her itinerary for the week, and the telephone only a reach away. A dozen times he passed it and thought how simple it would be to pick it up and dial Maggie's number. Talk about the show, the bookings they'd made, his week, her week – the things he should be talking to his wife about. In the end he resisted.

One day he went uptown to get the mail and passed Vera Pearson on the sidewalk. It was a windy day and she hurried with her head down, holding a scarf against her chin. When she heard his footsteps approaching from the opposite direction she looked up, and her footsteps slowed. Then her expression turned hard as she quickened her pace and moved on without any further acknowledgement.

During the third week of February he and Mike went to the Boat, Sports and Travel Show in Minneapolis. On the second day there a woman came into the booth who resembled Maggie. She was taller and had paler hair, but the resemblance was uncanny and brought Eric a sharp sexual reaction. He closed the button on his sports coat as he moved toward her.

'Hello, may I answer any questions?'

'Not really. But I'd like to take your brochure for my husband.'

'Sure. We're Severson's Charters, and we run two boats out of Gills Rock in northern Door County, Wisconsin.'

'Door County. I've heard of that.'

'Straight north of Green Bay, on the peninsula.'

Facts, pertinent questions, answers and a polite thank-you. But once, while they talked, their eyes met directly and though they were total strangers, a recognition passed between them: in another time, another place, given other circumstances, they would have spoken of things other than salmon fishing.

As she left the booth, the woman glanced back one last time and smiled with Maggie's brown eyes, and Maggie's cleft chin, leaving him with so strong an impression of her that it distracted him for the remainder of the day.

That night after he'd showered and switched off the television set, he sat on the edge of his bed, a white towel girding his hips, his hair damp and finger-rilled. From the nightstand he picked up his watch.

10:32.

He laid it down and studied the phone. It was beige – did any hotel in America buy phones in any other colour? – the luckless colour of things once alive. He picked up the receiver and read the instructions for long-distance dialling, changed his mind and cracked it back down.

Maggie knew him well, knew that even this indiscretion would create twinges of conscience.

In the end he dialled anyway and sat waiting with the muscles in his stomach seized up like a prize-fighter's fist.

She answered on the third ring.

'Hello?'

'Hello.'

Silence, while he wondered, is her heart slugging like mine? Does her throat feel like there's a tourniquet on it?

'Isn't it curious,' she said quietly, 'I knew it would be you.'

'Why?'

'It's 10:30. I don't know anybody else who'd call me this late.'

'Did I wake you?'

'No. I've been gathering data for my income taxes.'

'Ah. Well, maybe I shouldn't bother you then.'

'No, it's all right. I've been at it a long time. I needed to put all these papers away anyway.'

Silence again before he asked, 'Are you in the kitchen?'

'Yes.'

He pictured her there, where they'd first kissed, where they'd made love on the floor.

Another halting silence while they wondered how to proceed.

'How have you been?' she inquired.

'Mixed up.'

'Me, too.'

'I wasn't going to call.'

'I halfway hoped you wouldn't.'

'Then today I saw a woman who reminded me of you.'

'Oh? Is it anyone I know?'

'No, she was a stranger. I'm at the Radisson Hotel in Minneapolis –Mike and I – we're here for the sportsmen's show. This woman walked into our booth today and she had eyes so much like yours, and your chin . . . I don't know.' He closed his eyes and pinched the bridge of his nose.

'It's terrible, isn't it, how we look for traces of each other?'

'You do the same thing?'

'Constantly. Then berate myself for doing it.'

'Same here. This woman . . . something strange happened when she walked in. We couldn't have talked for more than three minutes, but I felt . . . I don't know how to put it . . . threatened almost, as if I were on the brink of doing something unholy. I don't know why I'm telling you this, Maggie, you're the last person I should be telling this to.'

'No, tell me . . .'

'It was scary. I looked at her and I felt . . . aw, shit, there's no other way to say it. Carnal. I felt carnal. And I realized that if it weren't for you and our affair, I might have struck up a conversation with her just to see where it would lead. Maggie, I'm not that kind of man, and it scares the hell out of me. I mean, you read about male menopause, guys who've been devoted husbands for years, and then in their forties they just lose it and start acting like morons, chasing kids young enough to be their daughters, having one-nighters with perfect strangers. I don't want to think that's what's happening to me.'

'Tell me something, Eric. Could you ever admit a thing like that to Nancy – about that woman, I mean?'

'Christ, no.'

'That's significant, don't you think? That you can tell me but not her?'

'I suppose so.'

'While we're baring our insecurities, let me confess one of my own: that I'm a sex-starved widow, and you were my feast.'

'Aw, Maggie,' he said softly.

'Well?' she demanded, self-deprecatingly, remembering the night on her kitchen floor.

'Don't worry about it.'

'But I do, because I'm not a user either.'

'Maggie, listen, do you know why I called you tonight?'

'To tell me about that woman you saw today.'

'That, too, but the real reason is because I knew I couldn't get to you, that it was safe to call you from three hundred miles away. Maggie, I miss you.'

'I miss you, too.'

'Next Friday makes four weeks.'

'Yes, I know.'

When she said no more, he sighed, then they listened to the electronic hum of the telephone line. Eric broke the silence.

'Maggie?'

'Yes, I'm here.'

'What are you thinking?'

Instead of answering, she asked a question of her own. 'Did you tell Nancy about us?'

'No, but I told Mike. I had to talk to somebody. I'm sorry if I violated a confidence.'

'No, it's all right. If I had a sister, I'd probably have told her, too.'

'Thanks for understanding.'

They listened to each other breathe for some time, wondering what lay ahead for them. Finally she said, 'We'd better say goodnight now.'

'No, Maggie, wait.' His voice turned abject. 'Aw, Jesus, Maggie, this is hell. I want to see you.'

'And what then, Eric? What will come of it? An affair? A messy breakup of your marriage? I'm not sure I'm ready to face that and I don't think you are either.'

He wanted to beg her, make promises. But what promises could he make?

'I . . . I really have to go now,' she insisted.

He thought he heard a tremor in her voice.

'Goodnight, Eric,' she said gently.

'Goodnight.'

For fifteen seconds they pressed their cheeks to the receivers.

'Hang up,' he whispered.

'I can't.' She was crying now, he could tell, though she did her best to disguise it. But her words sounded thick and quavery. Sitting on the bed, doubled forward at the waist, he felt his own eyes water.

'Maggie, I'm so goddamned much in love with you that I hurt. Like I've been bruised, and I'm not sure I'll make it through another day without seeing you again.'

'Good-bye, darling,' she whispered and did what he was unable to make himself do. She hung up.

He moved through the next day believing he would never see her again; her parting words had been sorrowful but final. She'd had a full, happy life with her husband. She had a daughter and a business and new goals in her life. She had financial independence. What did she need with him? And in a town the size of Fish Creek, where everybody knew everybody else's business, she was right to be cautious about involving herself in a relationship that was certain to bring her sideways glances from a segment of the population – whether they had an affair or he left Nancy for her. Already she'd suffered the censure of her own daughter and mother. No, their affair was over.

He had a miserable day. Walked around feeling like someone had stuffed a wad of rags down his chest cavity and he'd never draw another unrestricted breath. He wished he hadn't called her. It was worse since he'd heard her voice. Worse knowing she lived through the same four weeks as miserable as he. Worse knowing there would be no solace for either of them.

He went to bed that night and lay awake, listening to the sound of traffic on 7th Street below, now and then a siren. Thinking of Nancy, and Maggie's admonition to judge his marriage on the basis of it, and not his affair. He tried. He could not. To picture his future in any context was to picture it with Maggie. The hotel mattress and pillows were hard as sacks of grain. He wished he was a smoker. It would feel comforting to abuse his body with a little tar and nicotine right now, to suck it in and blow it out and think, to hell with everything.

His watch had an illuminable face. He pressed the stem and checked it: 11:27.

Is this what articles mean when they talk about stress? Don't men my age have heart attacks when they get into a situation like this? Worried, undecided, unhappy, not sleeping or eating properly? On a sexual tightrope?

The phone rang and he jumped so hard he skinned his

knuckles on the headboard. He rolled up on one elbow and found the receiver in the dark.

'Hello?'

Her voice was soft and held a touch of penitence. She spoke without preamble. 'I'd very much like to make dinner for you on Monday night.'

He sank back on the pillows, his heart drumming hard, the knot of yearning exploding into a thousand smaller knots that bound him in the unlikeliest of places – temples, fingers, shoulder blades. 'Maggie, oh, Jesus, Maggie, do you mean it?'

'I never meant anything more.'

So what's it to be – an affair or marriage? It wasn't the time to ask, of course, and for now it was enough to know he'd see her again.

'How did you find me?'

'You said the Radisson in Minneapolis. There are four of them, I discovered, but I finally got the right one.'

'Maggie . . .'

'Monday night at six,' she whispered.

'I'll bring Chardonnay,' he answered simply.

When he'd hung up he felt as if he'd been dragged free of a mudslide and flung up on solid ground, realizing he'd live after all.

On Monday night at six when he reached the top of her sidewalk, she stepped onto the back verandah and called, 'Put your truck in the garage.'

He did. And closed the doors before heading to the house.

He forced himself to walk, to descend the sidewalk at a casual pace, to climb the porch steps slowly, to keep his hands at his sides while she stood before him with her arms crossed, shivering, the light pouring from behind her and turning her into a celestial being with a halo.

They stood watching each other's breath puff out like white streamers in the chill February air, until he finally thought to say, 'Hello, again.'

She tipped her lips up and gave a timorous laugh. 'Hello. Come in.'

He followed her inside and stood uncertainly on the rug before the door. She had dressed in pink silk – a lissom raiment that seemed to move without prompting – and had hung a cord of pearls upon her deep, naked throat. When she turned back to face him the beads, the dress, and she seemed to tremble. But by some unspoken compact this greeting was to be the antithesis of the last. She accepted his green-glass offering and they tended to conventions.

'Chardonnay . . . lovely.' This as she examined the bottle.

'Chilled.' This as he removed his storm coat.

'I have the perfect glasses.'

'I'm sure you do.'

She stowed the wine in the refrigerator and he let his eyes drop to her legs. She was wearing high heels the exact shade of her dress. In the bright light of the kitchen they glistened. She closed the refrigerator door and turned to face him, remaining across the room.

'You look elegant,' he told her.

'So do you.' He had chosen a smoke-blue suit, pale-peach shirt and a striped tie combining the two colours. Her eyes scanned it and returned to his face. This, too, by unspoken agreement: lovers in finest feather, each seeking to please the other.

'We dressed,' she said with a fey smile.

He offered a grin. 'So we did.'

'I thought a little candlelight would be nice.' She led him into the dining room which was lit by only six candles, smelled of roses and had places set for two – the two at the near end, facing each other, at a table that would have held a dozen.

'You've finished the room. It's beautiful.' He glanced around – ivory wallpaper, swags above the window, china in a built-in glass-doored cabinet, the gleaming cherrywood table.

'Thank you. Sit here. Do you like salmon or do you only fish for it?'

He laughed, and they continued appraising one another, playing the game of restraint as he took the chair she indicated.

'I like it.'

'I guess I should have asked you. Would you like your wine now or later?'

'Now, I think, but let me get it, Maggie.'

He began to rise, but she touched his shoulder. 'No, I will.'

He watched her leave the room and return in the shimmering dress that caught the candlelight and sent it radiating along her curves. She poured the wine, and took her place across from him, beyond a white-lace runner and a low crystal basket holding an arrangement of fragrant coral roses. She had arranged them all at their end of the table, as if the remaining length did not exist, and had placed the candelabrum carefully to one side.

'So, tell me about Minneapolis,' she said.

He told her while they drank their wine and studied one another in the candlelight. While they lingered over tart endive salad and French bread so crusty the crumbs flew when they broke it. Once she wet a fingertip with her tongue, touched two crumbs, and carried them to her mouth while he watched in fascination.

'When will you open Harding House to the public?'

She told him while he refilled their glasses, then buttered another hunk of bread, ate it with great relish, and wiped his mouth on a flowered napkin, which her eyes followed.

In time she served him blushing salmon in apple-cider sauce; cheesy potatoes tubed into a garland of rosettes, browned on the tips; and spears of asparagus arranged like the stems of scarlet roses which she'd somehow carved of beets.

'Did you do all this yourself?' he asked, amazed.

'Mm-hmmm.'

'Does one eat it or frame it?'

'One does whatever one wants with it.'

He ate it, savouring each mouthful because it was the first gift she'd ever given him, and because across the table her eyes shone with promise, and because in the candlelight he could study her to his heart's content.

Later, when their plates were removed and the Chardonnay bottle drained, she came from the kitchen bearing a single, exceedingly heavy, hat-sized chocolate-frosted doughnut on a footed Fostoria cake plate with a floating candle rising from its centre in a matching Fostoria stemglass.

'Ta-daa!' she heralded.

He turned at her approach and burst into laughter, leaning back in his chair as she placed her *coup de grâce* before him.

'If you can eat it all you win another of the same size.'

She leaned before him to set it down, and his arm circled her hips as together they laughed at the gargantuan doughnut.

'It's a monster. I love it!'

'Think you can eat it all?'

He looked up, still smiling. 'If I do, I'd rather name my prize.'

His arm tightened and the laughter slipped from their faces.

'Maggie,' he whispered, and drew her around until her knees struck his chair seat. 'This month has seemed like a year.' He pressed his face to her breasts.

She closed her arms about his head, her eyes against the candlelight.

'This meal has taken days,' he added, muffled against her.

Her only answer was a smile, delivered while bending low over his hair, which smelled faintly of coconut.

'I missed you,' he said, 'I want you. First, before that doughnut.'

She lifted his face, and holding it, told him, 'My days seemed pointless without you.' She kissed him as she had so tried not to think of kissing him during their separation, his face raised as she bent above it. Freeing his lips she stroked his cheek with the backs of her fingers and felt the wretchedness of the past four weeks dissolve.

'How foolish and self-deluding we were to believe we could will away our feelings for each other simply to avoid complicating our lives.'

In the Belvedere Room her pink raiment drifted to the floor, and his suit was relegated to a small sewing rocker. Then, gladly, they gave up their wills to one another and celebrated the end of their self-imposed agony. Much later, lying with their limbs plaited, they spoke of their feelings during exile. Of feeling torn and lorn and incomplete when apart; of stepping into a room where the other waited and becoming immediately total, whole again.

'I read poetry,' she admitted. 'Searching for you in it.'

'I rode the snowmobile, trying to get you off my mind.'

'Once I thought I saw you uptown, from the back, and I ran to catch up with you, but when I got close and realized it was someone else, I felt tragic, like crying right there on the street.'

'I thought of you most in those hotel rooms, when I couldn't sleep and I wished you were with me. God, I wanted you with me.' He touched his index finger to the cleft in her chin. 'When I stepped into this house tonight, and you were here, waiting, in your pretty pink dress, I felt . . . I felt like I suppose a sailor feels when he comes home from years at sea. There was nothing more I wanted or needed than to be in that room with you, looking at you again.'

'I felt the same. As if when you left you took some part of me, like I was a puzzle, maybe, and the piece you took was right here . . .' She laid his hand over her heart. 'And when you walked in, that piece fell into place and I came back to life again.'

'I love you, Maggie. You're the one who should be my wife.'

'And what if I said I would be?'

'I'd tell her. I'd end it then and there. Will you?'

'Isn't it odd? I feel as if the choice isn't really mine, loving you the way I do.'

His face became amazed. 'You mean it, Maggie?'

She flung her arms about him, smiling against his jaw. 'Yes, I mean it, Eric. I love you . . . love you . . . love you.' She punctuated her pronouncement with kisses upon his collarbone, cheek, eyebrow. 'I love you and I'll be your wife . . . as soon as you're free.'

They clung together and celebrated, rolling side to side.

In time their exuberance changed to wonder. They lay on their sides, close, studying each other's eyes. He carried her hand to his mouth and kissed its palm.

'Just think . . . I'm going to grow old with you,' he said softly.

'What a lovely thought.'

And at that moment, they really believed it would happen.

Chapter 14

Nancy pulled into the driveway at 6:15 Friday night. Dusk had fallen, and from the kitchen window Eric watched her headlights arc around and disappear into the open garage. She'd always hated that garage door. It was old-fashioned, cumbersome, a son of a bitch to budge. Though it lowered with much less effort than it raised, he was nevertheless waiting to close it when she emerged from the garage.

A sharp wind bit through his shirtsleeves as he stood watching her lean into the backseat for her suitcase. She had good legs, always wore extremely expensive hosiery – aqua-green tonight, to match her suit. There had been a time when the sight of her legs had had the power to arouse him. He viewed them now with a sense of sorrow for his lost ardour, and with an unspoken apology for his stubborn insistence about this house – even this garage – which she'd hated so much. Perhaps if he'd given in on that one point alone she'd have given in on one, too, and they would not have reached this brink of dissolution.

She emerged from the car and saw him.

Immobility struck her: the lag-time of silence like that following a distant puff of smoke from a rifle before the sound catches up. These stagnant pauses had grown common to both of them in the weeks since his ill-advised sexual assault.

Nancy moved again. 'What are you doing out here?'

'I'll take that.' He stepped inside the garage and reached for her suitcase. She leaned into the backseat for a second load, coming up with a briefcase and a garment bag which she hoisted over her shoulder as he slammed the car door.

'Did you have a good week?' he asked.

'Fair.'

'How were the roads?'

'Okay.'

Their conversations had become sterile and halting since that night. They walked single file toward the house without attempting any further exchange.

Inside, she set down her briefcase and reached for her suitcase.

'I can take it upstairs for you,' he offered.

'I'll take it,' she insisted, and did so.

While she was gone he stood in the kitchen feeling shaken and apprehensive because he knew leaving her was the right thing to do and he dreaded the next hour.

She returned, dressed in a straight teal woollen skirt and a long-sleeved white blouse with a gold rose pinned at her collarbone. She crossed the room without meeting his eyes. He waited, leaning against the sink, watching as she lifted the lid from a pot of simmering chilli, found a ladle, spoons, bowls, and began to fill them.

'None for me,' he said.

She glanced up with the flat expression she had perfected since the night he'd drilled her on the sofa.

'I ate already.' He hadn't, but the hollow within could not be filled with food.

'What's wrong?'

'Eat your chilli first.' He turned away.

She set the bowl on the table and remained standing beside it, her stillness tinged with caution.

'First before what?'

He stared out the window over the kitchen sink at the dirty snow and the late-winter dusk. Nerves jumped in his stomach and bleakness weighted him like a heavy yoke. This was not something one did blithely. The major part of his life was invested in this marriage, too.

He turned to face her. 'Nancy, you'd better sit down.'

'I'd better sit, I'd better eat!' she retorted. 'What is it? Tell me so I can!'

He crossed the room and pulled out two chairs. 'Come on, will you please sit?' When she had, stiffly, he sat across from her, forearms on the table, studying the wooden fruit he'd always disliked. 'There's no good time to say what I've got to say – before you eat, after you eat, after you've had a chance to kick back. Hell, it's . . .' He linked his fingers and fitted the pads of his thumbs together. Lifting his eyes to her, he said quietly, 'I want a divorce, Nancy.'

She paled. Stared. Fought the sudden onslaught of panic. 'Who is she?'

'I knew you'd say that.'

'Who is she?' Nancy shouted, rapping a fist on the table. 'And don't tell me nobody, because I tried calling here twice this week, and when you're not home at eleven o'clock at night, there's somebody, so who is it?'

'This is between you and me and nobody else.'

'You don't have to tell me because *I know!* It's your old high school girlfriend, isn't it?' Her head jutted forward. 'Isn't it?'

He sighed and pinched the bridge of his nose.

'It's her, I know it! The millionaire widow! Are you screwing her, Eric?'

He opened his eyes and levelled them on her. 'Nancy, for God's sake . . .'

'You are, aren't you? You were screwing her in high school, and you're screwing her now! I saw it the first day she came to town. She wasn't on those church steps five minutes and you had rocks in your shorts, so don't tell me this is between you and me and nobody else! Where were you at eleven o'clock Wednesday night?' She thumped the table again. 'Where?'

He waited wearily.

'And last night!'

He refused to answer her anger with anger, which only incensed her further. 'You son of a bitch!' She lunged forward and slapped his face. Hard. So hard two chair legs lifted off the floor. 'Goddamn you!' She rocketed around the table and swung again, but he feinted and caught only the ends of her fingernails across his left cheek.

'Nancy, stop it!'

'You're screwing her! Admit it!' He caught her by the forearms and they grappled, bumping the table, spilling chilli, sending wooden pears rolling to the floor. His cheek began bleeding.

'Stop it, I said!' Still sitting, he gripped her forearms.

'You're spending nights with her, I know it!' She had begun to cry. 'And it didn't just start this week because I've called here before when you weren't home at night!'

'Nancy, cut it out!' A drop of blood fell onto his shirt.

Locked like combatants, he watched her struggle for control and find it. With tear-streaked cheeks she returned to her chair and sat facing him. He rose and got a dishcloth to wipe up the spilled chilli. She watched him move from the table to the sink and back again. When he was seated, she said, 'I don't deserve this. I've been faithful to you.'

'This isn't just about being faithful, this is about two people who never grew together.'

'Is that some platitude you read in the Sunday paper?'

'Look at us.' He pressed a folded handkerchief to his cheek, looked at the blood and asked, 'What's left anymore? We're apart five days a week and unhappy the two we're together.'

'We weren't until that woman moved back to town.'

'Could we leave her out of it? This began long before she moved back to Fish Creek and you know it.'

'That's not true.'

'Yes, it is. We've been growing apart for years.'

He could see her initial anger being replaced with fear, which he had not expected.

'If this is about my working, I said I'd ask about getting my territory cut.'

'But did you mean it?'

'Of course I meant it.'

'Have you done it?'

She hadn't. Both of them knew it.

'And even if you did it, would you be happy? I don't think so. You're happiest doing exactly what you're doing, and I've finally come to realize that.'

She leaned forward earnestly. 'Then why can't you just let me continue doing it?'

He released a huge, weary sigh and felt as if he was talking in circles.

'Why do you even want this marriage? What did we ever make of it?'

'You're the only one who thinks this marriage is a mistake. I think it's worth fighting for.'

'Aw, for heaven's sake, Nancy, open your eyes. From the time you started travelling, we started losing it. We stored our possessions in the same house, and we shared the same bedroom, but what else did we share? Friends? *I've* got friends, but *we* don't. I've come to the sad realization that we never made any because making friends takes an effort, takes time, but you never had the time. We didn't entertain because you were always too tired by the time Saturday night came. We didn't go to church because Sunday was your only free day. We didn't have a beer with the neighbours because you considered drop-ins gauche. And we never had kids of our own, so we never did the regular kind of stuff like taking turns in a car pool or going to recitals or Little League games. I wanted all of that, Nancy.'

'Well, why didn't you –' She bit off the sentence.

'Say so?'

They both knew he had.

'We had friends in Chicago.'

'When we were first married, yes, but not after you took the selling job.'

'But my time was so limited then.'

'That's what I'm telling you – not that what you want is

wrong, or what I want is wrong, but that what we want is wrong for each other. And what about pastimes? Yours is work, and mine – well, hell, we both know you've always considered my pastimes too unsophisticated to suit you. To ride a snowmobile you'd have to mess your hair. Fishing is too unrefined for an Orlane rep. And you'd as soon have a root canal as walk in the woods. What do we share anymore, Nancy, what?'

'When we started out we wanted the same things. It was *you* who changed. Not me.'

He considered, then admitted forlornly, 'Maybe you're right. Maybe it was me who changed. I tried the city life, the art galleries, the orchestra halls, but I found it more satisfying to look at a real wildflower than a painting of one. And I think there's more music at the Ridges Nature Sanctuary than in all the orchestra halls in the world. I was miserable trying to be a yuppie.'

'So you forced me to move here. Well, what about me? What about what *I* wanted and needed? I loved those galleries and orchestra halls!'

'What you're saying is what I'm saying: Our needs and wants are too different to make this marriage work, and it's time we admitted it.'

She rested her forehead on eight fingertips and stared at her bowl of chilli.

'People change, Nancy,' he explained. 'I changed. You changed. You weren't a sales rep then, you were a fashion merchandiser, and I didn't know my father would die and Mike would ask me to come back here and run the charter service. I admit, I thought back then that I wanted to be a corporate executive, but it took some years of experiencing corporate life before I found out it wasn't what I thought it would be. We changed, Nancy, it's as simple as that.'

She looked up with fresh tears in her eyes. 'But I still *love* you. I can't just . . . just turn away from that.'

The sight of her tears grieved him and he looked away.

They sat for some moments in silence before Nancy spoke once more.

'I've said I'd consider having a baby, too.'

'It's too late for that,' he said.

'Why?' She leaned across the table and clutched the back of his hand. He let it lie lifelessly beneath hers.

'Because it would be a desperation move, and it's not right to bring a child into a marriage to hold it together. What I did that night was unforgivable, and I want to apologize again.'

'Eric . . .' she appealed, still appropriating his hand.

He withdrew it and said quietly, 'Give me a divorce, Nancy.'

After a lengthy stretch of consideration, she replied, 'So she can have you? Never.'

'Nancy . . .'

'The answer is no,' she said firmly and slipped from her chair and began gathering the wooden fruit from the floor.

'I didn't want this to turn into a fight.'

She dropped four teakwood pears into the bowl. 'I'm afraid it's going to. I may not like this place, but I've got an investment in it, too, and I'm staying.'

'All right.' He rose. 'I'll go to Ma's for the time being.'

Abruptly she softened. 'Don't go,' she pleaded. 'Stay and let's try to work it out.'

'I can't do that,' he said.

'But Eric . . . eighteen years.'

'I can't,' he repeated in a choked voice and left her, with the pleading look on her face, to go upstairs and pack.

Ma's house was empty when he reached it. The light was on over the kitchen sink, spotlighting a dirty mixing bowl, a pair of beaters and two discoloured, dented cookie sheets.

'Ma?' he called, expecting no answer, getting none.

In the living room the television was black, her crocheting lay in a pile on the davenport with the hook projecting from the ball of thread. He carried his suitcases on through, up the creaky stairs to his old room under the eaves. It was a bleak room, by most people's standards, with faded scatter rugs on a linoleum floor and worn chenille spreads on its two beds. It smelled faintly of bat droppings; brown bats had lived under the eaves and behind the shutters for as long as he could remember. Occasionally one would get in and they'd bring it to the ground with a landing net. But even as children they'd never been afraid of the animals. Ma had always insisted they put them out instead of killing them. Bats eat mosquitoes, she'd said, so treat them gentle.

The dry, aged-attic smell of the bats was distinctly nostalgic, comforting.

He switched on a dim lamp in the 'boys' room', wandered through into 'Ruth's room' – the two arranged shotgun fashion so that Ruth had always had to pass through the boys' barracks to reach her own. Back then a flowered cotton curtain had served as a door between the two sections; it had since been replaced by a wooden door.

In Ruth's room he wandered aimlessly to the window. Through the naked trees, from his high vantage point he could see the lighted windows of Mike and Barb's house, undoubtedly where Ma was. She went over sometimes for supper. He had no desire to join them tonight. Instead he returned to the boys' room and flopped onto his back on one of the beds.

There in the gloom, he mourned the marriage that had for years seemed vacant; the mistakes he himself had made during it; his childlessness; the investment of years that had tallied only disappointment and regret; Nancy's refusal to end the relationship that had no future; the turbulence that lay ahead.

He reminisced about moments when he and Nancy had been wholly happy. Reflections flashed in his mind as vignettes upon a screen, each sterling in its clarity. The time they'd bought their first piece of furniture – a stereo, which they'd purchased on time. Certainly not the most practical first piece, but the one they both wanted most. They'd hauled it into the apartment together, then lain on their backs on the floor, listening to the two albums they'd chosen – Gordon Lightfoot for him, the Beatles for her. Those old albums were still around somewhere; he wondered if they'd each take their own when they parted. They'd lain on the apartment floor, feeling the music vibrate through them, and they'd talked about the future. Someday they'd have a whole houseful of furniture, all the best, and a house to put it in, too – all glass and redwood, in some affluent suburb of Chicago, probably. She was right. He'd let her down there.

Another time when they'd impetuously flown to San Diego – counted their money and decided on a Friday noon (via telephone between their two offices) and by ten that night were checking into a hotel in La Jolla. They had walked its hilly streets holding hands, and drunk cocktails in open-air lounges while watching the sun set over the Pacific, and had eaten famous split-pea soup at some restaurant in a windmill, and had explored Capistrano Mission, and made love in broad daylight in a hidden cove on the beach near Oceanside, and had promised one another they would never grow predictable, but would fly away often that way, at the drop of a hat. Now their lives were as predictable as the lunar cycle and Nancy travelled so much there was no incentive for impromptu weekends away.

Another memory came. It was their second year of marriage when Nancy fell one day on an icy sidewalk and sustained a concussion. He recalled his sick fear while waiting in the emergency room for the results of her X rays, the emptiness of their bed during the night she'd remained in hospital for observation, and the relief he'd felt at her return. In those days a single night apart had been a trial for both of them. Now, five days apart was the accepted norm.

He should have worked harder at finding a compromise that would have kept them together more of the time.

He should have built her a glass and redwood house.

They should have talked about children before they were married.

Lying on his boyhood bed, he found his eyes stung by tears.

He heard Ma come in downstairs, her footsteps pausing in the living room.

'Eric?' She'd seen his truck parked outside.

'Yeah, I'm up here. I'll be right down.'

He knuckle-dried his eyes and rose, blew his nose on his bloody handkerchief and clumped down the steep, wooden stairs, breaking his headlong plunge with both hands on the wall above which seemed permanently soiled from the thousands of descents it had slowed.

She was waiting at the bottom, dressed in a quilted nylon jacket of Halloween orange and a cotton scarf covered with dreadful purple cabbage roses, tied tightly beneath her chin. Her glasses were steamed. She raised them onto her forehead and peered at him curiously. 'What the devil were you doing up there?'

'Smelling the bat shit. Remembering.'

'You all right?'

'I've been crying a little, if that's what you're asking.'

'What's wrong?'

'I'm leaving Nancy.'

'Ah, that's it.' She studied him silently while he realized how little she'd cared for his wife and wondered what she felt. She opened her arms and said, 'Come here, son.'

He walked against her, took her short, stubby body against his much taller one, breathed the smell of late winter from her jacket, and the faint scent of fuel oil from her scarf and whatever Barb had cooked for supper from her hair.

'I'll need to stay awhile, Ma.'

'As long as you want.'

'I'll probably be a little grouchy.'

She pulled back and looked up at him. 'That's your right.'

He felt better after the hug. 'What happens to people, Ma? They change.'

'That's part of life.'

'But you and the old man didn't. You made it straight through.'

'Why of course we changed. Everybody changes. But we didn't have as many complications in them days. You young people now, you got two dozen different experts telling you how you ought to think and feel and act and how you ought to *find* yourself.' Long-lipped, she stretched the word. 'Stupid expression . . . *find* yourself. Give each other *space*.' Again she made mockery of the word. 'In my day, a man's space was beside his wife, and a wife's was beside her man, and what you gave each other was a helping hand and a little bit of loving if you weren't too tired at the end of the day. But nowadays they'd have you believing that if you don't come first you're doing it wrong, only marriage don't work that way. Oh, I'm not blaming you, son, I'm saying you were born in a time that was tough on marriages.'

'We always got along, Nancy and I. On the surface things seemed okay, but underneath we've been at odds for years about the most important stuff–jobs, kids, where we lived, what we lived in.'

'Well, sometimes that happens, I guess.'

He'd expected her to show maternal favouritism and was surprised by her neutrality, though he respected her for it, realizing again that she'd never warmed to Nancy.

She heaved a sigh and glanced toward the kitchen. 'Have you eaten yet?'

'No, Ma, I'm really not hungry.'

Again she surprised him by not nagging. 'Yeah, sometimes strife dulls the appetite. Well, I'd best get upstairs and change them sheets. They've been on since Gracie and Dan slept in 'em at Christmas.'

'I can do that, Ma. I don't want to be any trouble to you.'

'Since when was any of my kids a trouble to me?'

He went over and got her in an affectionate headlock, appreciating her with a freshness that healed.

'Y'know, the world could use a few more like you, Ma.' For good measure he gave her skull a knuckle-rub, the way they all had when they were boys.

'Let me go, brat!' she blustered.

He released her, and they went upstairs together to change the bed.

They'd put on the bottom sheet when he told her, 'I don't know how long I'll be here, Ma.'

She snapped the second sheet in the air with two deft flicks and replied, 'I didn't ask, did I?'

He went by Maggie's the next day at midmorning.

'Hi,' he said, looking forlorn.

'What happened to your face?'

'Nancy.'

'You told her?'

He nodded resignedly. 'Come here,' he said. 'I need to hold you.'

Against him, she whispered, 'I need to hold you, too, while you tell me.'

Each time he came to her their moods seemed a reflection of one another, as if a chord ran through both their hearts. Today they came together for reassurance. Passion had no place in their embrace.

'The news isn't good,' he said quietly.

'What did she say?'

'She won't hear of a divorce.'

Her hand moved lightly on his back. Her eyes closed. 'Oh, no.'

'I think she's going to make it as tough on us as she can. She says if she can't have me, you won't either.'

'How can I blame her? Could I give you up if you were mine?'

He drew back, his hands on the slope of her neck while brushing the corners of her lips with his thumbs. He studied her soulful eyes.

'I've moved into Ma's, so things are still up in the air.'

'What did your mother say?'

'Ma? She's the salt of the earth. She gave me a hug and said stay as long as you need to.'

She pressed close to him again. 'You're so lucky. I long for a mother I can be honest with.'

Each Tuesday afternoon Vera Pearson volunteered her time at the Bayside Nursing Home where she played piano while the old folks sang. Her mother had been a devout Christian who instilled in Vera the importance of charity, both at home and in the community. So on Tuesdays she played piano at Bayside; on Saturdays she arranged altar flowers at the community church; during springtime she helped with the church rummage sale; in autumn she helped with the bake sale; she attended regular meetings of her church circle and the garden society and the Friends of the Library. If at each of these functions Vera garnered any gossip that the *Door County Advocate* had missed, she regarded it as her beholden duty to spread it.

On this particular Tuesday afternoon Vera had whispered to one of the nurses that she'd heard the middle Jennings girl, only a junior in high school, was pee-gee. 'It's no wonder,' she added, 'like mother, like daughter.'

After the music they always had 'teatime'. The coffee was absolutely delicious today, and Vera had one cup with her chocolate-frosted cup-cake, two more with a slice of orange bundt cake and another with some coconut cookies.

She was in the restroom behind one of the two beige metal doors, struggling with her control-top panty hose when she heard the big door open and two women entered, conversing.

Sharon Glasgow – one of the nurses at Bayside – said, 'Vera Pearson's got a lot to talk about. Her own daughter is having an affair with Eric Severson. Did you hear he left his wife?'

'No!'

The adjacent stall door closed and Vera saw a pair of white shoes beyond the partition.

'He's living at home with his mother.'

'Are you kidding!' That was Sandra Ecklestein, a dietician.

'I guess they went together when they were in high school.'

'He's really good-looking.'

'So's his wife. Have you ever seen her?' On the other side of the partition a toilet flushed while Vera remained still as a broken watch. The dividing wall quivered as it was thumped by a door, and the white shoes went away. Another pair appeared. The faucet ran and the hand dryer whined and the routine was repeated while the two women went on to talk about other things.

When the room grew quiet, Vera hid a long time in her stall, afraid to go out until she was certain the two women had gone elsewhere in the building.

What did I do wrong? she thought. I was the best mother I knew how to be. I made her go to church, I set a good example by staying with one man my whole life, I gave her a clean home with good food on the table and a mother always in it. I set curfews and report card standards and made sure she never hung around with any riff-raff. But the minute she came back she ran off to that town meeting with him.

I warned her this could happen! Didn't I warn her?

Vera didn't drive. In a town the size of Fish Creek she didn't need to, but, trudging up Cottage Row on foot, she wished she did. Reaching Maggie's door, she was winded.

She knocked and waited, her purse handle over both wrists, which were pressed against her rib cage.

Maggie opened the door and exclaimed, 'Mother, this is a surprise! Come in.'

Vera marched inside, puffing.

'Let me take your coat and I'll put on some coffee.'

'No coffee for me. I've just had four cups at the home.'

'The weekly sing-along?'

'Yes.'

Maggie put the coat in the maid's room and returned to find Vera perched on a chair with her purse on her knees.

'Tea? Coke? Anything?'

'No, nothing.'

Maggie took a chair at a right angle to Vera's.

'Did you walk up?'

'Yes.'

'You should have called. I would have come down and got you.'

'You can take me back down after . . .' Vera paused.

Her tone warned Maggie something was wrong. 'After?'

'I'm afraid I've come here on unpleasant business.'

'Oh?'

Vera pinched her purse clasp with both hands. 'You're seeing that Severson boy, aren't you?'

Taken aback, Maggie took some time in replying. 'If I said yes, Mother, would you be willing to talk about it with me?'

'I *am* talking about it. The whole town is talking about it! They say he's left his wife and moved in with his mother. Is that true?'

'No.'

'Don't lie to me, Margaret! I didn't raise you that way!'

'He *is* living with his mother, but he left his wife because he doesn't love her anymore.'

'Oh, for heaven's sake, Margaret, is that how you excuse yourself?'

'I don't need excuses.'

'Are you having an affair with him?'

'Yes!' Maggie shouted, jumping to her feet. 'Yes, I'm having an affair with him! Yes, I love him! Yes, we plan to get married as soon as he gets a divorce!'

Vera thought of all the women in the altar society and the garden society and the church circle and the Friends of the Library, women she'd known her whole life long. She relived the sting of embarrassment she'd felt in the lavatory at the home this morning.

'How will I ever face the ladies of my church circle again?'

'Is that all that matters to you, Mother?'

'I have been a member of that church for more than fifty years, Margaret, and in all that time I've never had the slightest thing to hang my head about. Now this. You're not back in town but a few months and you're involved in this scandal. It's disgraceful.'

'If it is, it's my disgrace, Mother, not yours.'

'Oh, you're very smug, aren't you – just listen to yourself, believing everything he tells you, like some fool. Do you really think he intends to divorce his wife and marry you? How many women do you think have been told that line over the years? He's after your money, Margaret, can't you see that?'

'Oh, Mother . . .' Margaret dropped to a chair, overcome with disappointment. 'Why couldn't you just once in your life be a support to me instead of tearing me down?'

'If you think I'd support such goings-on –'

'No, I didn't think you would. I'd never think that, because in all my life you've never given me credit for anything.'

'Least of all good sense.' Earnestly Vera leaned forward and rested an arm on the table. 'Margaret, you're a rich woman, and if you aren't wise enough to realize that men will be after you for your money, I am.'

'No . . .' Maggie shook her head slowly. 'Eric is not after

my money. But I'm not going to sit here and defend him or myself because I don't have to. I'm an adult now, and I'll live my life the way I please.'

'And embarrass your father and I without the slightest thought for our feelings?'

'Mother, I'm sorry for that, truly I am, but I can only say again, it's my affair, not yours or Daddy's. Let me take responsibility for my feelings, and you take responsibility for yours.'

'Don't talk to me in your high-brow counsellor's talk! You know how I hate it.'

'Very well, I'll ask you something straight out, because I've always wondered.' Maggie looked her mother square in the face. 'Do you love me, Mother?'

Vera reacted as if someone had accused her of being a Communist. 'Why, of course I do. What kind of a question is that?'

'An honest one. Because you've never told me.'

'I kept your clothes clean, and the house perfect, and good meals on the table, didn't I?'

'A butler could do that. What I wanted was understanding, some show of affection, a hug when I came home, someone to take my side now and then.'

'I hugged you.'

'No. You allowed yourself to be hugged. There's a difference.'

'I don't know what you want of me, Margaret. I guess I never have.'

'For starters, you could stop giving orders. To both me and Daddy.'

'Now you're blaming me for something else. A woman's place is to keep the home running smoothly.'

'By dictating and criticizing? Mother, there are better ways.'

'Oh, now I've done that wrong, too! Well, your father

hasn't any complaints, and he and I have been together for forty-five years –'

'And I've never seen you hug him, or ask if he had a good day, or rub his neck. Instead, when he comes home, you say, "Roy, take off your shoes, I just scrubbed the floor." When I come home you say, "Why didn't you let me know you were coming?" When Katy drove up for Thanksgiving you scolded her because she didn't have boots. Doesn't it strike you, Mother, that we might like something more in the way of a greeting? That now, at this rather emotional time in my life, when I could use someone to confide in, I might appreciate your coming to me to ask how I feel instead of accusing me of shaming you and Daddy?'

'It strikes me that I came in here confronting you with your loose actions, and you've managed to turn the blame on me for something I've never done. Well, I can only repeat, in forty-five years your dad has never complained.'

'No,' Maggie returned sadly. 'He's just moved into the garage.'

Vera's face turned crimson. Roy was the wrong one for moving into the garage! And she didn't dictate and criticize; she only kept things in line. Why, if it were left to Roy the floors would be full of scuff marks and their meals would be eaten at any ungodly hour and they'd be late to church every Sunday. And here was this ungrateful child, whom Vera had given every advantage – hand-sewn dresses, Sunday school, a college education – telling Vera she could use improvement!

'I thought I raised you to respect your parents, but obviously that's another area where I've failed.' Summoning her shattered pride, Vera rose from her chair wearing a hurt look on her face. 'I won't bother you again, Margaret, and until you're ready to apologize to me, you needn't bother me, either. I can find my coat.'

'Mother, please . . . can't we talk about this?'

Vera got her coat from the maid's room and donned it.

Returning to the kitchen she attended to pulling on her gloves, never glancing at Maggie again.

'You needn't take me down the hill. I can walk.'

'Mother, wait.'

But Vera left without another word.

Closing the door upon her daughter, she felt her heart would surely break. That's all the thanks a mother gets, she thought, as she headed down the hill toward home.

That evening when Maggie saw Eric she said, 'My mother was here this morning.'

'What did she say?'

'She demanded to know if I was having an affair with "that Severson boy".'

He snapped shut a carpenter's rule and stepped down off a chair seat to gather her close. They were standing in one of the guest bedrooms where he was helping her insert a molly screw to hang a large-framed mirror.

'I'm sorry, Maggie. I never wanted that to happen.'

'I told her yes.'

He drew back in surprise. 'You *told* her that?'

'Well, I am, aren't I? I chose to.' With her fingertips she touched his cheek just below the fingernail marks where thin scabs had formed. 'I can accept it if you can.'

'An affair . . . aw, Maggie M'girl, what am I putting you through? What more will I put you through? This isn't what I wanted for you, for us. I wanted it to be legitimate.'

'Until it can be, I'll settle for this.'

'I filed for divorce today,' he told her. 'If everything goes right, we could be married a half year from now. But I've made a decision, Maggie.'

'What?'

'I'm not staying here overnight anymore. It looks too tacky, and I don't want people gossiping about you.'

In the weeks that followed, he came to her most days.

Mornings, sometimes, bringing fresh doughnuts; often at suppertime, bringing fish. Sometimes weary, falling asleep on her sofa, other times happier, wanting to eat, laugh, drive with the truck windows down. He came the day of ice-out, when the debacle on the lake signalled winter's end. And the day she got her first unexpected guests who'd got her name from the Door Chamber of Commerce and simply walked up to the door asking if she had a room. She was giddy with excitement that night and lit a fire in the guest parlour, making sure the candy bowl was filled and that there were plenty of books and magazines on hand. Her guests returned from having dinner uptown and knocked on the closed kitchen door to ask some questions. When Maggie introduced Eric by only his first name, the man shook his hand and said, 'Nice to meet you, Mr Stearn.'

He helped Maggie put the dock in and built a new arbour seat which she'd decided she wanted at the end of the dock instead of clear back by the tennis court, which had lost much of its charm as a parking lot. When the last nail was driven they sat on the new arbour seat holding hands and watching the sun set.

'Katy has agreed to come and work for me this summer,' she told him.

'When?' he asked.

'School is out the last week in May.'

Their eyes met and his thumb stroked the back of her hand. After a wordless exchange she quietly laid her head on his shoulder.

He came the day he put the *Mary Deare* in the water, sailing in below the house and bleating his horn, bringing Maggie flying down to the front porch to wave and smile as he'd often pictured.

'Come on down!' he called, and she raced down the verdant spring grass between rows of blossoming iris, and onto his deck to be borne away over the waves.

And again, later, when the Montmorencies and

McIntoshes were in full bloom, he came in his battered pickup, cleaned both outside and in for the occasion and bedecked with blossoms that held Maggie momentarily in thrall, and then brought tears to her eyes. He took her to an orchard in full bloom, laden with scent and colour and birdsong, but once there they shared only a melancholy silence, sitting wistful, holding hands again.

May arrived and with it warm enough weather to paint the unheated apartment over the garage. He helped her prepare it for Katy, furnishing it with familiar pieces from the Seattle house.

Mid-month brought a steady stream of tourists and fewer times together, then their last night before Katy came home for the summer.

They said good-bye on the deck of the *Mary Deare* at ten after one in the morning, loath to part, surrounded by blackness and the soft wash of waves against the hull.

'I'll miss you.'

'I'll miss you, too.'

'I'll come when I can, in the boat, after dark.'

'It'll be hard to get away.'

'Watch for me around eleven. I'll blink the lights.'

They kissed farewell with the same anguish they'd suffered when college had forced them apart.

'I love you.'

'I love you, too.'

She backed away, holding hands until their outstretched fingertips no longer touched.

'Marry me,' he whispered.

'I promise.'

But the words were mere pining, for though he'd filed for divorce immediately after leaving Nancy, the correspondence from her attorney remained unchanged: Ms Macaffee would not agree to a divorce, but desired instead a reconciliation.

Chapter 15

Katy had made up her mind she'd give her mother the benefit of the doubt. Grandma had written and said, your mother is having an affair with a married man, but Katy had decided she'd ask her mother straight out. She was sure Grandma was wrong; it was something she only suspected. After the words they'd had at Christmas, she didn't see how her mother could possibly have done anything except refuse to see her old boyfriend again.

She stopped in Egg Harbor and put the top down on the convertible. It was a hot spring day and she had to admit, it felt wonderful to leave Chicago behind. Living by the lake might not be so bad after all, though she wasn't too sure how she'd like being a cleaning lady. But what other choice did she have? Until she graduated from college her mother controlled the money, and her mother had not invited Katy as a guest. She'd invited her as an employee.

Cleaning. Shit. Scrubbing the pots after strangers had used them, and changing sheets with curly black hairs in them. It was still beyond Katy why her mother wanted to be an innkeeper. A woman with a million dollars in the bank.

Her hair whipped in the wind and she glanced around to make sure nothing was in danger of sailing out of the backseat.

She returned her eyes to the road, the countryside ahead. Crimeny, it *was* a pretty place. Everything getting green and the orchards in full bloom. She *did* want to get along with her mother. She *did.* But her mother had changed so much since Daddy died. All this independence, and it seemed as if she just forged ahead and did things without considering Katy's feelings. And if what Grandma had said was true, what then?

Fish Creek was back in full swing. The doors of the shops along Main Street were standing open, most without even screen doors. Tulips were in bloom out in front of the post office, and down by the town docks sailboats were already moored.

Up on Cottage Row the summer places had been reopened for the season and a man was out trimming shrubs beside a stone entry into one of them.

At her mother's, a new sign hung: HARDING HOUSE, A BED-AND-BREAKFAST INN. Next to the garage Maggie's Lincoln was parked beside another with Minnesota licence plates. Katy pulled in next to them, got out and stretched, and grabbed a load from the backseat.

She wasn't halfway down the steps before Maggie came charging out, smiling, calling, 'Hi, honey!'

'Hi, Mom.'

'Oh, it's so good to see you.'

In the middle of the walk they embraced, then Maggie took one suitcase and they headed towards the garage, chatting about the trip up, the end of school, the nice spring weather.

'I have a surprise for you,' Maggie said, leading Katy up the steps that climbed the outside wall of the building. She opened the door. 'I thought you'd like a place of your own.'

Katy looked around the room with wide eyes.

'The old furniture . . . oh, Mom . . .'

'You'll have to use the bathroom facilities in the house, and eat there with me, but at least you'll have some privacy.'

Katy gave her mother a hug. 'Oh, thank you, Mom, I love it.'

Katy loved her lodgings, but her enthusiasm quickly changed to dismay when she was faced with the realities of having guests in the main house, moving about at all hours. Maggie kept the kitchen door to the hall closed so that the portion of the house reserved for their private use seemed hemmed in. That afternoon there were no less than five knocks on the hall door, bringing bothersome questions from guests. (Can we use the phone? Where can we rent bicycles? What restaurant would you recommend? Where can we buy film, bait, picnic food?) The telephone rang incessantly and the overhead footsteps seemed an intrusion. In late afternoon a new party checked in and Maggie had to interrupt meal preparations to show them upstairs and get them registered. By suppertime Katy was totally disenchanted.

'Mother, are you sure this was the right thing to do?'

'What's wrong?'

Katy gestured toward the hall door. 'All the interruptions. People coming and going and the phone ringing.'

'This is a business. You have to expect that.'

'But why are you doing this when you have enough money that you wouldn't have to work for the rest of your life?'

'And what else should I do with the rest of my life? Eat chocolates? Go on shopping sprees? Katy, I have to be occupied by something vital.'

'But couldn't you have bought a gift shop or become an Avon lady – something that wouldn't bring your customers into the house?'

'I could have, but I didn't.'

'Grandma says this was a foolish move.'

Maggie bristled. 'Oh? And when did you talk to Grandma?'

'She wrote.'

Maggie took a bite of chicken salad without remarking.

'She said something else that's been bothering me, too.'

Maggie rested her wrist on the table edge and waited.

Katy looked square at her. 'Mother, are you still seeing that Eric Severson?'

Maggie took a drink of water, considering her answer. Setting the glass down, she replied, 'Occasionally.'

Katy dropped her fork and threw up her hands. 'Oh, Mother, I don't believe it.'

'Katy, I told you before –'

'I know you told me to butt out, but can't you see what you're doing? He's married!'

'He's getting a divorce.'

'Oh, sure, I'll bet that's what they all say.'

'Katy, that was uncalled for!'

'All right, all right, I apologize.' Katy held up her hands like a traffic cop. 'But I'm appalled just the same, and I think it's a hell of a shameful situation.' She jumped to her feet, took her plate to the garbage and spanked it clean with three loud whacks of a fork.

Maggie forgot about finishing her supper. She watched her daughter moving angrily to the sink. How was it that since last fall they had been on this merry-go-round of aggravation with one another? No sooner did they reach some truce, than up flared the tempers again. Other parents went through this during their children's teenage years, but for the Stearn family those had been surprisingly calm. Maggie had thought she'd made it through raising Katy with unusual luck only to find the distress beginning now at the time she'd thought they'd be most close.

'You know, Katy,' she said reasonably, 'if we're going to be at each other like this all the time, it'll make for a very long summer. Furthermore, our guests can sense if there's friction in the house, and they deserve to be greeted with genuine smiles. There'll be times when you'll be the one greeting them, so if you don't think you can handle it, tell me now.'

'I can handle it!' Katy snapped and left the room.

When she was gone Maggie sighed, propped her elbows on the table and massaged her forehead with eight fingertips. She sat for some time, staring down at her plate and the unfinished chicken salad.

Suddenly the pieces started swimming and a tear plopped onto a leaf of wilted lettuce.

Damn, not again! Why am I doing this so often lately?

Because you miss Eric and you're tired of all the duplicity, weary of fighting your family and afraid that maybe he never will get free.

She was still sitting there wet-eyed when a guest knocked on the hall door. *Go away*, she thought, *I'm tired and I need this cry*. Tired – yes, she'd been so tired lately. For a moment as she pushed to her feet her head felt light. Then she swiped her eyes with a sleeve, put on a cheerful face and went to answer the knock.

It became apparent with Katy's first day of work that maintaining discipline as an employer of one's own daughter would present problems for Maggie. Like the parent giving her own child piano lessons, she found her orders taken lightly and followed sluggishly:

'I'll be there in a minute.'

'You mean I have to dust the furniture every *day?'*

'But it's too hot to clean all three bathrooms!'

Though Katy's dilatory attitude incensed Maggie she refrained from badgering in hopes of minimizing the tension between them.

Then on the third day after Katy's arrival, her listlessness received a shot of adrenalin. She was stuffing soiled sheets into a canvas laundry bag when a lawnmower roared past the window, pushed by a shirtless young man dressed in red shorts and sockless Nikes.

'Who's that!' Katy exclaimed, staring, stalking him from window to window.

Maggie glanced outside. 'That's Brookie's son, Todd.'

'Mowing *our* lawn?'

'I hired him as my handyman. He comes two days a week to do the heavy work – mow, trim, clean the beach, take care of the garbage.'

Katy strained to watch him, her forehead bumping the screen as the mower moved beyond range and decrescendoed.

'Wow, he's cute!'

'Yes, he is.'

Katy made the dust bounce for the remainder of the morning and found countless opportunities to step outside: to shake the dust mop and rugs, to sweep the porches and carry trash up the hill to the dumpster beside the garage. She finished her cleaning in record time and careened downstairs, halting, breathless, beside Maggie who sat at her desk in their personal parlour.

'I scrubbed all three bathrooms, changed the beds, dusted the bedrooms *and* the guest parlour, including the windowsills. Can I be done now?'

Their agreement had been that Katy would work each day until two o'clock and after that would take turns with Maggie being available to check in arriving guests. During neither of her first two days had she completed her work by two; today, however, she was done by 12:15.

'All right, but I need to buy groceries sometime this afternoon, so be back here by three.'

Katy scudded across to the garage, appearing minutes later in the yard wearing clean white shorts, a red halter top and fresh makeup with her hair in a neat French braid. Todd was emptying grass clippings into a black plastic bag.

'Here, I'll hold that for you,' Katy called as she approached him.

Todd glanced over his shoulder and straightened. 'Oh, hi.'

Wow, what a build. And magnificent black hair, and a face that probably stopped girls in their tracks all the time. His bare torso and brow were beaded with sweat and he wore a white headband.

'Hi. You're Brookie's son.'

'Yeah, and you must be Maggie's daughter.'

'My name is Katy.' She extended her hand.

'Mine's Todd.' He shook it with a hard, dirty hand.

'I know. Mother told me.'

She held the bag open while he dumped the grass inside.

Standing close to him she caught the scent of tropical suntan lotion mixed with the green scent of the fresh grass cuttings.

'I saw you come outside before,' he told her, stealing a glance at her bare midriff.

'I clean for my mother.'

'So you're going to be here all summer?'

'Yup. I'll be going back to Northwestern in the fall, though. My second year there.'

'I'm going into the Air Force in September. Thanks.' He took the bag from her and knelt to replace the grass catcher on the mower.

From above, she studied his tan, sweating shoulders, the slope of his vertebrae and the wet black curls at his nape. 'Sounds like our mothers were pretty good friends.'

'Yeah. I suppose you heard the same stories I did.'

'The Senior Scourges, you mean?'

He glanced up and they laughed. She loved the way his face crinkled when he did that. He rose to his full height, wiping his palms on his shorts while they looked each other over and tried to appear as if they were not, then let their interest ricochet toward the lake.

'Well, I'd better let you get back to work,' she said reluctantly.

'Yeah. I've got another yard to do this afternoon.'

She turned her head and caught him eyeing her bare midriff again. Abruptly he lifted his eyes and they both spoke at once.

'I'll be –'

'Where do –

He flashed her a quick grin and said, 'You first.'

'I was just going to ask where the kids hang out around here.'

'And I was going to say that I'll be done with my afternoon job around five. If you want I could take you out to City Beach and introduce you around. I know just about everyone in Door – everyone but the tourists, that is, and I even know a few of them.'

She flashed him a bright smile. 'Okay. I'd like that.'

'After supper we pretty much hang out at the C-C Club down on Main Street. They have live bands in there.'

'Sounds fun,' she replied.

'I could come and pick you up around six.'

'Sounds great! See you then.'

Maggie noticed the change in Katy immediately. Her temperament mollified; she hummed and talked to her mother; she called a cheery good-bye upon leaving the house with Todd.

But by two A.M. Maggie hadn't heard Katy come in to use the bathroom. The following day Katy slept until ten and arose only under duress. For the next three nights she went out with Todd again, arising later and later each day, and when Sunday came, she grumbled about having to work at all. 'It's Todd's only day off and we wanted to go to the beach early.'

'You can go as soon as your cleaning is done.'

'But, Mom . . .'

'It would have been done already if you'd got up when you should have!' Maggie snapped.

During the days that followed, while Katy saw more and more of Todd, Maggie burned with indignation, not over her dating – Todd was a pleasant boy, a hard worker, prompt and unfailingly polite – but because of her daughter's cavalier attitude about work. Maggie resented being put in the position of having to revert to mothering tactics that harked back to Katy's young teen days. She resented becoming the night watch. She resented Katy's blithe assumption that she could bend her hours to suit her personal needs.

There was something else that bothered Maggie, too, something she had not expected. She missed her privacy. After so few months of independence she found she'd grown accustomed to eating – or not eating – when she wished; to finding the bathroom the way she'd left it, her cosmetics where she'd put them; to having the radio on the station of her choice, and the kitchen sink free of dirty glasses. Even though Katy slept in the garage apartment the house was not her own anymore, and many times she felt small and guilty for her reaction. Because she realized that it might all be a subterfuge to disguise the one greatest imposition Katy's presence had created; it had forced an end to her evenings with Eric.

Maggie wished she could talk to someone about these complex feelings, but her own mother had put herself off limits, and since Todd was involved, Brookie was out.

Then one night eight days after Katy's arrival, Eric came.

Maggie jolted out of a deep sleep and lay tense, listening. Some sound had awakened her. She'd been dreaming she was a child, playing Red Rover in the tall grass beside a square yellow-brick schoolhouse when the school bell rang and awakened her. She lay staring at the black ceiling, listening to the midnight chorus of crickets and frogs, until finally it came again – the faint ting not of a school bell, but of a ship's bell, close enough to be heard, distant enough not to disturb. Intuition told her it was he, calling her with the familiar brass bell hanging above the *Mary Deare*'s cabin.

With racing heart she leapt from bed and scrambled through a dresser drawer, yanking on the first shorts she found, beneath her hip-length nightshirt. The clock said eleven. Running through the dark house, Maggie felt her heart clubbing in anticipation. She slipped like a wraith down the hall and out the front door, across the deep front porch and down the steps between the fragrant bridal wreaths that hung with great white ropes of flowers; toward the vast blackness of the lake where the soft chug of the *Mary Deare*'s engines rippled the night water and diffused the reflection of the moon; downhill . . . barefoot . . . across the dewy grass . . . beneath the black lace of maple arms until she heard the engines cut, then the light swash of waves against the dock pilings, then her own bare heels thumping on the wooden platform, feeling it buck as the boat hove against it.

He appeared as an apparition in white, as silent and ghostly as the *Mary Deare* itself, waiting at the rail with arms uplifted as she sailed into them like some lost pigeon homing at last.

'Oh, darling, I've missed you. Hold me, please . . . hold me.'

'Ah, Maggie . . . Maggie . . .'

He hauled her tight against his bare chest, against the white trousers rolled to mid-calf. Straddle-legged, he braced against the faint roll of the deck, kissing her as if to do so were to heal from some awful abuse.

Like a sudden tropical shower, her tears came, bursting forth without warning.

'Maggie, what is it?' He drew back, trying to lift her face, which she, abashed, hid against his shoulder.

'I don't know. It's just silly.'

'Are you all right?'

'Yes . . . no . . . I don't know. I've been on the verge of this all day, for no good reason. I'm sorry, Eric.'

'No, no . . . it's all right. You go ahead and cry.' He held her loosely, rubbing her back.

'But I feel so silly, and I'm getting your chest wet.' She sniffled against his slick bare skin and gave it two wipes with the butt of her hand.

'Go ahead, get it wet. It won't shrink.'

'Oh, Eric . . .' After a halfhearted snuffle she began calming and settled comfortably against his widespread thighs. 'I don't know what it is with me lately.'

'Bad week?'

Her nod bumped his chin. 'Could I unload on you, please?'

'Of course.'

It felt so good to lean against him and spill out her feelings. 'It's not working out, hiring Katy,' she began. She told him everything – about Katy's late-night hours and how it affected her work; about the difficulty of supervising one's own daughter; about being unable to discuss it with Brookie; and her own sense of being trapped in a phase of motherhood she thought she'd outlived. She confessed her own abnormal irritability lately and her heartsoreness at losing even the thinnest line of contact with her own mother. She told him, too, that Katy knew she was seeing him and that they'd had words about it.

'So I needed you tonight . . . very badly.'

'I needed you, too.'

'Did you have a bad week, too?'

He told her about the grand hoopla at Mike and Barb's house this past week, first on Saturday when the whole tribe pitched in to throw a big graduation party for Nicholas; and last night when Barb had had a baby girl – two weeks late, but big and healthy and named Anna after her grandmother.

'In one week they send off one child into the world and bring another one into it,' he reflected sadly.

'And you have none – that's what's bothering you, isn't it?'

He sighed and shrugged it off, held her by both arms and looked down into her face. 'Something else happened last weekend.'

'Tell me.'

'Nancy came out to Ma's, begging for a reconciliation, and today my lawyer advised me it won't set well with the courts if I refuse to at least try a reconciliation when my wife is asking for one.'

Maggie searched his face, consternation on her own.

'Don't worry,' he added quickly, 'I love you. You're the only one I love, and I promise I won't go back to her. Not ever.' He kissed her mouth, tenderly at first, then with growing ardour, his tongue wet and sleek upon hers.

'Oh, Maggie, I do, I love you so.' His voice sounded tortured. 'I ache to be free so I can marry you, so you don't have to suffer your daughter's scorn and your mother's.'

'I know.' She took her turn at comforting him, touching his face, tracing his eyebrows. 'Someday.'

'Someday,' he repeated with an edge of impatience. 'But when!'

'Shh . . .' She calmed him, kissed his soft mouth, and coerced him into forgetting, for a while. 'I love you, too. Let's make some new memories . . . here . . . underneath the stars.'

The moon cast their shadow onto the wooden deck – one long spear against the lighter boards as they drew close and became one unbroken line. He opened his mouth upon hers, drew her hips flush to his, and ran his hands down the slope of her spine, flaring out and catching her buttocks to force her up hard against him. She lifted on tiptoe, running her nails up his skull, then down his naked shoulders. He captured her breasts beneath the loose-fitting T-shirt, caught her beneath the arms and lifted her toward the stars, holding her suspended as he closed his mouth upon her right breast. She winced and he murmured, 'I'm sorry . . . sorry . . . I get too impatient . . .' Softer, he opened his mouth upon her, wetting her shirt, and her skin, and the deepest reaches within her. She put her throat to the sky and felt his arms quivering, and herself quivering, and the night air quivering around them, and she thought, Don't let me lose him. Don't let her win.

When she slid down his body, her hand led the way, skimming his chest and belly, then cupping him, low.

'Come on,' he whispered urgently, catching her hand and leading her fore, where a canopy sliced off the moonlight and the panel lights illuminated their faces with a pale phosphorescence. Starting the engine, he perched on the hip-high stool and settled her between his thighs, facing Green Bay, slipping one hand inside her underwear, caressing her intimately as he took them away from shore.

Reaching back, she stroked him through his trousers, riding over the star-kissed waters, absorbing its slap and lap against the hull, and the smell of his warm hide and the brush of his hair as he lowered his face to the slope of her shoulder.

A mere twenty-five feet offshore he dropped anchor. They made love on the cool wooden deck, in a lunge and lift that matched the motion of the boat on the pliant night waves. It was as consuming as always, but beneath its wonder was an underlying thread of sadness. For he was not hers, and she was not his, and this above all they desired.

When it was over, he lay above her, his elbows braced on either side of her head. She studied his moon-shadowed face, what she could make out of it, and felt love inundate her once again with an immeasurable force. 'Sometimes,' she whispered, 'isn't it hard to express it? In words powerful enough or meaningful enough?'

He touched her moonlit brow, stretched her auburn tresses upon the decking until they lay like a nimbus around her. He searched for ways he might express it, but he was no poet or philosopher.

'I'm afraid "I love you" will have to do. That says it all.'

'And I love you.'

They carried the thought back to shore, captured it within for the days of separation ahead, reiterated it with their farewell kiss, clung to it as she bade him good-bye and left him standing on the end of the dock watching her up the hill.

At the top she turned and waved, then resolutely plodded up the front porch steps.

From the shadows came a voice. Hard. Condemning. 'Hello, Mother.'

Maggie started. 'Katy!'

'I'm here, too, Mrs Stearn.'

'Oh . . . Todd.' They'd been necking in the dark. It was obvious even without benefit of light. 'You two are out rather late, aren't you?'

Katy's clipped response dared her mother to challenge her. 'Seems everybody is.'

From below came the sound of the *Mary Deare*'s engine as she skimmed away from the dock. Maggie realized Katy had had a clear view of the dock and as her eyes adjusted to the shadows of the front porch, she saw Katy staring at her nightshirt and bare feet, judging, reprehending. Maggie blushed and felt guilt come nettling. She wanted to say, *But I'm older than you, and wiser, and I fully understand the vagaries of this course upon which I've embarked.*

All which served as a harsh reminder to Maggie that she was setting a double standard when she should instead be setting a good example.

After that night, the thought troubled her. She had not before given much thought to promiscuity. It was something against which girls were warned during adolescence, but upon maturity Maggie had considered the affair her choice and hers alone.

Perhaps it was not.

With an impressionable eighteen-year-old daughter in the house, dating a handsome, undoubtedly virile young man, perhaps it was not.

Katy's late nights continued and Maggie awakened often to lie and worry, wander to the bathroom and through the dark house, wondering if she should talk to Brookie about it after all. But to what avail?

Her interrupted sleep began telling, and she grew sluggish, occasionally queasy, sometimes weak. She had never been a snacker, but began snacking thoughtlessly, a nervous reaction to the stress, she figured. She gained five pounds. Her bras didn't fit. Then one day she realized the oddest thing: her shoes didn't fit.

My shoes?

She stood beside her bed, staring at her feet which looked like a pair of overgrown potatoes.

My ankle bones don't even show!

Something was wrong. Something was very wrong. She added it all up: fluid retention, tiredness, irritability, sore breasts, weight gain. It was menopausal, she was sure – the symptoms all fitted. She made an appointment with a gynaecologist in Sturgeon Bay.

Dr David Macklin had had the perspicacity to have the ceiling of his examination room painted with a floral motif. Lying on her back on the examination table, Maggie distracted herself by identifying the flowers. Tulips, lilacs and roses she knew. Were the white ones cherry blossoms? In Door County, how appropriate. The lighting was diffuse, illuminating the ceiling indirectly from the pale lavender walls, a restful room that put a patient as much as possible at ease.

Dr Macklin completed his examination, lowered Maggie's crackling paper gown and gave her a helping hand.

'All right, you can sit up now.'

She perched on the end of the table, watching him roll his stool to a wall-hung desk where he wrote in a manilla folder, a mid-thirtyish man balding too young but wearing a great, bushy brown moustache, as if to make up for Nature's slight on his dome. His eyebrows, too, were thick and dark, dropping like parentheses beside his friendly blue eyes. He glanced up and asked, 'How long ago was your last period?'

'My last real period – right around the time Phillip died, almost two years ago.'

'What do you mean by real period?'

'The way it always was. Regular, a full four days.'

'And after his death it stopped abruptly?'

'Yes, when I started experiencing the hot flushes I told you about. I've had some spotty periods off and on, but they didn't amount to much.'

'Have you had any hot flushes lately?'

She considered before answering, 'No, not lately.'

'How about night sweats, any of those?'

'No.'

'But your breasts have been tender?'

'Yes.'

'How long?'

'I don't know. A couple of months maybe. I really don't remember.'

'Do you get up fairly often in the middle of the night to urinate?'

'Two or three times.'

'Is that normal for you?'

'No, I guess not, but my daughter lives with me and she's been staying out rather late. I have trouble sleeping soundly until she gets in.'

'How has your temperament been lately? Have you been irritable, depressed?'

'My daughter and I seem to argue a lot. It's been a rather stressful situation with her living at home again.'

Dr Macklin hooked an elbow on the desk behind him and relaxed against it. 'Well, Mrs Stearn,' he said, 'I'm afraid this isn't menopausal, as you thought. Quite the opposite, as a matter of fact. My best guess is that you're approximately four-and-a-half months pregnant.'

Had he produced a ten-pound maul and bounced it off her head, David Macklin could not have stunned Maggie more.

For seconds she sat slack-jawed, gaping. When she found her voice it was incredulous. 'But that's impossible!'

'Do you mean you haven't had intercourse in the past five months?'

'No. I mean, yes, I have but . . . but . . .'

'Did you take any precautions?'

'No, because I didn't think it was necessary. I mean . . .' She laughed – a short, tense call for understanding. 'I'm going to be forty-one years old next month. I started having signs of menopause nearly two years ago and . . . and . . . well, I thought I was beyond that.'

'It may surprise you to learn that a good ten per cent of my patients nowadays are women in their forties, and many of them mistook their symptoms for menopause. Perhaps it would help if I explained a little bit about it and how it begins. Menopause is brought on by the body decreasing its output of the female hormone, oestrogen. But the reproductive system doesn't close shop overnight. In some cases it may last over a period of years, causing the system to vary from month to month. Some months the ovaries function normally and the body produces enough oestrogen to bring on a normal period. But at other times the ovaries fail to produce adequate hormones so ovulation does not occur. In your case, obviously, on one given month when you experienced intercourse, your system produced adequate oestrogen to trigger ovulation, so here you are.'

'But . . . but what about the hot flushes? I told you, I went to the emergency room thinking I was having a heart attack, and a nurse and an intern watched the hot flush happening and identified it. They watched the colour climbing my chest and they told me what it was. What about that?'

'Mrs Stearn, you must understand, hot flushes can be caused by conditions other than menopause. Your husband died a rather dramatic and untimely death. I imagine the newspapers were hounding you and there were lawyers involved, and a daughter to console, legalities to get in order. You were under a great deal of stress, weren't you?'

Maggie nodded, too upset to trust her voice, feeling her eyes begin to tear.

'Well, stress is one of the culprits that can trigger hot flushes and undoubtedly it did at that time. Because you were informed, and because you were of the age where you could expect menopause to begin, you took it for that. It's an understandable mistake and, as I said, a common one.'

'But I . . .' She gulped and swallowed. 'Are you sure? Couldn't you be mistaken?'

'I'm afraid not. All the symptoms are there – the wall of your cervix is slightly bluish in colour, the genitals are swollen, your breasts are enlarged and tender and the veins highly coloured, you've been experiencing water retention, tiredness, increased urination, weight gain, and probably a grab bag of other discomforts – cramps, heartburn, constipation, lower-back ache, leg cramps, maybe even a temper tantrum or two and a few unexplained tears. Am I right?'

Maggie recalled her many bouts of irritation with Katy, the outgrown bras and shoes, the nocturnal trips to the bathroom and the night she'd stepped onto the *Mary Deare* and burst into tears for no apparent reason. Glumly, she nodded, then dropped her eyes to her lap, abashed by the fact that she had begun to cry.

Dr Macklin rolled his stool nearer and fixed his sympathetic attention upon her.

'I take it from your signs of distress that you're single.'

'Yes . . . yes, I am.'

'Ah . . . well, that always complicates matters.'

'And I run a bed-and-breakfast inn.' She lifted brimming brown eyes and spread her hands in appeal. 'How can I do that with a baby in the house, waking for his night feedings?'

Dropping her head, she swiped at the tears with the side of her hand. Macklin plucked up three paper tissues and handed them to her, then sat nearby, waiting for her to collect her emotions. When she'd calmed, he said, 'You realize, of course, that you're beyond the stage of foetal development where abortion is either safe or legal.'

She lifted beleaguered eyes. 'Yes, I realize that, but it wouldn't have been a consideration, in any case.'

He nodded. 'And the baby's father – is he in the picture?'

She met his kind, blue eyes, dried her own, then rested her hands in her lap. 'There are complications.'

'I see. Nevertheless, I must advise you to tell him as soon as possible. In these days of human rights awareness, we realize that fathers have the right to know of the baby's existence and to have the opportunity to plan for its welfare, just as the mother does, and as soon as the mother does.'

'I understand. Of course I'll tell him.'

'And your daughter – how old did you say she is?'

'Eighteen.' At the thought of Katy, Maggie braced an elbow on her belly and dropped her face to her hand. 'How ironic. Here I've been lying in bed at night worrying about this happening to her, wondering if I should bring up the subject of birth control. Oh, Katy's going to be appalled.'

Dr Macklin rose and stood beside Maggie with a hand on her shoulder. 'Give yourself some time to adjust to the fact before you tell your daughter. It's your baby, your life, your ultimate happiness you should be concerned with. Certainly a barrage of accusations is not what you need right now.'

'No . . . it's . . . I . . .' Maggie's thoughts became disjointed by the enormity of her plight. Sadness and panic besieged her by turns. Myriad concerns flashed through her mind, one upon the other, in no specific priority.

I'll be fifty-seven before this child finishes high school.

Everyone will know it's Eric's and he's still married.

What will Mother say?

I'll have to close the business.

I don't want this responsibility!

Dr Macklin was speaking, instructing her to eliminate all alcohol and over-the-counter drugs from her intake, inquiring whether she smoked, handing her sample vials of prenatal pills, advising that she cut down on the use of salt and increase her intake of dairy foods and fresh vegetables, rest periodically with her feet elevated, do moderate low-impact exercise such as walking, and make an appointment for a return visit.

She heard his voice through a haze of thoughts that ran

like gurgling currents through her head. She replied distractedly, yes, no, all right, I will.

Leaving the clinic, she experienced a feeling of displacement, as if she'd assumed the identity of another, fluttering above and behind the woman below like some watchful angel, while that woman whose pumps clicked along the sidewalk was the one who had just learned she was carrying a child out of wedlock and would inherit all the complications of such a situation.

Suspended above herself she could remain aloof from the cares of the other. She could know and watch but remain beyond direct involvement, enveloped in this anaesthetized state of observant dispassion.

For a while she felt almost euphoric, divorced from the cloudburst of emotion she'd undergone in the doctor's office, as she passed two sweaty towheaded boys licking strawberry ice cream cones and riding skateboards, as she moved from sunshine into shade along the city sidewalks and crosswalks, smelling the peculiar mixture of smells emanating from the open door of a drugstore and the adjacent dry cleaner's.

In the parking lot she paused beside her car, feeling the summer heat radiate from its metal body even before she reached to unlock the door. Inside, the trapped heat seemed to have speed, so powerfully it struck. The steering wheel felt oily, as if it were being dissolved by the sun, and the leather seat burned through her clothing.

She started the engine, turned on the air conditioner, but as it emitted a hot blast, a wave of nausea struck accompanied by a billow of blackness, as of a curtain lowering behind her eyes. The sensations brought the bewildering truth back with vicious ferocity: *you* are the one who's pregnant! *You* are the gullible one who saw only what you wanted to see in the symptoms. *You* are the one who should have taken precautions and didn't, who *chose* an extramarital affair with a married man. *You* are the one who'll be attending school conferences in your forties, and be pacing the floor at night in your fifties waiting for your teenager to return from his first date. And you are the one who'll suffer the smalltown disdain of women like your mother for years to come.

The cold air rushed from the vents as she lowered her forehead onto the hot, hot steering wheel, and the hot, hot tears continued seeping from her eyes.

Four and a half months.

Four and a half, and I never even suspected – me, a Family Life teacher who spent years teaching high school students about contraception only to blithely ignore it myself. How stupid I was!

So what're you going to do, Maggie?

I'm going to tell Eric.

Do you think he can get divorced and married to you before this baby is born?

I don't know . . . I don't know . . .

Propelled by the hope that he could, she started the engine and headed home.

Chapter 16

Maggie had never called Eric at home, not since the previous summer when she'd been depressed and had unwittingly started all this at Dr Feldstein's prompting. Dialling the phone that afternoon, she felt transparent, vulnerable. What she feared, happened: Anna answered.

'Yeah, Severson's Charters,' came her gruff voice.

'Hello, Anna. This is Maggie Stearn.'

'Who?'

'Maggie Pearson.'

'Oh . . . Maggie Pearson. Well, I'll be jiggered.'

'How are you?'

'Me, I'm fine. Got a new granddaughter, you know.'

'Yes, I heard. Congratulations.'

'And a grandson just graduated.'

'One of Mike's.'

'Yup. And a son living back at home.'

'Yes, I . . . I heard that, too.'

'But fishing's good, business is good. You oughta come out sometime and try it.'

'I'd like to, but I don't get much free time anymore since I've opened the inn.'

'I hear your place is doing good, too, huh?'

'Yes. I've had guests nearly every night since I opened.'

'Well, that's just swell. Keeping 'em happy, you know, that's what brings 'em back. Ask me and my boys.'

A lull fell and Maggie could think of no way to break it but to inquire baldly, 'Anna, is Eric there?'

'Nope. He's got a party out. What did you want?'

'Could you have him call me, please?'

'Oh . . .' After a startled blank Anna added, 'Sure. Sure, I'll do that. Expecting him in around six.'

'Thank you, Anna.'

'Yuh, well, bye then.'

'Bye.'

When Maggie hung up, her hands were sweating.

When Anna hung up her mind was clicking.

Eric docked the *Mary Deare* at 6:05. Anna watched from the office window as he joshed with the guests, led them to the fish-cleaning shack, gutted their catch and hung seven salmon on the 'brag board' for photographing.

At 6:30 he breezed into the office, inquiring, 'Anything to eat, Ma?'

'Yeah. I fixed you a roast beef sandwich and there's iced tea in the fridge.'

He patted her on the butt as he circumnavigated the counter.

'Thanks, Ma.'

'Oh, by the way, Maggie Pearson called. She wants you to call her.'

He stopped as if he'd run into an invisible wall, and wheeled around, suddenly tense.

'When?'

'Oh, about four or so.'

'Why didn't you call me on the radio?'

'Why should I of? You couldn't call her till you got in anyways.'

He slapped the doorframe and hurried off with impatience in every movement. While the returning fishermen came in for cigarettes and potato chips, she heard him making the call from the kitchen, though his words were indistinct. Minutes later, he came out to the office, frowning.

'Hey, Ma, have I got a seven o'clock party?'

'Yup,' she replied, checking a clipboard. 'Party of four.'

'How about Mike?'

'Mike? No, he's open.'

'When's he due in?'

'About a quarter hour or so.'

'Would you call out and ask him if he'd mind taking my seven o'clock for me?'

'Don't mind at all, but what's so important it comes before customers?'

'I gotta run into town,' he answered vaguely, already hustling toward the kitchen. Minutes later she heard the ancient water pipes thumping as he filled his tub for a bath. When he came through the office fifteen minutes later he was freshly combed and shaved, smelling good enough to lick and dressed in clean white jeans and a red polo shirt.

'Did you get Mike?'

'Yup.'

'What did he say?'

'He'll take 'em.'

'Thanks, Ma. Tell him thanks, too.'

He slammed out the front screen door, jogged all the way to his pickup and took off spraying a rooster tail of gravel while Anna, with raised eyebrows, stared after him.

So that's the way the wind blows, she thought.

Maggie had said she'd meet him out at a little Baptist church in the country east of Sister Bay. The Door County countryside was dotted with churches such as this – tall-spired, belfried, white wood structures with four arched windows on either side, a pair of pines standing like handmaidens beside it, and an adjacent graveyard slumbering peacefully amid the weeds and wildings. On Sunday evenings the windows would be open and from them would drift the voices of worshippers raised in song. But it was Thursday night, no evening services in session, no cars save hers in the gravel patch out front. The church windows were closed and the only vespers were those being offered up by a pair of mourning doves calling dolefully from their perch on a nearby wire.

She was squatting on her heels beside one of the grave markers when he pulled up. She studied him as he opened the truck door, then returned to her preoccupation as she bent forward with her dress of lettuce green spread about her.

He paused, savouring the sight of her in the streaked light of evening, pouring water from a shoebox onto a clump of purple flowers, rising to wend her way between the ancient, lichened headstones to a black iron pump where she refilled the cardboard box before carrying it, dripping, back to the chosen plot. She knelt once more and watered the flowers while overhead the doves mourned, the day retreated, and the scent of wild sweet clover grew heavy in the gathering damp.

He moved without haste, across the crackling gravel which had trapped the day's heat, onto velvet grass which foretold the night's cool, picking his way toward her between the loved ones from the Old Countries whose names could scarcely be read on the weatherworn markers.

Reaching her, he stood in the long shadows and touched the top of her head.

'What are you doing, Maggie?' he asked, his tone low, in keeping with the doves.

Still kneeling, she looked up over her shoulder. 'Watering these poor withering phlox. This was all I had to carry water in.'

She set the damp cardboard box at her knee and bent forward to pull two scrawny weeds from among the purple blooms.

'Why?' he asked, kindly.

'I just . . .' Her voice broke, then resumed, pinched with emotion. 'I just . . . n . . . needed to.'

How quickly her distress could disturb him. The sound of her choked voice brought an anxious tightness to his chest as he squatted on his heels, catching her elbow gently, urging her to face him.

'What's the matter, Maggie M'girl?'

She resisted, keeping her face lowered, and rambled, distraught, as if to postpone some besetting subject. 'Don't you wonder who planted these? How long ago? How many years they've been coming up and surviving, unattended? I'd hoe around them a little bit if I had something to do it with, and try to get the qu . . . quack grass up. It's ch . . . choking them.'

But she was the one who was choking.

'Maggie, what is it?'

'Do you have anything in your truck?'

Confused by her obvious distress and her reluctance to talk about it, he relented. 'I'll see.'

His knees cracked as he rose and headed for the truck. A minute later he returned with a screwdriver and handed it to her before dropping again beside her to watch as she worked up the rocky soil and tugged at the crowded roots. He waited patiently until the pointless task was finished, then stilled her hand with his own, closing it over her fingers and the tool.

'Maggie, what is it?' he asked in a near-whisper. 'Will you tell me now?'

She sat back on her heels, rested the backs of her hands palm-up on her thighs and lifted sombre brown eyes to his. 'I'm going to have your baby.'

The shock ripped across his features, caught him like a kick in the chest and set him back on his heels.

'Oh, my God,' he whispered, turning white. He glanced at her stomach, back up to her face. 'You're sure?'

'Yes, I'm sure. I saw a doctor today.'

He swallowed once. His Adam's apple jumped. 'When?'

'In about four and a half months.'

'You're that far along?'

She nodded.

'So far that there's no mistake? And not much risk of losing it?'

'No,' she tried to whisper, though no sound came out.

A smile of sheer hosannah caught his face. 'Maggie, this is wonderful!' he exclaimed, flinging his arms around her. 'This is incredible!' He shouted to the sky, 'Did you hear that? We're going to have a baby! Maggie and I are going to have a baby! Hug me, Maggie, hug me!'

She could do little else, for he'd wrapped himself around her like a bullwhip. With her larynx flattened by his shoulder her voice came out reedy. 'My hands are dirty, and you're crazy.'

'I don't give a damn, hug me!'

Kneeling in the grass, she hugged him with her dirty hands pressing the middle of his back – screwdriver and all – soiling his red shirt. 'Eric, you're married to another woman who refuses to give you a divorce and I'm – *we're* – forty years old. This isn't wonderful at all, it's horrible. And everyone in town will know it's yours.'

He set her back by both arms. 'You're damned right they will, because I'll tell them! No more dragging my feet over that divorce. I'll have her off like an old shirt, and what's forty anyway? Jesus, Maggie, I've wanted this for years and I'd given up hope. How can you not be happy?'

'I'm the unmarried one here, remember?'

'Not for long.' Giddy, he held her hands and rushed on, his face radiant. 'Maggie, will you marry me? You and the baby? Just as soon as it's legally possible?' Before she could answer he was on his feet, pacing excitedly, the knees of his white trousers stained green. 'My God, four and a half months only. We've got some plans to make, a nursery to get ready. Don't we take some . . . some Mazda classes or something?'

'Lamaze.'

'Lamaze, yeah. Wait'll I tell Ma. And Mike. Man, is *he* going to be surprised! Maggie, do you think there's enough time that we could have another baby, too? Kids should have sisters and brothers. One of each would be –'

'Eric, stop.' She rose and touched him, a cooling touch of common sense. 'Listen to me.'

'What?' As still as the markers around him, he stared at her with an expression of utter innocence, his face flushed with exuberance, the same rosy gold as the western sky.

'Darling, you seem to be forgetting that I'm not your wife. That privilege,' she reminded him, 'belongs to another woman. You can't . . . well, you can't just go around shouting hallelujah all over town as if we were married. It would be an embarrassment to Nancy, don't you see? And to our parents as well. I have a daughter to consider, and she has friends. I understand your being happy, but I have reservations.'

He sobered as if some fatal accident had happened before his eyes, chilling his joy.

'You don't want it.'

How could she make him understand? 'It isn't a question of wanting or not wanting. It's here,' – she pressed her hands to her stomach – 'and it's nearly half-term already, which is much farther along than your divorce. And it will mean a tremendous interruption in my life, probably the end of the business I've been working so hard to get established. I'm the one who'll carry it from now until you're free, I'm the one who'll get the curious glances on the street, I'm the one who'll be called a homewrecker. If I need some time to adjust to these things, you'll have to be tolerant, Eric.'

He stood motionless, digesting her remarks, while overhead the doves continued mourning.

'You don't want it,' he repeated, devastated.

'Not with the unconfounded joy you do. That'll take some time.'

His face grew hard and he pointed a finger at her. 'You do anything to get rid of it, and it'll kill me, too, you understand?'

'Oh, Eric,' she lamented, drooping. 'How could you even think such a thing?'

He turned away, paced to a maple tree and stared at its smooth, grey bark. For seconds he remained stiff and unmoving, then slammed the tree with an open palm. Leaning against the trunk, he hung his head.

The stunning summer sunset continued to praise the sky. Among the sumac scrub on the rim of the adjacent wood a green, whiskered fly-catcher repeated his burry *fee-be, fee-be.* Beside the nearest headstone the phlox flowers nodded against the granite, while spiders and beetles hurried through the grasses and tiny green worms dropped on webs that shone like glass threads in the failing, final rays of the day. Life and growth flourished everywhere, even in a graveyard that marked the end of life and growth, even within the woman whose heavy heart amid all this summer splendour, seemed misplaced.

She studied the man she loved – the bowed back, the rigid arm, the sagging head.

How disconsolate he looked, lifted to the heights one minute, then mired in despair upon being forced to consider their dilemma.

She moved behind him and laid her palms upon his ribs.

'Conceiving it was an act of love,' she told him quietly, 'and I still love you, and I'll love it, too. But bringing it into the world outside of marriage is less than it deserves. *That's* what I'm unhappy about. Because I'm reasonably sure Nancy will give you enough resistance to keep us unmarried until long after this baby is born.'

He lifted his head and said to the tree, 'I'll talk to her this weekend, and tell her that a reconciliation is out of the question. I'll talk to my lawyer and give orders to get this thing going.' He turned to face Maggie, held from touching her by some new and unwanted constraint. He realized how prosaic their situation was, how classic his response appeared on the surface: a married man stringing his mistress along while keeping her pacified with promises of divorce. Yet she'd never accused him of lagging, never insisted, or demanded.

'I'm sorry, Maggie, I should have done it before.'

'Yes . . . well, how could we know this would happen?'

His expression turned thoughtful. 'How did it, Maggie? I'm just curious.'

'I thought I was safe. I'd had certain signs of menopause for over a year. But the doctor explained that even when regular periods stop, there are still times when a woman can be fertile. When he told me I was pregnant I felt . . .' She glanced at her hands self-consciously. 'I felt so stupid! Coming up unexpectedly pregnant at my age after I *taught* Family Life, for heaven's sake!' She turned away, chagrined.

He studied her back, the way she hugged herself, the way her pale-green dress pulled taut across her shoulder blades. The dark, uncompromising truth settled upon him. Sadly, quietly, he asked, 'You really don't want it, do you, Maggie?'

She seesawed her head – more of a shudder than an answer. 'Oh, Eric, if only we were thirty and married, it would be so different.'

It was different for her, he realized; she'd had a family. She couldn't begin to comprehend the impress of this child upon his life versus the relative unimportance of his age or hers. Once again disappointment deluged him.

'Here.' She turned and handed him the screwdriver. 'Thank you.'

The reserve remained between them, distancing them for some reason he could not fully fathom.

'I promise I'll talk to Nancy.'

'Please don't tell her about the baby, though. I'd rather she didn't know yet.'

'No, I won't, but I need to tell somebody. Would it be okay if I told Mike? He's no blabbermouth.'

'Of course, tell Mike. I may find myself telling Brookie, too, very soon.'

He smiled uncertainly, longing to reach for her, but they remained apart. This was silly. She was carrying his baby, for God's sake, and they loved each other so much.

'Maggie, could I hold you? Both of you?'

With a tiny cry that caught in her throat she flew to him and released them from their agony as she went up on tiptoe and clasped her arms across his neck. He held her hard and felt his heart begin beating again.

'Oh, Eric, I'm so scared,' she admitted.

'Don't be. We're going to be a family. We will, you'll see,' he vowed. He closed his eyes tightly and ran his hands over her pregnant body – her back, buttocks and breasts. He dropped to one knee and, cupping her stomach, pressed his face against it.

'Hello, little one,' he said, muffled against her soft, green dress. 'I'm going to love you so much.'

Through her clothing his breath warmed her skin. Through her sadness his words warmed her heart. But as he stood and closed her gently in his arms, she knew it wasn't enough. Enough was nothing less than becoming his wife.

There were times, Nancy Macaffee had to admit, when Door County was nearly tolerable. Now, in summer, at the end of a hot, hard week, returning to it wasn't quite as distasteful as in dead winter. It was, admittedly, cool here with the breezes wafting over the water surrounding the peninsula, and she liked the shade trees and the profusion of flowers in both likely and unlikely places. But the people were peasants: old women still went uptown in scarves and curlers and old men still wore their bill-caps tipped to one side. Fishing and the fruit crops were the primary subjects of palaver when locals met on the street. Grocery shopping was deplorable and the house she lived in was an abomination.

How could Eric have *liked* the decrepit little cracker box? When he'd moved her into it – nothing else was available – he'd promised it was temporary. Was it her fault she wanted something better? Returning to it when he was there, it had been almost tolerable. Now that he was gone, she found it disgusting, but her lawyer had advised her to stay in it for legal reasons, and to do anything else would have meant a disruption in her life which she didn't need at this time.

Returning home on Friday night she cursed, trying to open the damned garage door. Inside, the kitchen smelled stuffy. The same stack of junk mail lay where she'd left it on the kitchen cabinet last Monday. Nobody had washed the rug by the kitchen sink where she'd dropped a spot of mayonnaise. No game hens or chilli were cooking. Nobody offered to carry her suitcase upstairs.

But on the kitchen table was a note from Eric: *Nancy, I need to talk to you. I'll call you Saturday.*

She smiled and flew upstairs. All right, so he hadn't bought her a gleaming condo in Lake Point Towers with a view of the Gold Coast and all of Chicago at her feet, but she missed him, damn it! She wanted him back. She wanted someone to open the garage door, and to have supper cooking, and to take care of servicing her car and mowing the lawn and having the coffee perked on Saturday mornings. And when she slipped into bed, someone to reaffirm that she was a desirable woman.

Upstairs she threw her suitcase on the bed and stripped off a champagne-pink linen suit. Though sunset flooded the room, she snapped on the lights around her makeup mirror and leaned close, examining her pores, touching her face here, there, flicking a piece of fallen mascara from her cheek, testing her throat for tautness. She found a tiny brush and fluffed her eyebrows straight up. She traded that brush for another, removed her barrette and dropped it among the clutter on the dressing table, brushed her hair vigorously, bending sharply at the waist so its feathery tips whisked her shoulders.

Discarding the brush, she watched herself in the mirror, stripping off a peach-coloured petticoat, bra and panties, letting them drop at her feet like petals at the feet of a Madonna.

She ran her hands over her flat belly, down her thighs, up her ribs catching her cone-shaped breasts and lifting them high, pointing the nipples straight at the mirror.

Oh, how she missed the sex. They'd been so good at it.

But the thought of distorting her body with pregnancy remained repugnant. Some women were made for it and some weren't. Why couldn't he have accepted that?

In the cramped, ugly bathroom she drew a bath, laced it with bubbles and immersed herself with a sigh. Eyes closed, she thought of Eric and smiled. Tomorrow was too long to wait. She'd put on her new Bill Blass jumpsuit, and a spray of Passion – which he liked best – and she'd go out there to find out if he'd changed his mind.

Waiting for someone to answer her knock, Nancy glanced around in distaste. If there was one place she hated worse than her own house it was this stinking place. Fish – Jesus, she detested the very word. She could hardly eat a fillet of mahimahi since she'd been subjected to the smells around here. How anybody could work in such a stench was beyond her. The whole damned woods stunk!

Anna answered her knock, looking as tacky as ever in a horrible T-shirt emblazoned with the words *Grandma's Marathon '88.*

'Hello, Nancy.'

'Hello, Anna.' Nancy perfunctorily rested her cheek on Anna's. 'How are you?'

'Oh, you know . . . the boys keep me busy. Fishing's been real good. How about you?'

'Busy, too. Lonely.'

'Yeah . . . well . . . sometimes we have to go through

that. I imagine you came to see Eric. He's down at the fish-cleaning shed shutting down for the night.'

'Thank you.'

'Be careful in the dark in those high heels!' Anna called after her.

Nancy crossed the gravelled area leading to the dock and outbuildings. It was ten P.M. Beneath the trees all was dark, but near the fish-cleaning shed a single bulb beamed under a cymbal-shaped reflector. Inside the crude building another bulb oozed weak light onto the concrete floor and the rough board walls. Approaching it, Nancy covered her nose with her wrist and breathed the scent of Elizabeth Taylor's Passion.

Down near the lake a bullfrog belched relentlessly. Crickets whined everywhere. Insects buzzed and beat at the lights. Something hit Nancy's hair and she cringed and thrashed it away frantically. From inside the cleaning shack two men's voices could be heard while hose water smacked the concrete floor covering the sound of Nancy's approach on the gravel.

She stopped within feet of the door and listened.

'Well, she's not exactly ecstatic.' That was Eric.

'You mean she doesn't want it?' – and Mike.

'She doesn't want the interruption in her life.'

'Well, you can tell her from me that we didn't want it either, but now that we've got Anna we wouldn't trade her for the world.'

'It's a little different for Maggie, Mike. She doesn't think she can run an inn with a baby waking up and crying in the middle of the night, and she's probably right.'

'I hadn't thought of that.'

'Besides, she thinks we're too old to have a baby.'

'But shit, man – doesn't she know you've wanted one your whole life?'

'She knows, and she says she'll love it. It's just the shock.'

'When it is due?'

'Four and a half months.'

Nancy had heard enough. She felt scalded. In the dark her cheeks flushed and her heart bumped crazily. The water still splattered as she turned and retreated, leaving their voices behind. Beneath the shadows of the maple trees she slipped back to her car, closed the door stealthily and sat gripping the wheel with her eyes stinging.

He'd made another woman pregnant.

Devastated, she dropped her forehead on her knuckles and felt the blood rush to her extremities. Fear, shock and anger coursed through her. Fear of the unknown turmoil ahead, the uprooting of their home and their finances and their life pattern, which she'd wanted changed – yes – but by choice not by duress.

Fear of losing a man she had captured in her twenties and of being unable to catch another in her forties.

Shock because it had truly happened, when she had been so sure she could somehow get him back, that her beauty, sexuality, intelligence, ambition and her position as incumbent wife would be enough to pull him back to her after he'd come to his senses.

Anger because he'd turned his back on all that and made a laughingstock out of her with a woman everyone recognized as his old sweetheart.

How dare you do this to me! I'm still your wife! The tears came, burning tears of mortification for what she'd suffer when people found out.

Damn you, Severson, I hope your stinking boat sinks and leaves her with your bastard!

She wept. She thumped the steering wheel. The spurned woman. The one who'd let herself be dragged back to this loathsome place against her will. The one who'd given up life in the city she loved so he could come here and play Captain Ahab. The one who went out on the road five days a week while he stayed behind to screw another woman! If she lived in Chicago nobody would know the difference, but here everyone would know – his family, the postmaster, the whole damned fishing fleet!

When her tears slowed, she sat staring at the bleak light of the shack doorway as the men's shadows crossed and recrossed it. She could give him what he wanted, but she'd be damned if she would. Why should she make it that easy for him? Her pride was annihilated and he was going to pay for it!

She dried her eyes carefully, blew her nose, and flicked on the dome light and checked her reflection in the mirror. In her purse she found an eyeliner wand and did a quick repair job, then snapped out the light.

Down in the fish-cleaning shack the water stopped plopping and the light flicked out. As the brothers stepped outside, Nancy left her car, slamming the door.

'Eric!' she called, friendly, approaching the two men across the patchy darkness beneath the trees. 'Hi. I found your note.'

'Nancy.' His tone was cool, unwelcoming. 'You could have just called.'

'I know, but I wanted to see you. I have something important to tell you.' As an afterthought she tossed out, 'Hi, Mike.'

'Hello, Nancy.' Turning away, he added, 'Listen, Eric, I'll see you tomorrow.'

'Yeah. Goodnight.'

When Mike left, silence fell, broken only by the nightcalls of thick summer. Standing within her approachable radius, Eric felt threatened, impatient to be beyond her scope.

'Give me a minute to wash my hands and I'll be right back.' He stalked away without inviting her to wait inside. Hell, he'd finally admitted she'd never liked his mother or his mother's house. Why should he be noble at this late date?

He returned five minutes later, wearing clean jeans and a different shirt and smelling of handsoap, striding toward her as if he wanted to get this over with.

'Where do you want to talk?' he asked before reaching her.

'My, so brusque,' she chided, taking his arm, resting her breast against it.

He removed her hand with deliberate forcefulness. 'We can talk down in the *Mary Deare* or in your car. You name it.'

'I'd just as soon talk at home, Eric, in our own bed.' She rested a hand on his chest and again he removed it.

'I'm not interested, Nancy. All I want from you is a divorce, and the sooner the better.'

'You'll change your mind when you hear what I have to tell you.'

'What?' he snapped, with as much indulgence as a father removing his belt in the woodshed.

'It's going to make you happy.'

'I doubt it. Unless it's a court date.'

'What have you always wanted more than anything in the world?'

'Come on, Nancy, quit playing games. I've had a long day and I'm tired.'

She laughed, forcing the sound from her throat. She touched him again on the arm, knowing he resented her doing so, wanting the satisfaction of feeling the shock strike him. She had a momentary flash of doubt: what she was doing was reprehensible. But what he'd done was, too.

'We're going to have a baby, darling.'

The shock hit Eric like high voltage. He struggled for breath. Backed up a step. Gaped at her.

'I don't believe you!'

'It's true.' She shrugged with convincing nonchalance. 'Around Thanksgiving time.'

He did a quick calculation: that night he'd taken her on the living room sofa.

'Nancy, if you're lying –'

'Would I lie about a thing like this?'

He grabbed her wrist and hauled her to her car, opened the door and pushed her inside, then followed, leaving the door open so the dome light shone down.

'I want to see your face while you say this.' He gripped her cheeks and held them, forcing her to meet his eyes. To his great dismay he could tell she'd been crying, which increased his dread. Still, he'd make her repeat it so he'd be sure.

'Now tell me again.'

'I'm three-and-a-half-months pregnant with your baby, Eric Severson,' she said sombrely.

'Then why doesn't it show?' He released her cheeks and passed a dubious glance down her length.

'Take me home and look at me naked.'

He didn't want to. God forgive him, he didn't want to. The only woman he wanted to be that close to was Maggie.

'Why did you wait so long to tell me?'

'I wanted to make sure it wasn't a false alarm. A lot of things can happen in the first three months. After that it's safer. I just didn't want to get your hopes up too soon.'

'So why aren't you upset?' he grilled her, his eyes narrowing.

'About saving my marriage?' she asked reasonably, then did a superb job of acting puzzled. 'You're the one who seems upset, and I don't know why you should be. After all, this is what you wanted, isn't it?'

He sank back against the seat with a sigh, pinching the bridge of his nose. 'But goddamn it, not now!'

'Not now?' she repeated. 'But you're always pointing out that we're not getting any younger. I thought you'd be pleased. I thought . . .' She let her voice trail away piteously. 'I thought . . .' She conjured up several tears which prompted the response she expected. He reached over and took her hand from her lap and held it loosely, stroking its back with his thumb.

'I'm sorry, Nancy. I'll . . . I'll go in and get my things and come back home tonight, okay?'

She managed to sound even more beleaguered and pitiful. 'Eric, if you don't want this baby after all the years we've –'

He silenced her lips with a touch of his finger. 'You caught me by surprise, that's all. And considering the way our relationship has deteriorated, it's not the healthiest environment to bring a child into.'

'Have you really stopped loving me, Eric?' It was the first sincere question she'd asked. She was suddenly terrified at the idea of being unloved, of having to build a relationship from the ground up with some other man and go through all the exhausting groundwork it took to reach an amicable married status. Even more terrified that she wouldn't find one to do it with.

She received no answer. Instead, he released her hand and said heavily, 'Go on home, Nancy. I'll be there soon. We'll talk tomorrow.'

Watching him disappear into the shadows she thought, what have I done? How can I hold him once he learns the truth?

Walking back to the house, Eric felt as he had when the old man died – helpless and despairing. More: victimized. Why now, after all the years of coercing and convincing? Why now, when he no longer wanted her or a child by her? He thought he might cry, so he went out onto the dock and stood beside the *Mary Deare*. The aftershock quivered in his belly. He doubled forward, hands to knees, submitting to abject despair, letting it shake him so that he might move beyond it towards unemotional reasoning.

He straightened. The boat lay listless in the water, the rods upright in their quivers, the mooring lines drooping to the dock. He arched, looked high at the constellations which the old man, with wisdom brought from the old country, had taught him to identify. Pegasus, Andromeda, and the Fishes. The fishes, yes, they were in his blood, in his lineage as surely as the colour of his hair and eyes, passed down from some blond, blue-eyed Viking long before Scandinavians had last names.

She still hated his fishing.

She still hated Fish Creek.

She still wanted to be a career woman gone from home four nights a week.

Since he'd been at Ma's he'd done a lot of soul-searching and talking with her and Barb and Mike. They had admitted to having difficulty liking Nancy all these years. He had admitted that the joy he'd known with Maggie made him realize what a state of quasi-happiness he'd lived in with Nancy all these years.

Now Nancy was pregnant . . . and resigned if not happy about it.

And so was Maggie.

But he was Nancy's husband, and he'd been begging her for years to have this baby. To abandon her now would be the height of callousness and he was not a callous man. Obligation pulled with a gravity as powerful as the earth's: the child was his, conceived by a woman who would make a formidable mother, if not a disastrous, absentee one; whereas Maggie – loving, kind Maggie – would in time welcome her baby, and would be ever-present, and guiding and judicial in its rearing, he was sure. Of the two children, Nancy's would need him more.

He turned forlornly and shuffled up to Ma's house to pack and face his purgatory.

Chapter 17

He slept little that night. Lying beside Nancy he thought of Maggie, her image appearing keenly in a dozen remembered poses: with her chin raised, yodelling in a bathtub; laughing as she served him a plate-sized doughnut; kneeling before a clump of withering flowers in a country graveyard; lifting her sombre countenance while rocking his world with her news; gravely predicting that Nancy would keep them apart until well after Maggie's baby was born.

How right she'd been.

He kept to his side of the bed. Stacking his hands beneath his head, he made sure not even his elbow touched Nancy's hair. He thought of tomorrow; he would, of course, tell Maggie then, but he would not compound his wrongdoings by going to her fresh from even the slightest intimacy with the woman beside him.

He closed his eyes, assessing himself and the hurt he would bring to Maggie, suffering already at the thought of inflicting it upon her. His eyelids trembled. This was no venial offence. He was answerable to both women, guilty of all accusations, lower than either of them could even express. He could handle Nancy's wrath – and it would be vile when she learned the truth – but what of Maggie's hurt?

Aw, Maggie, what have I done? I wanted so much for us. You were the last one I wanted to hurt.

In the midnight blackness, he agonized. Some little creature scurried across the roof – a mouse, probably – leaving a trail of ticks as of acorns rolling down the shingles. Down on Main Street some teenager with a loud muffler let out his clutch and rapped his pipes up the deserted thoroughfare. Beside Eric the clock changed a digit with a soft *fup*.

Nancy's baby was one minute older.

Maggie's baby was one minute older.

He thought of the unborn children. The legitimate one. The bastard – what a harsh word when applied to one's own offspring. What would they look like? Would they have traces of the old man? Ma? Himself, surely. Would they be bright? (Coming from Maggie and Nancy, it seemed a certainty.) Healthy or sickly? Contented or demanding? What would Maggie's wishes be? To let her child grow up knowing who'd sired him or to conceal the father's name? If the child knew, he'd know, too, who his half brother or half sister was. They'd meet on the street, at the beach, in school, likely as early as in kindergarten. Somewhere along the line some kid would ask him, How come your dad lives with that other family? At what age do children become aware of the stigma of illegitimacy?

He tried to imagine himself taking both his children out in the *Mary Deare* and putting fishing lines into their hands, teaching them about the water, and the constellations, and how to read the depth finder screen. He'd boost them up, one on each knee (for they'd be small yet), and hold them by their bellies so their inquisitive hands could grip the wheel while he faced them toward the monitor and explained: *The blue is the water. The red line is the bottom of the lake, and that white line just above it is a school of alewife. And that long white line . . . that's your salmon.*

On a more real plane, the idea seemed unlikely, ludicrous even, that two mothers of two of his children would be so bending as to allow such a flaunting of tradition, even in today's enlightened era. How stupidly self-serving of him to even imagine it.

Well, he'd know tomorrow. He'd see Maggie tomorrow, would suffer right along with her.

Saturday dawned unseasonably chilly, with cloud racks scudding before a brisk wind. Nancy was already at work in her office as Eric prepared to leave the house. He stopped at her door, drawing on a windbreaker, his arms leaden from lack of sleep.

'I'll see you tonight,' he said, his first words to her since rising. He'd fallen asleep some time after four o'clock, and had overslept and awakened to find Nancy already dressed and downstairs. She looked very *downtown*, in oversized spectacles, a knobby linen jumpsuit with a belt that looked like coconut shell, two pounds of earrings, a container of yogurt at her elbow and her hair belling out behind her ears like a hoopskirt. At his appearance she sat back and raised the eyeglasses onto her hair. 'What time?' She picked up the yogurt and ate a spoonful.

'If this weather keeps up, early, maybe even this afternoon.'

'Great!' She arched a wrist and the spoon flashed. 'I'll fix us something loaded with calcium and vitamins.' She patted her stomach. 'Have to be extra careful about proper nourishment now.' She smiled. 'Have a nice day, darling.'

Mentally, he cringed at her endearment and rebelled at the reminder of her pregnancy.

'You, too,' he returned and headed for his truck.

The weather suited his mood. Rain began falling when he was halfway to Gills Rock, smacking the windshield with a sound like breaking plastic. Thunder grumbled and rolled an unbroken circle around the flickering horizon. He knew well before he reached Ma's that the morning's charters would already be cancelled, but he drove on anyway, checked in with Mike and Ma, had a cup of coffee but passed up a piece of sausage, too preoccupied to eat. For a while he studied the soiled kitchen phone, the phone book on its string, with Maggie's Seattle number still written on its cover, remembering the first time he'd called her.

Ma repeated a question then yelped, 'Boy, you got rutabagas in your ears or somethin'!'

'Oh . . . what?'

'I asked you if you wanted something else – some oatmeal maybe or some lunch meat on toast?'

'No, nothing, Ma. I'm not hungry.'

'Not revving on all cylinders this morning either, are you?'

'Sorry. Listen, if you don't need me for anything I've got to run back to Fish Creek.'

'Naw. Go ahead. This rain looks like she's settled in for good.'

He hadn't told either of them why he'd decided to move back home with Nancy, and though Mike calmly leaned against the sink, sipping coffee, watching Eric appraisingly, Eric chose not to enlighten him yet. Besides, Ma knew nothing about Maggie's pregnancy and he couldn't bear telling her yet. Maybe he never would. Guilt again: withholding the truth from Ma, who always found out everything, as if she had hidden antennae that twitched whenever her boys were bad.

When he was eight – he remembered the age clearly, because Miss Wystad had been his teacher that year, and it was the year Eric had been experimenting with his first cussing – he had laughed and poked fun at a boy named Eugene Behrens who had come to school with a hole in the seat of his overalls and bare skin showing through. Eugene also had a home-style bowl-and-scissors haircut that made him look like one of the Three Stooges.

Bare-ass Behrens, Eric had called him.

'Hey, Yoo-gene,' Eric had hollered across the playground. 'Hey Yoo-gene Bare-ass Behrens, where's your underwear, Yoo-gene?'

While Eugene turned away stoically, Eric had taunted in a sing-song,

Yoo-gene Behren's ass is bare
He ain't got no underwear
Looks like a stooge in his bowl of hair!

While Eugene broke into a run, crying, Eric turned around to find Miss Wystad five feet behind him.

'Eric, I think you and I had better go inside,' she'd said sternly.

Of that conversation Eric remembered little, except his question, 'You gonna tell my Ma?'

Miss Wystad hadn't told Ma, but she'd meted out a strapping that stung yet, as he remembered it, and had made him stand before the class and apologize to Eugene aloud while he was still red-faced and hurting and humiliated.

How Ma ever found out about the fiasco Eric never knew – Mike swore he hadn't told her. But find out she did (though she never alluded to the incident) and her punishment was even more ignominious than Miss Wystad's. He'd come home one day after school to find her cleaning out his chest of drawers. She had culled out some of his underwear, socks, T-shirts, corduroys. As he stood watching, she added to the stack a new T-shirt, his favourite, across its front a picture of Superman in flight. As she stacked the clothes, she spoke offhandedly. 'There's a family named Behrens – real poor, got ten kids. One of 'em's in your room, I think. A Eugene? Anyway, their Pa got killed in an accident at the shipyards a couple of years ago, and their Ma's got quite a struggle to raise 'em. My church circle's taking up a collection of used clothing to help them out, and I want you to take these to school tomorrow and give them to that boy, Eugene. Will you do that for me, Eric?' For the first time she glanced flat at him.

He'd dropped his eyes to his Superman shirt and gulped down a protest.

'You'll do that, won't you, son?'

'Yes, Ma.'

For the rest of that school year he'd watched Eugene Behrens come to school in his Superman shirt. He'd never again poked fun at anyone less fortunate than he. And he'd never again tried to withhold his misdeeds from Ma. If he got into a scrape, he'd march straight home and confess, 'Ma, I got into trouble today.' And they'd sit down and work it out.

Driving to Maggie's through the downpour on a black summer day, he wished for the simplicity of those problems again, wished that he could simply go to his mother and say, 'Ma, I'm in trouble,' and they could sit down and work it out as they'd always been able.

The recollection made him blue, and he forgave Eugene Behrens for wearing his Superman shirt, and wondered where Eugene was now and hoped he had a closet full of nice clothes and enough money to live in luxury.

At Maggie's the lights were on: yellow patches upon a purple day. Whipped by the strong wind, the arborvitaes swayed and danced. The wet yellow paint on the house had darkened to ochre. The daylilies beside the back stoop were beaten flat by the water sheeting from the roof. As he ran down the steps droplets plopped from the maples in great, cold blobs that struck his neck and head and shattered on his blue windbreaker. The rag rug on the back verandah squished as he leapt onto it. Inside, the kitchen was empty but bright.

To Eric's dismay, his knock was answered by Katy, wearing a curious expression that soured into censure the moment she saw who stood outside.

'Hello, Katy.'

'Hello,' she replied tightly.

'Is your mother here?'

'Follow me,' she ordered and went away. He hurriedly removed his tennis shoes and watched her disappear along the short passage into the dining room from where voices could be heard. He hung his head, shook the water from his hair and followed to find Katy waiting just inside the dining room doorway, the table surrounded by guests, and Maggie, at the foot.

'Someone to see you, Mother.'

The conversation ceased and every pair of eyes in the room settled on him.

Caught by surprise, Maggie stared at Eric as if he were an apparition. Her face turned brilliant crimson before she finally gathered her poise and rose.

'Well, Eric, this is a surprise. Won't you join us? Katy, get him a cup, will you?' She moved over to make room for him beside her while Katy got a cup from the built-in hutch and belligerently clattered it onto the place mat. Maggie tried to rescue the moment by performing introductions. 'This is a friend of mine, Eric Severson, and these are my guests . . .' She named three couples but in her embarrassment forgot the names of the fourth and coloured again, stammering an apology. 'Eric runs a charter boat out of Gills Rock,' she informed them.

They passed him the footed china coffee urn, and the plate of pumpkin muffins, and the butter, and a glass of pineapple juice which one of them poured at the far end of the table as if this were one big happy family.

He should have called first. Should have considered that she'd be with her guests over breakfast, and that Katy would be here and openly antagonistic. Instead, he found himself subjected to thirty minutes of chit-chat with Maggie tense as a guy-wire on his right, and Katy bristling with animosity on his left, and an audience of eight attempting to pretend they noticed nothing out of the ordinary.

When the ordeal ended, he had to wait while Maggie accepted cheques from two of her clients, answered several questions and quietly gave orders to her daughter to clean up the dining room and go on with her daily work. 'I won't be long,' she ended, finding a long grey sweater and tossing it over her shoulders as she hurried with Eric through the rain toward the truck.

When the doors slammed, they sat in their soggy clothes, breathing hard, staring straight ahead. Finally Eric blew out a great breath. His shoulders wilted.

'Maggie, I'm sorry. I shouldn't have come here at this time of day.'

'No, you shouldn't have.'

'I never thought about you being at breakfast.'

'I run a bed and breakfast, remember? Breakfast happens every morning here.'

'Katy wanted to slam the door in my face.'

'Katy's been taught some manners, and she knows she'd better remember them. What's wrong?'

'Can you come for a ride? Someplace away from here? Just out in the country a ways? We need to talk.'

She laughed tensely. 'Obviously.' Rarely had he seen her upset, but she was – with him – as she glanced toward the house where Katy's image could be seen moving about the kitchen beyond the lace curtains. 'No, I shouldn't leave. I have work to do, and there's no sense getting Katy any more antagonistic than she already is.'

'Please, Maggie. I wouldn't have come if it wasn't important.'

'I realize that. That's why I came outside with you. But I can't leave. I only have a minute.'

A man came out, the guest whose name Maggie had forgotten, carrying two suitcases, running through the downpour to his car across the road.

'Please, Maggie.'

She expelled a breath of exasperation. 'All right, but not for long.'

The engine sputtered, caught, and blustered as he pumped the gas, then put the truck in gear and drove up the switchback with the tyres hissing like brushes on a drum, and the windshield wipers thumping like a metronome. He drove the opposite direction of town, south onto Highway 42, then east on EE until he came to a narrow gravel track leading off into a copse of scrubwoods. At the end of the trail where the trees gave onto a fallow field, he pulled to a halt and cut the engine. Around them the heavens dripped, clouds glowered, and the heads of wildflowers drooped like penitents before a confessor.

They sat momentarily, each enveloped by his own thoughts, adjusting to the metallic resonance of rain on the cab, the absence of flapping wipers, the blurred landscape whose focal point was an abandoned farmstead viewed through ribbons of rainwater branching down the windshield.

In unison they turned their heads to look at one another.

'Maggie,' he said, forlornly.

'It's something bad, isn't it?'

'Come here,' he whispered hoarsely, catching and holding her with his cheek and nose against the pleasant mustiness of her wet hair and wool sweater. 'Yes. It's bad.'

'Tell me.'

'It's worse than the worst you've ever imagined.'

'Tell me.'

He drew back, met her brown eyes with an earnest, apologetic gaze. 'Nancy is pregnant.'

Shock. Disbelief. Denial. 'Oh, my God,' she whispered, pulling away, covering her lips, staring out the windshield. Quieter still, 'Oh, my God.'

Her eyes closed and he watched her battle with it, pressing her fingertips harder and harder against her lips until he thought her teeth must be cutting them. In time her eyes opened, and blinked once in slow motion, like an antique doll with lead-weights in its head.

'Maggie . . . oh, Maggie-honey, I'm sorry.'

She heard only a roar in her ears.

She had been a fool. She had played into the hands of a man who was typical, after all. She had not questioned or demanded, but had taken him at his word that he loved her and was seeking a divorce. Her mother had warned her. Her daughter had warned her. But she'd been so sure of him, so absolute in her trust.

Now he was leaving her for his wife, leaving her nearly five months pregnant with his child.

She did not cry; one cannot weep ice crystals.

'Take me home, please,' she said, sitting straight as a surveyor's rod, donning a veneer of dignity.

'Maggie, please don't do this, don't turn away.'

'You've made your decision. It's clear. Take me home.'

'I've badgered her for all these years. How can I divorce her now?'

'No, of course you can't. Take me home, please.'

'Not until you –'

'Goddamn you!' She swung, slapped his cheek hard. 'Don't you issue ultimatums to me! You have no more rights over me, no more say over what I choose to do! None! Start the engine this instant or I'll get out and walk!'

'It's a mistake, Maggie. I didn't want her to get pregnant. It happened before you and I even knew what we wanted, when I was so mixed up and trying to decide what to do about my marriage.'

She flung open the truck door and stepped into soggy grass. Cold water oozed into the lacing holes of her shoes. She ignored it and headed along the dirt track knocking aside a clump of tall milkweed which wet her slacks to mid-thigh.

His truck door slammed and he grabbed her arm. 'Get back in the truck,' he ordered.

She pulled free and stalked on, head high, eyes dry of all but rainwater which plastered her hair to her forehead and leached through her eyelashes.

'Maggie, I'm a damn fool but your baby is mine and I want to be its father!' he called.

'Tough!' she called. 'Go back to your wife!'

'Maggie, goddamn it, will you stop!'

She marched on. He cursed again, then the truck door slammed and the engine started. Killed. Started again, roared like a hungry giant before the truck shot backward, spraying wet muck onto its underbelly. She trooped along the worn track, as dogged as a foot soldier, preventing his bypassing her.

Bumping along behind her, in reverse, he hung his head out the window.

'Maggie, get in the damn truck!'

She gave him the flying finger, marching headlong toward the road.

He changed his tack, tried cajoling. 'Come on, Maggie.'

'You're out of my life, Severson!' she yelled, almost joyously. When she reached the blacktop he squealed backward onto the pavement on two tyres and changed directions with a grinding shift that dropped the truck's guts.

The engine killed for good. The starter whined five times without results. His truck door slammed. Maggie strode on, picturing him standing beside it with his hands on his hips.

'You goddamn stubborn woman!' he yelled.

She raised her left hand, bent the fingers twice: *bye-bye*, and tramped on through the rain.

He stood staring after her, absolutely flabbergasted and angrier than he ever remembered being. This was the reaction he'd expected from Nancy, not from his sweet-tempered Maggie. Damned unpredictable hussy, flipping him off like that. So she was pissed off. Well, that made two of them! He'd let her stew for a couple of weeks until she got good and lonesome for him, then maybe he'd get treated civilly!

He watched until he was certain she had no intention of turning around, then kicked the truck tyre, opened the door and pushed the damned old whore to the side of the road. When she was listing toward the ditch, he slammed the door and studied Maggie again, so distant he couldn't tell the colour of her clothes.

Go then, you stubborn little twit! But you'll have to talk

to me sooner or later. I've got a kid to support and it's bouncing along in the rain with you! You'd better – by God – take good care of it!

Maggie stopped at the first farmhouse she came to and asked to use the telephone.

'Daddy?' she said, when Roy came on the line. 'Did you drive to work?'

'Yes, but what –'

'Could you please come out and get me? I'm at a farm out on EE just a little east of 42 . . . just a minute.' She asked the greasy-haired adolescent girl who'd let her in, 'What's the name here?'

'Jergens.'

Into the phone she inquired, 'You know where the Jergenses live, out south of town?'

'I know it, yeah, Harold Jergens' place, used to belong to his folks.'

'I'm there. Can you come and get me, please?'

'Why, sure, honey, but what in the world –'

'Thanks, Daddy. But hurry. I'm soaking wet.'

She hung up before he could question her further.

When they were riding back to town together they encountered a hitchhiker just a short way down EE.

Roy began decelerating, but Maggie ordered, 'Drive on, Daddy.'

'But it's raining and –'

'Don't you dare stop, Daddy, because if you do, I'll get out and walk!'

They passed the man with his thumb up and Roy glanced over his shoulder.

'But that's Eric Severson!'

'I know it is. Let him walk.'

'But, Maggie . . .' Severson was shaking his fist at them.

'Watch the road, Daddy, before you put us in the ditch.'

She grabbed the wheel and averted a disaster. When Roy

faced front Maggie turned on the heater, fingercombed her hair and said, 'Prepare yourself for a shock, Daddy. This one's going to knock your argyle socks off.' She cast a steady glance. 'I'm expecting Eric Severson's baby.'

Roy gaped at her in amazement. She reached for the wheel again to keep them on the road.

'But . . . but . . .' He sputtered like a one-cylinder engine and cranked around to see the road behind them, oblivious to their direction or speed.

'Mother's going to shit a ring around herself,' Maggie said matter-of-factly. 'I expect this will end our relationship for good. She's warned me, you see.'

'Eric Severson's baby? You mean *that* Eric Severson? The one we just passed?'

'That's right.'

'You mean you're going to marry him?'

'No, Daddy. He's already married.'

'Well, I know that . . . but . . . but . . .' Roy again did an imitation of an old Allis-Chalmers.

'As a matter of fact, his wife is expecting their first baby, too. But if I've got it figured right, mine will be born first.'

Roy braked to a stop in the dead centre of the road and exclaimed, 'Maggie!' with all due astonishment.

'Do you want me to drive, Daddy? Maybe I should. You seem a little shaken.'

She was out and around the car before Roy could digest her intention. She shoved him over bodily. 'Move, Daddy. It's wet out here.'

He moved as if a door had slammed during his nap, scudding over into the passenger seat while Maggie put the car into gear and headed for town.

'We had an affair, but it's over. I have my own plans to make now and I may need your help from time to time, but I'm a strong person. You'll see. I've been through Phillip's death, and the move here, getting rid of the house in Seattle with all its memories, and all the hubbub of tearing apart the new house and starting the business, and I intend to make a go of it, baby or not. Do you think I can?'

'There's not a doubt in my mind.'

'Mother *will* be upset, won't she?'

'There's not a doubt in my mind.'

'She will probably, quite literally, disown me.'

'Probably . . . yes. Your mother is a hard woman.'

'I know. That's why I'm going to need you, Daddy.'

'Honey, I'll be there.'

'I knew you'd say that.' His shock was ebbing, in light of Maggie's decisiveness and steel intentions.

'Have you ever heard of the Lamaze method of giving birth, Daddy?'

'I've read about it.'

She sidled him a glance. 'Think we could do it? You and me?'

'Me?' His eyes grew round.

'Think you'd like to see your very last grandchild born?'

He considered a moment before answering, 'It'd scare the daylights out of me.'

'The classes would teach us both not be scared.'

It was the first time she'd admitted being so, while outwardly she continued as strong and dauntless as a steel I-beam.

'Your mother,' he said, eyes twinkling, 'would shit a ring around herself.'

'Tsk, tsk, tsk. Such shocking language, Daddy.'

They both laughed, conspirators with a sudden strong bond. Reaching the edge of town, Maggie confessed, 'I haven't told Katy yet. I expect some trouble when I do.'

'She'll get used to the idea. So will I. So will your mother. Anyway, my feeling is, you answer to no one but yourself.'

'Exactly. And I've just learned that today.' She pulled up at the top of her walk. The rain had stopped. Droplets quivered on the tips of leaves, and the air smelled like herbal tea – green, moist, earthen.

Maggie put the car in neutral and took her father's hand. 'Thanks for coming to get me, Daddy. I love you.' How easily she could say it to him.

'I love you, too, and I won't say I'm not shocked. I think my argyles are someplace back there on EE.'

When Maggie had laughed and quieted, Roy looked down at their joined hands.

'You amaze me, you know? There's so much strength in you. So much . . .' He puzzled before adding, '. . . direction. You've always been that way. You see what you want, what you need, and you go after it. College, Phillip, Seattle, Harding House, now this.' He raised his eyes quickly. 'Oh, not that you went after this, but look how you handle it, how you make decisions. I wish I could be that way. But somehow I always take the route of least resistance. I don't like it in myself, but that's the way it is. Your mother, she bulldozes me. I know it. She knows it. You know it. But this time, Maggie, I'm standing up to her. I want you to know that. This isn't the end of the world, and if you want that baby, then I'll go there to that hospital and show the world I got nothing to hang my head about, okay?'

The tears she had stubbornly dammed until now spurted into her eyes as she crooked an arm around Roy's neck and pressed her cheek to his. He smelled of raw beef and smoked sausage and Old Spice after-shave, an endearing and familiar combination. 'Oh, Daddy, I needed to hear that so badly. Katy's going to be so upset. And Mother . . . I shudder to think of telling her. But I will. Not today, but soon, so you don't have to think I'd leave that job up to you.'

He rubbed her back. 'I'm learning something from you. You watch. One of these days I'm going to make a move that might surprise you, too.'

She backed up and glowered at him. 'Daddy, don't you dare go fishing with Eric Severson! If you do, I'll get a new Lamaze partner.'

He laughed and said, 'Go on in the house and get into something dry before you catch a cold and cough that baby loose.'

Watching her go, he considered it, what he'd been considering for five years now. He'd see how Vera took the news, then he'd make up his mind.

Chapter 18

Maggie Stearn had a stubborn streak longer than the Door County coastline. She could do it! She'd show them all! She set about adjusting to the finality of this new, imminent presence in her life and to the fact that it would be raised in a fatherless environment. She fortified herself for the physical and emotional stamina it would take to do credit to both roles, those of mother and innkeeper. She altered her expectations to exclude a husband and groomed her courage to break the news to Katy and Vera.

A week went by, then two, but still she hadn't told them. She wore loose blouses, untucked, and beneath them kept her slacks unbuttoned.

One morning in early August, when Katy was less than a month shy of leaving for college, they awakened to the aftermath of a storm. The wind had strewn the yard with maple leaves and weeping willow branches from a neighbour's tree. Since Todd wasn't expected again for two days Maggie and Katy went outside to rake them up themselves.

Already at eleven A.M. the heat was sweltering, rising from the moist earth with tropical intensity while the breeze off the bay remained too warm to bring much relief. It brought instead the noisome odour of debris tossed onto the rocky shore by last night's storm, and more work: they'd have to rake up the seaweed and dead fish before the mess started decaying in the sun.

Maggie leaned over to scoop a handful of willow withes against her bamboo rake and straightened a little too fast. A twinge stabbed low in her groin and dizziness momentarily enveloped her. She let the twigs fall, flattened a hand to her pelvis and waited out the vertigo with closed eyes.

When she opened them, Katy was studying her, the rake idle in her hands. For seconds neither of them moved: Maggie caught in the classic pose of weary expectancy, Katy temporarily dumbstruck.

Katy's expression became quizzical. Finally she tipped her head and said, 'Moth-*errr* . . .', half questioning, half accusing.

Maggie dropped her hand from her groin while Katy continued staring. Her glance darted from Maggie's belly to her face, then down again. When comprehension dawned she began, 'Mother, are you. . . ? You aren't . . .' The idea seemed too preposterous to voice.

'Yes, Katy,' Maggie admitted, 'I'm pregnant.'

Katy gaped at her mother's stomach, aghast. Tears sprang to her eyes. 'Oh, my God,' she whispered after some seconds. And again, horror-stricken, 'Oh my God . . . this is horrible!' The ramifications of the situation settled upon Katy one by one, changing her face by degrees, as a flower withered by time-lapse photography. From stupefaction to displeasure to outright anger. 'How could you allow such a thing to happen, Mother!' she lashed out. 'You'll be forty-one years old this month and you're not that stupid!'

'No, I'm not,' Maggie replied. 'There *is* an explanation.'

'Well, I don't want to hear it!'

'I thought –'

'You thought!' Katy interrupted. 'What you *thought* is altogether too obvious. You thought you could have your little illicit affair without anybody being the wiser, and instead you turn up pregnant!'

'Yes, some five months now.'

Katy retreated as if something vile had insinuated itself in her path. Her face took on an expression of repugnance and her voice became sibilant with distaste. 'It's his, isn't it? A *married* man's!'

'Yes, it is.'

'This is disgusting, Mother!'

'Then you might as well hear the rest of it: his wife is pregnant too.'

For a moment Katy appeared too stunned to reply. Finally, she threw one hand in the air. 'Oh, this is just great! I've made new friends in this town, you know! What am I supposed to tell them? That my mother got knocked up by a married man, who also, by the way, happened to knock up his estranged wife at the same time?' Her eyes narrowed with accusation. 'Oh, yes, Mother, I know about that, too. I'm not ignorant. I've asked around! I know he hasn't been living with his wife since last winter. So what did he do, promise to divorce her and marry you?'

Stung by guilt and a sense of her own culpability, Maggie blushed.

Katy clapped a hand to her forehead, standing her bangs on end. 'Oh, good God, Mother, how could you be so gullible? That line is as old as VD! Speaking of which –'

'Katy, I don't need any sermons on –'

'*Speaking of which*,' Katy repeated forcefully, 'you're *supposed* to use condoms, or hadn't you heard? It's the *in* thing to do if you're going in for promiscuous sex. I mean, holy cripes, Mother, the newspapers are full of it! If you're going to snuggle up with some Lothario who's hitting on women all over town –'

'He is *not* hitting on women all over town!' Maggie grew angry. 'Katy, what's got into you! You're being purposely crude and cruel.'

'What's got into me!' Katy spread a hand on her chest, her face incredulous. 'Into me! That's a laugh! You want to know what's got into me when my own mother is standing in front of me five months pregnant with a married man's kid? Well, take a good look at yourself!' Katy railed. 'Look at how you've changed since Daddy died! How do you expect me to react? You think maybe I should start passing out cigars and spreading the news that I'm going to have a new baby brother?' Katy's face became distorted by rage as she thrust her chin forward. 'Well, don't hold your breath, Mother, because I'll *never* think of that bastard as my brother *or* my sister! *Never!*' She flung down the rake. 'All I can say is I'm glad Daddy doesn't have to be here to see this day!'

Crying, she ran for the house.

The door slammed and Maggie flinched. She stood staring at it until her tears began, Katy's renunciation resounding through her head. A dense feeling overtook her chest: fault and apology, weighted by the burden of wrongdoing. She deserved Katy's every rebuke. She was the mother, expected to be a paragon of irreproachability, a worthy role model. Instead, look what she'd done.

Oh, Katy, Katy, I'm sorry. You're right on every count, but what can I do? It's mine. I have to raise it.

Heavy-hearted, she stood in the dappled yard, quietly crying, wrestling with guilt and an overwhelming sense of inadequacy, for she didn't know, at this juncture, how to fulfil her duties as a mother. No case studies she remembered, no self-help books she'd read set precedents for a situation such as this.

The irony of it: she, a woman of forty being preached to by her daughter on the subject of birth control. Her *daughter* crying out, 'What will my friends think?'

Maggie closed her eyes, waiting for the oppression to lift, but it grew heavier until she felt as if it might drive her, like a steel spike, into the very earth. She realized she was still holding the smooth, warm rake handle. Turning listlessly toward the dock she let it slip from her hand and bounce to the grass.

She sat for a while on the wooden bench of the latticed arbour seat, the one Eric had built for her. During that time, while he'd worked on it, she'd had visions of waiting here for the *Mary Deare* at the end of the day. Of catching the mooring line as the engine died, and walking hip to hip with him, up to the house in the gloaming when the sky was pink and purple and the water as flat as a glass of cherry nectar.

The breeze was cooler here, out over the water. A pair of whitebanded plovers came flapping by, scolding, *chur-wee, chur-wee*, landing on the rocks to forage amid the flotsam. Far out on the water a sailboat with an orange spinnaker rode the wind. Maggie had meant to buy a new sailboat immediately after settling here. There were times when she'd imagined herself and Eric taking weekend jaunts up to Chicago, taking in shows, eating at Crickets, and ambling with joined hands among the slips in Belmont Harbor, admiring the craft that sailed in from points all around the Great Lakes. She'd meant to buy a sailboat, but now she wouldn't, for what pastime was lonelier than sailing alone?

She missed Eric in those moments with so intense a grip that it seemed to be crushing the breath from her. She wanted nothing so badly as to be strong, self-reliant, wilful even, and she would be again, but in her weaker moments, as now, she needed him with a stultifying desperation.

She found this appalling.

What, after all, did one person know of another's intentions? Analysing her and Eric's relationship, she realized he could have been amusing himself with her all along, without the slightest notion of leaving his extraordinarily beautiful wife. The story about Nancy's refusal to consider a family – was it false? After all, Eric's wife *was* pregnant now, wasn't she?

Maggie sighed, closed her eyes, and rested her head against the lattices.

What did it matter, his honesty or lack of it?

Their affair was ended. Absolutely. She had shunned him, had stalked away peremptorily in the rain, had refused his phone calls and icily asked that he not call again the once he'd shown up at her door. But her aloofness was a sham. She missed him. She loved him, still. She wanted to believe he had not lied.

The plovers flew away. The spinnaker became a black

speck in the distance. On the road above, a car rumbled past. Life moved on. So must Maggie.

She finished the raking alone, bagged the sticks and returned to the house to find Katy gone, a note on the kitchen table.

I've gone to Grandma's. No signature. No further enlightenment. Certainly no love.

Maggie's hand, bearing the message, dropped disconsolately to her thigh. *Mother*, she thought wearily. She tossed the note onto the table, pulled off her gardening gloves, and left them, too, before ambling around the perimeter of her kitchen like someone lost, riding the smooth Formica edge with one hip and one hand, postponing the inevitable.

She came, eventually, to the telephone on the cupboard beside the refrigerator.

The last great hurdle.

She backtracked and washed her hands at the sink. Dried them. Studied the telephone at ten paces, as a duellist studies his opponent before raising his arm. Finding no more logical delays, she closed the hall door and sat down on a small white stool next to the instrument.

Go ahead, get it over with.

At last she picked up the receiver and punched out her mother's number, drawing a deep, full-chested breath as she heard the ring, picturing the house – flawlessly clean, as usual – and her mother with her neat, dated hairdo, hurrying toward the kitchen.

'Hello?' Vera answered.

'Hello, Mother.'

Silence: *Oh, it's you.*

'Is Katy there?'

'Katy? No. Should she be?'

'She will be soon. She's on her way over, and she's very upset.'

'Over what? Did you two have another fight?'

'I'm afraid so.'

'What's it about *this* time?'

'Mother, I'm sorry to tell you this way. I should have come over and told you personally instead of dropping it on you like this.' Maggie inhaled shakily, released half the breath and said, 'I'm expecting Eric Severson's baby.'

Stunned silence, then, 'Oh, merciful lord.' The words sounded muffled, as if Vera had covered her lips with a hand.

'I just told Katy this morning and she left here in tears.'

'Oh, merciful lord in heaven, Margaret, how could you?'

'I know you're very disappointed in me.'

The imperious side of Vera could not be stunned for long. Abruptly she demanded, 'You aren't going to *have* it, are you?'

Had the moment been less monumental, Maggie would have registered her own dismay at Vera's callous reply. Instead, she answered, 'I'm afraid it's far too late to do anything else.'

'But they say his wife is expecting, too!'

'Yes, she is. I'll be raising this baby alone.'

'Not here, I hope!'

Well, you didn't expect sympathy, did you, Maggie? 'I live here,' she replied reasonably. 'My business is here.'

Vera made the expected remark. 'How will I ever be able to face my friends again?'

Staring at a brass drawer pull on the cabinets, Maggie felt the hurt mount. *Always herself. Only herself.*

Abruptly Vera launched into a tirade, her words crackling with censure. 'I told you – didn't I try to tell you? But, no, you wouldn't listen, you just kept running around with him. Why, everyone in town knows about it, and they know his wife is expecting, too. I'm already embarrassed to face people on the street. What's it going to be like when you're parading around with his illegitimate baby on your arm?' Without waiting for a reply, she rushed on with more narrow concerns. 'If you had no more self-respect than that, you might have at least considered your dad and me, margaret. After all, we've got to live here for the rest of our lives.'

'I know, Mother,' Maggie replied meekly.

'Well, how can we ever hold our heads up again after this?'

Maggie hung her head.

'Maybe *now* your father will stop defending you. I tried to get him to say something to you last winter, but no, he turned a blind eye like he always does. I said, "Roy, that girl is carrying on with Eric Severson and don't tell me she isn't!"'

Maggie sat silent, mollified, picturing Vera's face growing red and her wattle quivering.

'I said, "You give her a talking to, Roy, because she won't listen to me!" Well, maybe *now* he'll listen after he gets the shock of his life!'

Maggie spoke quietly. 'Daddy already knows.'

From clear across town she could sense Vera bristle.

'You told *him*, but you didn't tell me?' she demanded.

Sitting in silence, Maggie felt a glimmer of retaliatory satisfaction.

'Well, isn't that just ducky, when a daughter can't even come to her mother first! And why didn't he say anything to me about it?'

'I asked him not to. I thought it was something I should tell you myself.'

Vera snorted, then remarked sarcastically, 'Well, *thank you* for the consideration! I'm deeply touched. I have to go now. Katy is here.'

She hung up without a good-bye, leaving Maggie holding the receiver in her lap, leaning her head against the refrigerator, her eyes closed.

I won't cry. I won't cry. I won't cry.

So what is the lump in your throat?

Daddy said it best: she's a hard woman.

How did you expect her to react?

She's my mother! She should be my comfort and support at a time like this.

When was she ever a comfort or a support?

The electronic hang-up tone began whining but Maggie remained motionless, gulping at the wad in her throat until she'd mastered the compulsion to weep. From somewhere deep inside she found a reservoir of strength laced with a liberal shot of vexation and drew from it. Vehemently she replaced the receiver, picked up the phone book, found the number of the *Door County Advocate* and ordered, 'Want ads, please.'

After placing an ad under HELP WANTED, she emptied the dishwasher, changed four beds, cleaned three bedrooms, washed two loads of towels, swept the verandahs, mixed up a batch of refrigerator muffins, staked up the daylilies that had been flattened by the storm, greeted two incoming parties, answered eight phone calls, ate a piece of watermelon, gave a final coat of paint to a piece of used wicker, took a bath, put on clean clothes (comfortable ones this time, the maternity clothes she'd been hiding) and at 4:45 P.M. refilled the parlour candy bowl. All this, staunch as a midwife. Without a leaked tear.

I conceived it. I'll accept it. I'll overcome it. I'll be superwoman. I'll do it all, by God!

Her staunchness continued throughout that night, while Katy failed to call or return, and into the next morning as Maggie began her second day of innkeeping without help; through a lunch-on-the-run (a turkey sandwich in one hand, a dustcloth in the other); through the sign-out of guests and the blessed hours of silence following their departure, before the new batch arrived.

She was still suffering under her rigid, self-imposed drought when, at two o'clock, the kitchen screen door opened and Brookie walked in. She caught Maggie leaning over the half-empty dishwasher gripping a sheath of clean silverware. Standing just inside the door, samurai-fashion, Brookie pinned Maggie with a look of monumental pugnacity.

'I heard,' she announced. 'I figured you could use a friend.'

Maggie's fortifications crumbled like the pediments of a fortress under cannonade. The silverware clattered from her fist and she sailed into Brookie's arms, bawling like a five-year-old with a scraped knee.

'Oh, Brookieeeee,' she wailed.

Brookie held her fast, fierce, her own heart bounding with sympathy and relief. 'Why didn't you come to me? I've been so worried about you. I thought it was something I did, something I said. I thought maybe you weren't happy with Todd's work and you didn't know how to tell me. I imagined all kinds of things. Oh, Maggie, you can't go through this alone. Didn't you know you could trust me?'

'Oh, B . . . Brookieee,' Maggie wailed, releasing all her despair in a blessed rain of weeping, clinging to Brookie while her shoulders shook. 'I was s . . . so afraid to tell any . . . o . . . one.'

'Afraid? Of me?' Cajolingly, 'How long have you known old Brookie, huh?'

'I kn . . . know.' Maggie's words were choppy with weeping. 'But I m . . . must look like a t . . . total idiot.'

'You're no idiot, now stop talking that way.'

'But I'm o . . . old enough to know b . . . better. And I b. . . believeeed hiiiiim.' The words wailed like a siren as Maggie wept with abject totality.

'So, you believed him,' Brookie repeated.

'He s . . . said he'd m . . . marry me just as soon as . . . he . . . he . . . c . . . c . . . could get a d . . . div . . .' Maggie's words dissolved into an unchecked spate of weeping that echoed around the kitchen like a bagpipe through a glen.

Brookie rubbed Maggie's palpitating back. 'Bawl all you want. Then we're going to sit down and talk, and you're going to feel better.'

Childishly, Maggie claimed, 'I'll never f . . . feel better ag . . . again.'

Brookie loved Maggie enough to smile. 'Oh, yes, you will. Now come on. You're getting snot all over me. Blow your nose and swab your eyes and I'll make some iced tea.' She plucked two tissues from a box and guided Maggie to a chair. 'Sit down there. Empty those bilge pumps and catch your breath.'

Maggie followed orders while Brookie turned on the water and opened cupboard doors. During the making and drinking of lemon tea, Maggie gained control and spilled her emotions, omitting nothing, pouring out hurt, disillusionment and her own grave faults in one unbroken current.

'I feel so stupid and gullible. Brookie, I not only believed him, I thought I couldn't get pregnant anymore. When I told Katy she gave me a lecture on condoms and I was so embarrassed, I wanted to die. Then she screamed at me that she'd never consider my bastard her sister or brother, and now she's packed up and gone to Mother's. And Mother – God, I don't even want to repeat the tongue-lashing I took from her, and I deserved every word of it.'

'You through now?' Brookie asked dryly. 'Because I have a few comments to make. First of all, I've known Eric Severson all my life and he's not the kind who'd use a woman and lie to her deliberately. And as far as Katy goes, she's still got some growing up to do. She just needs some time to get used to the idea. When the baby is born she'll change her mind, just wait and see. And about Vera – well, nobody said raising our mothers was going to be easy, did they?'

Maggie gave a halfhearted smile.

'And you're not stupid!' Brookie pointed a finger at

Maggie's nose. 'I'd probably have thought the same thing about birth control if I'd had hot flushes and screwed-up periods.'

'But people will say –'

'Piss on people. Let them say what they want. The ones that matter will give you the benefit of the doubt.'

'Brookie, look at me. I'm forty years old. Aside from the baby being illegitimate, I have no business getting pregnant at my age. I'm too old for parenting and there's a real risk of birth defects at my age. What if something –'

'Oh, come on now. Look at Bette Midler and Glenn Close. They both had their *first* babies after forty, and no problems at all.'

Brookie's positive attitude was addictive. Maggie cocked her head and said, 'Yeah?'

'Yeah. So listen – what's it going to be? Natural childbirth? You need a coach or anything? I'm an old pro in a delivery room.'

'Thanks for offering, but my dad's going to do it.'

'Your dad!'

Maggie smiled. 'Good old Dad.'

'Well, good for him. But if anything comes up and he can't make it, just call on me.'

'Oh, Brookie,' Maggie said wistfully. The worst was over, the storm calmed. 'I love you.'

'I love you, too.'

Those words, above all others, healed, replaced self-esteem and gave a brighter outlook. The two women sat at right angles, their forearms resting on the scarred tabletop near a crockery pitcher of cosmos and larkspur Maggie had picked during her earlier spurt of angry energy. Maggie said quietly, 'I don't think we've ever said it before.'

'I don't think so either.'

'Do you think you just have to get old enough before you can say it comfortably to a friend?'

'I guess so. You just have to learn that it feels better said than unsaid.'

They smiled and shared a moment of silent affection.

'You know something, Brookie?'

'Hm . . .'

Maggie rolled her cold glass between her palms, studying her iced tea as she admitted, 'My mother has never said it to me.'

'Oh, honey . . .' Brookie took one of Maggie's hands.

Maggie lifted her troubled gaze, allowing herself to come to grips with the tremendous void Vera had left within her. She had been raised Christian. Everything from television commercials to greeting cards had instilled in her the canon that to do anything less than love a parent was depraved.

'Brookie,' she said solemnly, 'can I confess something to you?'

'Your secrets are my secrets.'

'I don't think I love my mother.'

Brookie's unwavering eyes held Maggie's sad ones. She gripped Maggie's hand reassuringly.

'I'm not shocked, in case you expected me to be.'

'I expect I should feel guilty, but I don't.'

'What's so precious about guilt that we all think we should feel it at times like this?'

'I've tried very hard, but she returns nothing, gives nothing. And I know that's selfish, too. You shouldn't evaluate love based on the returns it brings you.'

'And where did you read that, on some greeting card?'

'You don't think I'm degenerate?'

'You know me better than that. What you are is hurt.'

'I am. Oh, Brookie, I am. She should be the one holding my hand right now. Am I wrong? I mean, if it were Katy pregnant, I'd never turn her away. I'd be there for her every minute, and I'd hide my disappointments, because I've realized something in the last year or so. People who love one another occasionally disappoint one another.'

'Now, *that's* the kind of common sense I believe, too. It's much closer to reality.'

'I thought, when I moved back here, that it would be a chance for my mother and I to build some kind of a relationship, if not overtly loving, at least accepting. I've always had the feeling she never accepted me, and now, well . . . she's made it clear she never will again. Brookie, I pity her, she's so cold, so . . . so closed off from anything nurturing or caring, and I'm so afraid Katy is becoming like her.'

Releasing Maggie's hand, Brookie refilled both their glasses. 'Katy is young and impressionable, but from what I see of her around Todd, you don't need to worry about her being cold.'

'No, I guess not.' Maggie drew wet rings on the tabletop with the bottom of her glass. 'Which brings up something else I needed to talk to you about, the two of them. They're . . . well . . . I think they're . . .'

She looked up into Brookie's eyes and found a grin.

'Intimate is the word I think you're struggling for.'

'So you've seen it, too.'

'All I have to see is the hour he's coming in every night, and how he gulps his food at suppertime in a mad rush to get over here and pick her up.'

'This is awkward. I . . .' Again Maggie stopped, searching for a graceful way of expressing herself.

Brookie filled in the gap. 'How can you say to your daughter, be careful, when you yourself are carrying an unexpected bundle, right?'

Maggie smiled forlornly. 'Exactly. I've watched it happening and said nothing, because I'd look like a hypocrite if I did.'

'Well, you can stop worrying. Gene and I talked to him about it.'

'You did?' Maggie's eyes widened in surprise.

'Well, Gene did. We have an agreement – he'll talk to the boys and I'll talk to the girls.'

'What did Todd say?'

Brookie flipped up a palm nonchalantly. 'He said, "Don't worry. Everything's cazh, Dad".'

The two women's faces brightened and they found themselves laughing. They sipped tea awhile, filtering their parental experiences through memories of themselves and their first sexual encounters. At length Maggie said, 'Things have changed, haven't they? Can you believe you and I are sitting here calmly discussing the active sex life of our children as if it were the rising price of fresh vegetables?'

'Hey, who are you and I to point fingers? We, who once risked discovery on the same boat?'

'We? You mean you and Arnie, too?'

'Yup. Me and Arnie, too.'

As their eyes met, their memories harked back to a day after prom aboard the *Mary Deare*, when they were young and ardent and turning cornerstones in their lives.

Brookie sighed, leaned her jaw on a fist and absently rubbed the condensation off the side of her glass. Maggie took up a similar pose.

'Eric was your first, wasn't he?'

'My first and my only, besides Phillip.'

'Did Phillip know about him?'

'He suspected.' Maggie glanced up pointedly. 'Does Gene know about Arnie?'

'No. And I don't know for sure about any of his old girlfriends. Why should we tell each other? They were meaningless. Part of our coming of age, but meaningless today.'

'Unfortunately, my first one is not meaningless today.'

Brookie pondered awhile, then ventured, 'To think I was the one who gave you his phone number and said, "Don't be silly, why can't you call an old boyfriend?"'

'Yeah, it's all your fault, kid.'

They exchanged salty grins.

'So, how about if I dump the baby on you occasionally when I need to get away for an evening?'

Brookie laughed. 'That's the first healthy thing I've heard you say about the baby. You must be getting used to the idea of it.'

'Maybe I am.'

'You know what? I didn't want the last two I had, but they have a way of growing on you.'

Brookie's choice of phrases brought a second welcome laugh. When it faded Maggie sat up straight in her chair and turned serious again.

'I'm going to dump one more confession on you, then that's it for today,' she said.

Brookie straightened, too. 'Go ahead. Dump.'

'I still love him.'

'Yeah, that's the tough part, isn't it?'

'But I've given it some thought and I've decided it took six months for me to fall *in* love, I should give myself at least that long to fall out of it.'

How does one fall out of love? The longer Maggie went without seeing Eric, the more she missed him. She waited for the withering as a farmer awaits it during weeks of drought, watching over his struggling crops and thinking, just die and get it over with. But like weeds that can survive without nourishment, Maggie's love for Eric refused to wither.

August passed, a hot, tiring, oppressive month. Katy went back to school without a good-bye, Todd left for basic training, and Maggie hired an older woman named Martha Dunworthy who came in daily to do the cleaning. In spite of Martha's help, Maggie's days were long and regimented.

Up at 6:30 to bake muffins, prepare juice and coffee, set the diningroom table and make herself presentable. From 8:30 to 10:30 breakfast was available and she made sure she sat with each of her guests for a brief time during the meal, realizing that her friendliness and hospitality was the charm that would bring them back. When the last one had eaten, she put the dining room in order, then the kitchen, checked out guests (often a lingering parting since most of them went away feeling like personal friends). She accepted payment, filled out receipts and sent them away with picture postcards of Harding House, her business card, and hugs on the back verandah. Checkout usually overlapped inquiry calls which began around ten A.M. (numerous since autumn was approaching, Door's heaviest tourist season). The short-distance calls weren't bad; they were usually from the chamber of commerce checking on room availability. The long-distance ones, however, were time-consuming and required answering dozens of repetitive questions before most reservations were made. When the guests were gone she recorded the day's take in her books, answered correspondence, paid bills, laundered towels (the linen service did only bedding), picked and arranged flowers, supervised Martha's cleaning and went to the post office. Around two P.M. the next night's guests began arriving with their inevitable questions about where to eat, fish and buy picnic supplies. Between these daily duties, there were Maggie's own meals to be prepared and eaten, banking to do, and whatever personal task she had set for herself that day.

She loved innkeeping – she really did – but it was exhausting for a pregnant woman. She was at the beck and call of others nearly around the clock. Midday napping was impossible given the constant interruptions. If the last guest didn't pull in until 10:30, she was still up at that hour. And as for days off, they didn't exist. At night when she'd fall into bed, her legs aching and her body weary, she'd rest a wrist across her forehead and think, I'll never be able to do this and handle a baby, too. The baby was due around Thanksgiving and she'd accepted reservations through the end of October, but some days she wasn't sure she'd make it until then.

If only I had a man, she'd think in her weaker moments. If only I had Eric. Thoughts of him persisted, ill-advised as they were.

Then on September 22, Brookie called with some news that spun Maggie's emotional barometer.

'Are you sitting down?' Brookie began.

'Now I am.' Maggie plunked onto the stool beside the refrigerator. 'What is it?'

'Nancy Macaffee had a miscarriage.'

Maggie sucked in a breath and felt her heart whip into overdrive.

'It happened in Omaha while she was there on business. But, Maggie, I'm afraid the rest of the news isn't good. Rumour has it he's taken her on a cruise to Saint Martin and Saint Kitts to patch up her health and their marriage.'

Maggie felt her momentary hope plummet.

'Maggie, are you there?'

'Yes . . . yes, I'm here.'

'I'm sorry to be the one to tell you, but I thought you should know.'

'Yes . . . yes, I'm glad you did, Brookie.'

'Hey, kiddo, you okay?'

'Yeah, sure.'

'You want me to come over or anything?'

'No. Listen, I'm fine. Fine! I mean it. Why, I'm . . . I'm practically over him!' she claimed with forced brightness.

Practically over him? How could one ever get over the man whose only child you would bear?

The question haunted her during restless nights as she grew near term, when her body grew rounder and her sleep was interrupted by countless trips to the bathroom. When her ankles swelled and her face got puffy and she began attending Lamaze classes with Roy.

October came and Door County donned its autumn regalia – the maples blazing, the birches flaming, and the apple orchards hanging heavy with their blushing burden.

The inn was filled every night, and all the guests seemed to be in love. They came by twos, always by twos. Maggie watched them saunter toward the lake, hand in hand, and sit in the arbour seat studying the reflection of the maples which burned like live flames on the blue, calm waters. Sometimes they'd kiss. And sometimes risk a brief intimate caress before returning upyard with a look of replenishment on their faces.

Watching them, Maggie would retreat from the window, cradle her distended abdomen and relive the days of requited touches with a bittersweet longing. Observing the rest of the world passing two-by-two, she anticipated the birth of her child as one of the loneliest things she would ever live through.

'We'll do fine,' she'd say aloud to the one she carried. 'We've got your grandpa, and Brookie, and plenty of money, plus this grand house. And when you're old enough, we'll buy that sailboat, and I'll teach you to become a ragman, and *you and I* will sail to Chicago. We'll do fine.'

One afternoon in late October, during a spell of Indian summer weather, she decided to walk uptown to get her mail. She dressed in a pair of black knit slacks and a rust-and-black maternity sweater and left a note on the door: *Back at 4:00.*

The poplars and maples were already bare, and the oaks were shedding their leaves along Cottage Row as she headed down the hill. Squirrels were busy gathering acorns, racing across her path. The sky was intense blue. The leaves rustled as she walked through them.

Uptown the street was quieter. Most of the boats were gone from the docks. Some of the shops had already closed for the season, and those remaining open had little foot traffic. The flowers along Main Street were withered but for the marigolds and chrysanthemums which had withstood the first frost.

The post office lobby was empty – a tiny yellow space surrounding the service window, which was unmanned as Maggie entered. She went straight to her box, got her mail, slammed the door and turned to find Eric Severson not ten feet behind her.

They both came to a standstill.

Her heart began pounding.

His face flushed.

'Maggie . . ' he spoke first. 'Hello.'

She stood rooted, feeling as if the blood were going to beat its way out her ears and splatter the lobby wall. Spellbound by his presence. Absorbing the familiar – tan face, bleached hair, blue eyes. Decrying the unfamiliar – brown jeans, a plaid shirt, a puffy down vest – which created an absurd sense of deprivation, as if she'd been cheated of the time during which he'd acquired them.

'Hello, Eric.'

His eyes dropped to her maternity sweater, belled out by the protruding load she carried.

Please she prayed, *don't let anyone else walk in.*

She saw him swallow and drag his eyes back to her face.

'How are you?'

'Fine,' she replied in a queer, reedy voice. 'I'm just . . . just fine.' Unconsciously she shielded her stomach with a handful of mail. 'How are you?'

'I've been happier,' he replied, studying her eyes with a look of torment in his own.

'I heard about your wife losing the baby. I'm sorry.'

'Yes, well . . . sometimes those things . . . you know . . .' His words trailed away as his gaze returned to her girth as if it exerted some cosmic magnetic force. The seconds stretched like light-years while he stood rapt, his Adam's apple working in his throat. In the back room a piece of machinery rattled and somebody rolled a heavy cart across the floor. When he looked up her eyes skittered away.

'I understand you took a trip,' she said, groping for reasons to linger.

'Yes, to the Caribbean. I thought it might help her . . . us, to recover.'

Hattie Hockenbarger, a twenty-eight-year veteran of the postal service, appeared in the window, opened a drawer and replenished her supply of postcards.

'Beauty of a day, isn't it?' she addressed them both.

They shot her a pair of distracted glances, but neither of them said a word, only watched her depart around a high wall before returning to their interrupted conversation and their fixation with one another.

'She's having trouble getting over it,' Eric murmured.

'Yes, well . . .' Finding little to say on the subject, Maggie lapsed into silence.

He broke it after several seconds, his voice throaty, verging on emotional, too soft to be heard beyond the quiet lobby. 'Maggie, you look wonderful.'

So do you. She would not say it, would not look at him, looked instead at the WANTED posters hanging on the wall while firing a smoke screen of chatter. 'The doctor says I'm healthy as a horse, and Daddy has agreed to be my coach when the baby is born. We go to Lamaze classes twice a month, and I'm actually getting quite good at Kagel exercises, so . . . I . . . we . . .'

He touched her arm and she became silent, unable to resist the gravity of his eyes. Looking into them she became despairing because, clearly, his feelings hadn't changed. He hurt as she hurt.

'Do you know what it is, Maggie?' he whispered. 'A girl or a boy?'

Don't do this, don't care! Not if I can't have you!

In a moment Maggie's throat would close completely. In a moment her tears would well over. In a moment she'd be making an even greater fool of herself in the middle of the post office lobby.

'Maggie, do you know?'

'No,' she whispered.

'Do you need anything? Money, anything?'

'No.' *Just you.*

The door opened and Althea Munne walked in, followed by Mark Brodie, who was speaking. 'I heard Coach Beck is starting Mueller tomorrow night. Should be a good game. Let's just hope this warm weather . . .' He glanced up and seemed to go mute. He held the door open long after Althea passed into the lobby. His glance darted between Maggie and Eric.

She recovered enough poise to say, 'Hello, Mark.'

'Hello, Maggie. Eric.' He nodded and let the door close.

The three of them stood in a tableau of awkwardness, observed closely by Althea Munne and Hattie Hockenbarger who'd returned to her window at the sound of the door opening.

Mark's eyes dropped to Maggie's stomach and his cheeks turned pink. He had not called her since the rumours began circulating about her and Eric.

'Listen, I have to go, I have guests coming in,' Maggie extemporized, affecting a cheerful smile. 'Nice to see you, Mark. Althea, hi, how are you?' She rushed out the door in a welter of emotions, red-faced and trembling, unspeakably close to tears. Outside, she bumped the shoulders of two tourists as she hurtled along the sidewalk. She had planned to stop at the store and pick up some hamburger for supper, but Daddy would surely see she was upset and ask questions.

She plodded up the hill oblivious to the beautiful afternoon, the spicy smell of the fallen leaves.

Eric, Eric, Eric.

How can I live here the rest of my life, running into him now and then like I just did? It was traumatic enough today; it would be untenable with his child's hand in mine. A picture flashed through her mind: herself and their child, a son, entering the post office two years from now and encountering the big, blond man with the haunted eyes who would be unable to tear his gaze off them. And the child, looking up, asking, 'Mommy, who's that man?'

She simply could not do it. It had nothing to do with shame. It had to do with love. A love that stubbornly refused to wither, no matter how ill-advised. A love that, with each accidental encounter, would herald their feelings as unmistakably as these fallen leaves heralded the end of summer.

I simply cannot do it, she thought as she approached the house she had grown to love. *I cannot live here with his child, but without him, and my only alternative is to leave.*

Chapter 19

It had been a tense summer for Nancy Macaffee. Feigning pregnancy had put her on edge, and had not brought back Eric's affection as she'd hoped. He remained distant and troubled, scarcely ever touching her, speaking to her about only the most perfunctory things. He spent more time than ever on the boat, leaving her alone most of the weekends she was at home.

His only sign of remorse came when she had called him from 'Saint Joseph's Hospital' in Omaha to tell him she'd had a miscarriage. He had suggested the trip to the Bahamas to get her back on her feet, and had willingly cancelled a week of charter bookings to take her there. On the islands, however, beneath the spell of the tropics, where their love should have reblossomed if it were going to, he remained introspective and uncommunicative.

Back at home she had taken a month off, willing to try domestic science in a last-ditch effort to regain his esteem. She spent her days calling his mother for bread recipes, putting fabric softener in their laundry and wax on their floors, but she hated every minute of it. Her life felt pointless without the challenge of sales quotas and the high-tension pace of weekly travel schedules; without dressing up each day and jumping into the mainstream of the retail business where people had flair and style and the same kind of aggressiveness upon which she thrived.

Her time at home proved futile, for Eric sensed her restlessness and said, 'You might as well go back to work. I can tell you're going crazy here.'

In October she followed his advice.

But she continued searching for ways to win him back. Her most recent campaign involved his family.

'Darling,' she said, one Friday night when he'd come home at a reasonable hour. 'I thought maybe we'd invite Mike and Barbara over Sunday night. It's been my fault we haven't had friendlier relations with them, but I intend to remedy that. How about inviting them for supper? We could do linguini and clam sauce.'

'Fine,' he said indifferently. He was sitting at the kitchen table doing company bookwork, wearing glasses and a fresh haircut that made him look militarily clean. He had a wonderful profile. Straight nose, arched lips, pleasing chin – like a young Charles Lindbergh. The sight of him never failed to tighten her vitals when she remembered how it used to be between them. Would he never touch her sexually again?

She squatted beside his chair, crooked a wrist over his shoulder and flicked his earlobe with a finger. 'Hey . . .'

He glanced up.

'I'm really trying here.'

He pushed up his glasses. The pencil moved on. 'Nancy, I have work to do.'

She persisted. 'You said you wanted a baby . . . I tried that. You said I snubbed your family. I admit I have and I'm trying to make up for it. You said you wanted me to stay home. I've done that, too, but it didn't serve any purpose whatsoever. What am I doing wrong, Eric?'

Again the pencil stopped, but he didn't look up. 'Nothing . . .' he answered. 'Nothing.'

She stood, slipping her hands into her skirt pockets, crushed by the admission she'd been denying all these weeks, an admission that made her seize up with dread and insecurity.

Her husband didn't love her. She knew that as certainly as she knew whom he did love.

* * *

Maggie awoke at one A.M. on November 8 with a strong, knotting contraction that opened her eyes like a slamming door. She cupped her stomach and lay absolutely still, wishing it away, realizing it was two weeks early. *Don't let anything happen to the baby*. When the pain ebbed she closed her eyes, absorbing the prayer which had imposed itself without her conscious will. When had she begun wanting this child?

She turned on the light and checked the minute hand on her watch, then lay waiting, remembering her first birth, how different it had been with Phillip beside her. It had been a slow labour, thirteen hours total. At home they had walked, then danced, laughing between contractions at her ungainliness. He had carried her suitcase to the car and had driven with one hand on her thigh. When a hard pain snapped her straight as a switchblade, he'd rolled down the car windows and run a red light. His was the last face she'd seen before being rolled into the delivery room, and the first upon waking in the recovery room. How reassuringly traditional it had been.

How daunting, this time, to face it husbandless.

Another pain built. Eight minutes . . . pant . . . pant . . . call Dad . . . call the doctor . . .

Dr Macklin said, 'Get to the hospital.'

Roy said, 'I'm on my way.'

Vera told Roy, 'Don't expect me to show my face around that hospital!'

Reaching for his shirt and shoes, he replied, 'No, Vera, I won't. I've learned not to expect anything from you at the times that count.'

She sat up, her hairnet like a web over her forehead, her face pinched beneath it. 'See what this has done! It's driven a wedge between us. That girl has disgraced us, Roy, and I can't for the life of me see how you can –'

He slammed the door, leaving her braced up on one hand, still haranguing him from the bed they'd shared for over forty years.

'Hello, honey,' he said cheerfully when he got to Maggie's. 'What do you say we get this little person into the world?'

Maggie had not thought she could love her father more, but the next two hours proved differently. A father and daughter could not go through so intimate an experience without learning each other's true mettle and being bound by new, even stronger tethers.

Roy was magnificent. He was all the things that Vera wasn't: gentle, infinitely loving, strong when she needed strength, humorous when she needed reprieve. She had worried about certain moments – when he'd have to witness her pain, when her body was probed in one way or another, and above all, that of baring herself before him for the first time. He proved dauntless. He took her nudity in his stride – a surprise – talking her through the first minutes with a recollection while rubbing her abdomen, naked, for the first time.

'When you were little, oh, about five, six maybe, you delivered your first baby. Do you remember that?'

She wagged her head on the pillow.

'You don't?' He smiled. 'Well, I do.' His hand made soothing circles. 'That was back when we used to make home deliveries from the store. If somebody was sick, or if an old lady didn't have a car or a driver's licence, we'd deliver her groceries for her. So one day the doorbell rang and I went to answer it, and there you stood, with your dolly in a brown paper sack. "I gots a delibery from the hostible," you said, and handed it to me.'

'Oh, Daddy, you're making this up.' Maggie couldn't help smiling.

'No, I'm not. I swear upon this very grandchild, I'm not.' He patted her big, stretch-marked stomach. 'You must have overheard things about deliveries and hospitals and that's how you figured it was done, straight to the door in a brown paper sack like I delivered groceries.'

She laughed but at that moment a contraction began, closing her eyes, forcing a breathiness into her voice. 'I wish . . . it were . . . that easy.'

'Don't push yet,' he coached. 'Breathe short. Hold those lower muscles tight . . . just for a while yet. That's it, honey.'

When the contraction stopped he wiped her brow with a cool, damp cloth. 'There. That was a dandy. Things are coming along real good, I think.'

'Daddy,' she said, looking up at him, 'I wish you didn't have to see me in pain.'

'I know, but I'll be strong if you'll be. Besides, this is pretty exciting for an old man. When you were born I didn't get a chance to watch 'cause in those days they threw the fathers out in a smoky waiting room.'

She reached for his hand. His was there to grip hers tightly. For either of them to say 'I love you' would have been superfluous at that moment.

On the delivery table, when she called out, then growled with the effort of pushing the child from her body, he proved even more stalwart.

'That's the way, honey. Give 'em hell,' he encouraged.

When the baby's head appeared, Maggie opened her eyes between pains and saw Roy's eyes rapt on the mirror, a smile of excitement on his face.

He wiped her brow and said, 'One more, honey.'

With the next push they shared the moment in eternity toward which all of life strives. One generation . . . to the next . . . to the next.

The baby slithered into the world and it was Roy who rejoiced, 'It's a girl!' then added reverently, '. . . oh, my . . . oh, my,' in the kind of hushed tone often prompted by perfect roses and some sunsets. 'Look at her, look at that gorgeous little granddaughter of mine.'

The baby squalled.

Roy dried his eyes on the shoulder of his green scrubs.

Maggie felt with her hands the wet, naked bundle on her belly, touching her daughter the first time before the umbilical cord was severed.

Even before she was bathed they held her, together, the three generations linked by Roy's rough meat-cutter's hand which lay on the baby's tiny stomach, and Maggie's much more delicate one upon the infant's bloody, blonde-capped head.

'It's like having you all over again,' Roy said.

Maggie lifted her eyes and, as they filled with tears, Roy kissed her forehead. She found, at that moment, the blessing within the burden brought about by this unwanted pregnancy. It was he, this kind, loving father, his benevolence and goodness, the lessons he would teach her yet – both her and this child – about love and its many guises.

'Daddy,' she said, 'thank you for being here, and for being you.'

'Thank you for asking me, sweetheart.'

Mike called on November 9 and told Eric, 'Barb's cousin Janice called this morning when she got to the hospital. Maggie had a girl last night.'

Eric sat down as if poleaxed.

'Eric, you there?'

Silence.

'Eric?'

'Yeah, I'm . . . Jesus, a girl . . .'

'Six pounds even. A little small, but everything's okay.'

A girl, a girl. I have a baby girl!

'Is Maggie okay?'

'As far as I know.'

'Did Janice see her? Or the baby?'

'I don't know. She works on a different floor.'

'Oh, sure . . . well . . .'

'Listen, I hope it's okay to say congratulations. I mean, hell, I don't know what else to say.'

Eric drew an unsteady breath. 'Thanks, Mike.'

'Sure. Listen, you gonna be okay? You want me to come out or anything? Have a beer? Go for a ride?'

'I'll be all right.'

'You sure?'

'Yeah . . . I . . . hell . . .' His voice broke. 'Listen, Mike, I have to go.'

After hanging up he walked around feeling bereft, glancing out window after window, staring at objects without seeing them. What was her name? What colour was her hair? Was she lying in one of those glass cribs that looked like a big Pyrex bread pan? Was she crying? Being changed? Was she in Maggie's room being fed? What would they look like together, Maggie and their daughter?

His mind formed a picture of a dark head bent over a blonde one, the infant nursing from a baby bottle . . . or a breast. He felt as he'd felt within the hour after his father had died. Helpless. Cheated. Like crying.

Nancy came in from the grocery shopping and he forced himself to act normal.

'Hi, anybody call?' she said.

'Mike.'

'They're still coming tonight, aren't they?'

'Yes, but he asked me to come out and help him move Ma's old fuel oil barrel this afternoon. We're going to haul it out to the dump.' They'd finally talked Ma into a new furnace. It had been installed the previous week. It was a logical lie.

'Oh, that's all?'

'Yeah.'

He moved like a plane on automatic pilot, as if all will had been taken from him – upstairs to reshave, change clothes, recomb his hair and pat after-shave on his cheeks, thinking all the while, you're crazy, man! You keep your ass away from that hospital!

But he continued preparing, unable to resist, realizing

this would be his only chance to see her. Once Maggie took her home it might be months, years before she was old enough to walk and he happened to run into them uptown.

One look, one *glimpse* of his daughter and he'd hightail it out of there.

In the bedroom before Nancy's lighted mirror, he checked his appearance one more time, wishing he could have worn dress trousers and a sports jacket. *To haul Ma's oil burner to the dump?* His white shirt was tucked tightly into his blue jeans, but he smoothed the front another time, then pressed a hand to his trembling stomach. *What are you scared of?* He blew out a big breath, turned from his reflection and went downstairs to find his jacket.

Shrugging into it, avoiding Nancy's eyes, he inquired, 'You need any help with supper?'

'You're great with Caesar dressing. I thought I'd let you make it and toss the salad.'

'Right. I'll be home in plenty of time.'

He hurried out before she could kiss him good-bye.

He'd got a new Ford pickup. No advertising on its doors, nothing to disclose who owned it. Driving it through the drear November afternoon towards Door County Memorial Hospital he remembered a day much like this, only snowy, when he and Maggie had driven to Sturgeon Bay to attend an estate sale. That was the day they'd bought the bed on which their daughter had probably been conceived. The bed that stood now in the Belvedere Room at Harding House. Who was sleeping in it? Strangers? Or had Maggie kept it as her own? And was there a cradle in one corner? Or a crib against one wall? A rocking chair in one corner?

Lord, all he'd miss. All the sweet ordinary paternal milestones he'd miss.

The hospital was on 16th Place, north of town where the buildings thinned, a three storey brick structure with the maternity ward on the first floor. He knew his way to it without asking directions: he'd been here six times to see Mike and Barb's newborn babies. A half-dozen times he'd stood before the glass window, studying the pink-faced creatures, thinking, long ago, that one day he'd have one of his own; realizing, as the years advanced, that the chances of that happening were diminishing. Now here he was, taking the elevator up from the ground floor, entering the double doors into the maternity ward, a father at last, and having to sneak to see his own child.

At the nurse's station a plump fortyish woman with a dime-sized mole on her left cheek looked up as he passed, watching him through thick glass that magnified her eyes and tinted them pink. He knew the procedure – anyone wanting to view babies asked at the nurses' station for them to be brought to the observation window, but Eric had no intention of asking. Luck would either be with him or it wouldn't. He nodded to the woman and proceeded around the corner toward the nursery window without speaking a word. Passing open doors he glanced inside wondering which was Maggie's, telling himself, should he happen to catch a glimpse of her, he *would not* pause. But he felt an almost sick longing at the realization of how near she was. Within yards, behind one of these walls, she lay upon a high, hard bed, her body mending, her heart – what of her heart? Was it, too, mending? Or did it still ache at the thought of him, as his did at the thought of her? If he asked her room number and stopped in her doorway, what might her reaction be?

He reached the nursery window without encountering anyone, and looked inside. White walls trimmed with colourful rabbits and bears. A window on the opposite wall. A clock with a blue frame. Three occupied glass cribs. One with a blue nametag, two with pink. From this distance he could not read the names. He stood terrified, sweating, feeling an overload of blood rush to his chest and a shortage of breath as if he'd been tackled and gone down hard.

The baby beneath the pink card on the left lay on her back, crying, her arms up and quivering like newly-sprouted shoots in a stiff breeze. He stepped closer to the window and withdrew his glasses from his jacket pocket. As he slipped them on, the pink card came into focus.

Suzanne Marian Stearn.

His response was as swift and as total as passion. Such a wave, like a powerful breaker sweeping him to the ceiling and slamming him back down. It roared in his ears – or was it his own pulsebeat? It stung his eyes – or was it his own tears? It left him fulfilled and yearning, satisfied and empty, wishing he had never come this far yet certain he would have broken the limbs of anyone who'd tried to stop him.

Fatherlove. Mindless and reactionary, yet more real and swift than any love he had ever before experienced.

Her hair was the length, texture and colour of a dandelion seed. It erupted in a perfect crescent around her head, as blonde as his in his baby pictures, as Anna's, as Anna's mother before her.

'Suzanne?' he whispered, touching the glass.

She was red and disgruntled, her face tufted by temper, her eyes concealed in delicate pillows of pink as she cried. Within a white flannel blanket her feet churned in outrage. Watching, isolated by a quarter inch of transparent glass, he suffered a longing so intense he actually reached for her, flattening a palm upon the window. Never had he felt so thwarted. So denied.

Pick her up! Somebody pick her up! She's wet, or hungry, or she has a stomach ache, can't you see? Or maybe the lights are too bright in there or she wants her hands uncovered. Somebody uncover her hands. I want to see her hands!

Through the glass he heard her squall, a faint mewling sound not unlike that of a killdeer heard at a distance.

A nurse came, smiling, and lifted Suzanne from the sterile glass crib, talking to the infant in a way that shaped her lips like a keyhole. Her nametag said Sheila Helgeson, a pretty young woman with brown hair and dimples, a stranger to Eric. She cradled the baby on one arm and freed Suzanne's trembling chin from the folds of the undershirt, facing her toward Eric. At the touch, the baby quieted with amusing quickness while her mouth opened and sought sustenance. When none materialized, Suzanne howled afresh, her face pruned and colouring.

Sheila Helgeson bounced her gently then looked up and smiled at the man beyond the glass.

'It's time to feed her.' He read the nurse's lips and suffered an extraordinary deluge of loss as she carried the baby away.

Come back! I'm her father and I can't come here again!

He felt a thickening in his throat, a constriction across his chest closely resembling fear. He was grabbing air with quick, short breaths, standing with his entire body compressed in an effort at control.

He turned and walked away, his footsteps rapping like rimshots in the empty hall. A simple question was all it would take and he'd know Maggie's room number. He could walk in and sit beside her bed and take her hand and . . . and what? Mourn this impasse together? Tell her he still loved her? He was sorry? Burden her further?

No, the kindest thing he could do for her was to walk out of here.

In the elevator, riding down to ground floor, he leaned his head back against the wall and shut his eyes, battling the urge to cry. The doors opened and there stood Brookie, holding a big purple florist's sack.

Neither of them moved until the doors began closing, and Eric halted them, stepping out. The doors thumped together and the two stood before them, grave, uncertain what to say to one another.

'Hello, Brookie.'

'Hello, Eric.'

There was no use pretending. 'Don't tell her I was here.'

'She'd want to know.'

'All the more reason not to tell her.'

'So you've patched things up with your wife?'

'We're working on it.' His face held no joy while admitting it. 'What's Maggie going to do about her business?'

'She's closed the inn to guests for now. She's thinking of putting it up for sale in the spring.'

Another blow. He closed his eyes. 'Oh, Jesus.'

'She thinks it's best if she lives someplace else.'

It took a moment of silence before he could speak again. 'If you hear she needs help – any kind of help – will you let me know?'

'Of course.'

'Thanks, Brookie.'

'Sure. Now, listen, you take care.'

'I will, and please don't tell her I was here.'

She lifted a hand in good-bye, careful to make no promises as she watched Eric head for the lobby doors. On her way to Maggie's room, she reflected upon her responsibility as a friend – to divulge or not to divulge – which would Maggie have her do? Maggie still loved Eric, but she was working hard at surmounting and surviving his loss.

Brookie walked into Maggie's room just as a nurse was putting the baby into her arms.

'Hiya, Mag, how they hanging?' she greeted.

Maggie looked up and laughed, accepting the baby and a bottle.

'Not too bad right now, but in a day or so when the milk comes in they'll be hangin' like a couple of water balloons. But lookit here what I got.'

'Ah, the long-awaited offspring.' Brookie plunked down the plant and walked straight to the bed as the nurse left the room. 'Hiya, Suzanna Banana, how does it feel to be in low humidity? My God, Mag, what a looker. Crossed eyes and everything!'

Maggie's laughter bounced the baby. 'You brought flowers?'

'For the kid, not for you.'

'Then open them, so she can see.'

'All right, I will.' Brookie tore open the purple paper. 'Now look here, Suzanne, this is a gloxinia – can you say gloxinia? Go ahead, try it – glox-in-ee-a. What the hell, Maggie, the kid can't even say gloxinia yet? What are you raising here, a moron?'

Brookie always brought her own brand of love: impudence and humour. In time Maggie got a hug, and Brookie said, 'Nice goin', kid. She's beautiful.' A few minutes later Roy showed up carrying a teddy bear the size of an easy chair, and a bouquet of mums and daisies, which he discarded the moment he saw his granddaughter. They were all adulating the baby when Tani walked in followed fifteen minutes later by Elsie Beecham, a lifelong next-door neighbour of the Pearsons. Given all the commotion and visiting, Brookie never got the chance to tell Maggie about Eric's visit.

Maggie's happiness over the birth of Suzanne was shadowed by moments of great melancholy. During her hospital stay the absence of Vera cut deep. She'd tried to arm herself for it in advance, realizing it would be self-deluding to hope Vera might change her mind after all, but when Roy came on his second visit Maggie couldn't resist asking, 'Is Mother coming?'

His face and voice became apologetic. 'No, dear, I'm afraid she's not.' Maggie saw how he tried to make up for Vera's cold indifference but no amount of fatherly attention could ease Maggie's hurt at being shunned by her mother at a time that should, instead, have drawn them closer.

Then there was the matter of Katy. Roy had called her to tell her the baby had been born, but no call came from her. No letter. No flowers. Recalling Katy's parting riposte,

Maggie would find tears in her eyes at the idea of the two sisters who would be strangers to one another, and a daughter who apparently was lost to her.

And of course she thought of Eric. She lamented the loss of him as she had the loss of Phillip when he died. She mourned, too, for *his* loss, for the anguish he must be suffering, undoubtedly having heard of Suzanne's birth. She wondered about his relationship with his wife and how the birth of this illegitimate daughter affected it.

Late in the afternoon of the second day she was lying resting, thinking of him when a voice said, 'Ah, somebody loves you!'

Into the room came a pair of legs carrying a huge vase of flowers surrounded by green tissue paper. From behind it emerged a grey head and a merry face.

'Mrs Stearn?' It was a hospital volunteer dressed in a mauve-coloured smock.

'Yes.'

'Flowers for you.'

'For me?' Maggie sat up.

'Roses, no less.'

'But I've got flowers from everyone I know.' By now she was surrounded by them. They had come from so many unexpected sources – Brookie, Fish and Lisa (Brookie had called them), Althea Munne, the owners of the store where Roy worked, Roy himself, even Mark Brodie on behalf of the chamber of commerce.

'My goodness, there must be two dozen of them here,' the volunteer chattered as she set them down on Maggie's rolling table.

'Is there a card?'

The grandmotherly woman investigated the waxy green tissue. 'None that I can see. Maybe the florist forgot to include it. Well, enjoy!'

When she was gone, Maggie removed the tissue and when she saw what waited inside tears stung her eyes and she pressed a hand to her lips. No, the florist had not forgotten the card. No card was necessary.

The roses were pink.

He did not come, of course, but the flowers told her what it cost him not to and left her feeling bereaved each time she looked at them.

Someone else came, however, someone so unexpected, Maggie was stunned by her appearance. It was later that evening, and Roy had returned – his third visit – this time bringing Maggie a bag of Peanut M & M's and a book called *A Victorian Posy*, a collection of quaintly illustrated poems printed on scented paper. Maggie had her nose to a page, inhaling the musky scent of lavender when she sensed someone watching and raised her head to find Anna Severson standing in the doorway. 'Oh!' she exclaimed, experiencing an immediate flash of angst.

'I didn't know if I'd be welcome or not, so I thought I'd better ask before I came in,' Anna said. Her curls were extra kinky for the occasion and she wore a red quilted nylon jacket over polyester double-knit slacks of painfully royal blue.

Roy glanced from Maggie to Anna but decided to let Maggie handle the situation.

When she found her voice again, Maggie said, 'Of course you're welcome, Anna. Come in.'

'Hello, Roy,' Anna said solemnly, entering the room.

'How are you, Anna?'

'Well, I'm not exactly sure. Those damn kids of mine treat me like I haven't got a brain in my head, as if I can't figure out what's going on here. Makes a person get a little tetchy, don't y' know. I certainly haven't come here to embarrass you, Maggie, but it appears to me I've got a new grandchild, and – grandchildren being a blessing I'm particularly partial to – I wondered if you'd mind if I took a look at her.'

'Oh, Anna . . .' Maggie managed before she started getting misty and raised both arms in welcome. Anna moved straightaway to hug her, soothing, 'There, there . . .' patting her roughly on the back.

Roy's support had been welcome, but a woman's presence had been needed. Feeling the arms of Eric's mother close around her, Maggie felt some of the emotional void filled. 'I'm so glad you came and that you know about the baby.'

'I wouldn't of, if Barbara hadn't told me. Those two boys would've let me go to my grave none the wiser, the durn fools. But Barbara, she thought I ought to know, and when I asked if she'd drive me down here she was more than happy to.'

Drawing back, Maggie looked up into Anna's seamed face. 'So Eric doesn't know you're here?'

'Not yet he don't, but he will when I get home.'

'Anna, you mustn't be angry with him. It was as much my fault as his – more, in fact.'

'I got a right to be angry. And disappointed, too! Heck, it's no secret that that boy's wanted a baby worse than anything I ever saw, and now he's got one and damned if he ain't married to the wrong woman. I tell you, it's a sorry situation. You mind telling me what you're going to do?'

'I'll raise her myself, but beyond that I'm not sure yet.'

'You plan to tell her who her father is?'

'Every child deserves to know that.'

Anna gave a brusque nod of approval, then turned to Roy. 'Well, Roy, are we supposed to congratulate each other or what?'

'I don't know, Anna, but I don't think it would hurt.'

'Where's Vera?'

'Vera's at home.'

'She out of sorts over this, or what?'

'You might say that.'

Anna looked at Maggie. 'Ain't it funny how some people

will act in the name of honour? Well, I'd sure like to see my new granddaughter. No, Maggie, you just rest. Roy, you don't mind walkin' me down there to the nursery, do you?'

'I don't mind a bit.'

A minute later they stood together, studying their sleeping grandchild through a big glass window, an old man with a smile on his face and an old woman with a glint of tears in her eyes.

'My, she's a beauty,' Anna said.

'She certainly is.'

'My thirteenth one, but just as special as the first.'

'Only my second, but I missed out on a lot with my first one, being so far away from her. This one though . . .' His fading words told clearly that he had plenty of dreams.

'I don't mind telling you, Roy, that I never been partial to the wife my boy picked. Your daughter would've made a better one all the way around. It breaks my heart that they can't be together to raise this baby, but that don't excuse him.'

Roy studied the baby. 'Things are sure different than when you and I were young, aren't they, Anna?'

'That's for sure. You wonder just what this world's coming to.'

They thought awhile, then Roy said, 'I'll tell you something that's changed for the better though.'

'What's that?'

'They let grandpas in the delivery room these days. I helped my Maggie bring this little one into the world. Would you believe that, Anna?'

'Oh, pshaw! You!' She looked at him wide-eyed.

'That's right. Me. A meat-cutter. Stood right there and helped Maggie breathe right, and watched this one get born. It was something, I tell you.'

'I bet it was. I just bet it was.'

Studying the baby again, they contemplated the wonder and the disappointment of it all.

★ ★ ★

Anna got home at nine o'clock that night and called Eric immediately.

'I need you out here. Got a pilot light out and I can't get the blame thing lit.'

'Now?'

'You want that range to blow up and me with it?'

'Can't Mike check it?'

'Mike ain't home.'

'Well, where is he?' Eric asked disgruntledly.

'How the deuce should I know? He ain't home, that's all, now are you comin' out here or not?'

'Oh, all right. I'll be there in half an hour.'

She hung up the phone with a clack and sat down sternly to wait.

When Eric walked in twenty-five minutes later, he made straight for the kitchen range.

'There's nothing wrong with it. Sit down,' Anna ordered.

He came up short. 'What do you mean, there's nothing wrong with it?'

'I mean there's nothing wrong with it. Now sit down. I want to talk to you.'

'About what?'

'I went to the hospital and saw your daughter tonight.'

'You *what!*'

'Saw Maggie, too. Barbara took me.'

He swore under his breath.

'I asked her to because none of my boys offered. This is a real fine kettle of fish, sonny.'

'Ma, the last thing I need is to get my ass chewed by you.'

'And the last thing Maggie Pearson needs is a baby without a father. What the devil were you thinking, to have an affair with her? You're a married man!'

He put on a stubborn jaw and said nothing.

'Does Nancy know about this?'

'Yes!' he snapped.

Anna rolled her eyes and muttered something in Norwegian.

Eric glared at her.

'What the heck kind of marriage you got anyway?'

'Ma, this is none of your business!'

'When you bring one of my grandchildren into this world, I make it my business!'

'You don't seem to realize that *I* hurt right now, too!'

'I'd take a minute to feel sorry for you if I wasn't so danged disgusted with you! Now I may not think the sun rises and sets on that wife of yours, but she's still your wife, and that gives you some responsibilities.'

'Nancy and I are working things out. She's changing. She has been since she lost the baby.'

'What baby's that? I had four of my own and I lost two more, and I know what a pregnant woman looks like when I see one. Why, she was no more pregnant than I am.'

Eric gaped. 'What the hell are you talking about, Ma!'

'You heard me. I don't know what kind of game she's playing, but she was no five months pregnant. Why, she didn't have so much as a pimple on her belly.'

'Ma, you're dreaming! Of course she was pregnant!'

'I doubt it, but that's neither here nor there. If she knew you were stepping out with Maggie she probably told the lie to keep from losing you. What I want to make sure of is that you start acting like a husband – of which woman, I don't care. But *one at a time*, Eric Severson, do you hear me!'

'Ma, you don't understand! Last winter when I started seeing Maggie I had every intention of leaving Nancy.'

'Oh, so that excuses you, huh? Now you listen here, sonny! I know you, I know how that new daughter of yours is working on you, and unless I miss my guess, you're going to want to hang around Maggie's and see that little one now and then, and play father a little bit. Well, fine, you do that if that's what you choose. But you start doing that, and you know what else will start up again. I'm not stupid, you know. I saw those roses in her room, and I saw the look on her face every time she glanced at them. When two people got feelings like that for one another and a baby, to boot, that's a pretty tough thing to control. So, fine, you go see your daughter and her mother. But *first* you get yourself free and clear of the woman you got! Your dad and I raised you to know right from wrong, and keeping two women is wrong, no matter what. Do I make myself understood?'

His jaw was set as he answered, 'Yes, clearly.'

'And do I have your promise that you won't darken Maggie's door again unless you got a divorce paper in your hand?'

When no reply came she repeated, 'Do I?'

'Yes!' he snapped, and slammed out of the house.

Chapter 20

It took monumental control for Eric to keep from accosting Nancy with his mother's suspicions the minute he walked in the house. His emotions were too raw, his confusion too fresh, and as it turned out, she was asleep. He lay beside her, wondering if Ma was right, going back over the dates. It had been sometime in early July when she'd told him she was four months pregnant, and he'd commented about her not showing. What had she said? Some passing remark about him looking at her when she was naked. He had, in time, and he'd wondered about her thinness, but she'd explained it away by reminding him that she exercised daily, was extremely fit and diet-conscious and that the doctor had told her that the baby was small. By late August when she claimed to have miscarried she would have been in her fifth month. He tried to remember what Barb looked like in her fifth month, but Barb was a bigger woman all around, and what man besides a father is assessing a woman's girth in terms of months? What about Maggie? She'd been almost five months pregnant when she'd stormed away from him in the rain, and, like Nancy, she hadn't been wearing maternity clothes either. Maybe Ma was wrong after all.

In the morning he went into Nancy's office under the guise of filing the stubs from the bills he'd paid three days earlier. He was standing before the open drawer of a tall metal file cabinet when she passed in the hall. 'Hey, Nancy,' he called, forcing an offhand expression, 'shouldn't we be getting a bill from that hospital in Omaha?'

She reappeared in the doorway looking trim and chic in a pair of grey trousers and a thick Icelandic wool sweater.

'I took care of it already,' she answered, and started away.

'Hey, wait a minute!'

Impatiently, she returned. 'What? I've got to be at the beauty shop at ten.'

'You took care of it? You mean the insurance didn't cover it?' She had excellent insurance through Orlane.

'Yes, of course it did. I mean, it will when I send in the forms.'

'You haven't done that yet?' Nancy was the most efficient book-keeper he knew. For her to neglect paperwork for three months was completely out of character.

'Hey, what is this, some kind of inquisition?' she returned, piqued.

'I'm just wondering, that's all. So what did you do, pay the hospital by cheque?'

'I thought we agreed, you take care of your bills and I'll take care of mine,' she replied, and hurried away.

When she had gone he began searching the files more thoroughly. Because of her travelling it made sense for them to have separate cheque accounts but since her paperwork had always been heavy they'd agreed that he'd take care of paying their household bills. The insurance was one of those grey areas that crossed boundaries since he too was covered on her policy, therefore the paperwork for both of them was filed together.

He flipped through the folder but found only their dental claims for the past several years, a two-year-old claim for a throat culture he'd had, plus those for her annual pap smears. He searched every folder in the four-drawer file cabinet, then turned and sat down at her desk. It was a sturdy, flat-topped oak piece probably eighty years old. She'd bought it at a bank auction years ago, and he'd never snooped in it for anything beyond an occasional paper clip or pen.

Pulling open the first drawer, he felt like a burglar.

He found her cancelled cheques with no trouble, neatly

filed and labelled, the most recent covering the month of October. He went back to August's and opened up the summary sheet, laid it on the desk and scanned it. Nothing to St Joseph's Hospital, or to any strange doctors or clinics. He scanned it again, just to make sure.

Nothing.

He checked September's. Still nothing.

October's. Still no hospital.

He took off his glasses and dropped them on the blotter, spread his elbows wide on the desktop and covered his mouth with both hands.

Had he been that gullible? Had she lied to him as Ma suggested, to keep him away from Maggie? With his misgivings mounting, he searched on.

Cheque stubs from Orlane. Clothing receipts from stores he'd never seen. A correspondence file containing business letters with New York return addresses and carbon copies of her answers. Visa stubs for all her gasoline. Maintenance records for her car. And inside a hanging folder labelled *Sales Profiles*, a plastic zippered case with the name and logo of some real estate company he'd never heard of: Schwann's Realty.

He zipped it open and recognized the computer printout of a hospital bill even before he withdrew it from the pouch. Extracting the folded sheets, he glimpsed code words – Pulse Oximeter, Disp Oral Airway – that immediately diluted his suspicion. He unfolded the four connected sheets, saw the name of a hospital at the top and breathed easier.

Wait a minute.

The hospital was not St Joseph's in Omaha, but Hennepin County Medical Center in Minneapolis. The admit/discharge dates were not August 1989, but May 1986.

Three years ago?

What the hell?

He frowned over the codes and descriptions, but most of them meant little to him.

Halcion Tab 0.5 MG
Oxyto3 In 10U 1C3
Ceftriaxone Inj 2 GM
Drugs, he surmised, and read on, frowning.
Chux Pkg of 5
Culture
Delivery Room Normal
D & C Post Delivery

D & C? He didn't know what words it stood for, but he knew what it meant. She'd had a D & C in May of 1986?

Dread filled his throat as he read the remainder of the list. By the time he reached the end his insides were quaking. He stared at the corner of an aluminium picture frame on the opposite wall while tremors spread down his legs and up his arms. His lips were compressed. His throat hurt. The sensation spread until he felt as if he were on the verge of choking. After a full minute of escalating distress he leapt from the chair, catapulting it backward as he stalked from the room with the bill in his hand. Out to the truck. Started it angrily. Ramming it into reverse. Digging up brown grass as he backed from the yard. Roaring down the hill and around the corner doing thirty in first with the transmission howling. Speed shifting into second an instant short of blowing up the engine, then thundering down the highway like a World War II bomber on a runway.

Fifteen minutes later when he stormed into Dr Neil Lange's office in Ephraim, he was in no mood to be waylaid.

'I want to see Doc Lange,' he announced at the receptionist's window, his fingers rapping the ledge like a woodpecker at work.

Patricia Carpenter glanced up and smiled. She was plump and cute and used to help him with his algebra when they were in the ninth grade.

'Hi, Eric. I don't think you have an appointment, do you?'

'No, but it won't take more than sixty seconds.'

She glanced at the appointment book. 'He's really full today. I'm afraid the best we can do would be four this afternoon.'

His temper erupted and he shouted, 'Don't give me any shit, Pat! I said it would only take sixty seconds, and he's only got one patient left out here before he goes to lunch, so don't tell me I can't see him! You can charge me for a goddamned office call if you want but I've got to see him!'

Patricia's mouth dropped open and her cheeks coloured. She glanced toward the waiting room at an old woman who'd looked up from her magazine at Eric's outburst.

'I'll see what I can do.' Patricia pushed back her rolling chair.

While she was gone he paced and felt like a goddamned heel, remembering how Pat used to have a crush on him. Tapping a thigh with the rolled-up papers, he nodded to the white-haired woman who gawked back as if she recognized his face from the WANTED posters.

In less than sixty seconds Patricia Carpenter returned to the front, hotfooting it to a step behind a long-striding giant in a flapping white lab coat who pointed a finger at Eric as he strode past the receptionist's window. 'Get in here, Severson!' He flung the door open, his face grim with anger, and thumbed toward the end of the hall. 'Down there.'

Eric walked into Neil Lange's office and heard the door slam behind him.

'Just what the *hell* do you mean by coming in here and harassing Pat? I've got a mind to toss you out on your ass!'

Eric turned to find Neil with his hands on his hips, his lips pinched, his dark eyes irate behind square horn-rimmed glasses. He was the second generation Doc Lange, only three years older than Eric, had delivered all of Mike and Barb's babies, had diagnosed Ma's high blood pressure and had at one time dated his sister, Ruth.

Eric took a deep breath and forcibly calmed himself. 'I'm

sorry, Neil. You're right. She's right. I owe her an apology and I'll make sure she gets it before I leave, but I need to have you explain something for me.'

'What?'

'This.' Eric unrolled the computer printout and handed it over. 'Tell me what this bill is for.'

Neil Lange began reading it from the top down, giving it his total attention. When he reached the halfway point, he glanced up at Eric, then read on.

Finishing, he let the sheets fall into their accordion fold and looked up. 'Why do you want to know?'

'It's for my wife.'

'Yes, I see that.'

'And it's from some goddamned hospital in Minnesota!'

'I see that, too.'

In silence the two men stood face to face. 'You know what I'm asking, Neil, so don't give me that look. Does D & C mean what I think it means?'

'It means dilation and curettage.'

'An abortion, right?'

Lange paused a second before confirming, 'Yes, it looks that way.'

Eric stepped back and collapsed to the edge of Lange's desk, catching himself with both hands, dropping his chin to his chest. Lange folded the bill with his thumbnail and dropped his hands to his sides. His voice softened.

'You didn't know about it until now?'

Eric shook his head slowly, staring at the brown flecks in the thick Berber carpeting.

'I'm sorry, Eric.' Lange put a comforting hand on his shoulder.

Eric lifted his head. 'Could there be some other reason for her having it?'

'I'm afraid not. The lab indicates serum pregnancy and surgical tissue II – that always means abortion. Also, it was done in a county hospital rather than a private or religious-affiliated hospital, which generally don't perform abortions.'

Eric took a minute to absorb the anguish before drawing a deep sigh and pushing to his feet. 'Well, now I know.' He reached tiredly for the bill. 'Thanks, Neil.'

'If you want to talk, call Pat and set up a time, but don't come barging in here this way again.'

Chin down, Eric raised a hand in farewell.

'Listen, Eric,' Lange went on, 'this is a small town. Talk gets around, and if what I hear is true you need to get your life in order. I'd be more than happy to talk about it, even away from the office where there are no interruptions. If you prefer, forget about calling Pat. Just call me, will you do that?'

Eric lifted his head, studied the doctor with a look of flat despair, nodded once and headed out. At the reception desk he stopped.

'Listen, Pat, I'm sorry for that . . .' He waved the scrolled papers towards the other side of the window. 'Sometimes I can be a son of a bitch.'

'Oh, it's all right. It –'

'No. No, it's not all right. You like salmon? Smoked maybe? Steak?'

'I love it.'

'Which kind?'

'Eric, you don't have to –'

'Which kind?'

'All right, steaks.'

'You'll have 'em. I'll drop off a package tomorrow, by way of apology.'

He drove home slowly, feeling bleak as the November day. Cars piled up behind him, unable to pass on the curving highway, but he rolled along unaware of them. Endings – how sad they were. Particularly sad to end eighteen years of marriage with a blow like this. His child . . . Jesus, she'd disposed of his child as if it were of no more consequence than one of her outmoded dresses.

He stared at the highway, wondering if it had been a boy or a girl, fair or dark, with any of Ma's features or the old man's. Hell, it would be riding a trike by now, begging to have stories read, riding on his father's hand high overhead, learning about the gulls.

The white centre lines became distorted by tears. His child, her child, who might have grown to be a fisherman or a president, a father or a mother someday. Nancy was his wife, yet she cared so little about him that the life he'd sired was absolutely dispensable. Eighteen years he'd hoped, a good half of that time he'd begged. And when it had finally happened, Nancy had killed it.

She wasn't home yet when he arrived so he put her office in order, growing angrier by the minute now that his first spate of melancholy was gone. He packed her suitcases, unpacked them and packed his own (he wasn't going to give her a single thing to come back at him on), loaded the truck and sat down at the kitchen table to wait.

She arrived shortly after one P.M., coming sideways through the door with her arms full of packages, her hair oriental black.

'Wait till you see what I bought!' she exclaimed above the crackle of bags as she set them on the cabinet. 'I went into the little shop next to the –'

'Shut the door,' he ordered coldly.

In slow motion she looked back over her shoulder. 'What's the matter?'

'Shut the door and sit down.'

She closed the door and approached the table warily, drawing off her leather gloves.

'Whoa, you're really bummed out about something. Should I get my whip and my chair?' she cajoled.

'I found something today.' Icy-eyed, he tossed the hospital bill across the table. 'You want to tell me about it?'

She glanced down and her hands stalled, pulling off the gloves. Her surprise registered as a mere tightening of her brow before she disguised it beneath a look of hauteur.

'You were going through my desk?' She sounded affronted.

'Yes, I was *going through your desk!*' he repeated, his voice rising, his teeth bared on the final word.

'How dare you!' She threw the gloves down. 'That's *my* personal file, and when I leave the house I expect –'

'Don't you get high-handed with me, you lying bitch!' He leapt to his feet. 'Not with the proof of your crime lying right there in front of you!' He jabbed a finger at the bill.

'Crime?' She spread a hand on her chest and affected an abused expression. '*I* go off to get my hair done, and *you* dig through my personal files, and *I'm* the criminal!' She thrust her nose near his. 'I'm the one who should be upset, dear husband!'

'You killed my baby, *dear wife*, and I don't give a goddamn what the law says, in my book that's a criminal act!'

'Killed your baby! Don't be ridiculous.'

'In 1986. D & C. It's all there on the bill.'

'You have a fixation with babies, Eric, do you know that? It makes you paranoid.'

'Then explain it!'

She shrugged and spoke nonchalantly. 'My periods were getting irregular. It was a routine operation to straighten them out.'

'Done secretly, in some hospital in Minneapolis?'

'I didn't want to worry you, that's all. I was in and out in one day.'

'Don't lie to me, Nancy. It only makes you more despicable.'

'I'm not lying!'

'I showed the bill to Neil Lange. He said it was an abortion.'

She stretched her neck like a gander, her mouth taut, and said nothing.

'How *could* you?'

'I don't have to stand here and listen to this.' She turned away.

He spun her around by an arm. 'You're not walking away from this one, Nancy,' he shouted. 'You got pregnant, and you didn't even bother to tell me! You made a decision to snuff out the life of our baby, the baby I begged you for years to have. Just – *pfft!*' He brandished a hand. 'Scrape it out, like you'd scrape out some . . . some *garbage*. Killed it without a thought for what I was feeling, and you think you don't have to stand here and take this?' He grabbed her by the coatfront and pulled her to her toes. 'What kind of woman are you anyway?'

'Let me go!'

He jerked her higher. 'Can you imagine what I thought when I found that bill? What I felt? Do you even *care* what I felt?'

'You, you!' she shouted, shoving him away and stumbling backward. 'It's always you. What *you* want, when it's time to decide where we'll live! What *you* want when we decide what we'll live in! What *you* want when we crawl into bed at night. Well what about what *I* want?'

He advanced nose first. 'You know something, Nancy? I don't give a damn what you want anymore!'

'You don't understand. You never did!'

'Don't understand!' His face turned red with rage as he controlled the urge to smash a fist into her beautiful face. 'Don't understand you having an abortion without telling me? Jesus Christ, woman, what was I to you all these years, nothing more than a good lay? As long as you got your orgasms that's all that mattered, wasn't it?'

'I loved you.'

He pushed her away in revulsion.

'Bullshit. You know who you love? Yourself. Nobody but yourself.'

Coldly, she demanded, 'And who do you love, Eric?'

They faced each other in deliberate silence.

'We both know who you love, don't we?' she insisted.

'I didn't until you became unlovable, and even then I came back here and tried to make a go of it with you.'

'Oh, thanks a lot,' she said sarcastically.

'But you lied then, too. You were no more pregnant than I was, but I was so gullible I believed you.'

'I lied to keep from losing you.'

'You lied to suit your own twisted needs!'

'Well, you deserved it! The whole town knew you were the father of her baby!'

The fight left him and guilt tempered his voice. 'I'm sorry about that, Nancy. I never meant to hurt you that way, and if you're thinking I did it deliberately, you're wrong.'

'But you're going to her now, aren't you?'

He watched her mouth turn sad and said nothing.

'I still love you.'

'Nancy, don't.' He turned away.

'We each made some mistakes,' she said, 'but we could start from now. A new beginning.'

'It's too late.' He stared out a window without seeing a thing. Standing in the kitchen of the house he'd loved and she'd hated, he felt momentarily overwhelmed by sorrow at their failure.

She touched his back. 'Eric . . .' she said imploringly.

He swung away from her and plucked his leather jacket from the back of a kitchen chair, pulling it on.

'I'll be at Ma's.'

The zipper closed with the sound of finality.

'Don't go.' She began to cry. To the best of his recollection he'd never seen her do that.

'Don't,' he whispered.

She gripped his jacketfront. 'Eric, this time I'd be different.'

'Don't . . .' He removed her hands. 'You're embarrassing both of us.' He picked up the hospital bill and put it in his pocket. 'I'll be seeing my lawyer tomorrow and giving him the order that either he gets this thing pushed through fast or I'll find another lawyer who will.'

'Eric –' She reached out one hand.

He put a hand on the doorknob and looked back at her. 'I realized something while I was waiting for you today. You shouldn't have a baby and I should never have tried to talk you into it. It would have been wrong for you, just like it's wrong for me to be without a family. We changed – somewhere along the line both of us changed. We want different things. We should have seen that years ago.' He opened the door. 'I'm sorry I hurt you,' he said solemnly. 'I mean it when I say I never meant to.'

He walked out, closing the door softly behind him.

There were no secrets in a town the size of Fish Creek. Maggie heard about Eric leaving Nancy within days and lived on tenterhooks after that. She found herself stopping and cocking her head each time a vehicle passed on the road up above. Whenever the phone rang her heart shot into double time and she scurried to answer it. If anyone knocked on the door her palms were sweating long before she reached the kitchen.

She trimmed the leaves from the pink roses Eric had sent and hung them upside down to preserve them, but they were dry and bound with a mauve ribbon and still she hadn't heard a word from him.

To Suzanne she murmured, 'Do you think he'll come to us?' But Suzanne only crossed her eyes and hiccuped.

Thanksgiving came and still no word from Eric. Maggie and Suzanne spent the holiday at Brookie's.

On December 8 it snowed. Maggie found herself wandering from window to window, watching the white fluff cover the yard in a soft, level blanket, and wondering where Eric was and if she'd hear from him soon.

She began making Christmas preparations and wrote to

Katy, asking if she'd be home. Her reply was a brusque note: 'Mother . . . I'm going to Seattle with Smitty for Christmas. Don't buy me anything. Katy.' Maggie read it fighting tears, then called Roy. 'Oh Daddy,' she wailed. 'It seems like I've made everybody unhappy having this baby. Mother won't talk to me. Katy won't talk to me. You're going to have a miserable Christmas. I'm going to have a miserable Christmas. What should I do, Daddy?'

Roy replied, 'You should put Suzanne in a snowsuit and take her for a buggy ride and get her acquainted with winter and spend a little time yourself looking around at the snow on the pines, and the sky when it's the colour of an old tin kettle, and realize there's a lot out there to be grateful for.'

'But, Daddy, I feel so bad that I've driven Mother away, and where does that leave you on Christmas?'

'Well, I may have to take a walk and look at the pines and the sky every now and then myself, but I'll get by. You just see after yourself and Suzanne.'

'You're such a good person, Daddy.'

'There, you see?' Roy replied with jocularity in his voice. 'That's one thing you've got to be grateful for right there.'

So Roy and Brookie saw her through.

For Maggie it was a Christmas of mixed blessings – with a new daughter but without the rest of her family. And still with no word from Eric. She spent the holiday at Brookie's again and on New Year's made a resolution to put Eric Severson behind and accept the apparent fact that if she hadn't seen him by now she wasn't going to.

One day in January she was taking Suzanne to the doctor for her two-month checkup, sitting at a red light in Sturgeon Bay when she glanced idly to her left and found Eric staring down at her from behind the wheel of a shining black pickup. Not a finger, not an eyelid moved on either of them.

Maggie stared. And Eric stared.

The middle of her breastbone ached. Drawing the next breath became a milestone.

The light changed and behind her a car horn honked, but she didn't move.

Eric's gaze shifted to the pair of tiny hands beating the air with excitement – all he could see of Suzanne, who sat strapped into her infant seat, watching a paper cutout revolve in the breeze from the windshield defroster.

The car horn honked again, longer, and Maggie pulled away from the light, losing sight of his truck when he made a left-hand turn and disappeared from her rearview mirror.

Desolate, she told Brookie about it later. 'He didn't even wave. He didn't even try to stop me.'

For the first time, Brookie had no words of consolation.

The winter grew harsher in every way after that. Harding House seemed oppressive, so big and empty with only two in it and not a prospect of more. Maggie took up needlework to fill her time, but often dropped her hands to her lap and rested her head against the back of the chair. *If he's left her, why doesn't he come to me?*

February was bitter and Suzanne got her first cold. Maggie walked the floor with her at night, haggard from loss of sleep, wishing for someone to take the baby from her arms and nudge her toward bed.

In March letters began arriving requesting reservations for the summer and Maggie realized she'd have to make her decision about whether or not to put Harding House up for sale. The best time to do so, of course, would be when the spring rush began.

In April she called Althea Munne and asked her to come over and appraise the house. The day that the FOR SALE sign went up in the yard, Maggie took Suzanne and drove clear down to Tani's in Green Bay because she couldn't bear to look at the sign and wait for strangers to come poking and prodding through the place into which she'd poured so much of her heart.

In May Gene Kerschner came and hitched up the dock to his big green John Deere tractor and rolled it back into the water for the summer. The following day while Suzanne was taking her afternoon nap, Maggie set to work giving it a coat of white paint.

She was on her knees with her backside pointed toward the house, her head wrapped in a red bandanna, peering up at the underside of the arbour seat when she heard footsteps on the dock behind her. She backed up, turned, and felt an explosion of emotion.

Coming down the dock, dressed in white jeans, a blue shirt and a white skipper's hat was Eric Severson.

She watched him moving toward her while adrenalin shot through her system. Oh, how the appearance of one person could change the complexion of a day, a year, a life! She forgot the paintbrush in her hand. Forgot she was barefoot and dressed in faded black sweatpants and a baggy grey T-shirt. Forgot everything but the long-awaited sight of him approaching.

He stopped on the opposite side of the paint can and looked down.

'Hello,' he said, as if heaven had not suddenly shown itself to her.

'Hello,' she whispered, her pulse drumming everywhere, everywhere.

'I brought you something.' He handed her a white envelope.

It took moments before she could force her arm to move. She took the envelope wordlessly, staring up at him as he stood silhouetted against a sky of crayon blue – the same blue as his eyes. The sun glinted off the black visor of his cap, lit his shoulders and the tip of his chin.

'Open it, please.'

She balanced the paintbrush on the edge of the can, wiped her hand on her thigh and began opening the envelope with trembling hands while he stood above her, watching. Watching. She drew the papers out and opened them – a thick white sheaf that wanted to spring together at the folds.

As she read, the tremor from her hands twitched the corners of the sheets.

Findings for Fact, Conclusion of Law, Order for Judgment, Judgment and Decree.

She read the heading and lifted uncertain eyes.

'What is it?'

'My divorce papers.'

The shock rushed up pushing tears before it. She dropped her chin and saw the lines of type wash sideways before two huge tears plopped onto the paper. Abashed, she buried her face against it.

'Aw, Maggie . . .' He went down on one knee and touched her head, warm from the sun and bound by the ugly red hanky. 'Maggie, don't cry. The crying's all over.'

She felt his arms pull her close and realized he was on his knees before her. He was here at last and the agony was over. She threw her arms around his neck, weeping, confessing brokenly. 'I th . . . thought you weren't c . . . coming back.'

His wide hand clasped the back of her head, holding her fiercely against him. 'My mother made me promise I wouldn't until I had my divorce papers in hand.'

'I thought . . . I thought . . . I don't know what I thought.' She felt childish, babbling so, but she'd been totally unprepared, and the relief was so immense.

'You thought I didn't love you anymore?'

'I thought I'd b . . . be alone for the rest of my l . . . life, and that Suzanne would n . . . never know you, and I d . . . didn't know how to face it without you.'

'Oh, Maggie,' he said, closing his eyes. 'I'm here and I'm staying.'

She cried awhile, her nose against his neck, his hand stroking her hair beneath the scarf.

At length he whispered, 'I missed you so much.'

She had missed him, too, but adequate words had not been coined to express the complexity of her feelings. To have him back was to taste the bitter turn to sweet, to feel the missing piece of herself settle into place.

Drawing away, she looked into his face, her own glossy wet in the sun. 'You're really divorced, then?'

He dried her eyes with his thumbs and answered quietly, 'I'm really divorced.'

She attempted a quivering smile. His thumbs stopped moving. The pain left his dear blue eyes and his head slowly lowered. It was a tender first kiss, flavoured with May and tears and perhaps a tinge of turpentine. His mouth dropped soft and open upon hers – a tentative first taste, as if neither could believe this reverse of fortune, while he held her face in his broad hands. Their tongues touched and his head moved, swaying above hers as their mouths opened fully. Still kneeling, he drew her hips flush against his and held her there as if forever. Great cotton clouds moved across the blue sky above, and the breeze touched her hair as he removed her scarf and cupped her head firmly. To kiss was enough – to kneel beneath the May sun with tongues joined and feel the agony of separation dissolve and know that no law of God or man stood between them any longer.

In time he drew back, found her eyes, told her eloquent things with his own, then folded her against him more loosely. For moments they remained so, motionless, empty vessels no more.

'I went through hell after I saw you in Sturgeon Bay,' he told her.

'I wanted you to stop me, force me over to the side of the road and carry me away.'

'I wanted to leave the truck there in the middle of the street and get into your car and drive off someplace, to Texas or California or Africa where nobody could find us.'

She chuckled shakily. 'You can't drive to Africa, silly.'

'I feel like I could right now.' With an open hand he rubbed her spine. 'With you I feel like anything is possible.'

'A thousand times I stopped myself calling you.'

Side by side Maggie and Eric watched her come awake, making faces, rolling up like an armadillo, and finally coming up on all fours like a shaky cub bear, peering at the strange man standing beside the crib with her mother.

'Oops, there she is. Hi, sugar.' Maggie reached into the crib, lifted the sleepy baby out and perched her on her arm. Suzanne immediately curled and rubbed and burrowed. She was dressed in something pink and green and her backside was puffy. One of her socks had slipped down, revealing a small, pointed heel. Maggie tugged it up while Suzanne finished her rooting.

'Look who's here, Suzanne. It's your daddy.'

The baby looked up at Maggie with her lower eyelashes clinging to the soft folds of skin beneath, then shifted her regard to the stranger again, still a little shaky on Maggie's arm. As she stared, steadying herself with one hand against Maggie's chest, her thumb kept crooking and straightening against Maggie's T-shirt.

'Hi, Suzanne,' Eric said quietly.

She remained as unblinking as a fascinated cat, until Maggie bounced her a time or two on her arm and rested her face against Suzanne's downy head. 'This is your daddy come to say hello.'

As one mesmerized, Eric reached and took his child, lifting her to eye level where she hung in the air and stared at his black, shiny visor.

'My goodness, you're a little bit of a thing after all. You don't weigh as much as the salmon we catch off the *Mary Deare*.'

Maggie laughed while one happiness seemed to crowd in upon another.

'And you're no bigger around either.' He brought the baby close and touched his dark face to her very fair one, and caught the infant scent of her powdered skin and soft clothing. He set her on his arm, braced her back with one long hand and rested his lips upon her silky hair. His eyes closed. His throat seemed to do the same.

'I thought I'd never have this,' Eric whispered, his voice gravelly with emotion.

'I know, darling . . . I know.'

'Thank you for her.'

Maggie put her arms around both of them, laid her forehead against Suzanne's back and Eric's hand while they shared the sacred moment.

'She's so perfect.'

As if to prove otherwise, Suzanne chose that moment to complain, pushing away from Eric and reaching for her mother. He relinquished her but hovered close as Maggie changed her diaper and pulled up her stockings once again and put on soft white shoes. Afterward, they lay on the bed, one on each side of the baby, watching her untie her shoes and blow spit bubbles and grow fascinated with her father's shirt buttons. Sometimes they studied the baby, and sometimes each other. Often they reached across the baby to touch one another's faces, hair, arms. Then they would lie still, with contentment dulling the need to move at all.

In time Eric took Maggie's hand.

'Would you do something for me?' he asked softly.

'Anything. I would do anything for you, Eric Severson.'

'Would you go for a ride with me? You and Suzanne?'

'We'd love it.'

They walked outside together, Eric carrying Suzanne, Maggie bringing a bottle of apple juice and Suzanne's favourite blanket – enchanted beings still somewhat awe-struck at the grandeur of happiness in its simplest form. A man, a woman, their child. Together as it should be.

The breeze touched the baby's face and she squinted her eyes.

A warbler trilled in the arborvitae hedge.

They ambled slower; time was their ally now.

'You got a new truck,' Maggie remarked, approaching it.

'Yup. The old whore finally died.' He opened the passenger door for her.

She had one foot on the running board before she looked up and saw the blossoms.

'Oh, Eric.' She touched her lips.

'I could have asked you back there in the house, but with all the cherry trees in bloom, I thought we might as well do this right. Get in, Maggie, so we can get to the best part.'

Smiling, beset once again by the urge to cry, she climbed into Eric Severson's shiny new truck and gazed around at the cherry blossoms stuck behind the visors and the rearview mirror, jammed behind the backseat until they nearly covered the rear window.

Eric climbed in beside her. 'What do you think?' he asked, grinning at her, starting the engine.

'I think I adore you.'

'I adore you, too. I just had to think of a way of telling you so. Hang on to our baby.'

They drove through the Door County springtime, through the blossom-scented air of late afternoon, past sloping orchards rimmed with rock walls and birches shining white against new green grass, past grazing cows and bright-red barns and ditches filled with singing frogs. And came at last to Easley's orchard, where he stopped the truck between the billowing cherry trees.

In the quiet after the engine had stilled, he turned and captured her hand on the seat between them.

'Maggie Pearson Stearn, will you marry me?' he asked, his cheeks flushed, his eyes steady upon hers.

In the moment before she answered, all the sweet bygones came rushing back, filling her senses – the place, the man, the smell of the orchard around them.

'Eric Joseph Severson, I would marry you this very minute if it were possible.' She leaned across the seat to kiss him, with Suzanne on her knees struggling to reach the blossoms in the ashtray. He lifted his head and they searched each other's eyes, smiled their gladness once more before Eric braced up and dug into the left pocket of his tight white jeans.

'I thought about buying you a great big diamond, but this seemed more appropriate.' He came up with his class ring and took her left hand to slip it on her ring finger, where it still fitted loosely. Holding the hand aloft, she studied it, adorned as it had been twenty-four years before.

'It looks so familiar there,' she said, smiling.

'All except for the blue yarn. I don't know what happened to that.'

With the beringed hand she touched his face. 'I don't know what to say,' she whispered.

'Say, "I love you Eric, and I forgive you for all you've put me through."'

'I love you, Eric, but there's nothing to forgive.'

They attempted one more kiss, but Suzanne interrupted, wriggling off her mother's lap to stand on the seat between them. When she was on two feet she closed one chubby fist around a branch overhead and flailed the air with it, a sharp point of one stick narrowly missing Eric's eye.

He pulled back – 'Whoa there, little lady!' – and planted one hand beneath her diaper, another on her chest and returned her to her mother's lap. 'Can't you see there's a courtship going on here?'

They were both laughing as he reached for the ignition and headed toward Fish Creek, holding Maggie's hand.

Chapter 21

They were married five days later in the backyard of Harding House. It was a simple ceremony on a Tuesday evening. The groom wore a grey tuxedo with lilies of the valley in his lapel (from the bed on the north side of the house), the bride wore a pink walking suit and carried a bouquet of apple blossoms (from Easley's orchard). In attendance were Miss Suzanne Pearson (wearing Polly Flinders and eating Waverly Wafers), Brookie and Gene Kerschner, Mike and Barb Severson, Anna Severson (having forsaken slogans in favour of blue polyester from Sears Roebuck) and Roy Pearson, who walked his daughter down from the front verandah to the yard while from the porch came a scratchy monophonic recording of the Andrews Sisters singing 'I'll Be with You in Apple Blossom Time'.

On the fresh spring grass stood an antique parlour table holding a bouquet of pink apple blossoms in a milk-glass vase. Beside the table a judge waited in a black robe, its sleeves filling and emptying as breezes drifted in off the bay. When the song ended and the wedding party stood before him, the judge said, 'The bride and groom have requested that I read the poem they've chosen for this occasion. It's of the same vintage as the house, and it's entitled "Fulfilment".

'Lo, I have opened unto you the
gates of my being
And like a tide, you have flowed
into me.
The innermost recesses of my spirit
are full of you

And all the channels of my soul
are grown sweet with your presence
For you have brought me peace;
The peace of great tranquil waters,
And the quiet of the summer sea.
Your hands are filled with peace as
The noon-tide is filled with light;
About your head is bound the eternal
Quiet of the stars, and in your heart
dwells the calm miracle of twilight.

I am utterly content.

In all my being is no ripple of unrest
For I have opened unto you the
Wide gates of my being
And like a tide, you have flowed into me.'

After the reading, Eric turned to Maggie. She laid her apple blossoms on the table and he took both her hands. In the late, low sun her face appeared golden, her eyes the pale brown of acorns. Her hair was drawn back from her face, and her ears held delicate pink pearls. In that moment she might have been seventeen again, and the branches she'd laid aside were those he'd first picked to express his love. No single act of his life had ever seemed so appropriate as when he spoke his vows.

'You were my first love, Maggie, and you will be my only love for the rest of our lives. I will respect you, and be faithful to you, and work hard for you and with you. I will be a good father to Suzanne and any other children we might have, and I will do all in my power to make you happy.' Softly, he ended, 'I love you, Maggie.'

In the brief silence that followed, Anna wiped her eyes and Brookie fitted her hand into Gene's. A glint appeared in the corner of Maggie's eyes, and her lips held a wistful smile.

She dropped her gaze to Eric's hands – broad, strong fisherman's hands; looked up into his blue eyes, the first she'd ever loved, blue as blooming chicory; into his dear windburned face that would only grow dearer in the years ahead.

'I love you, Eric . . . again.' The merest smile touched their eyes and disappeared. 'I will do all within my power to keep that love as fresh and vibrant as it was when we were seventeen, and as it is today. I will keep our home a place where happiness dwells, and in it I will love our child and you. I will grow old with you. I will be faithful to you. I will be your friend forever. I will wear your name proudly. I love you, Eric Severson.'

Out over Green Bay a pair of gulls called, and the sun rested at the end of a long golden path on the water. Maggie and Eric exchanged rings, plain gold bands which seemed to catch the fire from sunset and warm beneath it.

When the exchange was complete, Eric lowered his head and kissed the backs of Maggie's hands. She did likewise, and they moved to the scroll-footed table, accepted a pen from the judge and signed their names to the wedding certificate. Their signatures were witnessed by Brookie and Mike and the simple ceremony was over less than five minutes after it began.

Eric smiled at Maggie, then at the judge, who extended his hand and a hearty smile. 'Congratulations, Mr and Mrs Severson. May you have a long and happy life together.'

Eric scooped Maggie into his arms and kissed her.

'Mrs Severson, I love you,' he whispered at her ear.

'I love you, too.'

The circle around them closed. Brookie was crying as she kissed Maggie's cheek and said, 'Well, it's about time.'

Gene embraced them each and said, 'Good luck. You deserve it.'

Mike said, 'Little brother, I think you got a winner.'

Barbara said, 'I couldn't be happier. Welcome to the family.'

Anna said, 'It's enough to make an old woman cry. At my age, getting a daughter-in-law and a new grandbaby all in one day. Here, take her, Eric, so I can hug Maggie.' When she'd handed Suzanne to her daddy, Anna told Maggie, cheek-to-cheek, 'I seen this day coming when you were seventeen years old. I can see you made my boy happy at last, and for that I love you.' Hugging Eric, she said, 'I wish your dad was alive to see this day. He always favoured Maggie and I did, too. Congratulations, son.'

Roy told Maggie, 'You look pretty as a picture, honey, and I'm awful glad that this all happened.' Thumping Eric's back, he said, 'Well, I finally got me somebody to go fishing with and, by golly, I plan to do it!'

They turned toward the house, everyone happy and chattering as they ambled up the front lawn. Suzanne rode on her daddy's arm, with her mother pressed close to his side.

In the dining room champagne and cake waited.

Mike proposed a toast. 'To the happy bride and groom who started on our back porch when they were seventeen. May they be as much in love at ninety as they are today!'

There were gifts, too. From Brookie and Gene a pierced-work tablecloth long enough for the mammoth dining-room table, with ten matching napkins. From Barb and Mike a pair of antique candleholders of etched crystal with six white fluted candles to fill them. Anna brought a grab bag: embroidered dish towels, crocheted doilies, six pints of Eric's favourite thimbleberry jam and a china tea set that had belonged to Eric's Grandma Severson. The latter brought tears to Maggie's eyes and a great big hug for Anna. Roy's offering was a small Louis XIV antique chair for the front parlour, which he had stripped, refinished and re-upholstered. It also earned him a hug from his daughter and a round of enthusiastic inspection and compliments from all the guests. There was, too, something from Suzanne (though nobody would confess to having brought it): a greeting card with a picture of a Victorian family – father, mother and child – setting a toy boat asail beside a grassy-banked pond with a willow tree in the background. Inside, someone had written, *To my mommy and daddy on their wedding day . . . With lots of love, Suzanne.*

When they'd read it, Maggie and Eric exchanged a look of such expressive love that every eye in the room became misty. They were sitting on the window seat of the dining room at the time, with their gifts strewn about them and Suzanne nearby in her grandpa's arms. Eric touched Maggie's jaw, then reached for the baby.

'Thank you, Suzanne,' he said, taking her, kissing her cheek. 'And thank you all. We want you to know what it's meant to us to have you all with us tonight. We love you all and we thank you from the bottom of our hearts.'

Suzanne started rubbing her eyes and whining, and it seemed an appropriate time to end the festivities. Each good-bye was emotional, but Roy lingered till last. Hugging Maggie, he said, 'Honey, I'm so sorry your mother and Katy weren't here. They both should have been.'

There was no denying their absence hurt. 'Oh, Daddy . . . I guess we can't have everything perfect in this life, can we?'

He patted her shoulder, then drew back. 'I want you to know something, Maggie. You've taught me a lot during these last few months that I wish I'd have learned when I was a much younger man. Nobody can make you happy but yourself. You've done it, and now I'm going to do it. I'm going to start by taking a little time off work. You know, in all the years I worked at that store I don't think I took more than four vacations, and I used all of them to paint the house. I'm going to be gone for a few days – take a little time for myself.'

'Isn't Mother going with you?'

'No, she isn't. But I don't want you to worry. I'll talk to you when I get back, okay?'

'Okay, Daddy. But where –'

'You just keep on being happy, will you, sweetheart? It does my heart good to see you that way. Now I'd better say goodnight.' He kissed Maggie, rubbed Suzanne's head and thumped Eric between the shoulders. 'Thank you, son,' he said with tears in his eyes, and left.

They stood on the back verandah and watched him climb the steps to the road, Eric holding Suzanne, Maggie with her arms crossed.

'Daddy is troubled,' Maggie said reflectively.

Eric dropped an arm around her shoulders and tipped her against his side. 'Not about us though.'

She smiled softly and looked up. 'No, not about us.'

For a moment they lingered in each other's eyes before Eric said, low, 'Come on. Let's put Suzanne to bed.'

Suzanne was tired and grumpy and fell asleep before her thumb reached her mouth. They stood awhile looking at her, holding hands.

'I feel like I've never lived before,' he said quietly. 'Like everything began with you . . . and her.'

'It did.'

He turned her into his arms and held her in a loose embrace. 'My wife,' he whispered.

She pressed her cheek against his lapel and replied in matching quietude, 'My husband.'

They stood motionless a moment, as if receiving a blessing, then walked across the hall to the Belvedere Room where the great carved bed waited.

Roy Pearson drove home slowly. He went the long way around, by way of the switchback, up the hill from Maggie's, and out between the up-country fields, then down the curving highway to the stop sign at Main. He turned right, passed the store where he'd worked all of his adult life, recounting its sights and sounds and smells – ageing fruit and garlicky sandwich meats, the tangy stink of pickled herring. The rumble of the old-fashioned door on the meat case when it rolled open. The *bing* of the cash register up front. (Actually, the old cash register had been gone four years and the new one went *dit-dit-dit-dit*, but when Roy thought of cash registers he still thought of bells.) Helen McCrossen coming in every Tuesday, promptly at eleven A.M., so promptly you could set your watch by her, asking, 'How is the liverwurst today, Roy, is it fresh?' The feel of the cleaver in his hand, thudding against the butcher block. The cold, tallowy smell of the cooler.

He would miss the store.

At home, he pulled around the rear, parked before the closed garage doors and crossed the backyard to the house. The grass was dewy and his shoes got wet – Vera would scold if she were up. But the house was quiet and dim. He disregarded the back rug and crossed the kitchen floor, heading directly for the storage space beneath the stairs. He emerged with a flimsy cloth suitcase and a cardboard box which he carried upstairs to his bedroom.

Vera was awake, swathed in a hairnet, reading by the light of the bedlamp which was clamped to the headboard above her shoulder.

'So?' she said as one might order a dog, 'Speak!'

Roy set down his suitcase and box and made no reply.

'Well, she's married to him, then.'

'Yes, she is.'

'Who was there? Was Katy there?'

'You should have come and seen for yourself, Vera.'

'Hmph!' Vera returned to her book.

Roy snapped on the ceiling light and opened a dresser drawer.

For the first time Vera noticed the suitcase. 'Roy, what are you doing?'

'I'm leaving you, Vera.'

'You're what!'

'I'm leaving you.'

'Roy, don't be a fool! Put that suitcase away and get to bed.'

He calmly began emptying drawers and loading the suitcase. The box. Carried three hangers from the closet and laid them across the foot of the bed.

'Roy, you're going to wrinkle those trousers and I just ironed them yesterday. Now, put them away this minute!'

'I'm all done taking orders from you, Vera. I've been taking them for forty-six years, and now I'm done.'

'What in the world has got into you! Have you gone crazy?'

'No, you might say I've come to my senses. I have at the most maybe ten, fifteen good healthy years left, and I'm going to try to get a little happiness out of them the way my daughter did.'

'Your daughter. She's behind this, isn't she?'

'No, Vera, she's not. You are. You and all forty-six years of being told where to take off my shoes, and how to put the Christmas tree in the stand, and how much fat to trim off the pork chops, and where I can't put my feet, and how loud the television can be, and how I never did a thing right. I want you to know I didn't just decide this overnight either. I've been thinking about it for five years. It just took Maggie's courage to finally make me work up a little courage of my own. I've been watching her the last year, forging ahead, making a new life for herself, making herself happy against all the odds, and I said to myself, Roy, you can learn something from that young woman.'

'Roy, you're not serious!'

'Yes, I am.'

'But you can't just . . . just *leave!*'

'There's nothing here for me, Vera. No warmth, no

happiness, no love. You're a woman who's incapable of love.'

'Why, that's ridiculous.'

'Is it? If I asked you right now, Vera, do you love me, could you say it?'

She stared at him, tight-lipped.

'When have you ever said it? Or shown it – to either me or Maggie? Where were you tonight? Where were you when Suzanne was born? You were here, nursing your bitterness, congratulating yourself on being right once again. Well, I made up my mind when that baby was born that I'd give you just so long to come to your senses and be a mother to Maggie and a grandmother to Suzanne, and tonight when you failed to go to your own daughter's wedding, I said to myself, Roy, what's the use? She'll never change. And I don't believe you will.'

Roy laid a folded shirt in the suitcase. Vera stared at him, incapable of moving.

'Is there another woman?'

'Oh, for pity's sake. Look at me. I'm old enough to collect Social Security, I'm damn near bald, and I haven't had a good hard-on in the last eight years. What would I do with another woman?'

It began to dawn on Vera that he really intended to leave.

'But where will you go?'

'For starters, I'm going down to Chicago to see Katy and try to talk some sense into her and make her see that if she keeps on the way she is, she's going to turn out just like her grandma. Then I don't know. I've quit at the store, but I asked them not to say anything about it up till now. I may just retire and collect that Social Security after all. I may take my tools and set up a little fix-it shop somewhere and make doll furniture for my new granddaughter. I'd like to do some fishing with Eric. I don't know.'

'You've quit the store?'

He nodded, stuffing a stack of socks into the box.

'Without even telling me?'

'I'm telling you now.'

'But . . . but what about us? Are you coming back?' When he continued packing without looking up, she asked in a quiet, shaken voice, 'Are you saying you want a divorce?'

He looked at her sadly. His voice, when he replied, was quiet and deep. 'Yes, I am, Vera.'

'But can't we talk about it . . . can't we . . . can't we . . .' She made a fist and pressed it to her lips. 'Dear God,' she whispered.

'No, I don't want to talk about anything. I just want to go.'

'But, Roy, forty-six years . . . you can't just turn your back on forty-six years.'

He latched the suitcase and set it on the floor.

'I've taken half the money out of our savings account, and cashed in half of our certificates of deposit. The rest I left for you. We'll let the lawyers work out details about our retirement account. I'm taking the car but I'll be back when I find a place, to get the rest of my clothes and my power tools. The house you can have. It was always more yours than mine anyway, the way you kept me from soiling and using things.'

Vera was sitting up on the edge of the bed, looking bewildered and scared. 'Roy, don't go . . . Roy, I'm sorry.'

'Yes, I'm sure you are now. But it's a few years too late, Vera.'

'Please . . .' she pleaded, with tears in her eyes as he left the room to collect some toilet articles in the bathroom. He returned in less than a minute and dropped them into the cardboard box.

'One thing you should make sure you do right away, Vera, is get yourself a driver's licence. You're going to need one, that's for sure.'

Vera's eyes looked terrified. She had one fist folded tight between her breasts. 'When will you be back?'

'I don't know. When I decide what I want to do next. After Chicago I may check out Phoenix. They say the winters down there are mild and there are a lot of folks our age down there.'

'Ph . . . Phoenix?' she whispered. 'Arizona?' Phoenix was on the other side of the world.

He propped the box on one hip and picked up the suitcase with his free hand.

'You never asked, but Maggie and Eric had a real nice wedding tonight. They're going to be mighty happy together, and our granddaughter is a real beauty. You might like to walk up there and meet her someday.' The last time he'd seen Vera cry this way was when her mother passed away in 1967. He thought it was a good healthy sign: she might manage to change after all.

'I imagine the minute I walk out of the door you'll want to call Maggie and cry on her shoulder, but for once in your life would you think of somebody else first and remember it's her wedding night? She doesn't know I'm leaving you. I'll call her in a few days and explain to her.' His glance circled the room once and came to rest on her. 'Well . . . good-bye, Vera.'

Without an angry word or a trace of bitterness, he left the house.

He surprised the daylights out of Katy when he rang her from the lobby of her dorm. 'This is Grandpa. I've come to take you out to breakfast.'

He took her to a Perkins Restaurant and bought them each a ham and cheese omelette and told her with a great deal of caring in his voice and eyes what he'd come to say.

'We missed you at the wedding, Katy.' He waited, but she made no response. 'It was a real nice wedding, in your mother's backyard by the lake, and I don't believe I've ever seen two happier people in my life than your mother and Eric. She wore a pretty pink suit and carried apple blossoms, and they said their own vows. They just kept it simple, then afterwards we had some cake and champagne. It was just a small group – the Kerschners, Eric's mother, and his brother and wife . . . and me.' Roy took a sip of coffee and added, as if it just occurred to him. 'Oh, there was someone else there, too.' He leaned forward and laid a photograph on the table. 'Your little sister.' He sat back and hooked a finger through his cup handle. 'Myyyyy, that's a darling little girl if I do say so myself. She's got that Pearson chin all the way. Cute little dent in it just like yours and your mom's.'

Katy's downcast eyes remained riveted on the picture and her cheeks turned pink.

The waitress came and refilled their coffee cups. When she moved away, Roy leaned his elbows on the table.

'But that's not the reason I'm here. I came to tell you something else. I've left your grandma, Katy.'

Katy's eyes shot to his, disbelieving.

'Left her? For good?'

'Yes. It's all my idea, and she was feeling pretty bad when I left her. If you could find the time to run up there one weekend soon, I think she'd really love to see you. She's going to be pretty lonesome for a while . . . she'll need a friend.'

'But . . . but you . . . and Grandma . . .' It was inconceivable to Katy that her grandparents could part. People their age just didn't!

'We've been married forty-six years, and during that time I watched her grow colder and harder and more unforgiving, until it seems like she finally just forgot how to love. That's a sad thing, you know? People don't get like that overnight. They start in little ways – fault-finding, criticizing, judging others – and pretty soon they think the whole world is mixed up and they're the only ones who know how it ought to be run. Too bad. Your grandma had a nice chance lately to show a little compassion, to be the kind of person other people like, but she turned your mother away. She condemned Margaret for something that nobody's got the right to condemn another for. She said, if you don't run your life the way *I* think you ought to run it, well . . . then that's it, I don't want anything to do with you anymore. She never visited your mother in the hospital when Suzanne was born and she hasn't visited her since. She hasn't even seen Suzanne – her own granddaughter – and she refused to go to the wedding. Well, a man can't live with a woman like that, I know I can't. If your grandma wants to be that way, she can be that way alone.' He ruminated awhile and added as an afterthought, 'People like that are bound to end up alone eventually because nobody likes to be around bitterness.'

Katy had been sitting for some time, staring at the table. When she looked up, tears lined her eyelids.

'Oh, Grandpa,' she whispered in a trembling voice, 'I've been so miserable.'

He reached across the table and covered her hand. 'Well, that should tell you something, Katy.'

The tears magnified her eyes, growing plumper until they finally tumbled over and streaked her cheeks.

'Thank you,' she whispered. 'Thank you for coming and for making me see.'

Roy squeezed her hand and smiled benevolently.

On the Saturday following their wedding, Maggie was feeding Suzanne her lunch and Eric had been gone since early morning. The infant seat perched on the kitchen table and Suzanne's mouth was lined with applesauce when the phone rang.

Maggie answered it holding the jar of warm baby food in her free hand.

'Hello?'

'Hi, honey.'

'Eric, hi!' she replied, breaking into a smile.

'What're you doing?'

'Feeding Suzanne her applesauce.'

'Tell her hi.'

'Suzanne, your daddy says hi.' Into the phone Maggie said, 'She waved a fist at you. Are you in for lunch?'

'Yup. Had a good morning, how about you?'

'Uh-huh. I took Suzanne out in the sun with me while I thinned the day lilies. She really seemed to . . .' Maggie stopped speaking, mid-sentence. A moment later her voice returned in a stunned whisper. 'Oh, my God . . .'

'Maggie, what's wrong?' Eric sounded alarmed.

'Eric, Katy is here. She's coming down the sidewalk.'

'Oh, honey,' he said understandingly.

'Darling, I'd better go.'

'Yes . . . all right . . . and, Mag?' he added hurriedly. 'Good luck.'

She was dressed in blue jeans and a Northwestern sweatshirt, a thin purse strap over her left shoulder. Her convertible was parked at the top of the hill behind her, and as she descended the steps her eyes were fixed upon the screen door.

Maggie stepped to it and waited.

At the foot of the verandah Katy stopped. 'Hello, Mother.'

'Hello, Katy.'

For the moment only the most mundane question came to Katy's mind. 'How are you?'

'I'm happy, Katy. How are you?'

'Miserable.'

Maggie opened the screen door. 'Would you like to come in and talk about it?'

Head down, Katy entered the kitchen. Her eyes went immediately to the table where the baby sat in ruffled blue breeches with suspenders, sucking one fist, her ankles crossed and a bib flaring up around her ears. Letting the screen door close softly, Maggie watched Katy halt and stare.

'This is Suzanne. I was just feeding her her lunch. Why don't you sit down while I finish?' – painfully polite, as if a church elder had come to call.

Katy sat, mesmerized by the baby, while Maggie stood beside the table and resumed spoon-feeding Suzanne whose regard was centred on the strange newcomer in the room.

'Grandpa came to see me on Wednesday.'

'Yes, I know. He called.'

'Isn't it awful about him and Grandma?'

'It's very sad to see any marriage break up.'

'He told me some things about Grandma, about what kind of person she is . . . I mean . . .' Katy stammered to a stop, her face a reflection of anguish. 'He said . . . he said I'm just like her, and I don't want to be. I really don't, Mom.'

She was half-woman, half-child as her eyes began to glisten and her face crumpled.

Maggie set down the baby food and went around the table with open arms.

'Oh, Katy, dear . . .'

Katy fell against her, crying. 'I was so awful to you, Mom, I'm sorry.'

'This has been a trying time for all of us.'

'Grandpa made me see how selfish I've been. I don't want to lose the people I love like Grandma did.'

Holding her daughter, Maggie closed her eyes and felt another of the complex joys that were so much a part of motherhood. She and Katy had been through such a catharsis in the past two years. Bitter at times, sweet at others. While Katy clung, all but the sweet dissolved.

'Darling, I'm so glad you've come home.'

'So am I.'

'Katy, I love Eric very much. I want you to know that. But my love for him in no way diminishes my love for you.'

'I knew that, too. I was just . . . I don't know what I was. Confused and hurt. But I just want you to be happy, Mom.'

'I am.' Maggie smiled against Katy's mousse-stiff hair. 'He's made me so incredibly happy.' The exchange, like a solemnization, brought the proper moment for Maggie's next question. 'Would you like to meet your sister?'

Katy backed up, drying her eyes with the edge of a hand. 'Well, why do you think I came?'

They turned toward the baby.

'Suzanna Banana, this is Katy.' Maggie took Suzanne from the infant seat and perched her on her arm. Suzanne's blue eyes fixed upon Katy with uncomplicated curiosity. She looked back at her mother, then at the young woman who stood by uncertainly, and finally gave Katy a spitty smile and a gurgling sound of approval.

Katy reached out and took the baby from Maggie's arms.

'Suzanna, hiiiii,' she said wonderingly, then to her mother, 'Oh, wow, lookit – Grandpa was right. She's got the Pearson chin. Gol, Mom, she's just beautiful.' Katy held the baby gingerly, bounced her experimentally, gave her a thumb to hang on to, and smiled into Suzanne's rosy face. 'Oh, wow . . .' she said again, captivated, while Maggie stood back and felt favoured by all the right forces.

The two were still getting acquainted when a truck door slammed outside and Eric came down the walk.

Maggie opened the screen door and held it while he approached.

'Hi,' he said with uncharacteristic quietness, dropping a hand on her shoulder blade.

'Hi. We have company.'

He stopped just inside the door, let his eyes find Katy, and waited. She stood on the other side of the table, her face a mixture of sombreness and fear while Suzanne's broke into a smile at his appearance.

'Hello, Katy,' Eric said at last.

'Hello, Eric.'

He laid his skipper's cap on the cupboard. 'Well, this is a nice surprise.'

'I hope it's okay that I came.'

'Of course it is. We're both happy you're here.'

Katy's eyes flashed to Maggie, then back to Eric. Her lips quirked up in a doubtful smile. 'I thought it was time I met Suzanne.'

He let his smile shift to the baby. 'She seems to like you.'

'Yeah, well, that's a miracle. I mean, I haven't been too likeable lately, have I?'

An awkward pause fell and Maggie stepped in to fill it. 'Why don't we all sit down and I'll fix us a sandwich.'

'No, wait,' Katy said. 'Let me say this first, because I don't think I'll be able to swallow anything until I do. Eric . . . Mom . . . I'm . . . I'm sorry I didn't come to your wedding.'

Maggie's eyes met Eric's. They both looked at Katy and searched for some reply.

'Is it too late to say congratulations?'

For a moment nobody moved. Then Maggie shot across the room and put her cheek to Katy's while Katy looked over her shoulder with tear-filled eyes at Eric. He followed his wife across the room, and stood uncertainly nearby, studying the face of the young woman who looked so much like his infant daughter perched on her arm.

Maggie drew back, leaving Eric and Katy poised, caught in one another's regard.

He was not her father.

She was not his daughter.

But they both loved Maggie, who stood between them with her lips trembling while Suzanne studied the scene with wide-eyed innocence.

Eric made the final step and laid one hand on Katy's shoulder.

'Welcome home, Katy,' he said simply.
And Katy smiled.

King's Oak

Anne Rivers Siddons

Leaving behind a disastrous marriage, Diana Calhoun and her young daughter Hilary seek refuge in the comforting security of a small Southern town – Pemberton, Georgia, a close-knit, aristocratic community bordered by a primeval forest.

What she discovers, though, is not serenity but Tom Dabney, a magical, passionate man who has renounced his patrician heritage to live close to the land and who worships the wilderness surrounding Pemberton. Despite warnings from friends, Diana abandons herself to a fiery affair that releases within her unforeseen strengths.

She soon comes to realise that Tom will do anything to protect and preserve his world. When an explosive confrontation involving a sinister threat to his cherished wood pits Tom against even his closest friends, Diana must decide if she can follow . . .

'A wickedly good love story, one that soars'

New York Daily News

ISBN 0 00 617922 3

Homeplace

Anne Rivers Siddons

Bestselling author of *King's Oak*

'*Homeplace* is the crowning achievement in Anne Rivers Siddons' brilliant career. She breaks your heart and writes with such astonishing lyrical beauty that you will want to read it aloud to everyone you ever loved. *Homeplace* is a fantastic book, one that changes the way you look at the whole world.' Pat Conroy, author of *The Prince of Tides*

On the eve of her fortieth birthday, Micah Winship has returned to her home in the South, to confront the places and characters she left behind twenty years before. At last, she would come to terms with her unforgiving father, John; she would rediscover the passion that had brought her and Bayard Sewell together; and she would finally try to leave the old family homeplace forever in the past.

But her father and Bay Sewell were quite different men now. The homeplace had stronger ties than she imagined, especially since it was under threat. And standing in the shadows was the appealing but enigmatic young lawyer Sam Canaday . . .

'Sheer seductive power . . . She knows the lay of the land and of the human hearts and delineates both with a lush lyricism that seems to grow from the very soil.' *Chicago Tribune*

ISBN 0 00 617514 7

Fortune's Child
William Gill

She had everything. She wanted more . . .

Marcus Ackerman is a gold-digger. Fabulously rich and powerful from prospecting in the mines of Chile, he cannot control the one love of his life – his daughter, Leonora. Creative, insecure, and all passion, Leonora adores her father. But nothing, not even his threats, can get in the way of her need to paint.

At art college in London, Leonora meets three men: David, Oliver and Nick. As diverse in character as in their skills, they are bonded by two desires: to succeed as world-class architects, and to win Leonora. For all three it is a question of balancing ambition with love – a combination only one can achieve . . .

'Intelligent, pacy and well written' *Sunday Times*

'A brilliant storyteller' Rosie Thomas

ISBN 0 586 21531 X

Trespassing Hearts
Julie Ellis

Betsy Bernstein is a young Jewish graduate living in New York. An aspiring interior designer, she meets wealthy Gentile Paul Forrest and falls in love. But Paul's mother, a grasping socialite, will never accept her beloved son's choice of a Jewish girl. Nevertheless, when Betsy becomes pregnant, she and Paul throw caution to the winds and marry – but in secret.

With a young son, and Paul away, Betsy is determined to make a success of her interior design business. What she hasn't counted on is the astonishing wilfulness of her mother-in-law, or the prejudices of New York society – or the horrors of the Second World War.

From the bestselling author of *The Only Sin*, *Loyalties* and *No Greater Love* comes this stirring saga of courage, character and love.

ISBN 0 586 21854 8

Ellie

Frankie McGowan

She's smart, she's sexy, she's going places

Eleanor Carter is a top magazine journalist with her own column. It's a glamorous, easy life, for Ellie is politically correct, sexually adjusted and socially skilled. But her past is about to catch up with her, in the shape of property tycoon, Theo Stirling.

Suddenly, without reason, Ellie is fired. Her diary is empty, lunches are cancelled, doors are closed. But Ellie is that glorious mix of an alluring lady with the heart of a street-fighter. Having started at the bottom and climbed to the top, she's not going to fall down again . . .

'Recommended, it's a good read!' *Essentials*

'A sure winner' *Company*

ISBN 0 00 647312 1

Bygones
LaVyrle Spencer

Bess Curran is a lively and successful interior designer, happy with her role as mother of two, content to be divorced from her ex-husband Michael. It's when her daughter, Lisa, asks her to an intimate dinner, that she senses something is up. Lisa is about to drop a bombshell: she wants to marry, she's having a baby, and she wants both her parents at the wedding.

Both for Bess, and for her teenage son, Randy, it's a terrible blow. They adore Lisa, they can't abide Michael, yet protocol demands that the family presents a united front.

Ever the professional, Bess decides to bless her daughter's day with love. That means meetings with her ex-husband: the man whose perfect teeth she could rearrange with a chisel; whose looks and wit make her spit and catch her breath all at once. For Michael is the man who has wounded her son yet loves him dearly; who irritates Bess but still causes a stir. Michael: once a husband, always a lover . . .

ISBN 0 586 21848 3

Forgiving
LaVyrle Spencer

A magical new novel in the glorious Spencer tradition.

It is 1876 and young Sarah Merritt is a woman with a mission: to set up the only newspaper in the dusty gold-rush town of Deadwood, Dakota. But determined Sarah hasn't reckoned on the rawness of the town, or of its people, and she soon finds herself at loggerheads with the headstrong and arrogant local sheriff, Noah Campbell.

Enemies can be friends in the face of adversity, and when Noah discovers Sarah is also in Deadwood to find her sister Adelaide, he vows to help her. For Addie is working as an 'upstairs girl' in the bordello of Mrs Hossiter . . .

ISBN 0 586 21324 4

November of the Heart

LaVyrle Spencer

A commodore's daughter must be careful who she loves.

It is a warm summer's evening in 1895 at Rose Point Cottage on White Bear Lake. But Commodore Gideon Barnett's planned victory dinner has been spoilt – his team lost the boat race, and he just can't figure out why. Against his principles, he agrees to let his kitchen hand try to solve the problem.

Jens Harken is no ordinary odd-jobs man. Working 'below stairs' to pay his way in the New World, he happens to be a master boat builder. Soon he is designing a boat bound to win – the *Lorna D*. But he's not bargained for the enthusiasms of Barnett's daughter, the real Lorna.

Lorna, beautiful and determined, with lush auburn hair and a heart-shaped face, can't help falling for the charms of the blue-eyed, open-hearted Norwegian. Their love sets their world spinning. But it can only bring sorrow and shame to the family that holds Lorna so dear . . .

'This is a novel to cherish!' *Affaire de Coeur*

ISBN 0 00 647608 2